# THE INDUSTRY OF HUMAN HAPPINESS

## A NOVEL

## JAMES HALL

Lightning Books

Published by
Lightning Books Ltd
Imprint of EyeStorm Media
312 Uxbridge Road
Rickmansworth
Hertfordshire
WD3 8YL

www.lightning-books.com

First edition 2018
Copyright © James Hall 2018
Cover design by Ifan Bates

British Library Cataloguing in Publication Data
A catalogue record for this book is available from the British Library

Printed by CPI Group (UK) Ltd, Croydon CR0 4YY

ISBN 9781785630804

For Zanna

Forward, forward let us range,
Let the world spin for ever down the ringing grooves of change

**Alfred, Lord Tennyson, 'Locksley Hall' (1842)**

ഗ഻ൟ഻ൟ഻ൟ

# Part One

❧❧❧❧❧

# Overtures

## London, July 1899

# 1

**M**ax bit his knuckle, aware of a gloved hand hovering inches above his head. It disappeared momentarily before returning to linger once again. Sharp sticks jabbed through the murk amid a thunderous cacophony. He could do nothing to halt the creeping agony as the arch of his foot involuntarily contracted; the slightest movement would result in disaster. Sultry air clawed at his face, heavy with the sulphur tang of human toil. A crash. A wince. The bone stay in his collar cleaved into his chin, his own clothing turning against him in the stifling darkness.

He had hidden in orchestra pits before, but never among the second violins.

Four hours of darkness, three acts of Verdi and a bout of severe cramp. And for what? A brittle disc, liquorice black, seven inches across. He smiled. Alfredo Balducci was there for the taking. His Rigoletto was the talk of Covent Garden. Every thud of the baritone's feet rumbled down through the wooden boards above as his hunchbacked jester traversed the stage, deceived and cursed. The Italians back home called him The Big Beast. With every movement, Max shrank deeper into himself.

But that voice. Never had he heard such purity and truth. Its rich shimmer resonated and echoed through the theatre, like God yawning.

Music, Max thought. The joyous din of people letting go. The calling card of cultures. The universal language. What else was there beyond music and love? Drudgery and disease, reality and regret.

In a city full of noises, this was the one he needed. And he had to strike the deal tonight, before Balducci returned to Milan. The baritone's singing would provide that elusive breakthrough. Another jewel off the list. He pictured committing Balducci to the corkscrewing glory of shellac: the anticipatory crackles, the piano, that rich tone, the crescendo, all bringing pleasure to thousands of people.

Caressing his deformed finger, he prayed that Franklin's men hadn't spotted him. His neck tightened against his trenchant collar as he imagined the hot sting of piano wire. Those monsters wouldn't hesitate in stringing him up. He'd been careful. He'd had to be. Like the stench from the Fleet River, Franklin pervaded every nook of the city. Like the stench, he caused stomachs to curdle.

The gloves fell still, the instruments silent. Heat from the flaring footlights brought a fresh sheen of perspiration. The opera had ended. Max squinted into the light. He usually found curtain calls moving; the mutual exchange of gratitude between audience and performer, life-affirming. But that was when he could see it. In the pit as a stowaway, twisted like a bent screw, it was simply frustrating. Twice as the applause rose he prepared to manoeuvre himself towards the pit's rear door from where he would intercept Balducci on his way back to his dressing room. But his attempts to leave were thwarted by waves of adulation and the endless whirring of the curtain wire. Back and forth

Balducci tramped, drawn by praise from the stalls, the last night of the run merely heightening the audience's enthusiasm.

As the cheers died away Max received a knee in the shoulder from a sympathetic fiddler. His legs prickling and heavy, he pulled them from beneath a music stand. Hauling himself to his feet he limped through the pit's thick air to its door, pausing to tuck his curls behind his ears. He tapped his moustache. Despite the heat his pomade had held. Reaching forward, he pulled the door open and hovered in its frame. Just metres in front of him, below dangling entrails of ropes and stage flats, he watched the barrel-chested Italian stomp down the stairs from the stage above. He remained in the shadow of the doorway, eyeing his quarry.

The singer's green cape occupied the width of the stairwell as he shouted congratulations to the mezzo-soprano behind him, dabbing his forehead. Big Beast indeed. The vast expanse of white greasepaint on his face mocked the feeble silk handkerchief in his hand.

Max swallowed. As Balducci reached the bottom stair he stepped out from the darkness and softly grabbed his arm from beneath the cape. The Italian edged backwards in alarm.

'Signore. I am Maximilian Cadenza of The London Gramophone Corporation.' He leaned in. 'Your Don Giovanni at La Scala changed my life. Did you receive my letters in Milan? It would be an honour to capture your voice.' He was struck by the infantile quality of Balducci's face: it was innocent and expressionless like a porcelain doll. Tear tracks diluted the paint around his eyes. Tread carefully, Max thought. 'I implore you, Signore, remain in London for two more days and record for me.'

With a conspiratorial cock of the head, he motioned Balducci back towards the pit door. Reaching into his trouser pocket, he pulled out a bundle of white notes secured with a brass clip. Fresh beads appeared on the singer's forehead as he craned in and eyed the paper. Max caught a whiff of a sweet but musky broth. *Come on, my friend, bite.* He held the money out, ignoring his own dry throat, aware that the wedge represented a significant chunk of his dwindling reserves. He flashed the smile that had opened so many doors for him over the last two tumultuous years. The Italian's expression remained impassive. Max was starting to think he had misjudged the situation when the oval of Balducci's mouth flinched, then broadened into a crescent.

'Aaaah, Signor Cadenssssa...' Pencil-thin eyebrows followed the arc of his voluptuous whisper.

'Yes, Signor Balducci?'

Balducci's face suddenly drooped as though he was still emoting on the stage. 'No.' He shook his head, holding Max's gaze, his chin gently wobbling. 'Tomorrow, ah, *torno a Milano.*'

*Clever dog.* Max knew that look. Everything about the 'no' meant 'yes'. It was an issue of quantity.

'Signor, you simply must stay.' He imagined the bundle of notes doubling in thickness with his next words. No matter. This was Balducci. 'I will put you up in any hotel you desire. Just say the word.'

A frown was followed by a faint smile. 'Any hotel?'

I'm not so unintelligible now. To hell with it. 'Yes.' His view darkened as the Italian leaned in further.

'The Savoy.' Balducci's eyes widened.

Inevitably. London's finest. And its most lavishly priced. 'As you wish.'

He felt a tug to his hand as the baritone squeezed the bundle to assess its worth. Balducci paused. His chin juddered as he confirmed the transaction he had entered into. '*Bene,*' he whispered.

*Beautiful beast.* Max let go of the money and raised his finger to his lips. 'Secrecy is key. Do not under any circumstances tell Mr Franklin. Understood?'

Balducci nodded.

'I'll make the necessary arrangements. Go to The Savoy in the morning. I'll come to your room in the afternoon and take you to my studio.'

Once again Balducci's face drooped like a leaky balloon. 'But not tomorrow. Three days.' He pointed to his throat.

The rest days. Max sighed. Of course. He ran through the figures in his head. What were another few days of expense when they were assuring their immortality? He nodded.

'In which case, until then.' Max reached behind his knees, raised the tails of his jacket and bowed.

He was about to turn back to the gloom of the orchestra pit when he halted and beckoned Balducci towards him. 'You won't regret this, Signor. It could prove momentous for us both. *Momentous.*' Without losing eye contact, he edged backwards. 'Good night,' he said, backing through the open door.

Squeaking gas lamps showed him that the pit was now empty. He tiptoed to the conductor's rostrum, stepped up and peered out into the auditorium; the audience was still filing out. Crouching, he pressed his calloused finger to the pouch in his breast pocket. There, as ever. His list of twelve musical jewels; the world's most unique sounds. He closed his eyes and thrilled at the possibilities. Capture these twelve and you have music's essence. In this dozen's combination of beauty and melancholy, superstition and virtuosity, the exotic and the spiritual, lay life's code, greater than all philosophy and wisdom. Individually they sparkled. Together, they formed the complete picture. An aural jigsaw of the truth. Capturing them was all that mattered. Riches

– *immortality* – would follow. Three down. With Balducci, four. He stood and peered over the rostrum. The theatre was now almost empty. He heaved himself from the pit and caught up with the last of the patrons in the aisles.

With his head down but his heart dancing, he followed them into the foyer and out into the London night.

෬෮ඁ෬ඁ෬ඁ

'Stop it, Max. You're teasing me again.'

'My dear Delilah, I'm not joking. Soon they will be in every house in the land.'

Max twitched his toes, relishing the freedom to manoeuvre after the evening he had just had. His tie was off, his collar unstudded and his blond curls – previously parted and tamed – tumbled spaghetti-like over his forehead. The cigarette wedged between his lips leapt around as he talked, always threatening but never quite managing either to tumble onto the table or to singe the buffalo horns of his moustache. He loved Simpson's on nights like this. It was not the restaurant's stained-glass opulence or the pianist's Gaiety Theatre tunes that attracted him. Nor was it the lush carpets and mellow lighting that provided such relief from the stinking clay and churning hordes outside. It wasn't even its accountant's magnificently relaxed approach to the settlement of bills. No, Simpson's thrilled him because it was within three minutes' walk of eight theatres and two minutes' walk from his studio. These streets lay at the heart of Covent Garden. And the Garden itself set the city's pulse. Wedged between the courts and trading houses to the east and the palaces and grand squares to the west, its throb drew everyone in. Most escaped its dark pleasures. Some didn't.

'You and your silly toys. So how many people – at this very

moment – are using gramophones in their drawing rooms?'
Delilah drained her glass.

'More than yesterday but not as many as tomorrow.'

A sharp push to his shoulder forced him back into the red banquette. He smiled. He had liked Delilah Green since he'd spotted her playing the waitress Mi Mi in *A Chinese Honeymoon* at the Royal Strand Theatre three weeks previously. She was as memorable as the show was forgettable; a sugared almond in a tray of breadcrumbs. She was even more captivating off stage than on, with a wild mass of chestnut hair piled in a high bun, deep jade eyes and an ever-present scent of cherries and summer lawns. He supposed that some people would call her direct manner vulgar. He'd call her caring but fierce; she had a steely ambition, a wicked smile and was just the right side of flighty. She was also in possession of a thrilling décolletage. But it was now late and her drawl – Stepney by way of every stage east of Seven Dials – was slow and loud.

'Well I don't like those talking machines.'

Max leaned in. 'Delilah, think about any room you like. Until recently every sound heard in that room had to be *created* in that room. Not any more. Isn't that outrageous?'

'It's daft.'

'In place of the rustle of a newspaper or the scratch of a nib you can listen to choirs, orchestras or marching bands. Gramophones make walls melt away. Magic and passion flood in. Have you never had opera for breakfast?'

Crotchet-shaped dimples punctured her cheeks, honeying the air like a joyous trill. I must use that line again, Max thought. He wondered how that first kiss might taste. An early attempt to find out had resulted in a slapped cheek.

'What about all the people who go out to shows to see people sing? To hear me sing? They'll just stop? Even you can't charm them that much.'

'Delilah, my dear, don't you see? Our recording machine enables us to go anywhere in the world to capture any sound we like, from Covent Garden to Siam. Javanese gamelan players, Welsh choirs, Zulu warriors; just name it. Music makes people happy.' Stubbing out his cigarette, he raised his palms skywards. 'And I am in the industry of human happiness.' He didn't mention his deeper compulsion: that since he'd stopped playing himself, other people's music was all he had.

During similar discussions with other sceptics, it was around now that he pointed out that in the twenty-five years of his lifetime, the world had been introduced to the telephone, the blot-free fountain pen and the light bulb. In his opinion, the talking machine was another step in this relentless march forwards, as revolutionary as the railways. He had used this tactic three months ago on Papa, just before he died. He still hadn't understood. Wretched man, still warm in the ground but not a day missed. He decided to spare Delilah such a history lesson. Instead, he gazed at the constellation of freckles dancing on her forehead in the candlelight.

'Well I'll tell you what will make *me* happy, Mr Music Man,' she said, sliding her hand under the table.

'What's that?' He raised his knee into the squeeze.

'Get me another Old Fashioned.'

Max turned from the table to beckon a waiter. The room was dotted with people he knew. Under a wall of muddy portraits and mounted antlers he saw a table of musicians from the Vaudeville, Franklin's newest establishment. There was barely a theatre from Blackfriars to Piccadilly that he didn't now own. Next to them were two theatre promoters of note. He avoided eye contact; human happiness was in short supply from the musical fraternity. At best, they thought him peculiar. At worst, he was an irritant to be dealt with. A pesky disrupter. The arsenic in the wallpaper.

A crash at the bar startled him. He felt Delilah jolt on the banquette and they turned their heads in unison. Across the room, a man around Max's age was sprawled on the floor surrounded by broken glass and glowing pipe embers. He growled at a waiter before kicking him aside with a brutish swipe of his leg.

'Oh,' Delilah said. 'That person's an animal.'

'Ignore him.'

He watched as the man sat up and hooked his ankle around a dining chair. Using it as a crutch, he stood. Delilah's hand rose to his thigh as the fellow stumbled backwards and surveyed the room. The man was stocky like a prize fighter, with a shock of red hair and a nose like a ripening strawberry. A weathered sack coat hung loosely from his shoulders. He performed a drunkard's waltz as he orientated himself. Max placed a protective hand on Delilah's when he saw the man stagger towards their corner table.

'He's coming over,' she said.

Max glanced up and saw the jagged-haired figure loom closer towards them. Seconds later he felt Delilah's grip tighten. The man, enveloped in a peppery fug of sweat and alcohol, hovered over them.

'And what precisely are you two looking at?' he said, leaning in so close that Max could trace the scars left among his freckles by some childhood ailment. His voice was deep and gruff, as if he'd swallowed wire wool.

Max said nothing. He watched the visitor's coarse lips crack as his eyes traced Delilah's outline from her chest to her head and back again.

The man stood upright, steadying himself on Max's shoulder.

'Not even talking to me now, Maximilian? Too busy at your precious opera?' He fumbled with his pipe.

He could sense Delilah looking at him.

'Do you *know* this beast?' she whispered.

Max picked up his empty brandy glass and rocked it back and forth on the table. 'I do.'

'Who is he?'

He coughed to clear his throat before a faint smile tickled his lips. As introductions went, he supposed it was pretty memorable. He looked at Delilah before leaning back and beckoning the man in.

'Rusty, come and meet Delilah. Delilah, this is Rusty. My chief sound engineer.'

'Oh.'

'And my cousin.'

# 2

**M**usic hid in everything. Hooves on clay would become clattering castanets. The rumble of a distant locomotive would become a swelling brass section. Buckets emptied over stoops, cymbals. Once insinuated in his head, Max had little control over the music's duration; sounds germinated, budded, flourished then shrivelled, only to emerge again at a later date. The piercing flute suggested by a braking horse bus might lie dormant for a week, only to pop up when Max was bathing, or laughing, or eating. But the scrub of a sponge or the munching of teeth would add an extra element, transforming the sound yet again. His mind was a restless orchestra, a revolving carousel of snippets. It was twelve years since the accident. Twelve years since he'd played. But the music had never left his head. This morning, as he walked the three miles from his childhood home in Highbury to Tavistock Street, trilling larks in the silver maples had become a sweet viola sonata.

He knew the levity's source: Balducci. Another jewel, guaranteed. His first stage star. One by one he'd cross the names off his list. Soon, handsome houses from Mayfair to Morningside would echo with arias and laments, pipers and shanties. Tomorrow afternoon, the Italian would form the bedrock of this library. They'd press thousands.

The desire to prove everyone wrong burned like splendid pain. The high hopes of the previous year had yet to bear fruit. The very earliest recordings had been pitched at music hall audiences, none of whom, he and Rusty discovered, could afford the gramophones on which to play the shellacs. They'd wasted the little money they had recording unsellable music. In one way the failure suited Max; he'd never liked those simple tunes. They were flimsy. Forgettable. No roots. So he'd compiled his list. Those twelve songs – curated, the best of the best – would convince people to buy, he was sure of it. *Music of the Sands*, a scorching flamenco, had been their sole success to date. Over two hundred copies sold. It was a tentative step. But it gave succour to the notion that they were on the right path. Balducci, though. With him, they'd be running. Riches would follow. They had to. Max had already hired an extra body to help him and Rusty, against all financial reasoning. But he sensed breakthroughs. So long as he watched his back, the Big Beast would change everything.

As he stepped into High Holborn the sonata in his head intensified. He thought of Claude Debussy, of fresh beginnings and of hope. London was a city on the cusp; a metropolis straining for change. Above him, navvies hoisted steel cables onto pylons for the new electric tram system. He felt the ground beneath his feet gently buzz from the sunken boring machines creating tunnels for the Underground. That motor car. How right it felt that the carriages and horses were giving way to it; the older and slower had always yielded to the younger and sleeker. He loved being boxed in by the relentless chaos of improvement. Change was life's great agitator: advancement shunted people's stagnant behaviour along; progress rearranged the established order of things. Would those French artists be painting in dots today had the camera not come along and filched their livelihoods? Of course not. Would former blacksmiths be manufacturing his gramophone parts had the motor car not diminished their incomes? He doubted it.

But darkness and entrenched interests were never far away. At the mouth of a junction, he watched a knot of costers guarding their patches, barking over each other next to carts piled high with herrings, cabbages and potatoes, another of London's unscrupulous tribes out to get what they could. Muggers' music, Max called it. They stood in the shadow of the Southampton Theatre, another of Franklin's. That man, the biggest entrenched interest of them all. As Max knew, succeeding in London depended on degrees of virtue, shades of decency. On some days the city was a fecund orchard. On others, a spilled bin.

He arrived at 22 Tavistock Street, a blackened sliver of a building tucked behind Covent Garden's market. Behind its dusky façade was a warren of garment workshops, furnace-hot in summer and bitter as Alaska in the winter. On a high floor among the workshops – and little bigger than a modest scullery – was his office and second home. At least three nights a week, by design or default, he slept on the battered chaise squeezed into the space between his desk and the wall. It was a short stumble from his haunts and just a few flights up from his recording room in the building's basement. The set-up suited him: everything was under one roof, the rent was cheap and the lease was long. And for those nights when he wanted the luxury of space, bathing facilities and clean clothes – as he had last night – he had his room up in Highbury at Mama's house. The arrangement afforded his life, in his head at least, the perfect balance of convenience and duty, of the seedy and the proper.

As he climbed the building's narrow stairwell he wondered which arias he would ask the Italian to sing. Before he reached the fourth floor he was hit by a tell-tale smell: Rusty's baccy smoke. It always struck him as borderline rotten, like moist wood. For years the odour had followed his cousin around like an obedient mongrel. Its presence was surprising: after Simpson's two evenings ago he had not expected to see Rusty for a few more days. He usually took longer to recover. The smell was accompanied by a slow, dull drumbeat.

Max arrived at his office and pushed open the door. Lying on the threadbare chaise, Rusty was throwing a flick knife into the back panel of Max's desk. Born a cousin, raised a brother, forever a handful. His dirty boots were wedged between the piles of paper and gramophone parts on the desk.

The knife's discordant refrain snuffed out Max's viola. As he paused in the doorway his first instinct, as so often, was to clench his fists and box Rusty's ears; clatter him so hard that his lobes bled down his pockmarked cheeks. However he knew that such a move would create more problems than it solved. Rusty was a spill to be contained. Breach the walls and chaos would seep out. But he was also a fortress to be protected. Those defences were as weak as eggshells.

'Blimey. Back in the world of the living so soon?' Max ruffled the man's coarse hair. 'You daft soak.'

'Oi.' Rusty ducked away as if dodging a fly.

Ignoring the air's stale sweetness, Max hung his bowler on a stand he'd recently bought in the misguided belief that more furniture would suggest a bigger room. He closed the door and skirted around his desk, ducking beneath the warped sitar hanging from a nail on the wall.

Rusty removed his feet from the desk and cleared the scree from his throat. 'Yeah... Simpson's. I needed to blow some cobwebs away. I think she warmed to me eventually, did, er...'

'Delilah. I'm not sure she knew what to make of you, old boy,' Max picked up a pile of post. 'She could probably have done without the joke about the gravedigger and the umbrella. I know I could have.' He chuckled, careful not to berate. Rusty may have been two years his junior, but he was the more developed when it came to sulking. And he was the stronger. Besides, they had bigger things to rail against than each other: they shared a purpose, a business, and blood. On top of this, Rusty was his best friend.

'Where d'you find her anyway? Out on the randy?' A gruff cackle was followed by a wheeze, rising in pitch like a stove-top kettle.

He hated Rusty's use of dockside vernacular. Magnified when drunk, it was still appalling when sober. He used foul language like a cloak, as if pretending to have been raised on the hip of a syphilitic vulgarian would disguise his other character defects. Max sometimes wished he carried in his wallet a photograph of young Rusty on the rolling lawn of Chaveley; he'd whip it out to puncture the guttersnipe illusion whenever he became overly fruity. The lad had always been a tangle of contradictions: a needy misanthrope; a bat craving light.

'Actually, I like Delilah.' Max rifled through the post. 'And you know she's a singer. Or perhaps you've been at the tail end of a carouse every time I've told you that.'

Rusty shrugged. 'Anyway, why do you look so perky? And why no black tie? Aren't you still in mourning?'

'Don't joke. I didn't like the man but there's still Mama to think about. Besides, where's yours? He was your uncle.' Dear Mama. She'd put up with the pair of them for years. The least they could do was respect her grief. 'But to your point, I look perky because...' Max paused deliberately. The dramatic interlude elicited no reaction. '...I look perky, you ginger rotter, because, as I told you two nights ago, Signor Balducci' – he raised his empty palm to the ceiling – '*ha detto di sí.*'

Rusty stared back, impassive.

'He said *yes*. His voice is ours. Room 522 at The Savoy is currently sheltering our operatic jewel. Isn't that marvellous?'

'Smashing.'

'Less of that sarcasm, please. It was a coup to get him *and* Franklin doesn't know.' He hoped this was true. Some form of warning would surely have landed on his desk had Franklin got wind of the plan. He'd often let it be known that he thought talking machines would suck the money out of his theatres and challenge his livelihood. He made no bones about snapping limbs.

Max recoiled as a thud shook the room.

'Sod Franklin. I'll do him over.' Rusty prized the knife from the back of the desk.

'Behave.'

'Hate opera anyway. What's wrong with trying Lillie Langtry or Marie Lloyd again? You know, people's music. They'd get the punters wet.'

Max shook his head. Rusty knew full well that that experiment failed. He pretended not to notice the mocking kiss. Whenever he mentioned opera to his cousin he knew to expect an indifferent response. It was one of life's great ironies: although they ran a gramophone company, Rusty did not possess a musical bone in his body. It was the machines that enthused him, not the sound. It had always been that way. While Max did the music, Rusty did the mechanics. Somehow the division of labour worked. Max never doubted they'd end up working together; their roles had been ordained for years.

'Remember, tell no one about Balducci. We can't allow

anyone to hear of this. Utter secrecy is imperative.'

Rusty smiled. 'Of course. I think you're wrong, though. Franklin'll never hurt us. Too close.'

Max scoffed. It was nonsense and Rusty knew it. Family ties were weaker than the man's ruthless streak. And with Papa no longer here, Franklin had no reason for loyalty. 'We'll see. Anyway, what did Mary make of your state when you got home the other night? Kill the fatted calf, did she?' It was still strange seeing Rusty married. Max always imagined he would be the first cousin with a wife. He suspected that Rusty enjoyed the petty triumph.

'I wish she had killed the fatted calf. I was fucking starving.'

The trouble with having grown up together was that nothing was unsayable. Max considered it a by-product of a close but troubled family. These days, he tended to let Rusty get on with things: the skittish and contrary outbursts, the ill-judged comments, the occasional bragging that he stood to inherit Chaveley. The poor boy had known enough suffering. His rage was best left unstoked; like an underground spring, latent anger ran deep and hidden, only to burst into the open at some unexpected place where the ground was weak and vulnerable. And while Rusty vented and simmered, Max took all business decisions on their behalves. Both knew instinctively that he only acted with their mutual interests at heart. Like links in a chain, they were permanently yoked.

'Oh, and remember that new fellow's arriving this morning. Joe Langley.' Max said. 'He'll be here shortly. Having an extra person should help us no end.'

Rusty lit his pipe and sat back in the chaise. 'Thought we were brassic.'

'We are, but if we're to capture our jewels we need more than just the two of us.'

He watched as Rusty blew a smoke ring.

'If we're so skint, how can we afford all this? You a bloody magician as well?'

Max leaned forward on his chair and mimed the sweep of a wand. 'We've got enough.' They hadn't. Particularly after the Balducci outlay. But a spike in sales was just around the corner.

'When's the tubby lump coming in?'

'Tomorrow.'

Rusty pulled the pipe from his mouth. 'Tomorrow?'

'Well, starting tomorrow. One or two recordings in the afternoon and a few more the next day. He sails for Italy at the end of the week.'

'Christ.'

'Indeed.' Two days left scant room for mistakes.

Rusty hauled himself from the chaise. 'I'll go down and get started.'

'Spick and span.' He knew he needn't have said it. For one so turbid, Rusty was unduly tidy and methodical in the studio. 'And please be enthused, old boy. I know he's not your thing but we need to make this work. It's us against the bastards, remember?'

Rusty winked as he opened the door. 'Have I ever let you down?'

'Often.'

The gust from the slammed door caused the sitar to wobble on its wire. As air passed over its remaining strings, it emitted a dissonant hum. Max surveyed his desk but could not see the surface for ledgers, bills, stylus boxes, tone arms and a broken toy xylophone. There was, he supposed, some poetry in the fact that the mess before him mirrored the state of the company. He removed his jacket. It was one of three pre-made suits he'd recently bought from Pontings Department Store, all hewn under the hammering needle of an electric sewing machine. Glorious technology. As a result, all three cost less than a single hand-tailored waistcoat from a Burlington Arcade boutique. And all were in the latest short-jacket style. He hung it on the hatstand and picked up a well-thumbed copy of *Primitive Culture* by Edward Tylor. He'd read it a dozen times, and a dozen times it had enthralled him. Sitting, he leaned back and raised his feet. This was the blueprint. Forget music halls. Tylor's writings had convinced him that the entire world was a fertile musical field to be ploughed.

*Culture or civilisation,* he read to himself, *is that complex whole which includes knowledge, belief, art, morals, law, custom, and any other capabilities and habits acquired by man as a member of society.*

'The most important of which,' Max said, as the sitar's vibration looped into a soft raga in his head, 'is music.'

☙❧☙❧☙

The church hall behind the Paragon Theatre of Varieties would have made an adequate rehearsal space were it not for the odour of decaying mice. The smell stuck in Delilah's nostrils like poison. She deposited her hat and bag on a bench and walked to the piano, late, inhaling in shallow half-breaths. Seemingly oblivious, Mr Wilson bashed away at the stained keys with a vigour she'd forgotten about. She glanced around. Here again. Whenever new sets were being built in the theatre, Wilson made them practise in the hall, dead rodents or not. Delilah joined the three other girls at the piano.

'Sorry,' she mouthed to no one in particular, nudging herself into the centre of the group. As she claimed the space, she swept an errant coil of chestnut hair from her forehead. Over the piano she watched Wilson's wandering fingers, the black and yellow of his nails matching the keys he so keenly dominated. She flattened the embroidery down the front of her dress. It was her cream one, a favourite but fiddly. It was also, she happily noted, prettier than the other ones on display today. She composed herself and stifled the smirk that had stubbornly played on her lips since Max bid her farewell two nights ago with a surprise sprig of lavender from his hat.

The hall may not have changed, but she hoped that she had. And yet everything suddenly felt so familiar, as though the last few months hadn't happened. She'd sworn she'd never return to the Paragon after her spell at the Royal Strand. Wilson counted them in with buttery teeth. She looked down. From *A Chinese Honeymoon* in Covent Garden to his glossy face in Mile End in less than a week. But she always knew that her world was a porous one; a world in which luck and fortuitous timing played as big a role as talent. That, and knowing when to smile prettily at a pianist. Her role had come to an end, there was nothing else out there and Wilson had asked her back. Money was money and she needed it. Her digs weren't cheap. Work was work. Her father had taught her that before he turfed her out; he'd depart for Smithfield's abattoirs every day before dawn no matter the season, no matter the workload. If something better turned up, she'd just leave. Loyalty counted for buttons in this game. Besides, she loved singing. And East London wasn't so bad. It was home.

She'd forgotten Wilson's knack of playing while gazing at the closest female chest. In every curve a tune, it seemed. Still, she wished she could play that well. Owning a piano would be a start. He coughed as the verse came around. Although unfamiliar with most of *The Drunken Judge*, she inhaled as much as the air allowed and sang the feather-light ditty.

'Lovely.' Wilson flicked a curtain of oily hair from his eyes. 'Now, one at a time. A line each.'

There was one singer around the piano whom Delilah had not met. But she did know Clara Pattinson, who sang first. She was notorious on the circuit for not stopping at a pretty smile when it came to pianists.

'Good, Clara.' Wilson's eyes darted up from the keys.

Delilah saw Clara redden. The two had clearly exchanged more than smiles recently. Judging by Clara's stance, she was trying to forget. Judging by Wilson's, he wanted to remember.

A Welsh girl called May whom Delilah had beaten to the Mi Mi role sang next. Too precise, too loud. As May went, her imploring eyes flicked sideways to check that the other girls were watching her. Delilah ignored her. Wilson clearly felt the same; he moved on, maintaining the song's rhythm.

'*And* Miss Braithwaite.'

Delilah heard the new girl, who was standing to her right in a plain blue dress, inhale deeply. Sincere with tar-black hair, her voice caught as she sang. A meek cough filled the gap. Delilah reached across and touched her arm. It happened all the time. Besides, it always paid to get the fresh ones onside early. The new girl tried again. Her singing, while tender, was only a qualified success. It seemed to be guided by technique rather than talent. However rather than admonish her, Wilson grinned.

'Well recovered, Molly. Touch more passion next time please.'

Delilah received the nod. 'And our returning starlet,' Wilson said.

She briefly poked her tongue out before taking a breath. Time stopped as she sang. In that moment, nothing else mattered. It was just her and her voice, alone, each in turn leading and controlling the other. '*There once was a judge whose intellect fine, Was often strengthened by a jug of wine.*' As she sang, she soared, oblivious to the world. Air rushed through her. She was as free as a starling heading for the clouds. She'd been told that her voice had developed. Through Mi Mi, her confidence, projection and clarity had improved. While she sought no affirmation from anyone around her, she nonetheless glowed when Wilson winked in approval.

The song ended and Delilah found herself clapping with the group.

'Well done, ladies, well done. I think that'll do for today. Thank *most* of you for arriving on time.' Wilson raised a brow at Delilah.

Dirty sod, she thought, smiling back.

'And remember to start thinking about your frocks for Victoria Park. It's some time away, but I'd like you to choose something bright and' – Wilson flicked his hair – 'fetching.' He caressed the keyboard and lowered the lid.

Delilah struggled to picture him and Max together. She knew that Wilson played in his studio occasionally, paid by the session. As men, they couldn't be more different. But everyone knew – and used – everyone else in this game.

She walked to the bench to retrieve her belongings. Even though she'd known him for less than a month, she found her thoughts turning to Max with alarming regularity. She'd never met anyone quite like him. He was different from the others; there was respect there. His eyes were kind, always assessing, quick to sparkle. And he came from a different world, one of relative privilege: he had grown up in a townhouse in North London and used to take holidays in an uncle's house by the sea. Not that a stranger would know any of this by spending time with him. He had a beguiling ability to float among all people, appearing to be of no social standing and all social standings at the same time. He amused her. But most of all, he excited her. Being with him, she imagined herself strapped to the grill of a speeding locomotive; he was thrilling, dangerous, enlivening. The redhead was strange, mind. A tangled coil of petulance. Stank like a damp sack.

Delilah turned to leave and saw May hovering close by in the hope of finding a companion to walk with. Not likely. She knew her type too well; overly keen and inadequately talented. Ignoring her, she walked briskly to the door and exited the hall. The air on Mile End Road was delightfully fresh. She lifted her head to the summer sun and closed her eyes. She had walked fewer than five paces when she collided with something at thigh height. She looked down; a crouching figure was gathering the spilled contents of her handbag. Delilah recognised the blue dress. It was the new girl, the one who'd stumbled as she sang.

'Here, darling, let me.' Delilah knelt. 'Molly, isn't it?'

The girl looked up, flustered. 'Yes.'

'I'm Delilah.' She handed Molly a glove – worn, simple – and a vial of perfume. Petunia. Sweet and dependable. Delilah stood.

'Much obliged.' Molly straightened up and exhaled sharply before looking across at Delilah and smiling. 'Thank you very much.'

Delilah liked her unassuming nature. She was shorter than Delilah herself, with a slightly thicker waist, and a few years younger; probably around twenty. Her face was open but she had the innocent air of someone who'd spent too much time reading and not enough time experiencing the world. No threat here. Delilah definitely liked her. They walked on.

'Haven't you got a pretty voice?' Delilah said.

'Oh, I was terrible. I still get so nervous. But that's kind of you to say so.'

'He likes you too. I can tell.' Delilah nodded towards the hall and saw Molly try to obscure a slight shiver. It was charming. 'Where are you going now?'

'Dalston.'

'I'm heading that way too.' Delilah slipped a hand around Molly's arm and led her down the row of stalls lining the street; tables laden with fruit and coloured thread spools in fancy piles. 'Him aside, are you enjoying it?'

Molly nodded. 'It's my second week now. I like the Paragon. I'm looking forward to the shows.'

The shows. For a second Delilah considered telling her about the catcalls and the stench from the crowds, about the soiled costumes and dirty dressing rooms, about the meagre earnings at the end of the week. But she bit her tongue. Dreams were like gold dust. It would be cruel to blow them to the wind. 'The shows are fun. Hard work, mind.'

'Mr Wilson mentioned you at my audition. You've been performing on the Strand. I think he was showing off a bit,' Molly said. 'He didn't say you were coming back.'

Delilah laughed. 'He didn't know. Nor did I until a few days ago.'

'Why did you choose to come back?'

Delilah looked at her. Unassuming *and* naïve. Poor girl. It won't last. If it does, she'll be back making hat boxes or selling pincushions within weeks. 'You sing wherever they'll have you, darling. I finished *A Chinese Honeymoon* and there's not much around. But there's always room for me at the Paragon. I'm like a bad penny.'

They walked on.

'So, how long were you at the Paragon before shows like that came up?' Molly said.

'*A Chinese Honeymoon*? Two years. Three.' Delilah felt Molly's gaze. It was four. She gave her arm a reassuring squeeze.

'A word of advice.'

'Please.'

'If I can get to Covent Garden, so can you. The trick is to push at every door. You won't get to Drury Lane by being meek.'

Molly nodded. 'Don't be meek.'

'And remember that once you're there, the journey back to dives like the Paragon isn't a long one. Look at me,' she chuckled mirthlessly and imagined how she'd have felt two years ago if she'd known she'd still be there. Still, in imparting something she felt useful. 'Be careful who you trust. London's full of crooks. Can't move for crackpots and liars in our world.'

With their arms still linked, they continued down Mile End Road.

'So what about this Victoria Park event that Mr Wilson mentioned? What happens there?'

'It's a fête. We go there to sing to drum up custom for the show. He likes to make it special. All the theatres have stalls there.'

'It sounds fun.'

'It's certainly noisy. It'll be even more so this year. My Max will be there demonstrating his blessed machines.'

'Who's Max?'

Hearing his name made her smirk again. 'Max Cadenza. He's *half* a crackpot. Thinks he's seen the future. Makes me laugh though.'

'What kind of machines?'

Delilah raised her eyebrows. Perhaps she'd overspoken. Her typical impulsive self, assuming this girl would be interested. 'Talking machines.'

'Talking machines?'

'Yes. He's got some opera man in this week.'

'What? Gramophones?'

'Ye–' She turned to see Molly staring at her. 'Oh, not you and all.'

'What?'

Delilah shook her head. 'They're ridiculous, sweetheart. Scratchy ugly hulks of machinery.' Everyone knew that. 'You know, in France they make the discs out of chocolate so people can eat them after two listens. Best use for them.'

Molly spoke quietly. 'My uncle has one. I think they're extraordinary. Such power.'

Delilah peered across. Molly's face had a quiet authority to it. Normally, she would have ignored any mention of talking machines but there was something about the girl that made her think twice. She didn't seem built to exaggerate. 'What do you mean *power*?'

'For people like us, for singers. The power to reproduce our voices so everyone can hear them. I think it's incredible. Wouldn't you want to make a disc?'

'Me? Na. Not unless I was hungry.' Delilah chuckled.

'I would.'

Delilah thought back to the nights when Max had held forth about opera for breakfast, about walls melting and about the magic and passion of gramophones. She'd always dismissed it as Max being Max. The eccentric ramblings of a dreamer. Somehow, though, the words sounded different coming from a stranger, someone whose livelihood did not directly depend on the machines being a success. It was like hearing about them in a different language.

'So does Max run this gramophone business?'

'Yes.'

'And you haven't asked him to record you?'

She shook her head.

They turned down White Horse Lane in silence. Delilah felt

strange, as though the conversation had slipped away from her. It was a rare sensation and she didn't like it. Control was important. Yet in a few brief exchanges, she felt like the naïve party. This unassuming girl by her side had quite thrown her. Although their arms were still linked, Molly was staring down at the pavement as she walked.

Delilah may have imagined it, but she could have sworn that as they wove among the stalls and carts towards Bethnal Green she felt a faint, reassuring squeeze to her elbow.

⚮⚮⚮

Max was eighty pages in when he heard a knock.

'Come.'

The man who poked his head around the door was unnaturally tall, clad in tweed and looked disappointed. The narrow corridors and small rooms at Tavistock Street often had this effect on people. The poor soul was probably expecting a gleaming office with a plaque outside.

'Joe Langley. My good fellow. Welcome.' Max stood as the man gingerly entered. Leaning over his desk, he shook his hand. 'Please sit.'

Langley lowered himself into the chaise. He moved tentatively, as though he feared insulting the furniture. As with most people who did not know Max, he tried hard not to let his gaze linger on the man's shortened finger. In trying not to stare, he ended up doing the opposite.

Max raised his copy of *Primitive Culture*.

'Have you read him?'

'Excuse me, sir?' Langley said in a soft Scottish lilt.

'Edward Tylor.'

'Er, no.'

'Most enlightened fellow. Turns out that primitives don't remain primitive. Culture evolves. We're all the same underneath.'

'I see,' Langley said, looking for all the world like he'd never seen anything.

'And music lives in all of us. Imagine the recording opportunities out there. *Imagine.*'

He looked exactly as Max recalled: clean-shaven and eager, although his bulbous nose and long torso gave him a vaguely cartoonish air, as though his features had been exaggerated by a satirist's pencil. There was a sense of lofty bafflement in the way he held himself.

'Glad to be here, sir.' Langley looked up at the sitar on the wall.

'To remind us of the musical opportunities out there.'

Max watched him survey the rest of the room. Freshly graduated, he was looking for noticeboards and timetables, for structure. He'd learn. There was something about this chap's enthusiasm that he liked. He was young – around nineteen – and was unashamed to ask questions about the company. Following a brief interview at the Trocadero a month ago, Max had offered him the job on the spot.

'How was the journey down from Edinburgh? I was up in the Highlands last year recording bagpipers. They're on my list,' Max said. A heavenly drone buzzed in his ear.

'The journey was fine, thank you, sir.'

'Excellent. You've actually joined us on an auspicious week. Tomorrow we have Alfredo Balducci coming in to record.'

'Yes, I heard he was in London.' Langley drew breath as if to say more, perhaps a fact about Balducci or a nugget about his impressive range. But he said nothing.

'Well I'm thrilled,' Max continued. 'Now let's get you started.

It's a small operation here. Just myself and Rusty. The best sound engineer around. When he behaves.'

'I hope I shall pick everything up quickly.'

'Dear chap, you'll be fine. I employed you for your enquiring mind. Craft can be learned. Curiosity cannot.'

'Thank you, sir.'

'Please don't call me sir. You're not that much younger than I. Now, you're clear on your role?'

'To help you establish and grow the market here and overseas. Record. Help with playbacks.'

Max clapped his hands. Hearing other people talk about his aspirations lent them credibility. 'Yes! Well put. Establish and grow. As I outlined to you at the Troc, our mission is to hunt out the best music and commit it to disc, here, there, anywhere. Our library is basic at the moment. It's time to cast our net wider. Exciting, no?'

'Extremely.'

'I hope you have a thick skin. We're not popular. The world is rather against us at the moment.'

'Oh.'

'We'll be travelling soon. Russia probably. Rusty and I did Spain recently. Marvellous place. In the meantime, I need you to go fabric shopping for me this afternoon.'

Langley suppressed a frown. 'Fabric shopping?'

'I need a very particular length of muslin. Heavy weft. You'll probably need to head east.'

'East?'

'East London, Mr Langley.'

'Yes, of course. Understood.'

Max stood. 'But before you go, let me show you the studio.'

'Oh, I almost forgot.' As Langley stood from the chaise, he reached into his trouser pocket. 'Someone outside asked me to give you this.' He held a small envelope over the desk.

Max opened it and removed a business card. One side was taken up by elaborate interlocking letters: B and F. His stomach turned as he recognised the initials. Barnabas Franklin. He turned the card over. There, scrawled in jagged ink, was a message.

'Do not record the Italian. It would displease me greatly.'

෬෨෩෪෫෬෨

Max was still clasping the card when he opened the basement door and led Langley into the studio. The only light came from two rectangular windows high on the opposite wall. Through them, feet of passers-by clipped past on the pavement outside. He inhaled the distinctive odour: pipe smoke, chemicals and the musty damp of a semi-sunk room.

'Welcome to London's finest recording studio. Such as it is.'

He hovered by the door and let Langley walk towards the rig in the room's centre. Without fail the apparatus drew in the uninitiated like a magnet. It loomed like a mechanical totem, all improvised spindles and crooked cranks, its needles and cones jutting and slotting about each other. From its side protruded a long horn, like a vast megaphone. A billowing canopy, the lining of an old Bedouin tent of Papa's, taken from Chaveley, hung above the contraption. This room, his cradle of creation, was where physics met alchemy; a wondrous confection.

Two white flashes from a recess illuminated the studio. Max saw Langley recoil. He looked over to see his cousin's broad frame hunched over a soldering iron at his workbench in the corner, his pipe clasped between his teeth.

'Rusty,' he shouted. There was no reply. '*Rusty.*' He waited for three more bursts of stuttering fluorescence before Rusty set down the iron. 'Didn't you see us? Come and meet Mr Langley.'

Rusty unhurriedly rubbed his palms on his leather apron and walked to Langley. Stocky insouciance met lanky gaucheness. He scowled up at his new colleague. 'My, my. You're a long streak of piss, aren't you?'

'How do you do?' Langley offered a hand.

Max smiled. Under his jacket's heavy twill, the poor chap looked as willowy and exposed as a lone tree on a heath, almost inviting a hungry gust of wind to do its worst.

'Rusty. A word.' Max struck a match to light a pair of gas sconces on either side of the door. He watched Langley turn to examine the rig again and beckoned his cousin towards him. 'Look. From Franklin.' He gave Rusty the card, his hand softly quivering.

Langley was bending over the machine, examining its spindles.

'That's right, Mr Langley, it's a spring-loaded turning table with a wind-up motor. Mahogany. That horn protruding at head-height is five feet long, the longest we could make. Impressive, eh? Watch you don't knock the stand supporting its end.' Max looked back to Rusty, his fingers now whirring like a cyclist's legs. 'Well? What do you think?'

There was no doubt that the message was a threat, and he usually responded to those by doing precisely what he was being warned against. But this was Franklin.

Rusty's lips were pursed in concentration. 'How did he hear?'

'It may be a wild guess. I certainly wasn't aware of being spotted with Balducci the other night. But *how* is hardly the point. It's what we do now that matters.'

Over the years, they'd crossed Franklin. They'd nipped and sniped and cocked a snook at the man. But they'd never done anything in contravention to a specific warning from him.

Nor, Max knew, had London's army of judges, constables and newspaper editors. The man was as active, alert and vile as ever, and his grip on Covent Garden's circuitry was total. It had started twenty-five years ago with a penny gaff, unspectacular but profitable. He traded the gaff for a theatre. One became three, three became five. In a grab for respectability, he opened an opera house. He also reached down, buying up taverns, supper rooms and casinos. When the creation of New Oxford Street sliced through the Garden's Holy Land slum, ripping apart decades of squalor, he promised the Metropolitan Board of Works he'd drain the swamp and rebuild the area. The promise was partial. But the area became his. Today, whether punters were sitting in the stalls, eating, whoring or gambling, their pennies went to Franklin. Worse than his rackets was his cloak of respectability. Rumour was he kept a photo of him and Bertie on his desk. Max rubbed his callous and squeezed his eyes shut. *Franklin.* Quite unexpectedly, he saw Papa's brutal, pinched face. That grim axis. He opened his eyes and looked at Rusty.

Neither man moved from the doorway, their glares fusing them to each other. Neither blinked, nor spoke. They stood, bound by a silent connection forged over two decades.

'Franklin's bluffing. He can't know,' Max whispered. Only the men in this room and Balducci himself were aware of the arrangement. He'd ensured that. It was in none of their interests to bleat. And in two days Balducci would be gone. The chance over. As he looked into Rusty's eyes, he saw the hint of a glint. He felt one growing in his own. Opportunity overrode fear. They teased the look from one another, their faces morphing into agreement. Max wiped his moistening palms on his trousers. 'Shall we do it?'

Rusty nodded. It lasted for less than a second. But in that

fleeting moment they shared an unbelieving smile, thick with conspiracy.

Max saw Langley peering into the long recording horn. He walked towards the rig. 'Everybody looks into that, Mr Langley. Nothing in there but air and potential. And at its thin end, a very sharp cutting stylus.'

The apparatus never failed to fill him with pride. Rusty had calibrated the recording box's motor to rotate the turning table precisely seventy-eight times in a minute; the uniformity of the speed at which the stylus cut sound vibrations onto the master disc was crucial. Meanwhile they'd welded the blade of an ice skate to an old music stand to create the frame to support the horn. The cleverly adapted canopy above was designed to guide noise into the horn rather than up to the roof. Magic and passion, Max thought. He imagined Papa's disapproving face and smirked.

Walking beyond the machine, he stroked the lid of the upright piano that sat on a wheeled platform. 'And *this* is my portable orchestra. We can position it anywhere in the room.'

The studio may have been dark and scruffy but Max would wager that there was more possibility contained within its four walls than anywhere else in London. He looked from Rusty to Langley and back again. Were they a rag-tag team? For sure. Did they face possible humiliation? Certainly. Punishment? Possibly. But someone had once told him that the path of least resistance was the path of the loser. It wouldn't do to buckle under pressure, particularly in front of the new man.

He raised Franklin's business card. Silhouetted against the rig it looked insignificant, pathetic even. The status quo versus progress. The past versus the future. 'Remember I told you that we're not very popular, Mr Langley?'

'Yes.'

Max held up the card by its long side and ripped it in two, relishing its pathetic *shhh*. He folded the halves together and tore them once more, its pleads for silence becoming shorter with each rip. He repeated the ritual until the card resembled confetti. Dropping the pieces to the ground, he rubbed his hands together. No one could tell them what to do.

'Come on, chaps,' he said. 'It's time to prepare for a special visitor.'

# 3

Rusty rounded the corner onto Drury Lane with a swagger in his step and rig oil in his hair. 'Quick one in the Lion?'

Max could sense the pre-record jangle. He felt it in himself, too.

'Not tonight.' He looked around. It was his favourite time of day. Covent Garden was undergoing its dusk scene-change. Costers and hawkers were being replaced by a thickening whirl of people, some heading to the theatre, others to a tavern or club, a chophouse or casino. Crossing-sweepers cleared manure from the clay, bent low and scuttling backwards as if paying homage to the impending revelry. Their brush strokes scarred the earth with a rhythmic thrum. Although the light was fading, London's essence was stirring.

Rusty spun on his heel but carried on walking, backwards. He looked up at his cousin as a child would his father in a sweet shop. 'Just one?'

'Stop it. Need to be alert tomorrow.' Rusty always did this. And it was never just one. Besides, they were about to peel off on their respective routes home; Max north to Highgate, Rusty east to Hackney.

Rounding a bend, Max abruptly stopped. 'Will you look...'

Across the Lane, a vast crowd, dozens thick, had gathered outside the Imperial Theatre. The sea of bonnets and trilbies was illuminated from above by dozens of flaming gas brackets on the theatre's awning. Above them, in dazzling yellow, a sign. *The Golden Sun*. Franklin's new musical. A seat-filler. The talk of the town. But Max had seen the score; it was watery and derivative, did nothing for him. In the excitement over Balducci, he had forgotten it opened tonight.

The crowd was the thickest he'd seen for months. And for every punter looking to spend money, Max wagered there was a swell mob or prostitute looking to relieve them of it. Covent Garden was a perfect democracy like that.

A blast of hornpipe caught his attention. In the thinning fringe of the crowd, on one of the pavement stages that Franklin rented to street performers, an organ-grinder in a patched-up suit wound a box hanging from his neck. Max knew every busker in the area and he'd never seen this fellow before. He was joined by family; his wife plucked a banjo while a chained marmoset leapt between two children's shoulders. As the monkey bared its teeth to passers-by, the children shook a cap in time to the music.

Max smiled and fingered a ha'penny in his pocket for when he passed. Forget *The Golden Sun*; here was fun. He lit a cigarette, aware of Rusty's demented jig next to him. The tune suddenly thickened as Blind Ted, a bearded fiddler as old as sound itself, joined in from the other side of the theatre's entrance. His bow bouncing from the strings, he followed the hornpipe's melody, filling gaps with intricate flourishes. Max smiled at the three-person orchestra. This was how music should be: spontaneous and unencumbered. A number of hats under the awning gently bobbed and a whoop rose from the crowd. Somewhere in the throng people were dancing.

A whistle of warning. Rusty nodded towards the theatre.

Standing taller than the milling crowds, two of Franklin's patrolling blackguards surveyed the scene. Of course, thought Max. Joyous interludes rarely lasted unchecked, not around here. He watched the blackguards' steely faces and wondered if they were the ones who'd handed the warning to Langley outside the studio. It was no surprise they were here. Franklin's henchmen were known to circulate around his theatres before shows, watching for disruptive influences. It wasn't just ticket touts, pickpockets and whores in the blackguards' sights – it was anyone who clogged the theatre's entrance or caused a distraction. The patrolmen's sole role was to safeguard their employer's interests. Nuisances were dispatched with speed; first relieved of cash then slung down the nearest alley, occasionally with an eye gouged or a thumb crushed. Max had once seen a sheet-music hawker garrotted for selling nursery rhymes outside a playhouse.

Raising his collar so as not to be recognised, Max cursed the men. Their routine was as dark as it was predictable; after curtain-up they'd head to the first floors of Franklin's taverns to oversee the gambling. After that they'd ascend further to the lavender-scented garrets, extracting lucre and pleasure until sunrise, often from women they'd already rinsed once that evening, each pound fattening Franklin's empire.

Max saw one of the men nod towards the organ-grinder and gesture to this colleague; he had spotted the family. The blackguards glided through the crowd towards the buskers' platform as though crawling through water. Max's hunch was right: the family had not paid their dues. They were busking illegally on Franklin's patch.

'Come on.' With his head lowered, he tapped Rusty's shoulder and strode towards the family. Underdogs stuck together in this part of town. It was their unwritten code. Approaching from over the road, rather than through the dense crowd, they arrived at the platform before the henchmen. Max dropped his ha'penny into the children's cap and caught the organ-grinder's eye. 'Leave. Now.' The marmoset pointed to the coin and stretched its mouth in delight.

'Sir?' The player's accent was thick, Germanic.

Once again Max motioned at Franklin's odious enforcers. 'You're not safe. Follow me.' The organ trailed off, leaving Blind Ted's fiddle the only sound.

Max walked from the theatre. As he turned he saw Rusty gather the children into his arms and guide them away. Behind them, bewildered, the organist and his wife followed.

Steps quickening, Max led the group north across Holborn before turning down a side alley, away from the street's chaos. The monkey mewled forlornly as they wove along the lanes between dank hovels and night houses. These putrefying rookeries of the old Holy Land had yet to be ripped down. They lingered unseen; London's filthiest relics. As Max walked, he heard the slush of feet and the gentle clanging of instruments behind him as his group kept pace. After a minute, as though drawing breath after being gagged, Max led them into the relative calm and order of Great Wild Street, where the city once again showed its face. Standing on a pavement, carriages rolling by, Max looked back down the alley. The blackguards were nowhere to be seen.

He beckoned the organ-grinder towards him and pointed east. 'I'd head that way. And maybe stay away from Covent Garden for a while.'

The musician laid a hand on his shoulder. 'Thank you.'

Rubbing the young boy's head, Rusty hurried them on their way.

'Well, well,' Max said as the family scuttled over the road, their instruments clinking as they went. It may have been small, but victories over Franklin were rare. 'Did you mention the Lion?'

๕๗๑๙๕๙

Standing on the threshold, Max heaved open the handle of the Black Lion's saloon door and waited for the blast. It came half a second later; a wallop of raised voices, dirty heat and baccy smoke. A staccato accordion cut through the drinkers' babble. It was urgent, fast, dirty. Max winced. The tavern was the offal to Simpson's rump steak. But like every man, he was partial to occasional offal; delicacies lurked among the gristle.

He let Rusty stride in ahead of him. The Lion was his domain. A regular, Rusty could often be found here in the bar or upstairs watching a bare-knuckle bout. With its cracked oil lamps and barrel tables, the place was a dump. But it was cheap and enticing. No one quite knew how, but the sweetest rum from West India Dock found its way to the Lion within hours of arriving in London. People rarely asked or complained. They just drank.

'Porter?'

'Please.' Max reached into his pocket and flicked Rusty a coin. At some point in the evening he'd ask for money. It may as well be now.

Gentlemen in white waistcoats skulked among the dark-suited drinkers, desperately but unsuccessfully trying to blend in, their opera hats stashed unconvincingly under their overcoats. Bare-shouldered women crowded around them or edged past with a polka swoop and a smile. Everyone moved with purpose. Max watched Rusty disappear towards the bar and found a seat. The lad's tail was up. This was good. People often asked him how two such different people remained so close. Sometimes he didn't understand either. But the bond was immutable. As boys they'd sworn allegiance to each other. They'd had to. The pact was in their blood. Just the one drink, he told himself. A furry head for the recording would not do.

Rusty's gruff laugh cut through the din. It was followed by a singing kettle, ascending. He barged his way back from the bar carrying two tankards in one fist. 'Hey, Max. Look who I met,' he shouted, waving his vast pewter boxing glove.

A man in a bowler and pressed white shirt was following him. Max didn't recognise the chap.

'This fella. Trumpet the night we recorded George Robey. Remember?'

'Ah yes, how do you do, Mr…?' Max offered his hand.

'Burton.'

George Robey had provided one of the early music hall recordings that Max was trying to forget. Four boxes of that costly folly still took up shelf space at their Acton warehouse.

'Bought him a beer,' Rusty said. 'Good health, gentlemen.'

Max sipped his porter. That's twice he'd paid Burton. Once in shillings and once in beer. He'd seen a return on neither.

Legs akimbo, Rusty lowered his tankard and smiled. It was a grin of petty triumph: he wasn't drinking to celebrate anything, rather he was celebrating drinking. A simple pleasure, wholeheartedly embraced. The taste of bitter hops, malt and water was enough.

'Burton's working at the Hall in Farringdon. Isn't that right, Burton?' Rusty said.

'It is. Twelve shows a week.'

Rusty grinned. 'Next round's on you.'

Max couldn't fathom why he'd dragged this bore over. There was so much he wanted to talk about: tomorrow's recording, whether they'd start with Verdi or Puccini, how to stay safe, young Langley's impressive debut. As the thoughts piled up he felt a flush rise, momentarily overwhelming him. He loosened his collar. 'Actually, chaps, I'm going for a smoke outside. Won't be long.'

Walking to the door, he yanked the handles open and let the street's cool air envelop him. Outside, he stood on the cellar flap, where he patted a cigarette into his palm. Perhaps Verdi first. Something from *Rigoletto*. It'd warm Balducci up nicely. He had just struck a match and inhaled deeply, wondering what treasures tomorrow held, when he heard a yell from inside followed by a rumble. Rusty.

'Not tonight.' Dropping his cigarette, he strode to the door. He walked in to see Rusty standing over Burton's prone body, his face transformed. Curious punters coiled around him.

A bitter grimace had replaced Rusty's carefree smirk. He was breathing in heavy bursts, eyes wild. His blood-flecked fist pumped at his side sending ripples up his forearm; an empty tankard hung from his other fist. On the floor, the trumpeter touched his hand to his mouth and looked up in disbelief.

Max ran to them. 'Jesus. What happened?'

Teeth bared, Rusty was leaning over Burton, whose white shirt was dotted crimson. 'Next time I'll split more than your lip.'

'Calm down.' Max positioned himself between the two men and offered his hand to the musician. 'I do apologise, Mr Burton. Come on.' Refusing the hand, Burton remained on the floor. He repeatedly dabbed his lip. Frowning. Stunned.

Max ripped the tankard from Rusty's hand and slammed it on an upturned barrel. As he bundled him towards the door, he threw a handful of coins to the musician.

'Wrong way, darlings,' shouted a bare-shouldered girl when they passed. Laughter ripped through the tavern as he guided Rusty out into the street.

With a protective arm over his shoulder, he walked his cousin away from the building. 'What happened? You were having a fine time.'

'I was.' Rusty glanced back at the pub.

'And?'

'He smiled when I told him gramophones aren't selling.'

Max slowed, then stopped completely. He looked at Rusty askance. 'Hold on. You smile when I tell you gramophones aren't selling.' The Corporation's woes were a constant source of amusement to him.

'Yeah. But I'm allowed to. He's not.'

Max pursed his lips as he tried to stifle a laugh. It came anyway.

'What?' Rusty said.

'Stupid contrary idiot.' He lifted his arm from his cousin's shoulder and ruffled his hair, pushing him away as they walked. 'Honestly.'

As they neared Drury Lane again, Max crossed the road to avoid the entrance to Kemble Street. Even from here, he could see The Den's flickering portico and the queue outside. Four premises knocked into one. Franklin's biggest accommodation house and casino. His headquarters. Best avoided at all times. As he walked he was aware of Rusty staring at him. He looked across; his cousin was gazing up with childlike sincerity, his earlier fury evaporated, his face a picture of innocent needfulness.

'But it's us against the bastards, isn't it? You and me.'

'Of course it is.' Max nodded. 'Always.'

A pinch of nerves as Delilah ascended the dim stairs, twisting to make way for jostling inebriates coming down. She'd never done anything like this before. The doorman downstairs had lifted the rope at the weakest of smiles. This dress always worked. Pink lace over pearl satin, short enough to reveal stockinged calves. The Den. Foul place, she'd heard. But she'd also heard that the money was easy. No strings. Just provide company. Make them look good and feel important. Talk and caress. No compulsion to lie on your back or lean against a wall. Up to five shillings an evening just for company. Five times what the Paragon paid. Everyone did it. Most did worse. She'd see.

At the top of the stairs, a corridor led to a set of double doors. A muffled carnival throbbed beyond. She tucked a wayward coil of hair behind an ear and paused outside to compose herself. With a sudden crash the doors opened from within. A mob of girls, all pink ribbons and clicking heels, burst from the light, while a surge from revellers behind Delilah forced her into the supper room, carried like a rose on a landslide. Staggering to steady herself, she flattened a crease in her lace appliqué. It made no odds. No one was watching. As she stepped in, she saw no eyes; just a riot of backs and shoulders and thighs and nipples. Shadows and shapes danced under the quivering gasoliers suspended from the ceiling. The hall was a thick concentration of the self-interested; diners, shaggers, dollymops and dancing girls, either standing around tall tables, carousing along banqueting counters or sprawling on sofas. Lusty yells competed with a rowdy piano. Her eyes darted, her nostrils twitched. Even fortified wines and sweet gravies were unable to conceal the stench of fornication. Along one long wall, a series of doors opened and closed under the direction of a barking matron. The occupants of the dimly-lit chambers behind them were either shedding layers, writhing or rebuttoning garments. The perpetual motion of the gratification industry. Delilah turned. On the opposite wall was only one door, with two guards stationed outside. She'd been told about this. Barnabas Franklin's office. The centre of operations from where he ran his empire.

Straightening her back, she shouldered her way through the crowd. She walked with purpose to nowhere in particular, as though this was what she did. Flashes of faces. In every stranger she saw something familiar, something uniquely London. The tired perseverance of the girl just off stage, still in costume because punters paid an extra crown for role play. The quivering smile of the virtuous part-timer straining to sell filth, unable to shake the weight of shame. The layers of powder on the cheeks of the slum whore desperate to disguise her lesions. The men were acting too. Princes playing clerks. Clerks playing kings. Dandies playing paupers. Everyone trying to be a different version of themselves. She smirked at the daftness. Since when was ambiguity an asset, here or in life? The Den served one purpose. Money for pleasure. Why couldn't perverts be honest?

And yet she was assured this game had benefits. This room was a route up the ladder. Money bought choice. Money bought bigger digs. Money bought singing lessons, hot food and new boots. She may have had morals but she wasn't naïve. She knew how it worked. And the Den was best kind of establishment for this. The days of tarts being kept in brothels by madams were dying. In their place were rooms like this. Side chambers for hire at three shillings a night or one an hour. Sofas were half a crown each. Girls could come and leave as they pleased. Half their money went in their purses, the other half for the space they occupied. Here, girls were protected. Here, sofa covers and bedsheets were changed regularly. And they could go home at the end of the night. Franklin was protected too; in law, the place wasn't a whorehouse, it was a supper room, unlike some of his other establishments. It would be her secret. No one could ever know. Her father would kill her. Max would bin her. The Paragon girls would tilt their heads and feel better about themselves. She'd keep it a secret even from herself. She disliked Delilah Green for being here.

Air in her ear. She turned to see a puckered mouth inches from her face, its owner's eyes screwed shut as he blew at her. Beneath lank hair, a smile revealed a wooden peg among a crag of orange teeth. The warm stench of sour milk and rum. She jerked her head back.

'Aren't you delicious?'

He was in his forties, his accent suggesting a town house to the west rather than a tenement to the east. But the lapels of his once-pristine opera suit were smudged in grime, his shirt flecked with unidentifiable spillages. He handed her a wilted carnation and a coin. 'A crown for an hour. Sofa. Dance first.'

Delilah's eyes darted behind him. Dozens of other girls were in similar situations. To the individual, they were stroking cheeks, tugging on ties or cutting capers from their shows. She took a deep breath. A route up the ladder. Leaning back, she fixed her face with a determined smile and spun a slow pirouette. As she faced him again she rested a hand on his shoulder. A raspy groan. Sidling into him, she closed her nose, her mouth, her mind. She caught a flash of wooden peg as she put her lips to his ear and opened her mouth to speak. But no words came. The more she strained, the more her muteness grew. This rotting animal, half dead through liqueur, boundless opportunities squandered, deserved no words. Nor time. Nor pleasure.

Pausing where she was, she raised her hand from his shoulder and clasped her eyes shut. His hair was cold and moist against her fingers as she ran them up the back of his head. She cradled his crown, as a mother would a newborn's, her sealed lips still pressed to his ear. As she stood, imagining the tickle of soap and warm water on her hand, she saw movement outside Franklin's office. Two heavy-set men had dragged a third man to the door. He was wedged between them, head hanging, a pathetic link in the chain. One of the large men knocked. A pause. As the door opened, she caught a honeyed flash. Just a second, no more. In a bay behind a gilded desk, dressed in a gold-buttoned peacoat, a thick-set man sat completely still as a world of activity swirled around him. Franklin's gimlet eyes froze on the man dragged in. As the door swung shut, the man collapsed forwards as an arm the size of an ox leg thumped into his stomach. Then, no more. The room's activities were private once again.

Sour milk and rum, stronger than before. 'Come on then. What are you playing at?'

She started as a heavy hand pulled her dress's folds into her buttock. The hand circled as though kneading dough, its owner's breath growing heavier with every stroke. She coughed, suddenly deep in a world she'd only dallied with in her mind. Her pulse quickened and an unbearable itch pinched at her skin from head to toe. This was a misjudgement, a vile reality; being here was the difference between watching water from the shore and flailing in its choppy currents.

Lowering her hand, she reached for the man's trousers. Cupping the coarse wool beneath his crotch, she let his dangling triumvirate nestle in her palm. His lowest appendage swelled to the touch. Another rasp in her ear. She paused to ensure they were all there, thinking through the minutes ahead. With a grimace, she snapped her fingers together in a claw. Squeezing, she twisted his package before wrenching it down like a stubborn apple on a tree.

A howl screeched in her ear as the man's body jack-knifed. Bending with him, she gave her pitiful handful another yank before letting go and spinning away. She walked with pace towards the door, losing herself among the crowd's foul debauchery. As she heaved the door open she dropped the coin and threw the carnation to the floor. Fuck this. This wasn't the way.

# 4

Left a bit, signore,' Max said, eyeing Balducci's swaddled belly. He tapped the Italian on the shoulder to align him with the horn just inches from his face. The stretch of muslin encasing the baritone's stomach was causing him discomfort, but Rusty had refused to start the session until he was positioned correctly.

'There we go. Thank you, signore.' Max stepped back from the singer; the studio's heat magnified his deep-seated musk. He rubbed his hands and surveyed the room. The fire was stoked, the piano was in position. This was it. He rolled his shoulders and looked down to Langley, who was kneeling in his shirtsleeves behind Balducci. Flushed, he was preparing to take the strain with one end of the material, ready to heave the tenor backwards whenever he hit a high note. Max would take the other end.

'You see why your little shopping trip was so important, Mr Langley?'

High notes, they'd discovered, were sung with more gusto than low ones and therefore sounded louder. With no mechanical way of controlling a singer's volume, consistency of sound could only be maintained by varying the distance between the singer's mouth and the horn. A firm yank from the singer's rear did the trick. The muslin was one of Rusty's little inventions. The heft-heaver, he called it.

As Balducci warmed up, Max sat on the floor next to Langley and took one end of the muslin between his knees. 'When I pull, you pull.'

'Is it always this hot?' Langley said.

'Has to be or the wax on the disc hardens.' Max looked to the piano. 'Ready, Mr Wilson?'

He received an obsequious nod from the wheeled platform. Curious fellow, Wilson. Reliable player, mind.

'Ready, Rusty?'

Before they'd trussed him, Max had given the Italian the briefest of lessons. He had explained the importance of not stopping. Zincs were expensive. Despite nodding, Balducci seemed overwhelmed. Max supposed it was a common reaction to being bound up by strangers in a dark room. The setting was undeniably queer. Rather than send the notes over the heads of hundreds of rapt people, Balducci had been asked to send them down a cone. There was no orchestra, just a wheeled pianist. No matter. Balducci was certainly happy to accept a second bundle of notes. As far as Max was concerned, the arrangement was clear; he would make two recordings that afternoon and another four tomorrow. Six recordings for sixty pounds.

At the workbench in the corner, Rusty prepared the zinc master discs.

'Ready, Rusty?' Max repeated.

'No.'

Max turned and watched as his cousin coated the silver plates in the layer of beeswax and benzene that would capture the movements of the flickering stylus at the horn's end. The solution was far more impressionable than the old lampblack. On the bench in front of Rusty sat the steel tray of sulphuric acid into which he would briefly plunge the discs after the recording. The skull and crossbones on the acid's glass bottle always made Max nervous. But the acid was crucial; it burned the etchings in the wax onto the disc below. This would become the master from which all future pressings would follow.

'Signor Balducci,' Max said from the floor, 'I know it's hot but I suggest you stand with one leg in front of the other. For stability when you move backwards.'

Failing to move, Balducci shot him a withering glance. Max leapt from the floor and stood alongside him. He posed with one leg stretched in front of him like a limbering athlete. He slapped his front thigh and started to rock back and forth as he transferred his weight between his legs. 'Like this. Forward, back, forward, back. You see?'

The singer sighed and adopted the pose, his collar soaked with sweat. '*Sì.*'

Sitting once more, Max lifted his end of muslin and took the strain again. 'Sometimes,' he winked at Langley, 'this feels more like the industry of human haberdashery.' He glanced over as Rusty, now at the rig in the room's centre, placed a blank disc on the turning table and laid the stylus on its edge. 'Let's start with something from *Rigoletto*, eh Rus? To ease us in. How about *Pari Siamo*?'

The arioso about the jester lamenting similarities between himself and a murderer would be fresh in Balducci's mind.

Max waited for the nod from Rusty. 'Ready, Mr Wilson? *Pari Siamo*? Very well. On my count.'

Rusty wound the side-handle of the turning table and set the disc spinning.

The muslin tightened in Max's grip. '*Uno. Due. Tre.*'

A second's silence. Max's heart stopped as a thunderous rumble, intense and full of foreboding, shook the room. Volume dissipated in cavernous theatres. But here, Balducci's voice cannoned off the walls, its power almost overwhelming. Clasping his eyes shut, Max mouthed the words. *Pari siamo! Io la lingua, egli ha il pugnale.* He smiled. *We are two of a kind! My weapon is my tongue, his is a dagger.* His arms prickled as Wilson joined in with a low, dissonant piano. Covent Garden evaporated. He smelt the warmth of a Venetian evening. Geraniums burst from balconies, the air thick with drama.

'Now.' He nudged Langley.

As Balducci geared up for a high note they heaved on the material. A shadow loomed over them as Balducci tottered on his hind leg as though suspended, as likely to fall backwards as forwards. As the note sailed into the horn, Balducci slowly fell forwards onto his front foot. Max slackened the muslin. 'Perfect,' he mouthed.

He looked over to Rusty, who nodded that all was well as the needle scratched its grooves. The system, such as it was, was working. Between pulls on the muslin, Max conducted with his free fingers. When he signalled, Balducci was rocked.

Wondrous sorcery, he thought. Here in this room we have a group of people performing a range of tasks involving delicacy, passion, science and brawn to create an indelible record of the here and now. A beautiful warmth descended. This was the closest for years he'd felt to actually playing. He'd marshalled these elements and set the tone. He'd decided on the running order. In so many ways, this recording was his own composition. His own vicarious performance. Therein lay compensation.

The song ended too soon. Although hardly comfortable, Max could have listened for hours. He waited for Rusty to check that all was well with the zinc master on the turning table before he stood and patted Balducci on the back. The singer seemed befuddled, as though he had just completed some strange and dirty task.

'*Scandaloso*, Signor Balducci! *Scandaloso*!' he said. 'Take a moment and then we'll try something more recent. How about a tune from *Otello*?'

Balducci nodded. '*Era la Notte*?'

'Perfect. That brute Iago.' Max twirled his fists skywards as he imagined the evil turncoat, his phony kinship masking deception. At the side of the room Rusty dipped the completed master disc in the acid. The hiss of burning metal filled the studio. In destruction, creation. Max fetched a freshly waxed zinc from the workbench and placed it on the turning table. Although strictly Rusty's domain, he was capable of carrying out basic recording tasks. It was important not to keep Balducci waiting for too long.

When the rig had been reset, he and Langley re-assumed their positions with the muslin while Rusty stood by the machine. They went again. Balducci's rendition of *Era la Notte* was as glorious as he'd ever heard. It was delicate yet portentous and seemed to swell, once again filling their tiny basement, as it reached its climax. Magic and passion, Max thought as he drifted off again, magic and passion.

'Wait. Stop, *stop*...'

The piano trailed off, followed by Balducci. Max lowered the muslin and looked across to the rig. It was Rusty, agitated.

'What on earth is it?'

'The angle of the horn's wrong. Someone's knocked it.'

'No one's touched it. Are you sure?'

'Yes.' Scowling, Rusty walked round the machine and adjusted the ice skate cradle that supported the recording funnel. 'A cocked horn means weaker stylus vibrations. You know that.'

Max could not recall touching anything when he'd reset the machine. It must have been Balducci. 'But the singing was out of this world. Surely it'll do?' he said.

'No, Max. It won't *do*.'

'It's a waste of a perfectly good zinc. Really?' As he spoke he noticed that Rusty had started blinking. It was as if an internal wire had come loose.

'Are you trying to tell me what to do?'

It was a mere flash. But Max saw the same wildness dance across his pupils that he'd seen in the Lion the night before, and elsewhere all his life.

'*Are you trying to tell me what to do?*'

Max put out his hand and walked to Rusty. 'Please. Let's not cause a sce–' Before he knew it, Rusty had gripped his wrist. Max yanked his arm down and wrenched it free. His eyes watered as he rubbed the red tracks left by uncut fingernails. Cheeks warming, he looked his cousin in the eye. He spoke slowly and deliberately. 'Forgive me, Rusty. I'm sorry. You're absolutely right. Let's go again.' He turned and clapped to the room. 'Sorry everyone. A small technical issue. From the top.' Max retreated and watched as Rusty replaced the half-used blank disc with a fresh one. He blinked the confrontation away. 'Apologies, Signor Balducci. Let's go again when you're ready.'

'From the start?'

'I'm afraid so, signore.'

He sat next to Langley, ignoring the stare. 'Ready?'

The second rendition went without a hitch. Although it lacked some of the raw passion of the previous version, Max decided to keep his counsel. Petty squabbles escalated too easily.

It was with a heavy heart that, after the two songs and as per their agreement, Max called an end to the session and led the Italian out into the fading light of Tavistock Street. As he left the building he peered down the road for the prying eyes of Franklin's goons. There were none. The sweat on his back turned cool in the evening air. He knew it was pathetic but the goodbye felt bitter and premature. However, the next session was just fifteen hours away. Four more songs tomorrow, he thought. Four more shots at perfection. Some days, London was a fecund orchard.

'Now, be sure to rest your voice overnight, signore. I'll come to fetch you from your room in the morning.'

Balducci nodded as he pulled on a greatcoat, more relaxed than before. He leaned into Max. 'Tomorrow I give you Puccini.'

His arms tingled. 'And Mozart.'

'And Bizet!' Balducci bellowed a throaty laugh and clapped Max on the back. 'And Bizet!' he repeated as he walked down the cobbles towards the Strand.

Back in the studio, Max jigged in delight at Balducci's performance. As Langley folded the muslin, he wrapped the zinc masters in oilcloth in preparation for sending them to be copied and pressed onto shellac. Rusty was busying himself at his workbench.

'All well, Mr Engineer?' Max put the wrapped discs in a storage cupboard.

Rusty nodded. 'Never better. Look, don't worry about earlier.'

Max smiled. *Don't worry* meant *sorry*. It was Rusty's strange language. And it was the closest he'd get to an apology. Max wafted his hand in the air. The disagreement had evaporated in the heat. What mattered was that they had Balducci.

'That tubby lump delivered the goods, eh?' Rusty said.

'He certainly did.' Max pulled out his pocket watch. 'And I think we've all earned the right to celebrate. How does the Café Royal sound? Will you join us, Mr Wilson?'

Wilson was packing his sheet music in a holdall, seemingly

in a rush to leave.

'I'm afraid I can't, Mr Cadenza. Plans.'

'Very well. Until tomorrow.'

As Max wrote Balducci's name in the recording ledger, he thought of the singer's near-perfect rhythm and pitch. He slowly nodded. The voice may have belonged to the Italian but he had captured it.

He had caged the beast.

⚙️◈◈⚙️◈

Delilah placed her gloves in their usual spot between the jar of honey and the talcum powder on her chest of drawers. She turned and prodded the flannel bung in the impossibly-shaped hole in the window pane. The stench from the tyre factory on Ridley Road was always worse with a southerly wind.

She sat on the bed and unlaced her boots. This place was always going to be temporary. She'd dreamed of better digs almost as soon as she moved in. A bigger room across town. Perhaps with its own bathroom or a piano to practise on. But while the Mi Mi role had paid reasonably well, being back at the Paragon had delayed that dream by a few months at least. Even working fifteen-hour days, she'd be in this room for a while yet. It was, she supposed, tolerable. But who wanted tolerable? Ambition died at tolerable's lowly doorstep.

The Den had been a disaster. A ladder down, not a ladder up. The nape of her neck itched at the memory of the stinking place. What was she thinking? Apart from anything else, it would have played into her parents' flawed narrative, the reason she'd left home in Stepney in the first place. Everyone knew of actresses for whom the midnight swish of the curtain marked the start of the night not the end. But her father thought the jobs were one and the same. And there she was preparing to give succour to his prejudice. She was an actress. That was all. Still, it never stopped people assuming. She'd just have to act harder. Act better. Prove herself.

It had been a nice afternoon with Molly. Sweet girl, and not as soft as she'd thought. Reaching behind her, she picked up a cup from the windowsill. The pan downstairs would soon be boiling; she never missed her evening cup of hot water and honey.

She shivered as a cold gust breached the window's paltry defences. Twisting her body around on the uneven mattress, she took hold of the curtain's corner and dragged it across the window, being careful not to rip the moth-eaten material from its runners. An orange hue overlaid the piebald walls, at least suggesting warmth. It helped. She glanced around. Perhaps she'd decorate. The room needed something. The bed and the cupboard behind the door – containing her worldly wardrobe of five frocks, three petticoats, stockings, bloomers and her mother's fur coat – were all that the landlord provided. She'd had to buy the chest of drawers and the old oak dining chair. The oval mirror, the Chinese parasol and the lace cloth over the back of the chair were also hers; legacies of previous dalliances with assorted bastards, and the only remnants of those times worth a penny. Yes, she'd decorate. Give the room some colour. Max would help her. Maybe the room could incorporate something music-related. She'd seen the sitar on the wall in his office. She smiled as she imagined what he'd suggest. It would be something daft. He'd probably hoist a gaily-painted accordion over the bed or stick a gramophone under the mirror. Whatever his involvement, it would certainly be spirited. But then, no. She kicked off her unlaced boots and lifted her legs up into the folds of her petticoat. The chill crept up on her again, scattering her cosy thoughts as it spread. Of course Max would never see this room. Why would she let him? Her entire life was contained in this rented box on the second floor of a Dalston townhouse. One look and he'd know that the clothes he'd seen her wear were not the tip of a large and varied wardrobe but the wardrobe in its totality. Max was special. He was different from the rest. What if he took one look and ran? She cared about the silly fool.

Barely anyone knew about her basic accommodation or how little she owned, and as long as she kept working and striving and singing and pushing, then barely anyone ever would. This was London, her city. She'd spent years tramping through its squares, streets and alleyways. She knew the names of its theatres and music halls. Why shouldn't the city know her name in return? It would. One day. Something happened when she sang. She was free. Unstoppable. Holloway, Ealing, New Cross and Peckham all had brand new Palaces, Empires or Hippodromes. They were different from Franklin's Covent Garden theatres, independently-owned. There were auditions coming up. And Euston, the grandest palace of them all, was due to open in weeks. She'd heard it was drenched in gold from top tier to bottom. She reached down and gathered the corners of her bedspread. Pulling them over her shoulders, she wrapped the material around her. She'd get to these places as sure as she'd get out of this room. Some called her enthusiasm impulsive. She called it determined. She hugged the bedspread tighter. All this was temporary.

Downstairs, the kettle whistled. She stood to fetch the boiling water. As she reached for her slippers, a fist thumped on the outside of her door; her landlord's delicate touch. 'Visitor,' he shouted.

Delilah pulled on the slippers and tied her bedspread about her like a shawl. Odd. She wasn't expecting anyone. She walked into the corridor and descended the two flights, humming softly. As she heaved the front door open, she thought of Max and his sprig of lavender. Perhaps a visit wouldn't be so bad after all.

'Oh. It's you.'

Standing on the doorstep clasping a bunch of wilting delphiniums, his lips freshly licked and glistening, was Mr Wilson.

❦❦❦❦❦

'What happened to your finger?'

Max saw Langley nod at his right hand. He raised his shortened middle finger to his face and dragged on his cigarette. 'This? Cheetah in Sudan. Bit the tip clean off.'

'A cheetah?'

'Yes. Ask Rusty. Would've lost the whole hand were it not for his lightning reaction.' Max smiled. The Café Royal's plates and crockery chimed like a hundred pizzicato violins. Voices buzzed over the top.

Langley leaned over the table and repeated the question to Rusty.

'His finger? He got frisky with an adder in Devon.'

'But you said it was a chee–'

Max swiped the air. Games were unfair. 'I'm sorry, Mr Langley.' He placed a hand on his shoulder. 'An accident when I was a child. You'll stop noticing it soon enough.'

'What kind of accident?'

'A painful one.' Langley would find out one day. 'Now, more Moët?' He looked down at his hand. He'd lost so much more than a pink tip. The flesh itself was merely a quarter of one of twenty digits. The size of a bean. But something far bigger had gone with it; his ability to perform, his intended future, his means of expression. It was a heinous consequence for half an inch of bone. At least the accident was, he supposed, oddly responsible for the Corporation's formation.

Max checked his reflection in the restaurant's mirrored walls. He tucked his curls behind his ears and reshaped his moustache. 'Not conventionally handsome' was how he'd once heard himself described. He'd often disagreed, but that assertion felt particularly wrong this evening. Framed by the room's ornate mouldings and peach-hued gasoliers, did he look dashing and unstoppable? Or merely stylish and irrepressible? He couldn't decide. As he watched his reflection disappear into prism after prism, the second line of *Era la Notte* looped around his head. Balducci had sung it with such power; the way his voice strengthened as it sank made Max's ribcage tingle. He turned to the table and raised his glass. 'Gentlemen, to a good day's work. And an impressive start, Mr Langley.'

'Thank you.'

Rusty lit his pipe, saying nothing.

'Now. The moment I've been waiting for.' Max reached into his breast pocket and removed the leather wallet. He pulled out a dog-eared square of paper and set it on the table. 'My jewels. Rusty, a pen if you please.'

'Here we go.' Rusty shook his head.

'A pen!' The ceremony always irritated Rusty, but Max was banking on a show of solidarity in front of the new recruit. He smiled when he felt the weight of an ink pen drop into his palm. 'Observe.'

With the delicacy of a surgeon he unfolded the paper, its scrawny fibrous hinges connecting a loose patchwork of squares. On it, a list. Twelve items. Three had lines through them. Little had given him more pleasure than capturing the flamenco guitar of Miguel Sandoval in Seville the previous summer. Over two hundred people now owned that majestic cut. Max was thrilled at the figure, Rusty less so. Rusty had even joked about the relatively modest sales, saying that *Music of the Sands* had turned them into 'a household name – in a household'. But sales were sales. The bagpipers of Nethy Bridge and the baroque choir at Amiens had proven more arduous but no less rewarding, even though they'd shifted fewer than three dozen units between them. But the satisfaction Max took in striking a delicate line through his latest conquest trumped them all. In less than a second, Alfredo Balducci changed from an aspiration to a possession.

Eight to go, he thought. Carefully, he turned the paper to Langley. 'I spent months listening, reading and researching as I compiled this list. Individually, they cover every musical base. Taken together, they form the perfect library. Any truth worth expressing is in this music. Capture these jewels and you have the world.'

'Capture these jewels and you have the pox, more like,' Rusty said.

'*Please*. No one will resist once these are committed to shellac. By appointment or chance, we'll get them all. And the industry of human happiness will be ours. We'll also be friends with the richest men in London.' He felt his colleagues' eyes on him. '*Each other*.'

Langley scanned the list. 'Harlem.'

'A variation on ragtime. I hear something magical's brewing.' He smiled. Music bursting onto the street from sweaty backstreet boxes, he'd been told. Black faces from the South taking their brass to New York's piano bars. Life-affirming joy like little else.

'What's a Cornish crowdy-crawn?'

'Folk drum...'

'That,' Rusty craned in, 'is a hoop stretched with stinking sheepskin. A real jewel there.'

'Russian sea shanty. Serbian folk song,' Langley read.

'Soon. I hope,' Max said.

'Wilma Wagensperg?'

Max closed his eyes. 'Wilma. Vienna's finest violinist.'

'More Bach than Epping Forest.'

'Hush, Rusty. She's exceptional. Cripplingly shy. Rarely tours. Weaves magic from air.' Max turned to Langley. 'So, what do you make of my list?'

'I think you're going to be busy.'

'Wrong. *We're* going to be busy. Rusty thinks I'm mad. But capture them we will. No compromise, no exceptions.'

'You seem to have quite a system worked out in the studio,' Langley said.

'It's loose and unorthodox, but it works.' Max placed a protective arm around Rusty. 'He's a nut. I'm a bolt. Together we hold.' He squeezed his cousin in close. 'It's mainly down to him, to be honest. Tell me, Mr Langley, do you know the precise ratio of beeswax to benzene required to make the best recording solution?'

'No.'

'He does. Do you know how thick the solution needs to be – to the hundredth of an inch – to produce the least drag on a cutting stylus?'

'No.'

As he spoke, Max was aware of Rusty covering his face with his jacket in mock embarrassment. 'He does. What about the optimum size of a recording horn's diaphragm for the best transference of sound vibrations to the needle?'

Langley shook his head.

'Neither do I. I could guess, but he knows *precisely*. The man's a genius. I just pick the musicians.'

Rusty pulled his jacket back down and nodded at the list on the table. 'Truth is, I'm the only one who'll put up with him.'

Max smiled weakly. He didn't see it like that. Folding the paper, he replaced the list in the leather pouch.

'And guess what, Streak? I hate music. It's just dots on a page to me.'

Max nodded. 'A steel heart and a tin ear.'

He tried to duck as Rusty leaned across the table and placed his head in a lock. The hard ball of Rusty's bicep skimmed across his forehead, as tight and muscular as a coiled python. It was accompanied by the fusty odour of his sack coat, bought for beans from some rag fair. Max always scoffed at his argument that second-hand clothes were just as good as new ones. If taverns sold garments, Rusty would be the best dressed man in London. Max pushed him away and ran his hands through his hair. 'I say Mr Langley, why don't you tell Rusty your story about the musicians in Luxor? The one that enchanted me so when you told it at the Trocadero.'

'Well, it's really not of great significance…'

'Nonsense. It's charming.'

'Very well,' Langley sat up, nervous. 'We once – my parents and I, that is – had an Easter holiday in Luxor when my father was posted to the embassy in Egypt. He was a diplomat, you see. I was seven or eight. We were sitting on a patio by the river, my father was teaching me how to play vingt-et-un, when a boat – a felucca – carrying musicians sailed up the Nile. They wore bright blue robes and carried calabashes of water. A crowd lined the shore and people started singing and hollering and clapping. As the boat approached, the musicians started to play. Pipes and percussion. It was a magical clamour. It hooked me so I ran to the river's edge. It was glorious,' he tailed off, seemingly embarrassed at the lack of punchline.

'And…?' Rusty said.

'And my mother followed me and took me back to the house.'

'And?'

'Well, she sent me to my bedroom.' He stopped, reddening. In the Trocadero version he'd talked about his tears.

Max watched as Rusty slammed his fist on his thigh and rocked back in laughter.

'Fucking hell, Streak, you'd better improve your storytelling.' A wheeze then a whistle.

'Rusty! Did you not hear him? *A magical clamour.*' Max widened his eyes to suggest he calmed down. 'He's one of us.'

'So when did you get so interested in music, Mr Cadenza?' Langley said, diverting attention from himself. 'Do you play?'

Max shot Rusty a glance. At least telling him would stop the endless questions. 'My late father was a concert pianist. Of some repute, apparently.' He always played it down; Papa had been a virtuoso. Everyone knew. 'He played in theatres in the Garden for our friend Mr Franklin. And I played myself. I was rather good as it happens. But then I had to stop.' Once again he raised the shortened digit on his right hand. Mama's horrified face flashed before his eyes; she hovered above him, his head woozy on the carpet. 'Ever get the feeling that you've been cheated? Cripples don't tend to be known for their piano playing. The music's in here now.' He tapped his temple.

Langley tilted his head as though keen to probe further. But no words came. Instead he returned to his champagne and said nothing. Max wasn't surprised. If the tables were turned he would not have known what to say either. He swigged. In the weeks since Papa's death he had often thought about what had happened down at Chaveley. Mama had suggested to him that now would be a good time to let bygones be bygones. But he could not forgive, or forget. It was too late. The anger was too deep-rooted.

He heard Rusty explain to Langley that his own parents were dead. Poor chap, he thought. What must he think of us? He listened as the new boy expressed condolences. Then he saw Rusty shrug and say that everything would come right in the end. Max scoured the room for familiar faces. All this family talk was irritating. Tonight of all nights was not one for domestic matters. The pizzicato violins intensified; this was a profitable crowd.

A reflection caught Max's eye as the café's doors opened. As though sucked by a vacuum, the noise level suddenly lulled. Shouts were replaced by a ripple of whispers. Three men walked slowly towards the middle of the room, diners' necks craning in their wake like windswept barley. Max's stomach tightened. Chin down but eyes scouring, the short man in the middle prowled with the gait of a ravenous wolf.

'I don't believe it.' Max swallowed. 'Mr Langley.' He kicked his colleague under the table.

'Boss?'

He nodded towards the figure. 'Franklin.'

The noise picked up, as though diners were eager to downplay their reaction. Flanked by two blackguards, Franklin strode between the tables with an occasional shallow nod. Although in his seventh decade, his square jaw and unsmiling face had not altered in the years Max had known him. Nor had his love of immaculate tailoring. A green cravat, pinned with an ostentatious gem, matched the velvet collar of his black swallowtail jacket. Thin grey hair, die-straight and oiled back as though freshly wet, tickled his collar as he walked. I should have known, thought Max. Franklin was notorious for spending his evenings prior to curtain-up scouring the cafés and restaurants of theatreland for people of influence or debtors. Both received equal attention. These days, the few supper rooms that he didn't control were subject to the extortion rackets that he did. Max's eyes flicked to the two guards following him. One carried his hat, the other his coat.

As the unnerving trio patrolled the room, Max considered leaving. If they turned and crept out now, it was possible that Franklin wouldn't see them. He imagined the street's cool air on his face. He imagined sitting in Simpson's unencumbered. But as he looked to his men, Balducci's baritone echoed in his ear. Its overwhelming power. Its thunderous rumble. He remained seated. No one person could lay claim to that voice. Why should he run from Franklin? What they'd just achieved in the studio was unprecedented. He watched Franklin's sickening sense of entitlement as he paraded. A slam. Papa at his piano. Max didn't move from the table.

Tucking a curtain of hair behind his ear, he saw that Franklin had seen him. He ran his callous's twisted peak along the ridges of his teeth as he braced himself for contact. A tinny clash rippled through him as he secured armour. The men edged closer.

Franklin stopped. His glare froze the channel of air between them. Turning, he whispered to his guards. As he resumed his slow walk towards the table, all Max noticed was the light reflecting from his shoes. They'd been tallowed to become black mirrors. Unimaginably shiny.

When he was two tables away, Franklin raised a finger. 'Young man.' His flat Bow croak was so low that it was barely audible. He held his finger still, an arrow slowly homing in on its target.

Max stood from the table. From the corner of his eye, he saw Rusty do the same. He loosened his shoulders. They could either win this moment or let it crush them like wet cement.

Franklin was three paces away. 'You and your gewgaws are starting to irritate me.'

'Good evening, Mr Franklin. So I gather.' As he spoke, the knot in his stomach intensified. 'I received your little card.'

'I'm glad.'

Win or be crushed. 'And I ripped it up.' He heard a faint snort from Rusty, and stood still as Franklin edged closer to him. Unexpectedly, years tumbled. The waft of rose cologne jolted him back to Chaveley.

'Listen, Maximilian, my people have their ears to the ground. I know you've been sniffing around. If I hear that you've gone ahead and recorded the Italian there'll be consequences. Here, he's my property.' Reaching up, Franklin tapped Max's cheek, almost paternal in his softness. 'Is that clear, boy?'

Max was aware of Rusty bristling next to him but he threw him a darting glance; Franklin clearly had no idea about that afternoon's session. He was in the dark. News of the recording had eluded him.

'Consequences?' Max held Franklin's gaze and, emboldened, sunk his tongue into his cheek cavity. Ignoring his inner voice, he slowly shrugged.

'Your father would be ashamed of you.'

'Lucky he's dead then,' Max hissed. No one mentioned that man. Not to him.

Franklin raised a finger at his side to calm his men. 'If I didn't care for your mother so much I'd destroy you.'

'How terribly benevolent of you.'

Franklin inched so close that his nose disappeared from view. His eyes darkened. Rose cologne and intolerable pain. 'Give it up, sonny. Now.'

Max linked his hands at his waist to stop them shaking. 'Mr Franklin, you seem to think that people like us exist for your sport. But don't you see?'

'See what?'

He considered it for a second. Unclasping his fingers, he raised one and pointed from Franklin to himself. Thinking of Balducci, he raised a brow. 'That, in fact, people like you exist for ours.'

'We'll see.'

We will, Max thought, expecting at any moment the guards to reach forward and grab him. He watched Franklin. A slight tongue moistened mean lips. Max wondered when the impresario had last made a decision based on passion or creativity rather than box office receipts or lucre. There were more than just inches between him and this fool; there was a chasm of outlook, of mindset, of age. The compulsion to say it overwhelmed him. He shook his head. 'You're pretending the world isn't changing, Mr Franklin. Soon you'll understand that it is.'

Franklin stood on the spot, chewing on an unknown morsel. He nodded down to Max's curtailed finger. 'You want to be careful, boy.'

Then, to Max's surprise, he looked back to his men and signalled at the door. The duo turned and started to clear a path back across the café floor. Franklin held Max's gaze for a few seconds and turned himself. The departure was a bluff, surely. Max looked at Rusty and frowned; this felt strange, as though reading a book with a chapter missing. But the trio were now ten paces away, Franklin's thin hair bobbing on his collar as he went. They walked without stopping until they reached the door, a circle of silence accompanying them as they went. The blackguards heaved the doors open and, like an apparition, Franklin disappeared.

As the doors swung shut, Max reached into his pocket for

a cigarette. Quivering, he put it in his mouth. Elation like he'd never felt rose from his feet. It almost numbed. Soon his entire body was tingling as though he'd escaped from the path of a runaway carriage. He looked at Rusty, who was wearing his dirtiest of smiles.

Max roughly sparked a match, unsure of whether to bend double laughing or skip town. He reached for a drink.

As he sat, an exultant clattering filled his ears. A burst of tribal drums, triumphant and enlivening. He frowned and looked back at Rusty. They'd outgunned him. He had no idea about the recording. How can there be consequences when he's in the dark? He sat back. This was sweet. It was more than sweet; it was victory, pure and glorious.

Even though Max could feel the chair's seat beneath him he soared upwards, such was the joy of the moment. A giddiness overtook him and he felt curiously lightheaded. He saw Langley sit forward. The lad looked bewildered and slightly embarrassed at the scene he'd just witnessed. He looked as though he wanted to move the conversation rapidly on.

'Rusty,' Langley said politely. 'You were saying about your parents before... I'm sorry. What precisely happened to them? You never told me.'

Max yanked the cigarette from his lips and, thinking of Franklin, deployed his best menacing croak. 'They went swimming, boy,' he said, pointing his finger across the table.

As soon as the words left his mouth he regretted them. He blinked as Rusty turned to him, a look of disbelief on his face. It was as though some other person had spoken, a person so high on the fumes of the moment that they'd taken leave of reality. He crashed to earth. 'Rusty, I'm sorry.'

Rusty blinked. 'What did you say?'

'Nothing. I was being...ridiculous.'

'They went *swimming*?'

Max shook his head. He'd been caught up in his own excitement. Of all the spontaneous things he'd ever said, this was the most daft. He'd always assumed that Rusty blamed him for what happened, at least in part. Rusty's cheeks ruddied and his eyes took on a fiery, faraway look. A moist sheen overlaid his pupils' rawness.

'I'm going.' Rusty stood.

'I was being bird-brained. I'm sorry. Please.'

It was too late. Before he could work out what to do next, Rusty had punched his chair and was walking from the table.

*Fool.* What a stupid, needlessly rotten way to end the day. He cursed himself for hurting the man. And on a day of such considerable victory. He turned to Langley, who was looking sheepish.

'Sorry, old boy. We're too close. Sometimes I...lose perspective.' He picked up a champagne flute and clinked Langley's, a gesture as empty as the glasses themselves. Poor Rusty. He'd find him later and apologise. 'Anyway. Welcome to the company.'

# 5

The clean air of the Savoy's lobby soothed Max's head, still tender from last night's grog. He'd found Rusty in Rules after midnight, crawling into a bottle of whisky. A bootlick apology had made things all right. At least he'd hoped it had. For half an hour he sought to explain himself: he'd been elated, tired, daft. Swimming was such an insensitive word to use. He'd sealed his atonement with an embrace, which Rusty accepted. The chap still looked out of sorts, mind. No matter. They were all tired. A bridge had, Max was sure, been built.

The lobby was strangely quiet. As the hotel was among the first buildings in England to be lit entirely by electric bulbs rather than gas lamps, there was no rodent-like chirping from the orange flames. With no sound to cling on to, Max felt strangely bereft. He sped up his walk, fashioning a waltz from shoe leather on marble. Alfredo Balducci would be waiting. They'd be back in the studio within half an hour. Another few tunes like yesterday and we'll be there, he thought.

He walked to the lobby's western corner and entered an electric elevator. The bellboy pulled the cage door closed and the box rattled to the fifth floor. Max felt gravity's pull. An ascending box lifted by unseen cogs. He smiled at the audacity of it.

The elevator jolted to a halt and he stepped into the rich red of the corridor. He turned right; he'd booked Balducci into a river-facing room on the basis that it was quieter than a street-facing one. Room 522 was at the end of a long passage. With the final bill in mind, it was not the most lavish room but it was comfortable and commodious.

He neared the end of the corridor and saw that the door to Balducci's room was ajar. Through the crack he noticed that the curtains remained drawn; he pushed the door fully open and entered.

'Hello?'

Immediately he smelt the singer's unmistakable presence. But there was something else, something sharp. As the thick drapery across the windows prevented all but the dullest of light from illuminating the room, he reached for the switch next to the door.

He winced at the harshness of the chandelier's bulbs. As he slowly blinked himself back into the room, his eyes were drawn to the bed to his left. Sitting on the mattress with his nightshirt drenched crimson, starkly lit from above, sat the rotund figure of Balducci.

Slaughtered.

The singer's outstretched arms were lashed to the oak corners of the bedstead, his soiled nightshirt billowing below. Blood soaked his breasts. Bed sheets collected around the singer's legs; concentric circles of rust-coloured stains radiated around his crotch and thighs, suggesting that his unknown ordeal had been drawn out.

Max froze. The image of a war-damaged frigate flashed into his mind. His world darkened and his legs fell away.

He came to on the floor as if newly awakened. For a split-second he had to remind himself where he was. Raising himself, he looked back to the bed. Balducci's eyes stared straight ahead and his mouth hung open as if performing. Above his collarbone, the flesh of his neck had been carved open from one side to the other.

Edging towards the bed on his knees, Max hauled himself upright. As he stood, the full horror became clear. Once, when he was young, he had received a shock so sudden and brutal that he assumed it could never be trumped. But it just had. He knew that this was a sight he would never – could never – forget. He covered his mouth in an attempt to stop the vomit. It came anyway. Bile seeped through his fingers. Some caught in his moustache, most trickled down the inside of his shirt to his elbow. He wiped his lips and reached for his handkerchief. He exhaled through his nose with a strange mewling sound. Whatever noise he was making, he knew that he had never made it before.

So tight were the tethers on Balducci's arms that he appeared to be sitting up perfectly straight. His tongue hung low from his gaping mouth. The fat exposed by the slice to his neck had dried slightly, causing the opening to curl outwards like a nymph's pout.

Trembling, Max wiped his mouth. What had happened? Just last afternoon he was standing with Balducci in the studio, recording. And now he was confronted by this brutal savagery. He wondered what he should do. Not because he wanted to but because he thought it was right, he screwed his eyes shut and sent a silent prayer to Balducci's young wife in Milan and a second to his parents in their hamlet outside…where was it? Orton? Ancona? It really didn't matter. Poor wretches. He opened his eyes. How would he explain this to the police?

Glancing back at the corpse, he wondered how long the singer's torture lasted.

As he looked, he noticed something else. Above the slash across Balducci's neck, a cluster of metallic spots were catching light from the chandelier. The glistening looked to Max like the kind of reflection that would come from a women's choker or neck-brooch. And yet Balducci was wearing no such adornment. He covered his mouth once more and leaned in closer.

Into the skin around his protruding larynx – about an inch above his sliced neck – someone had inserted what appeared to be needles. Max counted five. They were pushed into his throat by around half of their full length, neatly encircling his voice box as if it was a pin cushion. As he took a closer look he noticed they had thick triangular bases. The bile rose in his throat once more. He recognised the implements. They weren't merely needles, they were stylus needles. What's more, they were the stylus needles made specifically for The London Gramophone Corporation's latest Empress model.

He lurched backwards as a black hood descended, smothering all thought. For a moment, he was once again absent from the world as a ghastly internal recalibration occurred. As the hood slowly lifted, the reality of the situation was obvious. This was no random act of violence. It was something far more sinister. This murder was a message. And it was aimed squarely at him. *Franklin.*

He grabbed the bedpost to steady himself, his mouth as dry as leather. What chaos had he caused? With a shake of the head he took two steps backwards. What he really needed now was for somebody to tell him what to do, for someone to gently guide him away and calm him down. But there was nobody there. Just himself and the gruesome cadaver.

Turning, he paced to the door. The hotel manager. He'd go

immediately to the hotel manager. Then he would alert the police. That was the correct way to do things. That is what he'd do.

Every instinct he had told him to keep moving. As he left the room he broke into a quick walk, then a run. Dashing down the corridor, he passed the entrance to the lift and crashed through the door of the stairwell beyond. His steps echoed as he ran down flight after flight.

All he craved was fresh air. All he wanted was to forget what he'd seen. All he needed was to tell the manager, then leave.

CRANGRANG

'But how did Franklin know? He didn't have a clue last night.' Hands shaking, Rusty poured two more brandies. Fair skinned anyway, he was more ashen than Max had ever seen him.

Max took the glass and sat on the office chaise. He was not sure whether his heart was pounding due to his run from the Savoy to Bow Street Police Station or due to the shock of what he'd seen. But his limbs were quivering between the thuds, convulsing his entire body. 'Goodness knows. He's got spies everywhere. It's the only explanation.'

'What did the peelers say?'

'Not a great deal. They're examining the room now. Sent me back here. Want me to go and talk to them later.'

I'm not right, Max thought. The second he saw the body he felt his world lose its shape. The second he saw the needles his world lost its colour too. Everything seemed bleached, monochrome, flat. Over the years he'd flirted with London's dirty underbelly, gently toyed with the city's dark side, but he'd never been caught up in anything like this before. It had all been an adventure. Until now.

'This wasn't your average nobbling. You should have seen him. He was flagellated.'

'Poor bastard.' Rusty leaned against the desk, sucking on his pipe. He looked different to Max today, as if the news of Balducci's death had somehow altered his features. It was his eyes. They looked as lifeless as he felt.

Max gazed ahead. 'His arms were tied. They mutilated the voicebox,' he raised a hand to his throat. 'Put needles in.'

Even though he had already described it to Rusty, the man flinched again.

'You're sure they were our stylus needles?' Rusty said. 'And surely if they're Empress needles we can track down whoever bought them? There must be a way.'

'How? Our stockists have got boxes of them, all over town. *Hundreds* of unsold boxes. Anyone could have picked some up.'

Rusty shook his head. 'Franklin,' he whispered. 'Evil bastard.'

'I never thought he'd actually do something like this.' Max hadn't even had to talk to Rusty about the perpetrator. They both knew. 'I thought last night was just...talk.'

In a macabre way, he supposed it all made sense. Balducci's run in Franklin's theatre was over so he had no use for him. In a single act of brutality, Franklin had punished the Italian for daring to record while at the same time robbing The London Gramophone Corporation of bona fide opera music. And as well as wreaking revenge, he had sent a signal: I'm as good as my word. Franklin was a clever man. His contacts in the force would ensure he escaped punishment. Max recognised that ruthlessness. It was the same ferocious quality that had turned him into London's most feared operator. He had seen similar ambition in the way he had spirited Papa from the polite salons of north London to the West End's grandest theatres.

Alternative perpetrators flashed through Max's mind but

none made as much sense. Were the owners of the other latent talking machine companies jealous at his star signing? Did they have murder in them? Possibly, but he doubted it. Could a crazed vagabond have ridden up in the elevator and stalked the floor until he found a victim? Perhaps, but there was solid security at the Savoy. Had Balducci picked up a Haymarket prostitute with a twisted sense of fun? Unlikely. The man was breathless after walking down a flight of stairs. He was too fat to fuck.

He looked at Rusty. The tell-tale ruddiness had flooded his cousin's jawline. He had always been a stormy soul, but now he seemed genuinely incensed.

'We should get Franklin.' Rusty stabbed the air.

'Calm down. And stop being daft.'

Every crook and ruffian in London had some form of loyalty to Franklin. By simply entering the music world, Max had dived into fairly murky water. He wouldn't last a day in even dingier surroundings. He wouldn't even know how to go about 'getting' someone. It was not an option.

'Do the police suspect anyone? What about the hotel? They must have seen something,' Rusty said.

'Who knows.' He signalled for another inch of brandy. He had to keep a clear head for the police but the drink helped. Time had stopped making sense. He thought back to that morning when he woke up. It seemed mere minutes ago. And yet when he thought of the events in Balducci's room, they unfurled at a glacial pace. Above anything else, he felt culpability. If Balducci had not recorded for the company then he would probably still be alive. If he had not been so insistent on the singer staying in London then maybe he'd be on the steamer back to Italy and not lifeless on a cold slab. It was almost as though Balducci had died at his own hand.

'Where's Streak?' Rusty asked.

'Sent him home.' The lad had been preparing the muslin in the studio for the day's session. Max wanted the unalloyed presence of his cousin.

Rusty glared into his glass. He contemplated saying something before stopping and draining his brandy. 'You don't think...'

'What?'

Rusty raised a hand in a plea for forbearance. 'Hear me. But how much do we actually know about the lad?'

'Who?'

'Langley.'

Realising what he was hinting at, Max smiled. 'You're not about to suggest that he tipped off Franklin, aren't you?'

'I'm simply asking the question. There's something about him. He's almost too timid.'

'Tish.' It was preposterous. The boy couldn't walk from Blackfriars to Bow Street without a map. 'There's nothing about him. Don't be silly.'

Silence descended, like a lull in a hailstorm.

'What do we do now?' Rusty said.

Max looked at his feet. He had no idea. Giving up was inconceivable. There was too much at stake. But carrying on as they had been seemed equally impossible.

'I don't know, Rusty.' He picked at the chaise's frayed arm with his fingers. Then he shook his head and emptied his glass. 'I just don't know.'

◌❀◌❀◌

Of all life's ironies, this was the grimmest: Bow Street police station stood directly opposite the opera house. While one entrance was grand, the other was a foul mirror image. One was the site of Balducci's apotheosis, the other the scene of his post-mortem. On entering the station, Max was guided down a corridor towards Detective Inspector Boot's office by the duty peeler. The building reeked; muffled shouts from the holding cells below were carried on air thick with piss and cheap perfume. The corridor itself was a rogue's gallery of skeletal hoodlums and stewed floozies. Max wondered if it was safer outside than in.

Even now, three hours after finding Balducci, he couldn't control his quivering hands. His head was equally scrambled. Events, so clear and stark before, had become strangely confused the more he thought about them. It was as though in swirling things around his mind, he'd muddied his memory. All he wanted to do was sleep.

Max walked into Boot's office to the sound of singing. A large man, the detective was sitting at his desk eating a bun. His vast white sideburns vibrated between chews as he pom-pommed some jovial tune. Max wondered if he'd got the right office.

Seeing Max, Boot rose from his chair. His thick uniform strained across his chest's lavish curvature as he wiped his hands on his sides. 'Mr Cadenza. Detective Inspector Frank Boot. Please sit.' His deep bass bounced off the bare walls.

'Thank you.'

'Do you like Gilbert & Sullivan?'

Even on a normal day, Max would have found the question strange from a policeman. Given the reason he was there, it was completely baffling. He pinched his eyes shut. 'I beg your pardon?'

'Being a gramophone man. I wondered if you liked Gilbert & Sullivan.'

'I am aware of their operettas, yes.'

'Did you know that the Savoy was built from the profits of

*The Mikado*? How about that? An English hotel financed by a Japanese musical. Curious world. Cracking tunes, mind. So. Alfredo Balducci.'

Max blinked, bewildered at the casual way in which Boot had leapt from one topic to the other.

With a final puff of his cheeks, Boot looked down at a notepad. 'Ten fifteen, you reported this crime. Tell me what happened before then.'

Crime. He made it sound like his pocket had been picked. 'I arrived at the Savoy at around ten o'clock and went up to Signor Balducci's room to pick him up for a recording session in our studio and I saw...it. You've seen the body, detective inspector. I don't need to tell you about that.'

'Your studio in Tavistock Street?'

'Correct. I suppose I spent around five minutes in the room and went to find the general manager. And they alerted you.'

Boot jotted down Max's movements. 'I used to prefer Iolanthe. Did you touch the body?'

'No.'

'And the needles in his throat? They've just removed them down on the slab. Your styluses?' Boot raised his hand from his notepad, frowning. 'Styl-*i*?'

'They're from our Empress model.' Max paused. 'You can buy them all over town. We have dozens of suppliers.'

After another jot, Boot put down the pen and closed the notebook. Max looked at him aghast. Was that it? There was so much more to talk about. He glared across the table, shaking his head. Telling him of his hunch had to be the right thing to do. 'You are clearly aware of Barnabas Franklin, aren't you, detective inspector?'

Boot dabbed a crumb of bun from his chin and popped it in his mouth, eyes on the desk. 'Of course I am.'

Max opened his mouth before halting. Inscrutable Boot. He had no idea if Franklin's tentacles extended into this station. He shifted on his chair. 'Two days ago Mr Franklin sent us a note via Mr Langley warning us not to record Balducci.'

Boot glanced at him. 'A note, you say?'

'Yes. A business card with his insignia on it. And on the other side, a warning.'

'May I see this card?'

'I destroyed it.' He pursed his lips. What would have possessed him to keep that silly business card? How could he have foreseen any of this?

An arched brow. 'Listen, Mr Cadenza. Unfortunately I have plenty of experience of this kind of thing. This is what I imagine happened. Signor Balducci was young and alone and fancied some company. But he picked the wrong person. Happens all the time.'

Max shook his head.

'Have you ever walked down the Strand after midnight?' Boot said.

Every night. 'Occasionally.'

'Then you'll know. You can't move for harlots tugging at your sleeves. Look, we'll talk to the porters, the bellboys, people in the foyer. Find out what happened. Someone will have seen something.' Boot sucked a clump of crystallised sugar from his finger. 'The trick, Mr Cadenza, is not to rush these things. Ice melts slowly, remember that.'

Ice? Max didn't know what he meant. He was about to speak when a wave of tiredness and nausea washed over him. His head fell forward. Pinching the top of his nose he tried to make sense of the day. But he could not. His mind drifted and he, strangely, found himself mulling the definition of sideburns instead. Had Boot grown actual sideburns? Or was it a full beard with an inch missing at the chin?

'Mr Cadenza…'

Max sat up, his head light. Boot had stood and was holding the door open.

'If you don't mind. I'm terribly busy.'

# PART TWO

# DISCORD

**August 1899**

## SUMMER 1878

*Music. Always music. In an attempt to create a breeze, Papa had jammed every door in the big house open. Air danced through the building, dispersing the music on its salty current, so that each room became its own concert hall. Even the house's thick Devonshire brick failed to absorb the noise. It carried through the open windows and out over the parched lawn. Max could see the man's shadow through the open drawing room doors from where he was sitting on the grass. Papa was hunched over the piano, sleeves rolled up, like a carpenter tending a block of wood. He imagined his pursed lips under his thin moustache. He imagined his heavy hands on the keys, rising only to inch those wiry round glasses back up his shiny nose. Papa was always working.*

*Max didn't recognise the actual tunes being played. As on other days, the endless sound cancelled itself out, its permanence creating a new level of silence. He was almost as oblivious to the boy sitting, silently, next to him on the lawn. Ronald. But he called him Rusty. His cousin. Just like last summer, he'd been thrown together with the boy at the holiday house on the presumption of rapport. At two, Max knew Rusty to be half his age. Too young to wear a cape. But he seemed even younger. Thickset and fat, with skin wan as rosewater, it was as though his upward growth* had already stalled. Although he could walk, he was prone to sitting still for long periods before embarking on some unforeseen activity with great intensity. His face was shielded from the sun by the comforting brim of his mother's bonnet.

Standing, Max stretched his arms behind him to provide the movement to his cape that the summer afternoon could not. Charting ragged circles down the lawn, he shouted a magician's incantation – nonsense, potent – and ignored the heat caused by the black velvet on his back. He ran past pink and orange flowerbeds, down to the bottom of the garden, to where the fence and The Forbidden Sty separated the lawn from the wild grass at the clifftop. This was his favourite place. He liked the glistening haze that coated the sea. Some days the sky and the water merged into one blue. Mama said that they were always separate but he knew that was a fib. When they merged, magic happened. He peered between the bars of the fence, looking at the narrow pathway along the cliff edge. Only grown-ups were allowed to walk on the path beyond. But one day he'd be on the path too. When he was old enough.

He ran back up the garden and, sitting, etched stars on his bare knees with his finger. In front of the open drawing room doors, three adults sat under a parasol. Mama had placed down her sewing and was pouring tea on a side-table. She looked calm. He liked that. Even the way she lifted the small jug of milk, delivered in a churn from the village that morning, was slow and caring. Max followed the shadow of her bun on the grass as her head bobbed as she poured. Next to Mama, Aunt Isabella was reading. The sunlight made her look even thinner than usual, as if she was half there. Her hair was more orange than Rusty's, like a disappearing sun. It dangled to her waist. Every so often she looked over to check that her son had not moved. Opposite Mama sat Uncle Tobias. He was surveying the house's exterior and saying something, a book wedged under his arm. Max followed his gaze and immediately looked away. The sun's reflection off the windows shone too bright. Unlike the sea it was violent, not calm. The house belonged to Uncle Tobias, Max knew that. He talked about it a lot: at mealtimes, on walks, when he pointed at pictures on the wall. Uncle Tobias was always busy; running or chopping wood or moving furniture. His arms were the strongest Max had ever seen. They were constantly full, as if he existed to carry things. As well as talking about the house, he often talked about the Royal Engineers, always standing to attention slightly when he mentioned them. It made Max laugh because it looked silly. Mama laughed too; she said he'd only been active for two years. Tobias was different to Papa. Papa didn't speak much. Mama said it was sometimes hard to believe they were brothers.

Every so often Max watched one of the three stand to walk around the garden or go inside only to return moments later. Grown-ups were always busy yet never seemed to do anything. They performed endless steps in some baffling ballet. Not like him. He looked at the toys scattered on the grass around him and lifted a wooden sailing boat. Skipping to where Mama was sitting, he held the vessel out to her. She reached across, touched its taffeta sail, and continued sewing. He ran around the parasol, shouting orders from the captain's cabin.

'Tack westward. About ship!'

He stopped in his tracks when he saw Papa appear at the drawing room door, a sheen on his forehead.

'Maximilian. In. Practice.'

He stepped back towards his mother, the sailing boat hanging low by his shorts. He sensed Mama lean towards him.

'Come now, Max. You know the rules. Daily practice. Even at Chaveley.'

He thought of the sea and wished he was down by the fence.

*But it was that time. The time every afternoon when he was ripped from what he knew and thrust into a different world, into their world, a colder place. He swallowed as Papa's figure loomed towards him. A hard hand gripped his arm and led him towards the house. The boat dropped sail first onto the grass.*

*As he walked, Max started to count out the four beats in a bar. He had to be ready. 'One, two, three, four. One, two, three, four,' he whispered in time with his steps.*

*Inside the drawing room, he splayed his elbows to let Papa lift him onto the leather stool. He caught his reflection in the brass plate screwed to the piano's heavy lid. Under the tangle of curls his face seemed stretched, ghoulish, like in those funny mirrors at the circus. With his legs hanging heavily, he looked up and down the keyboard. It stretched away on both sides, its span far greater than his arms'. He mouthed silently, 'One, two, three, four.'*

*'Scales first. C Major.' Papa hovered behind him, his breath warm on his neck. 'And let's take this off.'*

*Max felt the heat of Papa's hands at his chin. A gentle pull and the cape dropped to the floor behind him, its bow untied.*

*'That's better.' A ruffle to his hair. 'Now. C Major.'*

*Tentatively, Max lifted a hand to the keyboard. He stretched his digits out, spanning four keys. He held his longest finger above an ivory key, wondering if it was C. Unsure, he moved his entire hand, hovered, before moving it back to the first position. As he started to lay the finger down, Papa reached forward, took hold of his wrist and moved it back to the second place. After Papa let go, Max watched his wrist's white flesh slowly return to its normal shape and colour.*

*'There. There. Come along, Maximilian. You know this.'*

*He pressed down on the key with might. Yet the note had a watery tone, as though played next door. The second was no better. No matter how hard he pressed, he could not make the* same noise he had heard Papa make. Again, Max told himself. This time harder. He stiffened his finger to play the scale once more when a thud caused his reflection in the brass plate to shudder. Papa's fist had landed inches from his face on the top of the piano's lid.

'No! Like this.'

Max tried to move along the stool to let Papa sit next to him but the leather was tacky and his skin stuck in place. Instead, his head was pegged between Papa's shirtsleeves as he enveloped him from behind.

'Like this. Do you see?'

'Yes, Papa.'

'Now try again.'

He hit the keys harder, each successful note feeling like a small victory. Papa's approving hand enveloped his shoulder as he played four strong notes in a row. And yet with each one the fear of fouling up the next one grew. Towards the end of the scale he recoiled at another loud crash. He clasped his eyes tightly shut, wondering what he had done. But this time it was not Papa. The noise came from the garden.

Tearing his legs off the stool, Max ran to the open doors. Outside on the lawn, he saw Rusty sitting near the parasol, thumping his meaty thigh in satisfaction. Aunt Isabella's protective hat lay by his side, exposing weedy spikes of red hair. Under the parasol, Mama was scrambling on her knees, gathering cups and saucers.

Uncle Tobias glared down. 'Silly child.'

Max watched his cousin's face. White against the grass, it was etched with a look that he had never seen before: mirth. From what he could tell, Rusty had crawled to the table and pushed the entire thing over, sending crockery, tea and milk all over Chaveley's lawn.

Then he heard the noise. His cousin started to cluck like a hen, his shoulders rising and falling as he chuckled. The scene was strangely thrilling. Unable to help himself, Max laughed too. He caught the younger boy's eye. The child smirked back and cackled even louder. Max looked at the strange child anew. In disruption, a bond.

# 6

**M**ax squinted at the cramped stage. The finale was some kind of Wild West fight; a riot of war cries and cap guns. He counted seven squaws but their identical headdresses rendered them indistinguishable from one another as they circled a vanquished cowboy and hopped, crouching, into the wings. Delilah was in there somewhere. At the side of the stage Mr Wilson thumped away at his piano, oily and proprietorial, the tribe's self-styled chief. The staccato music wasn't helping Max's mood. The last thing he needed were jumpy rhythms and screeching hollers. Giving up, he jostled for space among the standing crowd and once again raised the newspaper in his hand. Occupying half the cover of the *Illustrated Police News* was an ink etching of the dead Balducci – arms outstretched, neck gruesomely sliced, gramophone needles protruding. The artist had let his imagination run wild. Next to the poor sod's bed, a figure recoiled, arms raised in horror. Him.

He'd yearned for front pages but not this kind. 'Hunt for the Opera Slayer', ran the headline. Beneath the Paragon's quivering gas lights, the picture looked even more murky than it had outside. The murder had captivated London. On streets, in salons and cafés, people were speculating about who was behind it. With grim gratuity, certain tawdry publications had mentioned the Ripper murders of a decade before in their copy.

He lowered the paper. The evening was supposed to be a pleasant diversion. But the air was devilish hot and every few minutes he flinched to avoid the pearls of human condensation dripping from the ceiling. Man-made rain; a drop down his collar, a spot on his forehead, a speck on his paper. But even here, in this hot box of brazen entertainment, he couldn't shake the memories of the week before. Discovering the body blackened his every thought. It had stolen his sleep and taken his appetite. Almost worse than memories of the mangled corpse – the angles, the expression, the rotten stench – was the guilt. Had he not persuaded Balducci to record then none of this would have happened. The thought chilled his bones. A man was dead due to his actions. It was almost unbearable. He'd even thought of leaving England for a while. A temporary escape. A recording trip to Russia, perhaps, to capture the Volga shanty. It would provide a new focus, if only fleetingly. London was toxic; too many hounds were scratching at his door.

A burst of activity from the stage caught his attention. The chorus had reappeared for the encore as shepherdesses, and this time Delilah's wild curls gave her away. His shoulders relaxed as the tension fell away and he smiled for the first time that day. As she had all evening, she'd occasionally peek into the auditorium as if searching for someone. It thrilled him that he was the possible target of her darting glances.

The show ended and Max waited for the stalls to empty before leaving the theatre. Thankful for the cool air, he walked down the Paragon's side alley to the artistes' entrance. He hated being a Stage Door Johnny, so was glad when Delilah emerged immediately – composed and confident, in a coat with a high fur collar over a blue dress. She giggled at something that Molly whispered in her ear. Max stepped out of the alley's gloom.

'Bravo.' He clapped.

'You did come! I wasn't sure you had.' Her eyes flashed like dark emeralds. 'Do you remember Molly?'

'Indeed.' He doffed his hat. Delilah had introduced him and Langley to her over sherry cobblers at Simpson's, before the incident.

'So where are you taking me?' Delilah took his arm. 'I'm famished.'

'I thought Covent Garden. Rules, perhaps?'

She rolled her eyes. 'I think we can do better than that.'

'Really?' Few places in London were better than Rules.

'Do you like Chinese food? There's a place in Limehouse.' She threw him a venturous grin.

He had no idea. But he liked the notion. And he loved that she knew parts of London that he did not. A secret side of the city, even darker than his version. It was enticing and deeply attractive. He nodded.

'Limehouse it is, then.' She rubbed Molly's arm. 'Goodnight, darling.'

Max said farewell to Molly, offered his arm to Delilah walked back down the alley to Mile End Road. She eyed the newspaper under his arm.

'You alright?'

'Not really.' He opened his mouth to say more but couldn't. Perhaps later.

'Guess what?' she said as they turned towards the river down a cobbled lane off Stepney Green.

'What?'

'Molly and your Mr Langley.' She smirked.

'The sly dog.'

'I saw him waiting for her after the show yesterday.'

'And?'

'He looked terrified.'

Max laughed.

'Took her to the Café Royal, he did.'

The boy was learning, and at least having some fun despite everything.

They walked across the Ratcliffe Highway, the street where London's dregs sought cheap thrills. Max was aware of it. A concentration of human vermin, its visitors were as likely to get ambushed as pleasured. Gun Lane was quieter, but he was glad to see the Thames glisten under cobalt moon as they got nearer. A maze of warehouses led down to the docks. They passed the occasional couple. A girl in boots with brass heels led a staggering lascar into an alleyway, his hat crooked on her head. Despite the noise, the place had a somnambulant rhythm, like a low hum from a warped cello. They wound down towards the water until they arrived at a wooden structure on a muddy promontory between two storehouses. The shack stood at the apex of one of the Thames's snaking undulations. Max looked out over the river and felt strangely liberated, as though he was standing over the mighty Amazon or the Orinoco. He glanced across to a second shed on a neighbouring pier. A line of hunched figures queued to get in.

'Opium-heads. Curdled, all of 'em. Come on. Food.' Delilah led him up the shack's steps, each greased with the lapping river's deposits.

Max stood for a second, curious at the sweet musk flavouring the air.

'*Max.*'

He followed her in. The hut was smaller than his studio, around the size of the potting shed at Chaveley. On entering he was hit by a fug of steam. His nostrils flared at the peculiar odour. It was not unpleasant, just different; simultaneously tart and warming.

Two tables were occupied; Chinamen at one, tug workers in filthy overalls at the other. Max and Delilah sat on benches at a table in the far corner. Through a hatch he saw Chinese women sitting on their haunches around a series of blackened pans. As the light danced from the table's candle stub, Max watched the pattern from the trim of Delilah's dress cast a lace shadow over her face.

'Who needs Covent Garden?'

She was right. She possessed this hut, filled it, as though it was the only restaurant in London. He looked at her and wondered if anywhere could be this enchanting or exotic. Every time they met he noticed something new about her. He liked the way she silently held his gaze after he stopped talking, and the way her mouth curled up at the sides before she replied, as though every conversation was a delicacy to be savoured. There was mischief here. And she was different to the previous girls. They'd all been like him; varying shades within the same milieu. Delilah was a new colour entirely. Bold and dazzling.

Food arrived quickly and unprompted in steaming bowls. Without flinching, Delilah picked up her chopsticks and inhaled from the dish in front of her. Max, his appetite returned for the first time in days, fumbled with his own sticks. He tried numerous times to clamp them into position, but his damaged finger made it impossible. Lowering his hand away from her gaze, he tried again under the table. It was no use. Within seconds he heard the knock of wood on wood: a freshly deposited spoon. Delilah pushed it across the table with a smile, saying nothing, as one of the cooks returned to the pans. Max blinked, overwhelmed at her casual kindness. As they ate –

rice with bamboo shoots and a root vegetable that numbed the throat – he relished the unfamiliar crunches.

'How do you know about this place?'

'Friend.' She spiked a chunk of vegetable with her chopstick and looked up from her bowl. Her face softened. 'Oh, Max. Tell me everything. I've been worried. You've been all quiet since...' She trailed off.

He smiled. 'You can say it.'

'Are you alright?'

He had been quiet. Shock did that to a man. He laid down the spoon. 'It's been hellish.'

Leaning forwards, she cupped his hand over the table.

'I saw the autopsy report today. Coroner said he was slain between ten and two. Just after Franklin left us in the Café Royal.'

'Won't that help the peelers get him?'

'It would. If they weren't in his pocket.' He had no proof that Boot was bent but he strongly suspected it.

'But you've told them of your suspicions? About Franklin?'

'Of course. But as far as I know he's not even been questioned. Boot's pursuing misadventure with a prostitute.'

'Could've been.'

It really couldn't. 'Doubt he's seen his cock in years. But at least Rusty and I have been absolved of involvement. We provided each other's alibi.'

Her head was down as she stifled a giggle. 'Sorry. It's not funny. That image.' She looked at him, the flush fading. She was as game as he'd hoped. 'How is Rusty?'

He shrugged. The murder had affected him in a strange way; he was more agitated and unpredictable than usual, as if a darker strain of misanthropy had taken hold. A stranger wouldn't have noticed, but Max did. His eyes darted with a touch more wariness. He drank to oblivion rather than merely to excess. His tools crashed down onto his workbench with greater force. It worried Max. And it thickened his desire to protect him from the horror.

'And listen to this.' He lowered his voice, barely hearing his own whisper. 'The cause of death was asphyxia. He was strangled and then his neck was slashed as some macabre form of window dressing. But the needles in his neck,' he paused, 'were probably inserted *before*.'

Her chopsticks slapped on the table and she covered her mouth. 'While he was still alive?'

'Nice touch, eh?'

She sat back, blinking. 'Poor sod. What will you do?'

'Gramophones? We'll carry on as best we can.' He tapped the list in his breast pocket. 'I've still got my jewels to record. The music remains.'

Further dishes arrived. One bowl contained sinewy leaves floating in a broth, another was some form of bean curd. Max listened as Delilah told him how her father had kicked her out of home in Stepney, how he saw singing as a dirty trade. She looked slightly uneasy as she told him. A proud man, her father was the third generation of butchers in the family. It was tough at first but she didn't mind no longer living at home. Occasionally he would drop into her lodgings to check she hadn't taken up with anybody.

'Talking of that, you'll never guess who turned up on my doorstep the other night,' she said.

'Who?'

'Mr Wilson. Flowers and everything.' She pulled a face.

A furrow, deeper than he'd have liked, pleated his brow. 'My pianist Mr Wilson?'

'My teacher Mr Wilson, yes.'

'I see.' He stopped chewing.

She stared at him for a moment, smiled and gently shook her head. 'No, Max. I'm more than capable of looking after myself. That's rule number one. And don't worry. I gave him what for.'

He fished a floating leaf from his bowl with his finger. The strength of his reaction had surprised him. But so had Wilson's presumption that he could pitch up at Delilah's door. He supposed he'd have to find a new pianist.

More food appeared: a plate of dumplings, hard fruits and – ultimately – a dish of fudge. Max picked rather than ate, preoccupied with his thoughts, transfixed by the spirit across the table.

'It really was a fabulous revue tonight, Delilah.'

She leaned in. 'How did I sound?'

Spirited and charming, he wanted to say. The truth was he'd only listened intermittently, so active was his mind. 'I'd say that your voice definitely has the 'three Ts': tone, timbre and tease. Prerequisites for any singing career.'

'Why, thank you.'

'I should tell your father.'

'Do you want to end up in sausages?' She rocked back on her bench.

As the bowls were cleared, she dabbed a speck of fudge from her lips and leaned in over the candle. 'Tell me something.'

'Anything.'

'Why do you like music?'

'*Why?*' He'd never been asked. He thought for a moment. 'Music transports you, lifts you. It has no boundaries.' He paused. 'It can't answer back.'

She smiled. 'So how does it work?'

'How does what work?'

'How do you capture sound?'

'Aah. Therein lies a tale.' His bench scraped on the floor as he pulled it close to the table. 'It all starts with waves and vibrations.'

'Waves.'

'Of sound.' He was about to expand on it when he stopped and laid down his spoon. 'In fact, put on your coat. I want to show you something.'

❧❧❧❧❧

'St Paul's Cathedral?'

'Come.'

Max held Delilah's hand as she stepped down from the carriage. The cathedral stood monolithic against the clear sky, the only hint of three-dimensional form coming from the moonlight reflecting off its dome's lead ridges. He led her into the darkness of its south-eastern churchyard, well away from the beggars and whores who treated its grand entrance steps as their evening workplace.

'Max?'

'Shh. Don't worry. And watch your step.' He offered his arm.

He picked their way around the gravestones and trees that stood as sentinels to the looming building, until they reached the church's external wall. Creeping palm-over-palm along rough stone, he moved towards the corner where the transept intersected the nave, the occasional piqued giggle from Delilah the only noise to pierce the silence. When wall met wall and they could go no further, he checked that no one had seen them before striking a match. He illuminated a low nook; in it, a wooden door, its iron studs glistening in the light.

'Perfect.' He handed Delilah the match and bent to lift a rock at his feet. Underneath was a key. 'It pays to know the organist.'

He stood and, with a soft clunk, unlocked the door.

'Max!'

'Follow me.'

Air cooled by marble and flecked with dust from a thousand hymnals dried his throat as they entered, the most peaceful of sensory awakenings. He took her hand and led her through the gloom, their steps echoing up to unknown heights.

'Over here.'

Across a short stretch of the cathedral's floor they reached another door at the foot of an internal tower. Max turned to Delilah, her breath scented by mellow caramel, a lingering legacy of the fudge.

'Are you alright with steps?'

'What? Yes.'

'And heights?'

'Of course.'

He squeezed her hand and opened the door. As he started to climb the tight spiral steps he picked up and lit a lantern from a window recess. The chkk-chkk of shoes on stone told him Delilah remained close behind.

'Where we going?' she said, breathless, as they climbed.

He said nothing, just continued circling up and up, each step inching them further from profane concerns. He never counted the steps. But after a few minutes, when the thump of his heart intensified to thunderous, he looked to his right. A moment later it was there; the doorless entrance to a thin corridor. He turned, gestured, and led Delilah down it. After a few paces he felt a pang of cold air.

In front of him, beneath a flood of moonlight from a dozen vast windows, a perfect circle opened out, ominous and gaping. Around the circle's rim was a railed gallery the width of a table, and below, deep down in the darkness, the cathedral's marble floor.

'Hell,' Delilah said in awe.

He smiled. 'More like heaven, I'd say.'

He followed her eyes up. Above the windows, as if floating on their very light, a vast dome stretched upwards, its gold frescos glinting through the blue-grey. At the dome's apex, suspended again on its own light, rose another smaller dome.

'Is this…?'

He nodded. 'One hundred feet across.'

Dimples framed her mouth as she looked up. 'Incredible.'

He shuffled slightly, hoping she wouldn't think the exercise extravagant. 'So…that thing I wanted to show you.'

'Yes.'

'May I?'

She nodded, the curious grin still playing on her lips. He mouthed an apology as, in the tight space of the gallery's walkway, he placed his hands on her waist and turned her so the bustle of her dress gently pressed into his pelvis. Taking both her wrists, he slowly leaned her into the gallery's wall until her body was flush against its cold stone. 'Put your ear to the wall.'

She complied. 'Lucky I know you, Max, or you'd be flat on that marble floor.'

'Don't move.'

He stepped away and felt his way around the dome's gallery, steadying himself on its frail railing. When he judged that the circle's diameter was at its greatest and he was opposite her, he stopped and leaned into the wall himself. Cupping his hand over his mouth, he whispered her name into the stone. Twice he received no reaction. After the third attempt, his ear to the wall, he heard a fractured yelp.

He turned his mouth back to the wall. 'Delilah,' he murmured. 'Talk to me.'

'Max?' Although delayed, the sound was clear, as though emerging from the masonry.

'I'm here.'

'Where?'

'Across heaven.'

Silence. Then the distinctive crack of Delilah's laugh – splintered but enhanced and swollen – filled his ear. He whispered to the wall. '*This* is how sound works. It's merely waves disrupting air. And here, those waves cling to the wall. Sound, you see, it sustains and reverberates.'

She replied, elongating his words as if testing them. 'Sustains and reverberates.'

He clapped, each one echoing four times. Then, from the silence, he heard a tune. Quiet at first, he recognised it from the revue; it was the song about the drunken judge. Delilah's voice was thickened as if by an invisible choir. He pressed his ear to the cool wall, stretching out his arms as if to gather her into his embrace. The tune meant nothing; it was not the song he wanted, but its source. As he listened he knew. The girl over the chasm, the temporary angel throwing herself into her task as if the dome was a newly discovered toy, was the one he'd been waiting for. None of the others came close. The stone chilled his cheek. He felt a tickling energy as, out of sight, she probed the curio set before her. Closing his eyes, he imagined being the object of the same undiluted and intense interest. Fleetingly he resented the cupola for consuming her so wholly. His ear was now throbbing against the wall. He pushed further; wanting to be part of it, wanting to melt into its surface, wanting to reach around and touch her.

The ditty ended and he waited for the echoes' resonance to subside, arms still splayed.

A spoken word. 'Max?'

He started as if freshly woken.

'Max? Can I ask you something?'

'Of course.' It may have been a disruptive gust from the atrium but her voice sounded tougher, the earlier gaiety gone.

'It's just a question. But, I wonder,' she waited for the echo to end, 'could *I* record in your studio?'

That gust again. He can't have heard her correctly. 'What?'

'Some discs.'

Her words hung in the air, crystal clear this time, yet utterly unexpected. He lowered his arms, the spell fractured. The question had come from nowhere. He edged back from the wall, suddenly aware that he was standing on a precarious walkway, stranded in the air, in a dark cathedral, illegally.

'Record,' she repeated.

He said nothing.

'Max! Talk to me.'

'That would be...' he said into the wall, his mind filling with thoughts he never expected to have. He had his jewels; the mighty twelve; diverse and fragile. He'd vowed to see the list through. And he'd tried music hall. It hadn't worked. But then, this was her. This was Delilah. 'That could be wonderful. Will you allow me some time to think about it?'

He heard nothing. Then applause rippled up into the dome, ricocheting and multiplying as though from a hundred hands. He slowly felt his way back around the gallery to where she was standing, the applause still raining down. In the window's moonlight she was smiling.

'I thought you hated my machines.'

She shrugged. 'A girl's allowed to change her mind, isn't she?'

'Absolutely.'

She squeezed her hands together as if in prayer. 'Can you imagine? My voice, captured forever. Wouldn't it be splendid? If shops sold records with my name on them then all the theatres in London would want me. Promise you'll think about it?'

'Of course.' He peered over the railings into the gloom of the atrium. An icy chill whipped up as he imagined landing on marble. 'Now let's get down from here. I really must get you home before someone sees us.'

## SUMMER 1884

'Hide and seek, Rusty. Bet you your toffee apple you can't find me.' Max had coveted it since the Ilfracombe fair.

He flashed his cousin a smile and ruffled his hair, as coarse as a boot brush. The boy squeezed his eyes shut and jerked his head back. 'Gerroff.' Then he started to count.

Max knew he'd play. He always did.

He ran across the hall and, using the banister, hauled himself up Chaveley's staircase. He took the steps three at a time to avoid the rotten joists; their empty clunks would alert his would-be captor. He giggled as the sound of determined counting receded. He loved hiding. Even better was the excitement from the threat of being found. It made his stomach fizz.

Upstairs, compulsion took him into his parents' bedroom; the heightened danger of holing up somewhere forbidden was too much to ignore. It was certain they'd punish him if they knew, but he was hiding so they never would. Besides, he could hear Papa on the piano in the drawing room, too busy to notice. He scurried under the bed, making sure that the frame's patterned skirt concealed him from view. He positioned an imaginary ogre at his feet for protection. As doors banged downstairs he imagined Rusty's face as he prowled, puce and screwed up in frustration.

*He pictured his little frame, the baby fat gone, now just short and solid like a butcher's dog. As the doors sounded, Max ticked off the rooms: nursery, kitchen, pantry, boot room. A pause. Then the piano playing stopped. A shout from a grown-up male voice.*

*Max shivered in delight as he heard young feet ascend the stairs, accompanied by an elongated cry. 'Maa-aax'.*

*The voice grew louder in the corridor outside. Mindful that you can't always trust an ogre on sentry, Max raised his hand into the dark above him. Feeling for the cold iron of the frame's inner lip, he hooked his fingers and toes over its ledges and raised himself into the space under the mattress. His grip tightened as, close to bursting with excitement, he heard the door of the bedroom open. Lips pursed, he glanced down as the frame's skirt was raised. The silhouette of Rusty's head appeared. Tufts of hair turned one way then the next before promptly disappearing. The monster must've scared him. Max smiled. He'd done it. He lowered himself and rolled around his sanctuary.*

*Half an hour later, he was still there. There was no way he was moving. It didn't matter how long he stayed: summers were long at Chaveley. He thought about Rusty's toffee apple. It had sat on the bookshelf in the nursery for days, uneaten since the fair. It was his if Rusty failed to find him. Closing his eyes, he went through his piano scales on a pretend keyboard. Perhaps Papa would forgive his hiding if he knew he'd been practising.*

*Soft tinkles from the garden interrupted his D Major. They squeaked like feet crunching through frost-hardened snow. He counted three. They were followed by an almighty wail, breathless and unending. It was Rusty. He heard Aunt Isabella and Mama run into the garden. Then he heard his own name being called again, but this time by Papa and Uncle Tobias. Rusty's screaming continued between the men's shouts, but it now came from inside the house, from the nursery downstairs. Max didn't move. Why* should he? Rusty cried at anything. Yesterday he blubbed when Mama found him pulling the legs off a spider in the kitchen. Today, he was crying because he was losing.

Max curled into a ball as he heard big feet on the landing. He could detect no playfulness. Papa. Surely he'd be proud of him for finding somewhere so original to hide? The bedroom door creaked open. Glimpsing out, he saw heavy black boots approach. His sentinel deserted him as a rough hand gripped his ankle. Skin against floorboard, he was dragged from his den. In a flash he was hauled upright. His father's hard hand stung like angry fire as it met his thigh. Max bit his bottom lip as he was led out of the room and down the stairs. His leg throbbed but what really hurt was the disappointment. His ingenuity had been overlooked. There was no approval.

Down in the nursery, Rusty was sitting on Aunt Isabella's lap, red-eyed and gulping for air. His left leg was bound in cloth below the knee. A crimson dot peeked through.

Max ran to him. 'What happened?'

Rusty's head was buried low on his mother's chest, as though he was suckling her through the material of her dress. He turned suddenly. 'Where were you?' he shouted through a tangle of saliva and snot. 'I couldn't find you. I hate you.'

Isabella pulled Rusty in tight and cradled his head under her chin. Her long flame of hair hung limply, her face peeking through the centre like a nervous stagehand glancing between curtains. She doted on Rusty. It seemed to Max that he was her reason to be. And, in situations like this, she his. They sat there almost as one organism, a bundle of limbs and copper hair, his lips clamped to her chest, her lips now pressed to his crown. She rocked back and forth, whispering softly. 'Hush, Ronald. Hush.'

Seeing Papa and Uncle Tobias outside through the nursery window, Max ran over. They were standing outside the greenhouse.

A trio of panes along its lower half had been kicked in. Triangles of jagged glass littered the gravel. The men were talking in raised voices. Max leaned into the window.

Papa's finger jabbed at Tobias. 'I know Maximilian's disruptive, but for God's sake take control of Ronald. He'll be eight next year... Too upset... Every time.' He angrily removed his glasses and buffed them on his shirt.

He watched Tobias shake his head. His cheeks were reddening like his boy's. Max had seen this before. The men moved closer to each other. '...It's our bloody house, Chris. We'll stop inviting you...' Tobias said. Then he used a word that Max had never heard before. Something about heritance.

He turned back to Rusty, who was quietly sobbing. Max tapped him on the shoulder and playfully squeezed his cheek. The red peak held its shape after he'd withdrawn his fingers. Max walked to the bookshelf and picked up the toffee apple. As he rolled its long stem between fingers and thumb, light from the window reflected off its golden case. He moistened his lips and imagined its satisfying crunch and bitter juices. Max returned to Rusty and held the delicacy between them. Extending his hand, Max smiled. 'Yours. Because you're poorly.'

That afternoon, when Rusty had stopped crying, a man arrived from London to see Papa. He had a square jaw and oiled hair and strutted like a raven. He smelt sickly sweet, like cake icing. It was funny but the house seemed to cool when he arrived. Even when he smiled he looked angry. Papa sent the boys to the garden.

Sitting together halfway between the house and The Forbidden Sty on the clifftop, Max watched his younger cousin play with a wooden toy, his bandaged leg outstretched. The toy comprised three soldiers standing on a wooden frame. When Rusty turned a lever, a series of interlocking cogs danced the soldiers along the frame. Apart from Rusty's mottled tear troughs and the occasional pained wince, remnants of the earlier disagreement had vanished. It was as though the day had started afresh, at least until the next game. Max liked it with Rusty: he liked that they had regular fights but could never be enemies. Cousins couldn't be. It wasn't allowed. He enjoyed the fact that they only really saw each other every summer; for the whole year they lived separate lives in London – the older in Highbury, the younger in Putney – but spent the hot month at Chaveley. They always had time to catch up, and always had time to forgive each other.

'Here.' Max produced a sandy block from his pocket, broke it in two and gave the bigger part to Rusty.

'Shortbread. Thank you.'

As Max ate he wondered what Papa was talking to the visitor about. He was interrupted by an elbow in his ribs.

'Look.' At Rusty's feet, the wooden toy lay in pieces. He had disassembled it; the handle, cogs, spindle, frame and soldiers were laid out neatly on the grass.

'Not bad. Let's see how quickly you can put it back together. I shall count…'

Rusty wiped crumbs from his lips and counted. Before he reached fifteen, the soldiers were back jostling atop the wooden frame.

'Bravo,' Max said.

'Said I'm clever.'

'Let me have a go.'

'Very well,' Rusty said. 'If you do it in under ten, I'll let you stay at Chaveley after all.'

'I'm already here, silly.'

'No. When I'm older. When I own it.'

As usual, after not too long, Papa called Max into the drawing room for piano practice. He was singing under his breath. The London guest had departed although the strange sweet smell *lingered.*

*Max sat on the stool in front of the heavy grand and took a deep breath. He looked up and down the keyboard. This year, for the first time, he could almost touch both ends if he stretched his arms out as far as they could go. The instrument was nearly his. As he settled, he heard Papa pace excitedly behind him.*

*'Eight recitals, Maximilian,' Papa said. 'All in Mr Franklin's new theatre. There may be more come the winter. What do you think?'*

*'Who's Mr Franklin?'*

*'The gentleman caller.'*

*Max did not know what to think because he did not know what it meant. However, he nodded. 'Very pleasing, Papa.'*

*'It's wonderful news.'*

*Max lifted his hands to the keyboard and played Mozart's Allegro in G, almost perfectly. When he finished, he waited for minor errors to be picked up on. If he was lucky he'd have to repeat it until it was perfect. If he was unlucky he'd get a clipped ear. He tensed as he felt his father lean over him.*

*'Well...perhaps, my son, you will follow in my footsteps after all.'*

*A warm palm rested on his shoulder. It was his favourite moment of all the summers.*

# 7

Victoria Park clanged and trilled like a tuning orchestra. Max walked under its gnarled oaks, avoiding the children scurrying around their parents' legs, euphoric on air thick with bubbling honey and candyfloss. The patch of nature between stinking Bow and Bethnal Green had come alive for the day. He wove past the tobacco stands and puppet plays on the path, willing empathy with the revelry. But it was out of reach, untouchable, as though the fête was happening behind glass. As he swerved to avoid a hawker with a tray of rolled liquorice, the mocking laugh of recumbent trinket-sellers tumbled down the verge.

Rusty's handmade banner caught his eye across the park. 'Talking Machine Demonstrations'. Bright jagged lettering. Unmissable. The company's tent was shaded by sycamore trees in a far corner, the middle of three marquees erected for playbacks. As he walked towards them, Max recognised one of the other tents' occupants; a large painting of a white terrier sniffing a recording horn hung outside. The mutt had pissed on it, Rusty always joked. It was the logo of The Gramophone Company, a fledgling rival who'd tried for months to convince the public that *The Laughing Song* was a musical treat. Max didn't know who was in the third tent. Cutting through a cluster of fairground rides, he jumped as a midget parped on his battered trombone. 'Ghouls at every turn,' he cried, pointing to Swinford's Ghost Train.

As Max passed a big wheel – its occupants' whoops swelling then receding with each jolting rotation – he saw Rusty's arrangement outside their tent. He grinned; he'd have done the same. Standing to attention on a trestle table outside the marquee were three models of gramophone, ordered chronologically. The hand-crank, the coin-slot, and the new Empress model, its flowering horn gaping like a lily in bloom. Its teak petals almost beckoned something in. The future, possibly. Or oblivion. Max wasn't sure. He arrived at the tent but there was no sign of Rusty.

Walking behind the table, he selected a shellac disc from a stack. *Music of the Sands*, that propulsive flamenco. His eyes followed the letters curled around the label's centre: The London Gramophone Corporation. As though drawing nourishment from it, the letters clung to a picture of an eight-sided diamond. A sparkling jewel. His own logo. Better than a dog. Max's fingers tingled as he laid the record on the Empress's turning table. He was about to wind the machine's spindle when he heard Rusty's familiar grunt. It came from the third marquee.

Max gazed into the adjacent tent. The sackcloth of Rusty's jacket was instantly recognisable. He was bending over a table examining a contraption that looked like a sewing machine. Max frowned as he walked over. Phonographs had been around for years. Emile Berliner had invented the gramophone to wipe them out. He entered the tent.

Rusty turned. 'Look, Max. A new kind of phonograph. Single spring motor. Down from three.'

Clicking his tongue as he approached, Max ignored the wiry

besuited man standing next to Rusty. It was quite the ugliest contraption he had seen. Rudimentary, crude and wholly without mystery. Vapour-thin sound, too. He'd explained the difference to novices many times. Unlike gramophones, which recorded laterally, phonographs captured sound on wax tubes, which rotated on a central spindle like a rabbit on a spit. Also unlike gramophones, whose master discs could be replicated and stamped on a large commercial scale, phonograph cylinders had to be recorded individually. Max silently damned Rusty for being openly transfixed by a rival technology they both knew to be inferior.

'An office aid.' The phonograph's handle swung limply at Max's touch. He supposed that as dictation devices for clerks or elocution machines for teachers they had some use. The wiry man sprang on his heels and raised a hand.

'J. P. Hague. The International Phonograph Company. Engineer.'

'Maximilian Cadenza. The London Gramophone Corporation. Alchemist.' He noticed Hague rock expectantly on his feet, as though awaiting some kind of compliment. 'You do know, Mr Hague, that this is a music playback?'

'Oh, quite. Absolutely.' His delivery was artless, flat. 'I say, Mr Cadenza, tough luck.' Like a mime artist, Hague lifted his hand to his neck and turned away theatrically, as if to protect his voicebox from some unseen implement. Balducci. He let rip a high-pitched sneer as he dropped his arm. 'I've read all about you.'

'Come on, Rusty.' There was no time for this buffoon. As Max walked from the tent, he cursed the man; a fresh competitor and a murder were tricky enough to deal with without the former reminding him of the latter.

'Interesting man. Peckham way.' Rusty was at his shoulder

as they entered their own marquee. Max closed his nose to the covert tincture on his breath.

'Where's Langley?'

'Distributing posters.'

At least someone's not wasting time. It was only an hour before the playbacks were due to commence. Max had ordered the posters as a kind of insurance policy. As word of Balducci's slaying spread he'd wanted to do all he could to convince people to turn up to listen. He lifted a pile of papers from the floor and raised one. The size of a penny periodical, it pictured a laughing couple sitting in rocking chairs in front of a fire, ears cocked to a horn. He cleared this throat and read. "The gramophone is pleasing multitudes of people.' What do you think?'

Rusty curled his lip. 'Multitudes? That's an elastic definition even for you.'

Max shook his head and cradled the flyers in his arm. As he headed into the sunlight, he prayed that whatever sarcastic ember was smouldering in Rusty's belly would be burned out by the time the playback started. He'd been acting strangely since the murder.

Wandering from the tent towards the fair's centre, Max held the posters to passers-by. There were few takers. People either had their hands full or took his intentions to be religiously inclined. Religion. He supposed his fervour did feel spiritual most days. Or at least it did before events had cruelly defrocked him.

A burst of laughter from deep within the fête caused him to pause. One voice sailed above the others, as light and jolly as it was recognisable. The Paragon stand. Delilah. She said she'd be here. As if a tight coat had unexpectedly been unbuttoned, he found himself breathing more easily. Something had happened since the Chinese meal. Like some kind of crucial cog, she'd become impossible to dislodge. Her request to record still sat uneasily, mind. Life in the studio and his time with her were two distinct entities; different compartments, equally precious but separate. She'd understand. He smiled as a second burst of laughter rang out. Perhaps he'd go to find her now, before the playback commenced. His stomach warmed at the thought. That spirit, that mischief, would pep him up. A piano glissando interrupted the girls' chatter. Of course. Mr Wilson. The warm sensation evaporated. Every songbird had its hawk. Max hoped the confrontation he'd had with Wilson in Simpson's a week earlier had squared things between them. Wilson had sworn he'd never had any ill intentions towards her. Max had given him the benefit of the doubt and they'd shared a bottle afterwards. They'd shaken hands. Max didn't want to lose him as an accompanist. On some days, London was a spilled bin.

He headed towards the sound, its pull too great. A moment at the Paragon stand would prove a tonic. Just a minute or two exchanging glances with her. As he made his way to the noise, a brightly-coloured juggler to his left caught this eye. A harlequin, she was pacing outside a preposterous open-sided marquee. The tent was lavishly-draped in an Arabic style: outside, around the harlequin, an army of workers set easels with vast poster boards advertising coming attractions; inside, there was some kind of commotion around a low platform at its centre. Max froze as the subject of the fuss became clear. Sitting on the platform like a monarch on a durbar dais was Franklin.

That jutting jaw was instantly recognisable. But so was the stillness. Apart from his scanning eyes, he was utterly static on his chair. A cravat pinned with a gem bulged between lapels of a dark green frockcoat. Black-clad acolytes circled around him, tiny planets orbiting a sun.

Max dropped the posters. In a deafening rush, a thousand

wasps descended. The bed. The bound wrists, the soiled sheets, the gamey stench of spilled blood. All present, as fresh and gruesome as on that morning. The swarm intensified, nullifying the Paragon's piano. Franklin can't be here. Not in this park. Not advertising his wares. Not after what he did. One by one, the wasps stung. With each burn, he took a step towards the tent. Franklin belonged in Newgate among the sodomites, rapists and pimps.

Balducci's contorted face. The rubber-like dryness of his ruptured flesh. A nymph's pout. Legs throbbing and acting independently of sense, Max strode towards the tent. He had no idea of his purpose beyond following raw instinct. But it was the right thing to do. It had to be. As he passed them, the easels bellowed about imminent shows. 'Franklin Entertainment presents *Jack and the Beanstalk* at the Theatre Royal.' '*Cavalleria Rusticana* at the Palace.' '*Treasure Island* at the Strand, now with hydraulic scene changes'. The posters were vivid but almost without meaning; a jumble of loud announcements. Beanstalk Island. Jack and the Cavalleria. Treasure Rusticana. Around the easels, tent tassels cast latticework shadows on the grass. Max's angry daze carried him over them and into the tent.

The swarm still buzzing, he stopped and looked to the dais. Although lively, the tent was not full. Max had a clear view of Franklin, and Franklin of him. Still the wasps stung. He clenched his teeth and prepared to speak.

A hand crunched onto his shoulder from behind. He shambled forwards before being pushed towards Franklin, whose face was cold and stony. He turned. The man was black-clad, humourless. Jerking his body away, Max walked with a free will, his intent his own. His strides lengthened as he approached the dais, nodding. Franklin's nose twitched. Max paused at the foot of the platform, his nods intensifying.

A smile spread across Franklin's jowls, as if a switch had been flicked. The menace disappeared. Franklin looked around the tent in mock bewilderment before he spread his hands to his side, a pontiff blessing a pilgrim.

'Maximilian.' His voice was softly gruff.

'I know what you did,' Max hissed as he inched forwards.

Franklin tutted. 'I hope you're not making another scene, sonny.' He looked either side of Max. 'Where's the beetroot?'

'We know it was you and we'll prove it.'

'I don't know what you're talking about.'

The silence gaped. Max vowed not to fill it, vowed not to be the one to bring up the details. But a shrug goaded him. 'The opera singer.'

'Aah, Mr Balducci. Sad, that.'

'How did you find out where he was?'

Franklin chuckled then leaned forward. His eyes narrowed. For the first time since entering the tent, Max really understood just how treacherous this intervention was. 'Now why would I do something like that?'

'You warned me off him. Twice.'

Franklin swiped the air. 'Games. How's your mother?'

Max clenched his fists at his side, wasps swarming. But the more his internal rage grew, the stiller Franklin seemed to sit. He was so imperious, so rooted on his throne, that Max could not imagine that he ever walked to the seat. It was as though the park had been built around him and unfurled like an offering.

Suddenly, Franklin looked bored as if an internal shutter had fallen. 'Listen, why don't you skip off? I'm simply here to promote my shows. Meet agents. Thrill the public.' He nodded at the various easels and laughed. 'What do you think, by the way? Exciting season ahead?'

'You'll fucking pay.'

A heavier silence. The swarm evaporated.

'What, boy?'

Max glanced around. He had never felt so brutally exposed. The uncomfortable stillness enveloped him. Standing on the spot, he heard the crinkle in his ear as he swallowed. Franklin glared down, his pupils slowly distending. With a slow shake of the head, Max held his gaze for as long as he dared. Seconds felt like minutes. Unable to remain, he turned and walked out towards the juggling harlequin. Rarely had an open expanse of grass looked so inviting.

'Oh Max.'

He turned back to Franklin. A thick scowl had returned.

'Don't do anything stupid. You know the rules.'

Spinning, Max walked out. Rules. What does that mean? Was that a threat? A joke? What rules? Outside, he spat on the ground as a heaviness clasped his stomach, lurching like mercury with every step. Had that been altogether wise? He peeked behind him to check he wasn't being followed. He wasn't. It hadn't been wise but it was needed. Someone had to lob rocks at Franklin's armour. If not him then who? The heaviness in his stomach subsided slightly. That had been the right thing to do. Hadn't it?

As he walked past the last of the tent's long guy-ropes he paused. An outlying easel carried a board about forthcoming attractions that he hadn't seen as he'd entered. He wasn't sure why but its words leapt out at him, as though the pattern of their letters was unconsciously familiar, somehow part of his being.

He read the board and his mouth dried.

'Coming soon to the Lyceum Theatre. Franklin Entertainment presents Wilma Wagensperg. Vienna's finest violinist.'

Max prowled in a loose circle outside the company's tent. He squeezed his eyes shut and thought of Wilma. He wondered how much money Franklin had offered to coax her from Vienna to London; how much lucre he'd dangled to make her forget her stage fright. Hundreds, no doubt. On seeing the board, in anger, he'd indulged the most impossible thought: how to record her. He'd immediately dismissed it from his mind. It would be like baiting a monster. Stealing a crown from a king. He'd focus on his other jewels. As he prowled a Russian shanty swirled around his head; a love song to Mother Volga, all deep harmonies and primordial passion. It faded, to be replaced by hymnals and crowdy-crawns, Harlem rags and Serbian folk songs. The cacophony in his head became more pronounced. As it grew in intensity, he stretched out his arms and splayed his fingers. There was no crowd to speak of at the tent. It mattered not. They'd come. He nodded to Rusty and Langley behind the table. As *Music of the Sands* played from the Empress he cleared his throat and, still circling, spoke over the noise.

'Ladies and gentlemen. Will the gramophone mean the end of the opera, the artiste, the concert and the music hall? No. But will it bring music from around the world into your house? Yes. That's right, *into* your house on one seven-inch disc. Louder, Rusty!'

As he circled he saw that two people had paused to watch. Rusty removed a material bung from the horn and the volume intensified. Max started to shout.

'I present to you a new technology for a new century. Music from Covent Garden to Cornwall, from Seville to St Petersburg. In. Your. House. *Louder!*'

He watched Rusty reach into the gramophone's horn and pull

out a second rolled up ball of fabric. He placed it next to the second pair of old socks on the table. The frenzied flamenco guitar increased in volume. A handful more people stopped on the grass. Max stopped circling and pointed at the closest person to him, a lady in a shawl.

'You, madam. Have you ever had opera for breakfast? No? Then such pleasures could be yours tomorrow.'

Like a ringmaster, he gestured at the array of gramophones on the trestle table outside the tent. He pointed at each of them one by one.

'In two short years we have come so far. But we are merely at the start. We will do all in our power to bring you...exclusive... music...from around the world.' As the flamenco reached an impossible tempo, he spread his arms as wide as he could, thrust his head back and clasped his eyes shut. 'Ladies and gentlemen, welcome to the industry of human happiness!'

The disc ended to total silence from the small crowd. He opened his eyes, straightened his head and took stock of the scene before him. About fifteen people had amassed. While the few children sat slack-jawed on the grass, the adults behind them stood still, some gawking, some talking behind their hands. It was as though he himself, rather than the machines, was the exhibit. He was about to turn to Rusty and Langley to demand a second disc when he heard the opening chords of a new song. It was *Daisy Bell*. And it was coming from the phonograph tent next door.

Some of the children in front of him nudged each other as they recognised the tune. They stood and ran across to the tent followed by their parents. Others joined from further afield. A few started singing.

'*There is a flower within my heart, Daisy, Daisy, Planted one day by a glancing dart.*'

Summoned by Mr Hague, the small crowd outside his tent grew. By the time the chorus came about, Max counted over twenty people huddled around its opening. His heart sank.

'*Daisy, Daisy, give me your answer do, I'm half crazy all for the love of you.*'

The sound from the phonograph was weak and wispy. The recording itself was so lacking in artistic merit that he quite wondered how it ever came to be captured. There was, he supposed, a certain communal bonhomie to the scene. Now alone, he turned to the gramophones. His cousin was dourly cleaning the Spanish disc, eyes down. Langley looked no happier but appeared to be waving at someone far away in the park, back among the stalls.

Max followed Langley's wave. The growing audience was not restricted to the mouth of the next-door tent. People had started to approach from a distance. It was then that he saw the objects of Langley's attention. Delilah and Molly were standing under an oak tree around thirty yards away, fresh from the Paragon stand. Arms linked, they were swaying and singing to *Daisy Bell*'s faint tune.

Max lifted his arm and waved along with Langley. The girls waved back, their grins broadening as they bobbed to the rhythm, oblivious to everything but someone else's music. Max continued to scan the crowd's fringes. A few yards along from the girls, a figure he recognised was standing with his arms behind his back. The shape and the colour jogged Max's memory first; the man was rotund and swathed in blue. His face was framed by two vast sideburns that almost met at his chin, which juddered to the music as he sang. Max jerked his head back as the stench of that interview room in Bow Street police station returned to his nostrils. It was Detective Inspector Boot.

'What was he even doing there?' Max thrummed his fingers on the sturdy pine table and waited for his tea.

Rusty turned from the cooking range, where Mary was setting down the kettle. Thin-lipped and faithful, she shuffled meekly between cupboard and grate. Max liked her; she leavened Rusty. She may have had the charisma of a nun but she also had the patience of an angel.

'Boot? Forget it. Means nothing.' Rusty passed a cup to Max.

Setting it on the table, he rubbed his temples. He was out of the park but still in the doldrums. Today had been awful. The flare-up with Franklin. You know the rules. What did that even mean? Then Boot. The murder hanging over everything like smog. Those awful machines. Their apparent popularity. Had he got it all wrong? Was this entire project a folly? 'Barely audible claptrap. Wouldn't you agree?'

A chair scraped on tiles as Rusty sat opposite him. 'You still on about the phonograph? Actually it's not a bad piece of kit. Easy to use. Cheap to manufacture, too.'

'Behave. The sound quality was frightful.'

Rusty shrugged. 'People didn't care, did they?'

But he did. Leaning back, Max eyed the vast dresser next to the range. Brought up to Rusty and Mary's house from Devon at Rusty's insistence. Max detested it. Its elaborately carved shelves reminded him of meal times after piano practice when his head either ached from missed notes or spun from praise. It held a gaudy pink china set bought recently just to fill it, each piece displayed like the priceless antique it would never be. The woven rug under his feet had the same provenance: brought up from the house. As Rusty often pointed out, the items would be his soon enough; he had merely pre-inherited them.

Max's eyes watered as the tea scalded the arch of his mouth. He was fleetingly glad of the distraction. The burn was not so bad with the second slurp, almost soothing. 'But where was the artistry in that machine?' He noticed that Rusty's hair was neatly combed; he had disappeared upstairs as soon as they arrived, as though here in the private space of his terraced house a few minutes from Victoria Park he was somehow tamed. He even smoked differently, sucking his pipe in a calmer way. For a second he wondered if this private Rusty was now the real one, and the gruff demeanour he had to cope with outside was an affectation. Or was something else at play? The man had been unreadable for days, even by his own standards.

'Actually, the feed screw mechanism next to the stylus is rather clever.'

Max glared at him. 'Who is this ghastly wind-up merchant anyway? Was it Hague?'

'Deep pockets. Was in bicycles.'

A chancer. No hope. At the range, whisk tinkled on copper pan as Mary beat an egg into milk. Her drop scones had soaked up many a belly of ale over the years. 'So, Mary, what did you think of the music?'

She turned from the pan, her face rouged from the coals. 'Oh, I love *Daisy Bell*.'

He'd meant *Music of the Sands*. The day was declining rapidly. He traced the grains on the wood of the tabletop with the tip of his finger. Free, they seemed to stretch to infinity. It was daft, but he envied their unencumbered passage and their artful swerves around the dark knots. Perhaps a spate of jewel-hunting in foreign climes was what was needed. Freedom of their own. It would take them away from the maelstrom. Sailors, ragtimers, villagers. London was a cesspool right now. He thought of Russia. An overseas tramp would bring them new energy and remind them why they were here.

Max thumped his elbows on the table. 'To hell with them all. Damn Franklin and his barbarous ways, and damn Mr J. P. Hague and his childish ditties. I won't let us be derailed from our mission. Not by murder, not by dictation machines and not by *Daisy Bell*. We push on.'

At the range Mary paused as if to consider a lingering thought. 'What's wrong with *Daisy Bell*?' Her rouge intensified.

'There's nothing wrong with it, Mary. Nothing at all. We're just aiming for things that are a bit *different*. A bit unusual. Music from around the world.' He ignored Rusty, who'd inched his nose in the air in faux haughtiness. 'It's the only way.'

Mary threw Rusty a glance. 'Most of it sounds like noise and nonsense to me.'

Max placed his cup down. 'I disagree. There are fascinating cultures out there. I genuinely believe this is the way forward. We capture exoticism wherever it may lie.'

Mary chuckled. 'Cultures? You're barking. Savages have no *culture*.' Her face pinched at the word. 'You'll come back with dysentery and lice and a whole load of wailing on your discs just like you did last time. I don't know.' She laughed again and looked to her husband for affirmation.

Wailing. Max weighed up his options. Prudence told him to hold his tongue. But passion prodded him otherwise. If the world was a musical meadow to be harvested then they were the ones to do it. They'd need money but they'd find it somehow. Perhaps he'd print up those Balducci masters. They would forever be the only recordings of the man; they could release them to the market posthumously. It was something to think about. World exclusives. Now there was beauty; there was lucre. Passion trumped prudence. 'Mary, have you heard of a chap called Augustus Pitt Rivers?' She shook her head. 'Lives in

Wiltshire. Has an enviable collection of musical instruments, spears, and artefacts from around the world. Last year, mulling the gramophone after our music hall disasters, I took the train down and knocked on his door. He was good enough to invite me into his home.'

She looked at him blankly.

'His artefacts demonstrate that, contrary to what many people think, primitive people – *savages* – have as much culture as you or I do. Some may seem less refined than us in our blinkered eyes, but we're all on the same path. Primitives view the world just as we do; they are not barbarians and they seldom *wail*. It inspired me.'

His words elicited no reaction. He nodded towards the Chaveley dresser.

'Take your china set up there. It is no different to the clay bowls that hang over natives' fires in Africa. That china is a tool of your culture, just as clay bowls are to theirs. There's really no difference.'

'But that china's from Derby.'

Rusty scowled as though he was also regretting this little family gathering.

'I'm not explaining myself. Your culture is everything you do: your habits, your music, your customs, these tea cups. All these ingredients make up the whole. No group of people is without their way of doing things – however strange we may find them – and therefore no group of people is without culture.' Max watched Rusty's lip curl in derision. He shrugged. 'We can't ignore the musical imperative out there in the world. Our business is predicated on it.'

Max looked at Mary to see if he was making more sense. But she was preoccupied with the dresser, no doubt wondering what her precious display had to do with African natives. He turned to his cousin and instantly recognised the look. He'd overstepped the mark.

Shaking his head, Rusty clamped his pipe between his teeth. He slowly clapped. 'Nice lecture, Max. You peculiar bastard.'

Silence descended on the kitchen, the heavy hiss of drop scones on the griddle the only sound.

## SUMMER 1887

*Two toys, similar in size. One, a monkey in naval uniform. The other, a bear with a Moorish hat. Both had silver keys protruding from their backs. Max's monkey, when wound, raised a cigarette to its lips. It held it there before lowering its arm and exhaling puffs of white powder. Rusty's bear, when wound, tipped a bottle in its right paw into a cup in its left. It then drank. The toys arrived at Chaveley from London, sent by Papa. He'd been absent for much of the summer, playing eight shows a week for Mr Franklin. Full theatres each night, Mama said. When they arrived, each toy was labelled; one said 'For dear Maximilian', other 'For Ronald'.*

*In the midday sun, Max and Rusty sat on the house's lawn, arguing about whose automaton was superior.*

*'But where does the monkey's smoke come from?' Rusty said.*

*'Magic.' It was obvious that a set of concealed bellows blew powder through the creature's mouth. Knowing this when Rusty did not gave Max power. Besides, he preferred the fantasy of magic to the dull reality of mechanics. What he also withheld from Rusty was the fact that he preferred the bear to the monkey. He liked the way its Fez sat at a strange angle, giving it character and charm.*

*Max missed Papa. It struck him as unfair that he had been*

ripped away from the family holiday. He didn't care how important Mr Franklin was. It wasn't the same without him. There were, he supposed, one or two upsides. That summer he'd found ways of creating new worlds in the ever-constant Chaveley. He put on a play, taking the lead role and convincing Rusty to arrange lighting and curtains until Aunt Isabella demanded he have a part. And he'd been able to skip the occasional piano practice. Although he enjoyed playing, the odd dropped hour was forgivable. Papa would never know. Besides, he was thirteen now and an accomplished player. He'd won a school prize the previous term. The news had made his parents happier than he'd ever seen them. He was an adult now. Mama and he took regular walks on which they talked in ways they had never done before. One morning, down by The Forbidden Sty, he asked her what would happen to Chaveley when Uncle Tobias and Aunt Isabella were no longer around. As they walked along the cliff top path she quietly explained that it would eventually pass to Rusty as Tobias and Isabella's son. But there would be a pause, she said. She and Papa had come to a special arrangement with them; they would be caretaker owners of the house initially. Chaveley would only pass to Rusty when both she and Papa had passed on. She called it a compromise arrangement and said that all families have them. Max looked out to sea thinking how unnecessary it all sounded.

The afternoon the toys arrived, Max looked for Rusty in the garden. He had seen neither his cousin nor the automatons since lunch; he assumed Rusty had hidden them as some form of treasure hunt. He eventually found him sitting on the ground behind a thicket where the lawn started to slope down to the clifftop. Rusty's face was specked with white powder. On the grass around him were scraps of fur and coils from a clockwork motor. A guillotined monkey's head lay at his feet. He had ripped the toy to shreds.

'What on earth have you done?' Max said.

'I wanted to know how it worked, and you wouldn't tell me.'

Lying at Rusty's side was a miniature set of bellows: the monkey's lungs. They were splayed open like a butterfly in flight.

'It's quite simple actually.' Rusty gestured at the parts. 'The smoke is chalk dust. It comes from these leather bellows, which are compressed and re-inflated by this lever when the spring motor is wound.'

'But that's my toy from Papa.' Max shook. He took a step closer. 'That's my toy from Papa,' he repeated, louder than before, anger rising. He was aware that his voice was deeper than in previous years. But it failed to intimidate his cousin. Rather it seemed to prod him. He flinched as Rusty leapt up, wiped his cheeks, and stood nose to nose with him.

'You wouldn't tell me so I found out myself,' Rusty shouted. 'Besides, I don't see why you should have got the better toy just because you're older.'

Max grabbed the boy's shirt and twisted it towards him. 'Papa gave it to me. It's mine.'

'Well, now neither of us can play with it.'

'You rotten…' Max drew back his arm to thump him on the nose. He imagined his face crumpling at the shot of pain. It was the least he deserved. Just as Max swung his fist forward he felt a larger hand smother his.

'Maximilian! Inside now.'

He turned. Papa loomed behind him, his hand wrapped around his own. He was still in his coat from the railway station.

'Papa,' Max whispered.

'Come up here with me. I have exciting news.'

As he turned to follow Papa back to the house, Max glared at Rusty. The fight was not over. He felt his father's hand on his back as they walked. He felt a little safer with him there, a little more protected.

In the familiar cool air of the drawing room, Max sat on an armchair adjacent to the sofa where Mama sat reading. Isabella and Tobias were playing cards on a table near the door. Papa paced.

'Maximilian, I have something to tell you. I have been speaking to Mr Franklin about your musical competence. He has suggested to me that you might make an interesting accompanist to me at my future piano concerts. A father and son show, if you will. He is keen.'

Max sat still. Performing publicly was something about which he'd always dreamed. However, he was aware that in Papa's absence he had barely played all summer. 'Thank you.'

'You're becoming an accomplished player. He thinks it would be…' Papa wafted the air with a flourish, '…an eye-catching show.'

Mama lowered her book. 'Gosh, can you imagine that, Max? How wonderful.'

'And when Mr Franklin has an idea it usually happens.' Papa stopped pacing and turned to him. 'Should you hit the mark, he has suggested a run in late October. How about that?'

Max glanced about the room, unsure of what to say. As he did so, he was sure he saw Isabella witheringly raise her eyebrow to Tobias. 'Wonderful,' he repeated.

'Come now, son. Play.' Papa pointed to the piano.

Max shrunk back into the chair as Papa leafed through a stack of sheet music. He picked out a Brahms waltz. It was one of the pieces that Max had not practised at all.

'Let's give this a go. Should be easy.'

Max wiped a clammy hand on his shorts. An urgent orange swish near the door caught his eye as Isabella pivoted her head towards a noise in the hallway outside. The needful sob was unmistakenly Rusty's. Isabella stretched her arms towards her son and – as if pulled by rope – her body followed their trajectory, carrying her seamlessly towards the commotion. Tobias followed her out of the room, muttering to himself.

'Maximilian.'

He turned.

'Come here at once.' Papa dragged out the stool from beneath the piano.

'But Papa. I don't feel ready. Not for that piece.'

'Nonsense. Sit. Play.'

Max looked to Mama, who failed to raise her head from her book. He slowly lifted himself from the chair and walked to the piano, his tummy turning in on itself. As he sat on the leather stool, Papa placed the waltz on the rack.

'As I've told you before, this piece requires precision and a lightness of touch. When you're ready.' Papa stood behind him.

Max slowly arranged his dank fingers on the keys, imagining himself in a circus, placing his head into the jaws of a lion. His eyes darted across the score. Although he could see precisely what notes he was supposed to play, he had no feel for how it was meant to sound. He took a deep breath and twisted around.

'I'm sorry, Papa. This piece is beyond me.'

A pause – ominous and long – then, 'Play.'

Max tried the opening bars. They sounded uneven, muddy. He winced. 'I am unable.'

He turned again and looked up at Papa, his nostrils gently flaring. Max knew that look. The expression hinted at a greater internal rage.

Papa leaned tightly over him, bearing his body weight on the keyboard's upright mahogany lid. 'Try again,' he whispered.

Max composed himself and repeated the opening bars. This time, he had more of a rhythm but there was little feeling there, little levity. He pushed on. As he was finding the song's pattern, he stretched the little finger of his left hand across to an A flat. But the finger's moistness caused it to slip off the ebony and land heavily on G. A discordant clunk interrupted the waltz. He played on for a bar before slowing then stopping entirely, leaving his hands resting on the mute keys. 'Sorry.' The word died in his mouth.

He heard Papa suck in air overhead. Inches in front of his face, he saw the man's knuckles slowly whiten as his hand gripped the piano lid.

'Ungrateful child.'

Max braced himself for the storm to erupt. He felt the warm body disappear from behind him as Papa spun away from the piano. As he moved away, he dragged forward the piano lid on which he had been supporting himself. For a split-second Max turned his head to watch the cyclone. Papa was striding across the room, talking to himself. It was a pained shout from Mama that made Max look forward again.

It happened so quickly. The piano's mahogany hood was plunging down towards his hands. Instinctively, he pulled his arms back; his left hand made it clear but his right was a little slower. He thought he'd managed to pull it clear too but as the lid crunched shut, it trapped the tip of his longest finger.

Max felt nothing at first, then a numb sensation, then warmth. He looked down, thinking that perhaps he had caught his fingernail in the piano. But a crimson and yellow pulp seeped from beneath the wood. When he tried to pull his hand free, a web of skin tethered him to the instrument. The white of bone peeped from beneath the lid. He looked closer. His middle finger had disappeared completely from its highest joint upwards.

Max thought of the dismembered monkey's head in the garden. He turned to look at Mama. She was lurching across the carpet towards him and silently screaming at Papa. Then, with the faintest of moans, Max keeled backwards off the piano stool and his world shut down.

# 8

It was only late morning but he needed his fix. Max selected a record, slipped off its paper sleeve and bore the disc's weight on the fleshy cushion between thumb and forefinger. His twisted callous protruded through the shellac's centre as he supported the disc. He carried it to the gramophone in the corner. A hand-cranked model. An early gift to Mama, presented in front of Papa. Intended to sit in the drawing room like some kind of omen, a gibbet to his father's trade. The record's spirals caught the sole shard of light peeping through the curtain crack; silver triangles danced around some unseen central anchor.

He placed the disc on the turning table and laid the stylus on its edge. Five turns of the crank, and a hiss filled the silence. As if in a trance, his eyes followed the label on its central stamp as it spun: Berliner Gramophone. The fingers that had moments earlier cradled the record prickled in anticipation as the needle began its inwards journey. He crossed the room and reclined into the sofa.

Three seconds of silence. All of them agony. As the needle locked into the record's dark inscription, he smiled. There was no sweeter disruption. A plucked scale from a Mesopotamian zither ascended for four-notes then retraced them. His unwaxed moustache swung limply as he followed the tune's course. After two bars a simple piano chord accompanied the first and third notes of the scale. The zither became more elaborate, filling the gaps in the rhythm it had helped to create. Textures not daubs. A skittery drum. *Baghdad 1897*, he thought. The earliest recording of its kind; shipped from Washington, the blueprint of all he was trying to achieve. The music became more urgent. Cymbals crashed like gannets. This was sensory distortion of the most delightful kind.

He imagined the series of processes going on in his head as he listened. A scientist had once explained to him how the brain digests music. Precise technical terms were forgotten in minutes, although he adored the cadence of the word cerebellum. He enjoyed, however, garnishing the parts of the lecture he did remember with his own interpretation. At that moment as he lay on the sofa, his eardrums were sending sparks of electricity to the pair of benevolent mittens encasing his brain. Like mystic clerks, the mittens ordered the pulses into notes and fired them around his skull like firecrackers on Hogmanay. His brain – awakened, alert – recognised the music and embraced it like an old friend. Gratification followed.

Max shivered as the record reached its clattering crescendo and firecracker after firecracker ricocheted around his head.

Then silence as stylus met barren core. Two minutes of challenge and pleasure, of peril and reward, were replaced by the familiar hiss of emptiness. He lay motionless as he gathered himself. Counting to ten, he let his mind run back over the rhythms he'd just heard. Then he reached into his waistcoat pocket and lit a cigarette.

He heard a key in the front door downstairs. Too soon, he

thought, too soon.

The door slammed shut and he heard the clunk of keys on the hallway sideboard. It was followed by the familiar progress of feet across the hall. He counted three limbs, all slow.

'Is that you?' he shouted.

He received no reply and rose reluctantly from the sofa. If it was her, he'd have another minute or so: she'd have to climb the stairs that led to the drawing room. He walked to the gramophone, set the stylus back to the beginning and turned the spindle five times. Releasing the disc, he sat back on the sofa. The second time was often even more enjoyable.

Drums followed piano followed zither as the song built. Just as the cymbals started to crash in, the lady entered the room's half light. As usual she was wearing the heavy grey dress from neck to floor. As soon as she heard the music, she raised her walking stick towards the gramophone.

'For goodness' sake, Max. Put a sock in it.'

He leapt up. She'd been quicker up the stairs than he'd expected. 'Of course, Mama.'

He extinguished his cigarette in an ashtray and walked to the machine. From a drawer in the table beneath it, he pulled out a rolled-up ball of material and stuffed it into the gramophone's horn. The sound muffled.

'Better?'

'Much.'

He walked to his mother and kissed her on both cheeks. He had not seen her in the days since Victoria Park.

'How was Medlock?' He took the stick from her. Almost daily, it seemed, she'd visited Papa's solicitor Harold Medlock to discuss his papers.

'Two weeks on Thursday. Here.'

'The will reading?'

She nodded.

At least they'd then be able to move on. Cradling her elbow, he helped her ease into an armchair and handed her a newspaper.

'Open the curtains, dear. Light. That's what you need,' she said.

He walked to a large bay and pulled the drapes apart. Crisp autumn sun illuminated the rich green walls of a room too lived-in to be austere yet just too formal to be homely. Papa's piano occupied the corner behind the sofa like a monolithic lump, untouched since his death. Max blinked before turning to look at Mama. Her hair was up in its customary generous bun. The purple trim around her hem was the only suggestion of dash about her entire wardrobe. It had been this way since Papa passed away. He lifted the stylus from the record. 'Anything?'

'Sherry. Thank you.' Her expression remained as it always was these days; outsiders said it was inscrutable, Max knew it was doleful. Her mourning had months to run.

'Have you seen this?' she said, raising the *Daily Telegraph*.

He glanced over. Another headline about the 'Opera Slayer'. She read the first paragraph of the article out aloud. Sources close to the investigation claimed that the police were pursuing new leads.

'I have seen it, yes.' He walked to the drinks table beside the window.

'Awful affair.' Disdain rendered her words barely audible.

He lifted the bulb off a decanter and poured in silence. As he crossed the room and handed a glass to her, his eyes caught the brooch on her collar. An oval no bigger than his thumb knuckle. Although Papa's eyes were the size of pinheads, their whites stood out – intense and cold. He turned back to the drinks table.

'I know you think Mr Franklin was involved,' she said. 'But

he's a good man. Helped your father. Helped us pay for this place.'

Franklin was rarely spoken of in the house. Everyone saw him through different lenses. He was like a language with two meanings. It was a mark of permanent shame to Max that his parents were friends with him. With his back to his mother, he poured himself a sherry and drank. 'I'm sorry, Mama, but I am almost certain he was behind it. And judging by the headlines it seems that the peelers are close to seeing sense.'

A bristle. He didn't see it but it infused the silence. He picked a fleck of shellac from his nail. Still she said nothing.

'We saw him that very evening. He threatened us. One of his people must have alerted him and he…did what he did.'

'He's a good man.' She repeated the phrase as though he'd said nothing.

'He's evil,' he snapped and turned.

He waited for the disapproving glance; that famous damning frown. But it never came. Before Papa's death it was sprayed like water. Eyes narrowed, head slightly tilted. She'd deployed it throughout his childhood, whether he'd fibbed about stealing an apple or lied about pissing in the bathtub before Rusty got in, and used it daily until Papa died. But the glance seemed to have gone the way of many of her mannerisms; spirited away by grief.

'I'm sorry. But you only know one side of Franklin. The charming one. Papa's champion. You didn't see what I saw in that hotel room.'

'I've known him since you and Ronald were children. Years. I don't believe it was him. I just don't. He may appear a little rough but he has a good heart. Jealousy's like rust, Max. It corrodes.'

'Jealous?'

'Of all he's achieved.'

'I'm not jealous,' he snapped. 'He's a crook. He runs London like it's his.'

Finally, the glance. 'He loved your father. I'm sure they'll catch some vagrant soon and the matter will be settled.'

He lifted an emollient hand. It was pointless talk. Somewhere deep down she surely knew that Franklin had not been carried to the top by charisma and sound judgement alone.

'Ronald's well?' she said, poorly plugging the silence.

'Rusty's Rusty.' He sat and sipped his sherry.

Momentarily he considered another record. Much as he hated them, he considered putting on one of the nonsense music hall numbers they'd captured the previous year. Mama had laughed when she first heard them. Levity might help.

'So who is it tonight?' Mama's tone altered once again. Maternal, slightly mocking.

'I beg your pardon?'

'Which of your friends are you taking out tonight? Lucy? Delilah?' She paused. 'The Queen of Sheba?'

No need for the record. He'd seen no one else since he'd started courting Delilah. She knew that. 'Tonight I'm taking Delilah for dinner at the Troc,' he said. 'I'm actually growing rather fond of her.'

He watched her blink. He knew what was coming. 'Progress, I suppose. Is she the marrying sort?'

'Oh, you know me. I see beauty in many things,' he said, deliberately vague. It was too early to set that particular hare running.

'Everything's always an adventure with you, isn't it? Wouldn't it be fun if, one day, you decided to do the right thing.'

'Oh, I plan to.'

Her mouth fell open.

'One day.'

He watched as crimpled crow's feet appeared around her eyes. He hadn't seen them for months. They spread like dawn rays after a stormy night. She started to chuckle. He joined in. They looked at each other. Soon their shoulders rose and fell in unison. The long-absent sound of mirth was only interrupted by a series of loud knocks at the front door downstairs.

'I'll get that.' Max stood and walked across the drawing room, catching Mama's eye as he went.

He was still chuckling as he descended the oval stairwell to the hall. The last few minutes had given him reassurance. She would, he knew, be fine. He reached the front door, pulled back the latch and heaved it open. Standing at the foot of three steps, with one hand on the black wrought iron railings, was the rotund figure of Detective Inspector Boot. He was flanked by two uniformed bobbies. Unlike when Max saw him in Victoria Park, Boot's jowls were not shaking in song. His face was stony.

'Mr Cadenza. I'd be grateful if you would accompany me to the station. I have some fresh questions regarding the murder of Alfredo Balducci.'

❦❦❦❦❦

'I've been digging, Mr Cadenza.'

Max had remained silent since he left the house. Partially it was the shock of seeing Boot at the door. But he'd spent most of the carriage ride south to Bow Street wondering what fresh questions the man could possibly have. Now, sitting back in Boot's small office, he could barely think at all. None of this made sense. As on his last visit, the stale odour wafted up from the cells below. And as on his last visit, Boot's voice boomed off the walls. But his rich bass had a velvety clarity that Max hadn't noticed the last time. It was as though he was speaking with greater purpose. He noticed another difference too; on a low table in the corner of the room sat an Empress gramophone.

'Digging, detective inspector?'

'Indeed. It has become clear that you have history with Mr Franklin. A history of antagonism, if I can put it like that.'

Max grabbed for words but none suited.

'Confrontation,' Boot said, as if to clarify.

Max gently puffed his cheeks. He saw no point in lying. Anyone who'd spent any time in Covent Garden after dark could have told him that. 'That is true.'

'And this antagonism has gone on for many years.'

'As you say, we have history.' As statements of fact, the detective inspector's comments were incontrovertible. He wondered how much digging they had actually required. And yet, sitting in a police station across a table from a detective possibly hinting at foul play, these words took on a different hue. Their delivery carried the implication of guilt. As well as feeling bewildered, Max felt vulnerable. Boot was making the truth sound like a hanging offence.

'You've constantly cajoled him and sought to disrupt his interests, haven't you?'

'Our business interests don't strictly align, no.'

Boot nodded to the gramophone in the corner. 'Of that, I'm aware. This antagonism stretches back, I believe, to his close relationship with your father.'

He bristled at the mention of Papa. Reaching into his pocket, he pulled out a packet of cigarettes and jammed one into his mouth. A match flared as he sucked.

Boot looked down at his notebook. 'You were seen on the night of the murder having an altercation with Mr Franklin in the Café Royal. Witnesses – and the *entire* restaurant saw it, Mr Cadenza – say you pointed and jabbed at him in a stand-off that lasted a number of minutes.'

He fired a plume of smoke across the table. 'We've often clashed.'

Boot clasped his arms behind his head and nodded slowly.

'What precisely are you saying, detective inspector?'

'I put it to you that as part of this long-held vendetta against Mr Franklin, you captured the voice of his star signing in an act of spite.'

'Not true.'

'Then you killed him.'

Max sat forward. 'Now hold on.'

'By ensuring that Signor Balducci's final act of singing was into your recording machine rather than into the audience from one of Mr Franklin's stages, you were getting some kind of macabre victory over him.'

'No.'

'You killed him so that he'd be unable to appear in Mr Franklin's theatres ever again.'

He stubbed out the cigarette.

'And you were sending Franklin a message that you're not to be messed with. Those needles in his neck. Elaborate. It's all part of your...*act*.'

'Act?'

Boot stretched his palms to his side and circled his fingers like a magician. "Exclusive...music...from around the world'. I saw you in Victoria Park, Mr Cadenza. You seemed like a man possessed. The industry of human happiness? Quite a show.'

This was preposterous. Max shook his head. 'You've got this the wrong way round.'

Looking at the gramophone again, Boot changed his tone. 'I'm enjoying that *very* much, by the way. I like the Spanish one. Most energetic. Not sure about the bagpipers though.'

Max looked at him, unsure of what to say.

'How are sales?'

'Eh?'

'Of discs. A little on the soft side?'

'Not at all...'

'You struggling?'

'No.'

'Ever thought of recording *The Mikado*, I wonder?'

'What?'

'Just a thought.'

Boot started as Max slammed his hand onto the table. 'Stop playing with me, Boot. The reason I targeted Signor Balducci...'

'*Targeted*?'

'To *record*. Targeted to *record*.' Max leaned forward on his stool. 'The reason is that I have a list, you see.'

Boot raised a brow.

'Here.' Max reached into his breast pocket and tossed the leather pouch containing his jewels across the table. 'It's a list of musicians I must record. Balducci's on that list. See for yourself. He was singing in one of Franklin's theatres. It's sort of inevitable when one man owns most of them.'

As though handling poison, Boot opened the wallet and tipped out the list. He unfolded it, scratching the bald inch of chin between his sideburns as he read its contents.

'What would you do?' Max raised his shortened finger.

Boot looked up. 'I don't follow.'

'I was robbed, detective inspector. Of the ability to play. Aged thirteen. That music in your hands is all I have.'

A shrug. The man wasn't interested in psychology. 'It's just a list. My theory still makes perfect sense to me.'

Max reached over the table and grabbed his wallet and the paper. 'Well it would, wouldn't it?' Anger pinched at his voice.

For a second he wondered who'd got at Boot. It seemed pretty obvious. He told himself to calm down. 'You have to believe me. Franklin killed Balducci to send a message to us.'

'To you?'

'Yes. He saw us recording him as an act of encroachment. You know, into his territory.'

Another raised brow.

'We'd only etched two masters, for God's sake. Why would I kill him?' Max could feel the conversation teetering away from him. He reached for another cigarette. This was a grim turnaround. Just a few weeks previously he had arrived at the station voluntarily to help Boot catch the slaughterer. Now he was being accused of the slaughter.

'This is how I see it.' Boot raised a hand and counted off his fingers. 'You and you alone knew where Signor Balducci was staying that night. You were, according to everything you've said to me, one of the last people to see him alive and the first person to see him dead. The styl-i in his neck came from your Empress model of gramophone. And he belonged to Franklin, a man for whom, you have just admitted, you have a strong and long-standing dislike. Furthermore, Mr Cadenza, just hours after the murder, you were in this very room trying to pin the blame on Mr Franklin with some deeply suspect story about a non-existent scrawled warning.'

Boot's cheeks juddered over his collar as he shrugged at the simplicity of it all. He leaned back on his chair and glared over the table.

Usually, Max deployed charm when he was in a corner. It almost always worked. But as he placed his unlit cigarette on the table, he opted for another tactic. Brinkmanship. He stared Boot straight in the eye and cleared his throat. 'And this is how I see it. You don't have one shred of evidence, not one ounce, to prove that I killed him.' He swallowed, raised his wrists and laid them on the table between them. 'Provide me with one piece, detective inspector. One piece of evidence. Then feel free to charge me, cuff me and sling me in a cell downstairs.'

## SUMMER 1891

*Max stamped on the smouldering cigarette and looked across the garden at Chaveley's windows, silently urging Papa to look out at him on the lawn. Goading the man had become a hobby. However he could see no sign of him. He imagined he was sitting inside somewhere, tinkering on the piano or talking to Uncle Tobias. He raised his collar against the rain and turned to Rusty, who was busying himself at his feet.*

*'Come on, chum, it's cold.'*

*'Almost there.'*

*Max put his hands in his waistcoat pockets and rocked back on his heels. He turned and looked down the rolling lawn towards the sea. Years of coming to Chaveley meant that he knew the garden's every contour intimately: every undulation, every bed, every shrub. The clifftop was shrouded in mist sent up from the water below. The cruel summer had rendered the lawn little more than a bog.*

*Rusty stood. 'Ready? Watch.'*

*Since last summer his freckles had become interspersed with the sore mid-youth pimples that Max had been fortunate enough to avoid. His cousin unscrewed the vinegar bottle and slowly poured it into the cup of baking soda on the ground. Almost instantly, the* cup filled with a thick brown substance. It oozed over the lip and onto the grass, a hungry volcano.

'See, it blooming reacts,' Rusty said.

Max bent forward, clapping in delight. 'You're a little genius. Again.'

'All right. Once more. I'll do more vinegar this time.'

The second cup overflowed next to the first with a greater fury. Max danced in a wild circle. As he did so his curtain of curls, grown long in recent years, fell in front of his eyes. He tucked them away and surveyed the glorious mess between them. 'Let's get a bucket and do a huge one.'

'Can't. Mother will notice what's missing.' Rusty lifted the half-drained vinegar bottle.

'Wimp.'

'And if either of our fathers see us they'll kill us.'

Max snorted. 'Don't care. I want mine to see.' He shrugged and looked up at the house again. 'Hate him almost as much as I hate this place.'

'Yeah. So boring,' Rusty replied unconvincingly.

Max suspected that Rusty actually enjoyed his summers of tinkering and soft rebellion. But Max didn't. Since the accident, he found everything about the house oppressive. Happy memories had soured. Like one of Mama's Dart trout, every room was stuffed with unsavoury scraps. He spat on the ground and watched his saliva slide through a crack in the paving stones. What could the fathers do anyway? Max knew that Papa was unlikely to lose his temper with him: he'd been beset by guilt after what happened. These days he was more likely to make an attempt to atone than to shout. In the last year alone, Max had been offered a bicycle and a trip to France. Both had been rejected. The offers made no odds. Whatever Papa did, he would never let him forget. He had vowed as much.

As he thought of his father, he caressed the nub of the middle finger on his right hand. The skin had grown back over the stump and the flaring nerve had calmed down. But his hand remained deformed; for three years now his middle digit had been squatter than all the others. His longest finger was his shortest. Despite trying, he had not been able to play the piano since it happened. He missed that ability to create, to interpret and to perform desperately. The stub's skin yielded under his thumb nail. He thought of all the other things he was no longer able to do: bowl a cricket ball, tie a shoelace or pick up a hand of cards without people staring. He kicked a cup into the hedge.

This summer was even worse than last. The hardest thing was the proximity to the man he loathed. At least in London he could avoid Papa. The man was giving concerts most evenings and it was easy to find distractions away from the house when he was in. He'd thrown himself into seeking out music with one criteria: that it was anything but the kind his father played. Away from the popular theatres and music halls, he'd discovered a wealth of curios; folk music in Bermondsey dives, choral ensembles in rehearsal rooms behind Hawksmoor's great churches, Japanese sailors plucking lute-like biwas in dark taverns. And opera. Its great slabs of emotion spoke to his soul. All provided peeks into a world greater than his own. As his musical horizons broadened, he read voraciously. The emerging anthropology. Pamphlets on myth, religion and ritual. Dizzying tales of exoticism in far off places. Every word, every note, was an invitation. As he roved, he discovered new parts of London: the chop houses of Covent Garden and the public houses of Mayfair. In London, he was relatively free. But down here at Chaveley, stuck on the sparse coastline of north Devon, the parameters were limited. The only gin bottle that he knew of was locked in a cabinet in the drawing room. The only music, that infernal piano. Numerous times during this stay *he'd asked himself why he'd bothered coming down at all. After all, he was a young man, he could do as he pleased. It was partly for Mama, who had asked him to. But the main reason, he knew, was bent over a bottle to his left: Rusty. It was a chance to spend time with the silly, impulsive fellow. He'd matured and thickened outwards, if not upwards. He was fun.*

*'Did you hear them bickering at the card table last night?' Rusty said.*

*'That's brothers for you. Always fall out.'*

*Max removed another cigarette from the carton in his pocket. 'Papa's so pompous. I dislike everything he stands for: his stupid theatre concerts, his ugly posters all over London. He might be a richer man now but he's not the virtuoso he thinks he is. Have you heard him play? It's so...' he struck a match hard and lit the cigarette. 'It's so narrow. All technique, no passion. I'd love to destroy that whole thing he and Mr Franklin have.'*

*Rusty looked at him.*

*'I'm serious. It's cosy and annoying. Theatre owner. Musician.' He mocked an amorous couple. 'Makes me sick.'*

*'Stick a blooming powder keg under them?'*

*'Precisely.'*

*Rusty laughed. 'At least we're strong, eh?'*

*Max nodded. If there was one upside to his falling out with Papa, it was that he and Rusty had become even closer. They were, in a strange sort of way, best friends. And they both now had things to rail against; Max against the injustice that his father had caused, and Rusty against people's attitudes towards his own physical awkwardness. Even at fourteen, his stocky frame and feral mop caused people either to look twice or keep their distance.*

*'Of course we're strong, chap. It's us against the bastards,' Max kicked him on the shin. 'Even if you won't do a bucket. Come on.'*

*He led his cousin up the path towards the glass doors of the* house's drawing room, past a sopping clematis. Inside, just as Max had predicted, he saw the silhouettes of the grown-ups. He immediately looked at the ground and slowly circled his tongue around the inside of his cheek in case they were watching. Without looking up, he led Rusty past the drawing room windows and in through Chaveley's back door.

He was about to unlace his boots when he stood straight and gestured to Rusty.

'I'm sick of here. Let's walk into Combe Martin. There's a hostelry there.'

'Can't. My mother'll have my guts for garters.' She was still his universe.

'She'll never know.'

'But I can't drink ale. Look at me.'

'You'll be fine. Hurry.'

Rusty cackled as Max drummed on his back. They scurried from the house through the front door, ducking behind hedges until clear from view. Max led the way, cupping a cigarette against the rain as they walked down the narrow lane. He felt a strange responsibility, and enjoyed telling Rusty what to expect.

'It'll be bawdy at the Pack o' Cards.'

Rusty nodded at every word.

'I'll buy the ale. Act as though you've been there before. There'll be shanties.'

The pub was set back from a shingle beach, ten minutes away, just off the track. To Max's surprise, the landlady welcomed them as they entered the low-beamed saloon. Settling Rusty on a corner bench, he walked to the bar. He allowed himself a smile; the hostelry was neither bawdy nor shanty-filled. There wasn't a fisherman in sight. Glancing back at Rusty from the bar, it was not his cousin that he saw. It was an older boy than the one he knew; almost a man, and one with a mildly threatening air about him. It was as though the alien surroundings of the saloon had stripped him of the fragile personality that Max knew. A ginger bulldog sat in his place. Max ordered two ales and returned to Rusty. Fifteen minutes later he was back ordering two more. His cousin matched him tankard for tankard. Rusty's eyes lit up every time that he brought another pair of ales. Fuggy freedom of the most joyous kind. He was glad that Rusty appeared to have taken to the hops.

'To your rotten health.' Max raised his tankard and clattered it into his drinking partner's.

'And yours.'

'It's us against the bastards. Always will be. Remember that.'

'Always,'

Max wasn't aware of the precise point at which the bar's clock stopped being a useful measure of time. It was somewhere between tankard three and four. After that, the time was measured by rounds of grog. Five, six. But even they were trumped, eventually, by the loudest chime of all: from Max's stomach. He was hungry. Desperately so. Ale swilling in him, he nudged Rusty, who seemed in another world entirely. It was time to head back.

'Do we 'ave to? Rusty's cheeks glowed blood-red.

'Yes we do. Come on. Chaveley.' Max stood unsteadily.

Max walked to the bar, thumped the empty tankards down and saluted the landlady like an old friend. They staggered from the Pack o' Cards into the near-horizontal rain. As they walked back down the path towards the house, he chanted in time to his footsteps. Rusty splashed ahead, kicking the heads off sodden dandelions on the verge. Both stopped to piss.

When they arrived at Chaveley, it was some time after Aunt Isabella normally served supper. Max crept through the front door and led Rusty into the hall. There was no sign of anyone. Head spinning, he raised a finger to his lips and beckoned Rusty into the drawing room. They sat heavily on the sofa as if they'd been there for hours. Max picked up a book. As he did so, he noticed that Rusty was trying to use his fingers to comb his hair into a parting. It didn't work.

The feet down the stairs sounded urgent. Max turned to see Mama enter the drawing room, breathless.

'Here you are.' She turned and shouted behind her. 'They're here!' It was rare for Mama to lose her temper, but Max knew precisely what was coming. 'Where have you been? We've been worried sick.' She took a few steps into the room. 'We've been looking all over for you. Did Isabella and Tobias find you?'

'No. We.' Max rubbed his face. Talking was an effort. 'We went fr'a walk.'

'A walk? Where? Look at you, you're sodden.'

'Combe Martin.'

Mama shook her head. 'So where are Isabella and Tobias?'

Max shrugged, letting Mama hold his gaze for just a second too long. She knew precisely where they'd been.

'Where are who?' Rusty glanced round the room, confused, when Papa strode in.

'Where in heaven's name have you two been?'

Max said nothing.

'I asked where you've been.'

He stuck his bottom lip between his teeth and bit down. He didn't want to argue with the man. It would only upset Mama.

'It's alright,' Mama said. 'They've just been for a walk.'

'You could have told us,' Papa said. There must have been a look, as Max noticed a change in his tone. It was probably the glance where Mama tilted her head to the side and squeezed her eyes. It seemed to Max that the only thing he shared with his father these days was the fear of the consequences of ignoring that flash. 'It would have saved us all having to look for you, *wouldn't it?' Papa added.*

*'Where's mother?'*

*'Don't worry, Ronald. They've gone for a walk. Boys, go upstairs and change. Then we should eat. The others'll be back shortly.' Mama left the room.*

*In fresh, warm clothes, Max and Rusty sat at the table. Max could not vouch for his parents, but supper for him was an amusing affair. He ate in silence and in haste, squiffy and eager to piss again, until he noticed that Rusty needed to go too. Once he'd cleaned his plate – mutton stew – he tried to play a silent game with Rusty to see who could remain seated the longest without going. But Rusty looked confused, constantly glancing around, before he bolted from his seat and ran to the bathroom. Max watched as Mama kept checking the carriage clock on the dining room dresser, fidgeting.*

*Checking Rusty was not in the room, she whispered to Papa, 'It's been three hours. It's most unlike them.'*

*'Very well.' Papa stood from the table. 'I believe they started looking on the cliff path. I'll have a look.'*

*He left the room, wearing his tolerance lightly. Max heard him open the back door from the hall, then saw him head down the garden through the dining room window. The contours of the lawn and the weather meant that he soon disappeared from view as he walked towards the sea.*

*'I'll go as well.' Mama stood.*

*When Mama had gone, Rusty reappeared. 'Where's everyone?' he asked.*

*Max gestured to the garden. Rusty immediately ran after them.*

*Max followed him into the hall and out onto the lawn. The rain was falling less hard now but the skies had grown a deeper grey as the light faded. The wind had picked up.*

*As Max walked down the garden towards the clifftop, he noticed* that both Papa and Mama had broken into a trot. He blinked rain away as he tried to follow their movements. But then Rusty, four paces ahead of him, started to run too. Cursing his drunkenness, Max crossed the lip where the lawn rolled down to the fence for the final time. He stopped in his tracks and a completely new sensation overtook him. It was a little like the bump he felt in his head after he'd drunk that first ale, only twenty times stronger. And there was no pleasure. The fence at the bottom of the lawn seemed closer to the cliff edge than before; beyond The Forbidden Sty, a whole section of land appeared to have collapsed into the sea.

Max walked on, his legs uneasy. After three steps he halted again. It was true. The weather had claimed a lip of ground from the end of the garden. Earth replaced by thin air. Mama and Papa were standing at the fence, just inches from the new edge, pointing down.

Suddenly, as if winded in the stomach, Papa bent double. Mama screamed and turned to intercept Rusty as he caught up with them. She clamped him by the shoulders before he could pass and fell to her knees. Max stood motionless as he watched his mother caress the boy's face. It didn't matter that the wind stole her words. Rusty's crumpled face told Max all he needed to know.

Slowly, Max edged his way to the fence, passing Mama and Rusty's huddle as he neared it. He clasped a crossbar with both hands and stood on his tiptoes to look down beyond. He could not make out much, but on the rocks at the foot of the cliff he saw that a heavy strip of fresh rubble was being ravaged by the water. The turf and wild flowers that once topped it were nowhere to be seen.

Among the debris lay two bodies.

# 9

**N**o evidence?' Rusty shifted on the battered chaise and wiped rig oil from his palms.

'None. All supposition. I challenged Boot to cuff me if he had any.' Max raised his wrists over his office desk as if to demonstrate his innocence. When pressed, the detective inspector had had little choice but to let him go.

'You poor sod.'

'It was horrible.' And humiliating. And sapping of his dignity. He hated the idea that the finger of suspicion could still be pointing at him. Allegations lingered unseen in this game, as stealthy and deadly as gas vapours.

'Just trying his luck, was he?' Eyes down, Rusty rubbed at a particularly stubborn oil spot.

'Of course he was. I tell you something though. It has stiffened my resolve to get out there and capture the rest of our jewels. Nothing focuses the mind like a chat with a policeman in an airless room.' A freshly unrolled map of Russia undulated over his desk's messy piles, the paper's jagged ridges suggesting a mountain range in miniature.

'I can imagine.'

'Somehow.' Max gazed at Russia's great river and imagined capturing a shanty's rough magic, its melody heavy and dark, as though heaved by stevedores from the depths of the Volga.

In the two days since his encounter with Boot, their conversation had rolled around his mind. He hadn't enjoyed recounting it to Rusty. It made it fresh again.

'But I don't understand why.' Rusty set down his chamois.

'Why what?'

'Why you? What does he know? He must know something.'

His questioning was almost as intense as Boot's. 'Nothing. He knows nothing. There *is* nothing.' He opened his mouth to move the conversation on to sunnier things when he saw Rusty's face slump. 'What on earth is it?'

Rusty glanced up. 'If I'm being honest, it's Streak.'

'Langley?'

'I don't trust him.'

'Not this again.'

'Look. This may just be me. But don't you think it strange that Balducci got done in just after he joined us? Funny coincidence, I'd say.'

Max rubbed his eyes. 'Don't be daft.'

'Think about it.'

'But we know it was Franklin. It's obvious.'

'And who delivered that business card to you? The one with Franklin's warning.'

'Well…Langley.'

'Exactly.'

'He was handed it outside. He told me.'

Rusty raised a brow. 'And who alerted Franklin to tubby's hotel room?'

'You think he's working for Franklin? Some kind of…what? Mole?' He shook his head. 'He's a good lad. Harmless. And look at him, for God's sake. He couldn't fight his way out of a paper bag.'

'You know that, do you?'

'Yes.'

'Well I don't trust him.'

'Fine. We'll agree to disagree.' Max reached for his pocket watch. It was a quarter past three. He needed to be in Kennington by four. Departing suited him; Rusty's skittishness was draining. 'Now I really must go. Delilah and I are going to see Mary Kingsley give a lecture.'

Rusty wobbled his head in mock wonder.

'Grow up. She canoed up the Ogooué river in a skirt with nothing but a box of tea and a pouch of tobacco for company. She's fearless.'

'Is she one of those *new women*?'

'She's simply a woman, Rusty. As glorious as all the rest.' Max stood and, ducking under the hanging sitar, squeezed around his desk to the hatstand. 'Oh, they've set a date for the trinket distribution.'

'Eh?'

'Papa's will reading.' His turn. He pulled a face of mock awe.

'I know. Highbury. Two weeks on Thursday. Don't you worry. I'll be there.'

Max pulled on his jacket and opened the door. Papa had left him next to nothing; he just knew it. Even on his deathbed he had beckoned his son in close and whispered something about changing the will. 'I can hardly wait,' Max said as he closed the door behind him.

෧෧෧෧෧

It was close to dusk when Max walked with Delilah over

Waterloo Bridge. Mary Kingsley's talk, in an Oddfellows' hall south of the river, had fired his imagination more than he'd hoped. Delilah was equally effusive, although she couldn't see why anyone would take to a canoe unaccompanied.

They stopped halfway over the bridge and leaned against its stone wall, watching the coal barges drift east down towards the Isle of Dogs. The sky was starting to bruise. For the first time in days Max felt relaxed. He turned to face Delilah. The breeze coming off the Thames had turned her hair into a delicate birds' nest. Without seeking permission, he caught a tangle and tucked it behind her ear. Somewhere behind him he heard the muted chimes of Big Ben. He counted six. She had a show that evening so they didn't have long to spare.

'Come.' He offered his arm.

They reached the north bank and turned left down the Embankment, the avenue's space and order in stark contrast with the Garden's anarchic tangle of streets quarter of a mile to the north. Like a slumbering serpent, the river alongside them glowed a lazy green in the fading light. As they walked Max deliberately bumped his shoulder into Delilah's. It was, he knew, a naïve way of seeking affirmation that there was something between them. Within two paces, she softly bumped back. He repeated. So did she. He smiled.

'He didn't hurt you did he?' she said.

'Boot? No. But he was hardly pleasant.'

'Want me to get him for you? Got a mean right hook on me, I'm told.'

He didn't doubt it.

'Anyway, forget the rotten peelers. I've been reading up.'

'Reading up?'

'On gramophones and records. You didn't tell me that shellac is what buttons are made from.'

He peeked across at her. She was becoming quite the expert. 'You mean the discs? Yes. Same material.'

'Crushed beetles' shells.'

'Mixed with a hot compound, yes.'

'But here's what I still don't understand. How do you actually put the music on them?'

'Magic an–' An elbow jabbed his ribs.

'If you say magic and passion I'll send you for a dip.'

'Very well,' he said. 'It's quite simple really. We take the master disc – the zinc one, the unique blueprint – and create a heavy stamp from it, a negative. Then we heat up a shellac patty until it's almost melted and, wham, drop the stamp on it. Voilà. Records.'

'Hot shellac?'

'Yes.'

'You're right. It does sound simple. Try running around a stage dressed as a squaw every night.'

'Given half a chance…'

'Stop it. Tell me more.'

He thought for a second and told her about a French bohemian called Charles Cros. Some twenty years previously, he explained, this fellow wrote a paper about reproducing sound. Cros had taken the idea of the telephone – then in its infancy – one step further. He believed that if sound could be transported down a wire as vibrations then it could also be captured and stored. 'People thought him mad. But he said that if a noise could somehow be made to leave some kind of physical trace – a scratched vibration, for example – then it could be replayed over and over again on a machine,' Max said. 'I was a mere boy when he wrote that. But what foresight, eh?'

'So did he invent the talking machine?'

'No. Poor old Cros,' he said. 'His paper got lost in a Parisienne academy, Thomas Edison had the same idea in New Jersey and Cros is now better known as the author of a silly poem called *The Kippered Herring*.'

She raised a hand to muffle a snort. 'You're all off yer chumps.'

They strolled in silence. Having her next to him still felt as surprising and uplifting as finding flowers on the doorstep.

'You won't forget, will you, Max?'

'Forget what?'

Her tone softened. 'To decide whether I can, perhaps...create a unique blueprint.'

'Stamp some hot shellac?'

'Record.' She smiled.

The word, he noticed, was accompanied by the slightest roll of the eyes, as though she wanted to seem embarrassed by it. The affectation was too deliberate; in trying to make light of it, she had underlined its importance to her. 'Of course. I promise to think about it.' He pointed to a bench. 'I can see you're keen.'

'I am.'

They reached the seat in the shadow of Cleopatra's Needle. It was ridiculous but he felt sad as he sat, knowing that in minutes she had to dash to the Paragon. Then that would be it until the next time. She'd run off to her show and his stomach would feel like a warm but empty husk, its warmth diminishing and its emptiness growing with every passing minute. He wished he could halt time's passage, just to be with her for a few more hours. He looked up at the looming obelisk and felt her head rest on his shoulder. On the breeze, he caught her scent. Cherries and cut grass.

'Delilah.'

Craning in to her turning head, he planted a single kiss on the constellation of freckles on her forehead. Slowly, she raised her head further. He kissed her again, this time on the lips.

Receptive and warm, she melted into him, reaching up to softly touch his cheek. He held her, savouring her supple lips and inhaling her blissful essence. Seconds passed, and an almost imperceptible movement caused him to edge back slightly; she'd opened her eyes. He was not even aware they'd been shut. An inch now between them, they both smiled.

'Slow coach,' she whispered and, once again, rested her head on his shoulder.

As his stomach fizzed, Big Ben struck a quarter past six. Delilah straightened up.

'Oh Lord, I've got to go or I'll miss my call.'

'What?' he said. 'So soon?'

He felt her tug at his lapel. Their lips merged even more snugly the second time. His hand sank into a forest of curls as he held the back of her head. Gently eager, she pressed herself into him. Max lost himself in the moment's euphoric blur.

She pulled back, smiled a faint smile and gestured east. 'I'm sorry. I really have to...'

He nodded. The moment's splendour trumped its cruel brevity. He watched her tidy her hair as he shook himself out of the moment. Then, still sitting, she briefly held his cheek again. As she stood she ruffled his hair.

In considering an appropriate response – now was the perfect time for a witty but heartfelt *adieu* – he found that he'd missed the chance to say anything. In a flash she was running back towards Waterloo Bridge.

It was not the goodbye he had hoped for. But then he raised his fingers to his mouth. Tentatively, he ran his tongue along his lower lip. He tasted the faint spice of poppy petals. They'd entered glorious new territory. There was no turning back. He grinned. *Finally.*

## SUMMER 1893

'Here he comes.' Max elbowed Rusty in the ribs. From his position behind a corkscrew column at the back of Wilton's stalls, he watched Papa stride slowly across the stage to the piano, applause echoing up to the music hall's ceiling. They were in the perfect position; it wasn't a question of hiding – they'd paid to enter – it was simply a case of being close to the exit. He didn't want to be there a minute longer than he had to.

Rusty wobbled next to him. Max knew the source; it was the little tap dance he did whenever he was fit to burst with excitement. He hadn't seen it for a while. Rusty turned, his face angrily red and oily, the physical manifestation of the early manhood feverishly coursing through him. 'This'll be something,' he shouted.

Max recoiled an inch at the whiff of musty clothing and warm rum. Sixteen, and he already smelt like a regular deckhand on a Cape-bound clipper. On stage, Papa was performing the routine Max had seen a dozen times before. How could a look of feigned surprise still be so joyless? It was followed by his customary half turn to the crowd. A weak smile. A bow. Papa then stepped around the piano stool and, with a flick of his tails, sat. Next came the shoulder rotations. Two in each direction, as predictable as the sun rising. And then, as the audience hushed expectantly, Papa reached into his tailcoat's inside right breast pocket. Max smiled as he watched him pull out a glasses case and cleave it open. It was his final, clunky act of building tension; an entirely selfish attempt to ramp up people's desire for him in the knowledge that, for these few measly seconds, he was the one thing they wanted. Reaching into the case, Papa removed his tortoise-rimmed concert glasses. Max nudged Rusty again and raised his clenched fist to chin height. They both leaned in and watched as, illuminated by the stalls' capering gas lamps, Max unfurled his fingers. There, gently undulating in his palm, no bigger than mice droppings, were two finely hewn screws. His eyes met Rusty's and their heads almost clashed in spasms of anticipatory elation.

There was a click from the stage like a baton on a rostrum. Max looked up to see one of the arms from Papa's glasses rocking on the ivory keys in front of him. He bit his lip and felt his legs quiver as though they were doing the laughing for him. Frowning, Papa quickly palmed his face to steady the frame now balanced precariously on his nose. But in saving the main body of his glasses, the second arm fell onto the keys. Another click. With cruel speed, whispers filled the hall's silence, gentle oohs and aahs at the public misfortune befalling the man on stage. Papa looked a picture of confusion sitting at the keyboard, brow furrowed, his little finger pointing skywards like a tea-drinker as he held the glasses to his face. Enjoy this you sod, Max thought. All would appear fine in a minute, no doubt. Papa would leave the stage, find his spare pair and continue the recital as usual. But the satisfaction in seeing control temporarily wrested from the man was immense. And Max knew that the sense of public humiliation would last far longer than the incident itself. They'd only witnessed the sting pierce the skin; the burning throb and swollen pride would take days to subside. Although what the man was feeling represented a thousandth of the humiliation that Max had carried with him since the piano incident, it was enough for today. Max dropped the screws on the floor. 'Skedaddle?'

'Skedaddle.'

Turning, feeling as tall as one of Wilton's twisted columns, Max strode towards the door to the foyer. Next to him, Rusty swaggered with a gibbon's gait. This, thought Max, is what friendship feels like. He smirked. Strength of an army, us two. On days like today, strength of a bloody army. He was too busy feeling imperious to seriously attempt to swerve the stout man in an immaculately tailored frock coat standing in his path in the foyer. Instead, he reached out his arms and clasped the fellow's shoulders on approach, attempting to palm past him. On contact, the man flinched and spun, his face as tight as a fist. Max recognised him immediately. Barnabas Franklin, Papa's champion and tonight's promoter.

'Better get in there, Mr F,' Max said, strutting on.

'What, boy?'

Max tipped his head back, not bothering to fully look behind him. 'Spot of bother.' He walked to the large double doors leading to the Whitechapel dusk outside. It was only Rusty's guffaw that made him turn. Two of Franklin's associates were standing with their mouths agape, like centurions watching Rome burn. There was a sudden stillness to the room as though some taboo had been violated, some uncrossable line crossed. As far as Max was concerned, he'd simply touched a theatre owner's clothing. The man was in his way so he moved him. Sometimes life really was that simple. 'C'mon, Rus,' he said.

Outside, he watched Rusty pull an orange out of his pocket and rip the skin off. Still walking, Rusty tore the fruit in two and handed half to Max. A gentle mulching sound accompanied the thump of their boots on clay. 'That,' Rusty said, juice trickling down his chin, 'is the sweetest fucking orange I've ever tasted.'

Max nodded. Tonight felt like one of those nights when any fruit would taste honeyed and plump, when every instinct would be correct, every action smart. He was glad Rusty was well today. So many evenings over the two years since Tobias and Isabella died had ended in tantrums or tears, including those of Mama. With Rusty now living in Highbury – through no choice of his own – Mama and Papa effectively had a new son, and Max a brother. They had become even closer. But the boy was lost and inconsolable after the awful events of that August night. Eye sockets like bruises spoke of permanent pain. So Max had taken it upon himself to protect him at all times. He'd also learned how to deal with him; when to indulge him, when to ignore him, and – occasionally – when to use his outbursts as a convenient yardstick to appear the better boy. Sometimes, Rusty became a useful decoy; while he was being difficult at home, Max would sneak out and find entertainment. More often than not, he'd return home and take a whimpering Rusty away with him again. Drinking helped. He'd watch Rusty get mortal and wait for the old Rusty – the merely tricky version – to crawl out of the hangover days later. They never spoke of that night at Chaveley. They just co-existed as an imperfect, damaged unit. Through all this Max had grown to accept the lad, just as a person would grow to accept an obvious and large birthmark; he was permanent, unchanging, a part of him. He could certainly never imagine life without him. More than that. In a funny way he'd grown to love him.

'Let's get some proper grub,' Max said.

Over chestnut-stuffed onions and a slice of game pie at The Broken Chair, a Whitechapel skittle dive, Max again felt his heart swell in his ribcage. He winked at the lad over the table. Strength of an army.

'How d'you think your father is?' Rusty wiped his mouth with his sleeve.

Max shrugged. 'Armless.'

The plate leapt on the table as Rusty's fist crashed down. He wheezed like a boiling kettle. Even once he'd stopped he wore the broadest smile Max had seen in months. 'I'll tell you what aren't harmless, though,' Rusty said. 'These onions. Taste of wood. They got no whitebait here?'

'Hush.' Max eyed the flagons sitting between them. 'Drink if you don't want to eat.'

'I will.' He raised the tankard and made an unclassifiable noise, like a barnyard fowl cooing under a bucket, as he emptied it. Max shook his head; as the older boy, it was mildly embarrassing that he'd long since given up trying to compete.

'Max?' Another sleeve of his lips.

'Yes.'

'You'll always look after me, won't you?'

Max snorted. 'Don't be soft.'

'Alright. Sorry.' Rusty stared down at the table, his cheeks gently flexing. After a moment he snapped his head up. 'Tell you what, get two more ales, eh? I've gotta...' He nodded to his crotch and motioned outside.

'Very well,' Max said as he watched Rusty bolt up from the table and cross the floor. He ambled to the bar, taking the empty flagons with him. 'Two ales, please,' he said to the barman.

As the full pitchers slopped back onto the bar, Max caught the publican's eye. 'I don't suppose you've got any whitebait, have you?'

# PART THREE

## KEY CHANGE

### August 1899

# 10

Irregular crackles from the fire pierced the drawing room's silence. Shadows cast by its flames danced up the rich green walls, providing the room's only significant movement. It irritated Max that the presence of officialdom could so alter a mood. As he watched Harold Medlock, short and solemn, lay ribbon-bound bundles on Papa's old bureau, he tried to calculate the hours that he, Rusty and Mama had spent in that room over the years. It stretched to days, and during that time their dynamics had rarely shifted: Mama was always at the centre of things, gently in charge; Rusty was generally tetchy, keen to convey that he didn't belong there; and Max was the perennially cheerful buffer, a lubricant between two cogs. And yet the solicitor's humourless manner re-ordered things.

Today as the three sat in a row on the sofa Mama was twitchy, Rusty's presence had swelled, and Max simply wanted to be elsewhere. This ceremony was pointless observance. The sole bit of new information that Medlock would impart was the impact of death duties on his estate. The rest was mere formality. Max picked at the sofa's arm and watched a spark leap from the grate.

He went over what he already knew. Mama would receive the bulk of Papa's estate bar a few chattels and perhaps a small amount of cash. Given his tangled relationship with Papa, the best he could hope for was enough money to buy a new recording horn or fund the food requirements for a future expedition. There would also, no doubt, be confirmation of Chaveley's passage down the generations. Again, this was known; the house would be held in trust by Mama until her death when it would pass to Rusty. The strange arrangement was struck to halt some beef between Papa and Tobias. The likely confirmation of this quirk of family politics probably explained Rusty's puffed-up state. Max supposed it made the whole charade worthwhile; he deserved to be happy.

Medlock coughed bumptiously and walked to the centre of the room, clasping a parchment bundle in his palms as a vicar would a bible. With undue earnestness he unwound its red ribbon. 'The last will and testament of Christopher Joseph Cadenza.'

Max settled back into the sofa as Medlock read, half listening and half willing it to be over. Everything was as he expected. Papa's fortune totalled two thousand three hundred pounds. Mama would get all of it bar fifty pounds for Max and thirty to Rusty. Max smiled. Four months' working capital, he reckoned. Papa would have earned that from three concerts. He folded his arms. That man; objectionable in life, stingy in death. Medlock moved on to chattels. As the flames quivered, the solicitor's silhouette leapt across the walls like a fairytale sorcerer. Max's mind drifted to his evening with Delilah. Perhaps when this was over he'd pay her a visit. He warmed at the thought. That's what he'd do. Medlock's outstretched arm caught his attention. Papa's grand piano in the drawing room's corner was to be donated to the Highbury Music Society. Best place for it, Max thought. The instrument dominated the room like a black tomb. To Rusty, Medlock continued, is bequeathed the collection of pewter tankards. Max exchanged a raised eyebrow with his cousin. This said it all. Tin cups for the surrogate son.

'And to my son Maximilian,' Medlock read, 'I leave my engraved pocket watch and concert suits. I also refer him to the separate Deed of Variation.' With that, he lowered the parchment and folded it.

Concerts suits. Max glanced at Rusty again. Tankards and togs for years of enduring the man. But Rusty was glaring at the floor. His face was etched with a frown, as though something he was expecting to happen had not occurred. Pink blotches crept across his cheeks, like droplets of blood diffusing through water.

Medlock received a nod from Mama and returned to the desk. He replaced the parchment and picked up a second bundle. The solicitor coughed away a discernible frog and Mama sat straight. Something strange was happening. 'Which brings me to the other matter that the deceased stipulated I discuss at this gathering. The Deed of Variation,' Medlock said. 'It relates to...'

Mama raised a hand. 'Actually Mr Medlock, I apologise. Perhaps you'd allow me to do this part.'

He looked surprised and stepped towards her. 'But Mrs Cadenza, it is a legal requirement that your late husband's wishes be relayed in their entirety.'

'I am aware of that. And I more than capable of doing it myself.'

'Very well.' He handed her the parchment and returned to Papa's desk.

'No, Mr Medlock.' Mama gestured at the door behind her. 'Please. Allow us some time alone. Return in half an hour.'

She glared at him. Reluctantly, he nodded. 'Half an hour,' he repeated as he passed her.

Whatever secret communication was passing between them, it didn't auger well. The flames wobbled as the door clicked shut. Max watched Rusty's cheeks ripple over his milling jaw.

'I need to tell you something, boys. It affects you both.' Mama stared straight ahead. 'This was set in stone years ago but Papa instructed me to wait until after he'd gone to tell you. It is about Chaveley.'

Rusty's head snapped up.

'As you know,' Mama continued, 'the house was to pass to Rusty when Papa and I are no longer around.'

Max nodded but, in a flash, Rusty rocked forwards.

'What do you mean *was*?'

He hadn't noticed the tense.

'Things have changed.' Mama nodded. 'Chaveley is yours, Max.'

He laughed and pointed at Rusty. This was a tease. 'No it's not.'

'Legally it is yours.' She lifted the second parchment bundle from her lap. 'It's all here.'

'What's that?' Rusty pointed at the bundle.

A frown clamped Max's brow. He rose from the sofa and took the bundle from Mama. Her eye briefly met his as she let go. She was serious. His hand shook as he held the parchment.

'I'm sorry Rusty,' she said, soft but resolute. 'Your father's wishes were altered. As Chaveley's trustee, Papa felt it would be better for all concerned if the house was owned by Max from the day he died.'

'What's that?' Rusty stood, still pointing at the paper in Max's hand.

'It's the Deed of Variation that changed your father's will.' Mama looked down.

'I don't understand.' Rusty looked from one relative to the other, a child confronted with a situation too big to comprehend. 'Max?'

Max put out a calming hand. 'Mama, this makes no sense. Chaveley goes to Rusty when you and Papa pass on.'

'No longer.'

'But you can't just change someone's will. He couldn't just do that.'

'The Deed of Variation is entirely legal. The house was not entailed. Papa could do with it what he wished.' She spoke as though she'd rehearsed the words. They sounded official, as if from Medlock's mouth. He wondered for how long she'd waited to say them.

Suddenly the room felt stiflingly hot. With his hands clasped to his head, Rusty walked in a tight circle in front of the fire, mumbling as he turned.

Max sat. 'Why?' he whispered.

'He was consumed by guilt after your accident. You never realised that. You wouldn't let yourself see it. But he was.' She took a deep breath. 'Gifting you Chaveley was his way of making amends. It was something he could do.'

Max looked at his hand. A house for the tip of a finger. 'When?'

'He altered Tobias's will shortly after he and Isabella died.'

'Gifting?' Rusty spat. 'It wasn't his to gift.'

Mama looked at Rusty with genuine sorrow. 'Dear Rusty. It is done.'

As he continued his bewildered pirouette Rusty started tugging at his hair. His eyes were glazed and fragile, like freshly cast marbles. Tugs became knocks as he bashed his head with this knuckles as if hammering on a door.

'But I never wanted Chaveley. I hate that place.' Max shook

his head.

As Mama opened her mouth to speak, Rusty cried out. A guttural scream, it was unlike anything Max had heard. There were no words, just a growl of pure rage. His hands had moved from the top of his head to the back of his neck, so his entire face was framed by bent arms. As the yell died he sprang on his heels and stormed to the door.

'Rusty.' Max leapt from his seat. 'We'll sort this out.'

The force of the slammed door caused Mama to flinch.

Max glared at her. 'What the hell have you done?' He rarely shouted.

She blinked heavily. 'He was never going to take it kindly.'

'Of course he wasn't. What was Papa thinking?'

'You know what your father was like. When he wanted to do something...' Her whisper faded.

'And you knew about this?'

'Of course. As a trustee I approved it.'

'And what about Rusty? What am I meant to do about that?'

She said nothing.

He picked up the Deed resting on the sofa's arm next to him. As he unfolded it, the whiff of conspiracy filled his nostrils. He wondered how much his father had paid for the will to be altered. Was it even legal? The calligraphy was dense and neat. He ran his eyes down the parchment, aghast that nothing more than formal language and a wax seal could so alter the presumed order of things.

*Deed of Variation, 20th May 1893*
*A Deed to amend the last will and testament of Tobias James Cadenza. Notice is hereby given that all beneficiaries and others having claims against the estate of Tobias James Cadenza formerly of Putney in the city of London, who died*

*on 18th August 1891, shall have regard to the following amendments...*

The document had been written two years after Tobias and Isabella died. Mama had sat on this secret for six years. He read aloud: 'The asset of Chaveley House in the county of Devonshire, held in trust by Christopher and Anna Cadenza for the duration of their lifetime and subsequently bequeathed hitherto to said Ronald Cadenza, son of the deceased, shall following this amendment pass to said Maximilian Cadenza, nephew of the deceased, on the death of Christopher Cadenza.' His eyes scanned downwards. 'This amendment has been made on grounds of need of said Maximilian Cadenza. This Deed over-rides any previous intent of the testator, said Tobias James Cadenza...'

Papa's signature was scrawled all over the page beneath the text, including next to where Rusty's name was printed as a beneficiary. 'In absentia,' Papa had written.

Max lowered the parchment. 'Papa forged Rusty's approval?'

'No!' Mama snapped. 'As Rusty's legal guardian he had a right to make decisions with the family's best interests at heart. As I said, the house...'

'Was not entailed.'

'Indeed. There was no legal requirement for it to pass to Rusty.'

Max imagined Papa handing a bundle of cash to Medlock, urging him to oversee the alteration. He thought back to those Chaveley summers; the endless rehearsals, the long days, the games, the fights, the pain. He felt queasy as the full picture emerged.

'He did it because he loved you, Max. He did it *for you.*' Mama paused. 'You were boys. He was beside himself.'

They stood in silence but he knew Mama wanted to add more. Twice she raised her head to speak before lowering it again. He knew precisely what she wanted to say. She wanted to say that Rusty never deserved Chaveley anyway, that he'd always been trouble and that he'd never appreciated the house. She wanted to say that she'd brought him up as her own after Tobias and Isabella died – changing his soiled sheets in those dark months afterwards despite his fifteen years, putting up with his outbursts – and that he'd never shown appreciation. And she wanted to say that he'd given her headaches, not love.

Max threw the Deed onto the sofa. In assuaging his own guilt Papa had caused another almighty stink. He had to go and find Rusty to try to repair the damage.

As he walked towards the door, Mama caught his arm. 'What's done is done, Max.'

He gently lifted her hand from his forearm and said nothing. The fire in the hearth had started to die down. But as Max opened the door, it angrily popped, spraying a shower of fiery sparks across the drawing room's neat carpet.

୧⁄ᢀᢁ᷁᷀ᢂᢁᢀᢁ

As they caught the lantern light, T-Bone McGregor's gleaming thighs shone through the smoke, as thick as carcases on a butcher's hook. Below them the ripples of the boxer's torso glowed like russet parcels, while on the ground his head bulged under the weight of his colossal frame. The crowd around him thrust notes at each other, betting on the duration of the headstand. The cacophony subsided then swelled as he slowly straightened his legs and, with the dexterity of a child, performed a perfect split, shaping his body into its own T. Max wiped the sheen from his forehead; sweat and condensation had turned the top floor of The Black Lion into a furnace. He tugged his moistened hair behind his ears and stepped in from the doorway, glancing around the pandemonium for Rusty. He had to find him. Like T-Bone, their world was upside down. But unlike the boxer, it could not be made right by simply rolling forward.

Max pushed his way in, the floor's cloying sawdust tugging on his soles. The stench of ale, piss and blood thickened with every step. The light was low but the lanterns and candles allowed the room's dimensions to become apparent. T-Bone's stunt occupied one half of the room. On the other, four posts were linked by rope: the fighting ring. All around Max, men in shirtsleeves bayed and roiled as though cut loose from civilisation, their flat noses and flailing elbows soon becoming indistinguishable from one another. Max jostled to a bar in the corner. If there were bottles, Rusty would be near them.

Next to the bar an elderly Irish man poured hot wax onto a fighter's raw knuckles as another minder kneaded his back. Max averted his eyes when he saw the old man slip a sharpened coin into the drying liquid. Being weak in this room made you poor. Being judgemental made you dead.

On a solitary stool on the other side of the bar, Max spotted him. Rusty rested a bottle on one knee and a glass on the other. His head was slumped forward so it hung low beneath his shoulder blade as though he was sleeping. But as Max approached he could see that Rusty's eyes were wide open; he was thinking in that position.

Pulling up a stool, Max sat next to him and leaned in so his words could be heard over the din. But before he could speak Rusty raised his head and glared at him.

'Fuck off, Max.' His words were jabbing and whisky-addled.

'Rusty.' Max placed his hand on his cousin's arm but it was

immediately knocked off. He leaned in further. 'This was a shock for me too.'

Rusty sneered and filled his glass. With the bottle resting back on his knee, he thrust his head back and drank.

'I never wanted Chaveley. We can work something out.'

Rusty glared at him as though his words were pure filth.

The room erupted in a cheer. Max looked around, aghast. The conversation would have been difficult enough in a quiet drawing room. But here it was almost impossible. 'Can we go somewhere else?'

With another shake of the head, Rusty topped up his glass again.

Feeling his emotion rise, Max decided to try again. 'I didn't ask for this.' His voice cracked as he shouted.

Another commotion erupted behind Max. Before he could register what was happening, Rusty stood from his stool and squeezed past him, joining the ringside throng.

The man who Max had seen having his knuckles coated in wax walked to the centre of the ring, his trousers buckled high. A second man, nimbler and slighter, danced towards him until they squared up. The noise rose to deafening as those watching barked encouragement and exchanged money. T-Bone was now at the crowd's epicentre, conducting proceedings; he ripped notes from hands and stuffed them into others with alarming speed. Rusty was close by, wide-eyed and manic; Max could not tell who he was backing but he screamed towards the ring, the veins in his neck straining as though he himself was engaged in the fight. Raising a white handkerchief, a referee in a mucky bowler stood between the men in the ring. The stiller he stood, the louder the shouting became. The referee stepped back and theatrically dropped his handkerchief. He had not had time to leave the ring before the smaller boxer thumped his opponent in the belly, forcing him to bend double. Rusty thrust his head back and mewled, utterly consumed in the moment. Again, Max could not tell whether he was yelling in joy or frustration. It hardly mattered. Such emotions changed within seconds in the room. A man who was down one minute was up the next; elation and despair balanced out in the tavern's squalid swirl.

Cursing Papa for creating the mess, Max watched the bigger boxer straighten and, with a twisted smile, smash his fist into his opponent's jaw. Max heard a crunch and saw shards of tooth fly across the ring in a sputum of bloody mucus. A fragment landed in the sawdust close to his stool, within seconds becoming another part of the room's foul carpet. The big boxer yanked his opponent up by the hair and hit him again with his other fist. An agonised scream overrode the crowd's noise as the nimble man fell to the floor, blood gushing from his gaping forehead. That concealed coin had been sharp.

The fight was over, as brutal as it was short. As the crowd sorted out their winnings like rabid stock-jobbers on a trading floor, Max tried to pick Rusty out. He caught flashes of his face; the smile etched across it suggested that he had bet big and bet well. A minute later, he was heading back at the stools, stuffing two folded white sheets into his breast pocket.

Max rose as he approached. 'Rust...'

'Forget it. Not interested. Do what you like.' Rusty's voice was trancelike. He picked the bottle from the floor and drank deeply. Wiping his lips, he threw the empty bottle against the wall and looked directly at Max for the first time since he arrived. 'Do what you like,' he repeated as he walked away. 'You always do.'

Max watched him weave his way to the door, sidestepping and stumbling as he went. One punter ruffled Rusty's hair and shouted something in his ear. He raised a hand in acknowledgement and carried on walking.

The monstrous room was getting hotter. Max's mouth was as dry as his shirt was moist. It clung to his body like the helplessness he'd felt since Mama read the Deed of Variation aloud. He wanted to rip it off but could not. Although he knew that in Rusty's eyes he was the villain in all this, he felt like the victim. He'd been thrust into a predicament by someone else's actions. He looked around the room. Unsure of what to do, he stood and walked to the bar, signalling for a cup of rum. As he relished its dark sweetness, he knew what he needed. It had helped him out of countless spots over the years. It would help him untangle the knot in his head. He thumped the cup on the bar and turned to the door. The Strangers' Home was calling.

⚜⚜⚜⚜⚜

Anonymity was like virtue in Covent Garden; it barely existed. But as Max walked the crooked lanes north to St Giles, he knew it was just minutes away. His head pounded with every step as though he'd just left that sordid boxing ring himself. He supposed he had been assaulted. By events. By family. By misplaced good intentions. He felt rotten for Rusty but seeking him out again would be a useless endeavour at this time of night. Although he could see why his cousin's anger was directed at him, Rusty must have known it wasn't his fault. He needed time to think. A few hours away from the world he knew – and the one that knew him – would help him make sense of things. He turned right at the bell foundry on Bucknall Street and squeezed past a pair of fresh-faced young women at the entrance of an alleyway. Maids newly out of service, he reckoned. Now that the season was over they had to find means to survive away from Mayfair. He ignored their purrs but silently wished them luck. Like their dresses, their smiles were doomed to fade.

Halfway down the alley he saw a smudge of light under a wooden door flanked by carved columns. A soft clattering rumbled within. He pushed open the door and was immediately enlivened by a flickering, musky energy. As he entered he tossed a coin to Bombay Jenny, sitting across an armchair next to a bucket of burning sandalwood. Originally from Billericay, she had worked at the Strangers' Home for Asiatics and South Sea Islanders for as long as he'd known the place. Her precise role was unclear, and he'd never asked. But she was always there. With a wink she nodded him through to the library.

Max entered the darkened room and winced at the brutal rhythm coming from a low stage in its centre. He tried to walk in but immediately had to stop; the library floor was crammed with men, fanned cross-legged around the stage. They clapped and hollered as the noise swelled, foot soldiers to the music's power. In lantern-light dulled by cigarette smoke, Max could just about make out faces. The array of nationalities always astonished him; Indians, Arabs, Burmese, Samoans, Chinese. Some wore stevedores' overalls, others *shalwars*; some suits, others rags. Dotted among them were a few Londoners; the drunk ones were there by default, the curious by design. Max tiptoed through the sea of men like a child on creaking floorboards. He'd find space around the side. Occasionally a hint of cumin or turmeric danced in the air before being overpowered by tobacco and the earthy tang of human bodies. The Strangers' Home was a crucible of the East; feared by most locals but loved by him. More fool them. Scared of native tongues, skin colour and otherness, Londoners took flight from this crowd. But as far as Max was concerned it was the locals who were the heathens. Most of the Home's temporary residents had left employment on ships from the Orient full of hope. They were robbed of that and all else within days of disembarking on the Thames' shores.

The real barbarians were back in that pub, beating the life out of each other for money. On top of everything else, this haven offered something transcendent that the taverns and casinos simply could not: music from Asia.

He found a square of free space on the floor a few feet from the stage. Sitting with his legs crossed, ignored by all, he suddenly felt blissfully invisible. This was the escape he craved; this was where he could think. He glanced up at the two portraits that dominated the wall. Queen Victoria gazed down. Next to her, the benevolent Maharaja who'd funded the Home stood proudly in native court dress, a cross around his neck. Beneath the paintings was a shelf laid with bibles, their covers embossed with gold-leaf Bengali, Mandarin and Urdu. Here was the benefactor's motive; Christianity for shelter. Some hope, Max thought; the bibles had never moved in the dozen times he'd visited.

At least ten musicians were crammed onto the stage, each playing loosely around the others. He recognised some of the instruments – two musicians plucked *esraj* violins while one sat with legs coiled around a vast cauldron drum. A number were new to him. On the far side of the stage a Polynesian held a nose flute to his face. Ascending in crooked harmony with the *esrajs*, its whistle was as haunting as Max had imagined. Two Chinamen, clinging for space behind the cauldron drummer, snapped bowl-shaped finger cymbals. He'd only read about them. Underlying it all was a smooth drone from a bagpipe-style instrument with a gourd-shaped neck. The music rumbled, unplanned, with no beginning or end. Lowering his shoulders, Max tried to tune his ears to the noise, to locate the heart of the rhythm. It was deep within the cacophony somewhere. It always was. This was a symphony for outsiders; democratic and as rich and varied as the humanity in that room. Somewhere in its chaos he'd find peace, like the calm centre of a hurricane.

As the music played he closed his eyes and tried to deconstruct the day's events. Could he have foreseen being gifted Chaveley? Absolutely not. But he knew what his starting point in sorting the situation out would be. He knew it instinctively as soon as Mama had spoken. He would not keep the house. It was a faraway prison; a repository of unwanted memories. In owning it, he'd forever be like the dusk slaughterhouse man, dragging a cart of unwanted off-cuts behind him. Besides, it wasn't his to own.

A high trill from the bagpipe led the symphony in a new direction. As far as Max was concerned the sensible option was also the simplest; he'd give the house back to Rusty as soon as possible. The poor sod was devastated. Engaging a solicitor and legally transferring it would be easy. It would be logical. Right. Fair.

And yet. *And yet.*

Max squeezed his eyes tightly and cast his mind to the other option that had buzzed into his mind as he'd walked up there. Aware of how outlandish it was, he'd initially swatted the rogue thought away. But it had not left him. He shifted on the floor, seeking greater comfort. Now he was alone, emperor of his own mind, he decided to grant this option a full audience. Indulge it. Give it the chance to lay itself bare and snuff itself out. It was only right. The second course of action was risky yet possibly, in the long-term, more rewarding for Rusty and himself. He concentrated. Did the situation with Chaveley present an opportunity to do something a little more ambitious? Sold on the open market, the house could net him and Rusty hundreds of pounds, possibly a thousand. Selling it was now in his gift. And selling it could provide enough funds to keep the company going for years. They could invest in new gear – it was only a matter of months until wax masters would replace zinc – and they could travel to Serbia and Russia to capture their jewels. Perhaps Japan, then India. They could blaze the trail they always envisaged, unencumbered. Was this not, in its own complicated way, even more logical than the first option? Throughout their lives, Max had always done everything with Rusty's best interests at heart. It was them against the world. Perhaps following this path would be Max's boldest commitment to that pledge? And selling the house would finally rid the family of a toxic asset forever. *Do what you like*, Rusty had said. There was something else. Giving the house to Rusty felt oddly – Max wasn't quite sure what – *regressive*. In following that path, the house would have transferred to all members of the family – from Tobias and Isabella to Papa and Mama to Max and then to Rusty – in less than a decade. Giving it to Rusty would merely perpetuate an endless game of pass the parcel. His mind numb, Max snapped his eyes open and tried to empty his head of thoughts.

A violent nudge from his neighbour's shoulder knocked him sideways. A wild cheer erupted all around him. The drummer had stood from his coiled position and was bending over this cauldron, beating an impossible rhythm using all parts of his hand; the base of his palm beat a meaty *dhaa* sound that shook the room, the nub of his thumb peppered the gaps with silvery *dhins*, while the tips of his fingers sprinkled tricksy flourishes over the cycle. Max watched the bibles vibrate across the shelf. Movement at last. Dancing to the new language. Like a barbed hook, the noise whipped Max into its path. The drummer sped up, maintaining the pattern as he went. Max smiled and shook his head in time; tentative at first, he grew more frantic as the momentum built. His curls bounced as he felt himself almost physically pulled upwards as the beat accelerated. This was the kind of spirit he yearned to capture. All the while the crowd's hollers grew in volume. The Chinamen joined in, their cup-cymbals frantically competing to be heard. Max wished time would stop to allow the sound to go on forever; he wished time would stop to prevent him from having to make a decision.

The drummer thrust his head back and wailed a throaty invocation, causing half the room to stand and cheer. As his shout sailed across the room, the drummer slowly straightened and slowed his rhythm by a fraction. Each cycle became less frenetic. Cooling it down in increments, he ensured he took the crowd with him. Max felt his heart slow as if he was being lowered from some holy platform. He filled his lungs and turned his mind to the house again, trying to look for answers in the gaps in the music. It felt daft. Sometimes wisdom lurked in rhythm. Knowledge prowled in melody. *Do what you like.* He wondered what Rusty was up to at that very moment. Glugging whisky in some saloon, no doubt, the only noise the oikish thrum of fists on the bar. *Do what you like.* He shook his head. Of course he wouldn't simply do what he liked. He'd do what was best for both of them. They were a team. He'd do what was right. Max thrust his head back as the drummer had a minute before. He let the slowing music envelop him. As the throb receded, something clicked deep inside. Everything suddenly became perfectly clear. He had the answer. He knew what his priority must be. Max looked around the room and thanked God for music.

# 11

Delilah hacked at the top of an iced bun with her fingernail, flecking the table with tiny sugar daggers. Auditions like this never got easier. Through the buttery's window she watched the queue of girls shuffling outside the Peckham Crown over the road, edging forwards like lambs to the slaughter. In minutes she'd be joining them.

'Are you going to eat that?' Molly said.

She glanced down and laughed. The bun looked like a cottage without a roof. Although famished, she couldn't eat. Not yet. 'Thanks for spending the morning with me. I appreciate it.'

Smiling, Molly poured more coffee.

'Are you sure you won't join me? There'll be plenty of roles going,' Delilah said.

'I think I need a few more months at the Paragon. But don't worry. I won't be far behind.' She pulled a face. Mr Wilson had a knack for inspiring the desire for career progression in his girls.

Nerves cast a curious spell. Delilah had never been the jittery type. It annoyed her that she allowed them to get the better of her in the few hours before an audition. The nerves were rarely about a specific role; there'd always be others. They stemmed from the fear of not performing as well as she could. Letting the director down with a lousy audition was acceptable; letting herself down with one was not. It was Delilah Green that she needed to impress. Wrapping her hands around her coffee mug, she relished the buttery's snugness. The street looked chilly.

But this was her strategy, and she was determined to see it through; she'd climb up rung by rung from the Paragon until she was back in the West End. Or in one of those new theatres away from Covent Garden with saloon bars and furnishings in three shades of gold and dressing rooms warmed by hot water pipes. The Peckham Crown was a necessary stepping stone.

'I'll wait for you after if you want,' Molly said.

'No, it's fine. You get on, darling. Plans.'

'Max?'

She shook her head. 'He's still away.' Business on the coast, he'd said. He was due back any day. 'Wilson's got me to do The Simple Pimple, hasn't he? Can't stand that show.' It required her to wear a large purple boil on her nose and cavort with George Roberts, an ageing singer whose stagecraft was almost as bad as his breath. At least in mentioning the show she felt her nerves briefly dissipate. It was another spur to leave the Paragon.

'Tell me. Does he mind?' Molly said.

'Who?'

'Max. Does he mind that you've asked to record?'

'Max? No. Why would he? He reckons it could be wonderful.' Just recalling his words relaxed her. She warmed at the thought of his kiss. He was good, strong. 'He's promised to think about it.'

'Has he said when?'

'Soon, I hope. Poor Max though. He's preoccupied with this slayer business. It's knocked him for six. There's some family issue as well. But it'll happen. I'm sure of it. I suppose there's no *immediate* rush.' She smiled, aware of her own qualification.

'Want me to ask Joe to ask him too?'

Delilah shook her head. No point in complicating things. '*Joe.*' She repeated with a mischievous grin. 'How is he?'

'Stop it.' Molly smirked and let a wall of black hair obscure her face. 'He's fine.'

'Mrs Molly Langley. Nice ring to it.'

Molly cocked her head to the side and they both giggled. 'Oh come on. Three meals we've had!'

Delilah had grown increasingly fond of Molly. Hours standing over the piano across from a clammy pervert bonded people. But it was more than that; she was sensible and kind. She was eager but not brash, in a way that Delilah sometimes faintly coveted. As she drained her coffee, Delilah thought about her question. Why should Max mind that she'd asked to record? She couldn't see how; it simply made sense. A few days ago when she'd imagined standing in front of his recording horn, she found herself inverting the situation. With a flip, she imagined that she was the one able to help, and that he was the one who'd asked for the favour. She pictured herself as a theatre-owner and Max as a singer. He'd asked for a role and she'd given him one. Of course she'd help. She'd clear the programme for the silly beggar. It's what people did in this game. Helped each other.

'Look, I'd still like Max if he punched tickets for a living.' Delilah looked out at the queue in the street. 'But he doesn't, does he? And if he can do anything to help me get ahead of this lot then that's a bonus.' She paused. 'I'm seeing this right, aren't I?'

Molly nodded. 'Of course.'

'Not being daft?'

'No.'

'Good. Thought so.' It was funny. Despite her early reservations, she couldn't remember wanting anything more. She flicked a shard of sugar from the front of her frock. Raising her chin, she pressed her lips together. 'Smudged?'

'All fine.'

'Fabulous.' She wrapped the decimated bun in a handkerchief and put it in her holdall, replacing it on the plate with two coins. Ensuring that her hair was neatly tied back, she threw a look of resolute determination at her companion. 'I'm off. Wish me luck.'

୧⁄ఠ౮౮⁄ఠ౮

Strange, Max thought as he pushed on the studio door. It would only partially open. He leaned against it but a piercing scrape forced him to stand back. Everything had been fine when he'd come down yesterday after his return from Devon, anxious but satisfied. He'd filed the papers upstairs and popped down on his way home; all had been spick and span. He pushed again. It was stuck, as if there was something blocking it from behind. With a shove of his shoulder it started to open. Ignoring the roar of metal against the wooden floor, he created just enough space to squeeze into the room.

It was dim – the only light came from the squat windows opening onto the pavement outside – but, looking down, he saw that a zinc master disc had become wedged under the door like a stop. Curious. Perhaps Langley or Rusty had been in this morning to catalogue recordings. But sloppiness was most out of character. Looking around in the gloom, everything else seemed in order: the recording rig loomed its usual eccentric self. The lingering trace of pipe smoke in the air added to the sense that all was well. He lit the gas sconces on either side of the door, dismissing the errant disc as a one-off. As the lamps fizzed to life, he recoiled. How cruel and misleading the half light had been. The studio was a scene of carnage; its floor was in total disarray. Wrenched into an S-shape, the padlock on the corner cupboard that housed all the masters had been ripped off. One of the doors was hanging loose, and the cupboard's contents were strewn across the room.

He stepped forwards. At his feet was an angular mess. Some zincs were dented, others were twisted like chrome butterflies. He picked up a disc. Running across its diameter was a jagged cross, scratched with a heavy point. He traced the X with his finger. It tore a crevasse across the disc's grooves, sabotaging their delicate trajectory like explosive charges on a thousand railroad tracks. It was ruined.

Bile stung his throat. All around him, dozens of zincs that once housed unique musical blueprints had been robbed of their function, meaning and life. This was no careless employee. The room had been sabotaged.

The unbearable screech of metal defiling metal filled his head. His woven spirals had been brutally neutered by a stronger force. A perpetrator flashed into his head. He tried to block him out. It was too foul a thought. Around Max, hours of music had been destroyed, incalculable legacies eliminated. Some of the masters had not yet been pressed onto shellac, meaning that their musical secrets had died in the very room where they were born. It was an act of vandalism meted out by a jackboot, hammer or blade on an unbelievable scale. Sucking a shaking knuckle, he strode through the mess. On the far wall one of the windows that opened into Tavistock Street flapped ajar.

It was when he thought of Balducci that something broke inside. The pair of recordings were among those yet to be turned into stamps. He'd held back from sending them to the factory to be pressed out of respect. Both masters had been stored in the cupboard, waiting. He ran to it and sank to his knees, yanking the hanging door from its remaining hinge. A buckled zinc clanged to the floor as he ferreted through its shelves. *Music of the Sands.* The master was ruined but at least they'd made a negative. He cleared out the rest of the cupboard's contents: blank discs that had been carefully dinked so as to render them useless, boxes of styluses, a bent spindle. Then he saw it; an oil cloth parcel on the bottom shelf. He pulled it out and unwrapped it. Closing his eyes, he thanked God. 'Balducci' was scrawled across a sticker at its centre. It was the *Rigoletto* arioso, *Pari Siamo*. Untouched. Intact. Wrapping it carefully, he cast his eyes round for the second Balducci but it was not in the cupboard. Arm over arm, he crabbed his way back across the studio, looking from mangled disc to mangled disc. Halfway to the door, his eye caught the Italian's name. Balducci's recording of *Era la Notte* had been stamped out of shape. The disc was a warped silver crater. The *Otello* aria had been brutally muted. Max creased as a sudden sickness, worse than the most intense hunger, tore at his stomach. That glorious music was no more. All that effort, all that money, the superlative singing. Taken. Crying out, he stood and kicked a crumpled plate across the room. The canopy overhead failed to absorb his primal howl; it echoed off the walls, the loudest noise the room had heard.

He walked to the fireplace. With an elbow on the mantelpiece, he thrummed his forehead. He pictured Franklin in his tent at the playback, affecting ignorance about everything. He imagined his taut face as he growled orders to his hooligans to trash the studio. A second, darker thought entered his head. As he shivered it away, his vision hazy with shock, he saw an object he instantly recognised on the mantelpiece's far end: one of Rusty's pipes. Must be a spare. He reached across to pick it up; he'd return it to him later. As Max wrapped his hand around the pipe, his arm instinctively recoiled. As he pulled his elbow into his body, the pipe dropped to the floor. Max froze, daring it not to be true.

The pipe's bowl was still warm.

⑥⑨⑨⑥⑨⑨

Dry and metallic. The sensation at the back of his throat became increasingly uncomfortable as the cab progressed from Covent Garden to the East End. Max hoped – prayed – that it would subside again once he'd confronted him. Rusty had done some stupid things in his time. But even he, even in his most frantic tantrum, wouldn't be so reckless as to do this. It wasn't just the studio, either. The office upstairs had been ransacked: the sitar had been pulled to the ground and stamped on; the contents of the desk drawers were strewn across the room; the chaise upended. As the cab turned into Rusty's street, Max wished he'd stayed to assess what had been taken. Instead, overwhelmed by the mess, he'd run downstairs and out onto the cobbles to hail the first hansom he saw.

The carriage pulled up outside Rusty's house. *Please don't let it have been him*, he muttered to himself. There had to be a different explanation. He climbed out and handed three coins to the driver. He swallowed, desperate to draw some moisture across his mouth, and knocked on the door. Go softly, he thought. Go softly until it's no longer a hunch. And then… And then what? He had no idea.

Mary, her face its usual picture of downcast disappointment, answered almost immediately. But rather than let him in, she stood defensively in the door frame.

'He doesn't want to talk to you.'

'Let me in, Mary.'

'He's resting.'

'Mary, please. I know what he did.'

She looked down from behind the door, defiant, and shook her head.

'In which case, tell Rusty to come outside now. I need to talk to him urgently.' He tried to catch her eye. 'I know what he's done.'

She said nothing.

He raised his voice a notch. 'I know what happened in the studio, Mary. If he does not avail himself to me immediately I'll...' He tailed off. Call the police? Storm into the house himself? He hadn't thought it through.

An internal door thumped. Behind Mary dull murmurings grew louder. Angry footsteps echoed within. Then, a shout.

'*Do what? You'll do what?*'

Max stumbled backwards as Mary was shunted aside and the front door was pulled open. Rusty advanced over the threshold at pace, his arm outstretched. He gripped Max around the neck without breaking stride.

Thumb and forefinger bore into the fleshy trench beneath his jawbone as Rusty applied upwards pressure. Had Max not been taken aback by the blizzard of fury, he would have fought his cousin off. But the strength from his arm was immense, and in his surprise Max found himself dancing backwards until he was pinned against the house's external wall.

'*You'll do what?*' Rusty raged.

Flecks of spit landed on Max's face. 'Please, Rusty.' His cousin's eyes were stained and blotchy, his face ruddy. 'The studio. Just tell me it wasn't you.'

Rusty leaned in. 'I've been nowhere near the studio. Ask Mary.'

Max forced Rusty's arm away and reached into his pocket. Perhaps he'd regret this. But he needed to know. He pulled out the pipe.

'You left this behind.' He held it up. Over the years, he'd come to learn Rusty's mannerisms. There was little that he could not deduce from a flicker of the eyelid or a tilt of the head. He watched as Rusty's nose twitched defensively.

'Means nothing.'

'It was warm.'

Rusty snatched the pipe from him and cradled it for a second. A hint of a smile peeked through the menace. 'It's not any more.'

In that instant, Max knew. It hadn't been Franklin. It had been Rusty.

As he stood there, one of life's great certainties disappeared. Rusty's friendship and loyalty had never been the straightforward sort. There were always blow-ups and jealousies, fisticuffs and feuds. But this went beyond playing and petty rivalry. This was the keystone crumbling. He fell back against the wall. 'Rusty.'

Their faces just inches apart, Rusty ground his teeth. 'Think I'm stupid? Some kind of clown?'

'Of course not.'

Rusty turned and strode back into the house, returning a moment later with a pile of formal papers. Max recognised them immediately.

'You bastard. I knew you were up to something.' He raised the papers to Max's face.

The letterhead was all too familiar. A. P. Clarke & Sons of Ilfracombe. Conveyancing solicitors. Max closed his eyes. He was going to tell Rusty this very afternoon. It was as he'd feared; the papers were from the drawers in his office, put there yesterday on his return from Devon. Of course Rusty had been there. It explained the carnage. Max bit his bottom lip and tried to summon the speech he'd carefully prepared. But the words, so precisely chosen on the journey home, evaporated like ethanol.

It was Chaveley. He'd sold it.

Rusty tightened his palm, screwing the paper into a messy flower, crushing the details of the £700 transaction. His face was contorted in a way that Max had never seen before; lips wide open, teeth clenched, as though his features were pulling in two directions. He breathed in shallow bursts through a puckered nose. 'It wasn't yours to sell.'

'I did it for us. Don't you see?'

'See what?'

'*Us*. This is freedom. Think of the music.' He'd bet big. He knew that. But that moment of epiphany in the Strangers Home had convinced him it was right. It would have been a dereliction of duty not to make that choice; not to put themselves in the best position to chase the music. Max knew that collecting the money from the sale was the easy half of the deal; telling Rusty would always be the challenging half. But it was the correct thing to do, he was sure of it. Straining, he stretched his mouth into a gambler's grin. Zeal tinged with hope. 'The music,' he repeated.

He watched as Rusty's eyes narrowed and he started to rock forwards on the balls of his feet, as if preparing to spring out of the moment. 'The house was *mine*.' His blotched face convulsed.

'Rusty. Think about it. We have money. *Money*. We can travel. Anywhere. We can buy gear. Capture jewels. It's us against the world.' There was something else. When he'd returned to London yesterday he'd bought the tickets to Russia. It was impulsive and perhaps reckless. But he had cash. And an immediate expedition would show their intent. Their ability. His pocket was lined and he'd gone ahead and done it. Swallowing, he watched Rusty seethe. 'You and me, Rusty. Against the world.'

Rusty rocked on his feet. 'Who?'

'What?'

'Who did you sell it to?'

'Local landowner. Cash. I thought you'd be happy. You hated the place as much as I did.'

Rusty's face contorted. Max had no time to react as an iron grip pinned him against the wall. He heard the front door click shut as Mary went back into the house.

Max heaved Rusty's arm back. 'Listen to me.' This wasn't how he'd imagined it. He'd convinced himself that he and Rusty would be out celebrating after he broke the news.

Rusty leaned in. 'My parents. Now Chaveley. Gone.' His anger was infused with something more reflective. Sadness. 'What are you trying to do to me?'

'Nothing. *Nothing*. I'm trying to help.'

'I've always just been a chore to you. An irritant.'

'No!' Hard work but never an irritant. Max's eyes glazed. He loved the boy. 'I know you're upset. But once you've thought about it, it will make perfect sense. I didn't do it lightly, Rus. This all but guarantees our future.' As he spoke he felt the downwards pressure of a heavy boot on his ankle. He pulled his foot free and slid down the wall into a sitting position. He could no longer look at Rusty's face. Should he have expected this reaction? Every decision he'd ever taken had been made with their best interests in mind. They were a screw and a nut; together they held. 'I've... I've booked us tickets. Russia.' A flinch. Confusion on anger. Max watched Rusty turn and walk to the front door, his head shaking. 'Rusty,' he whispered.

Silence. Then a shadow returned. Rusty hovered once more. A scraping sound filled the air. He could only cower as Rusty drew in air through his nose and collected the soggy debris from the back of his throat.

'N… *No.*'

He froze as a ball of fluid flew into his line of vision. Pinching his eyes shut, he felt the saliva hit his brow before dropping onto his cheek. He didn't see Rusty walk back into the house. But he heard the door slam. Mucus coated his eyelid like a warm oyster. He felt for a handkerchief and wiped his face before dropping the cloth on the pavement. Unsteadily, he stood and felt his way along the brickwork of the terraced houses. He passed two, three houses as he moved down the street before he broke into a run.

Stooped, he folded his arms across his chest as he went. He didn't look back and he didn't stop running. The man who had woken up that morning as Maximilian Cadenza felt like a stranger, flayed and dirty, stripped of himself. He sped up. He needed to get out of the East End as quickly as possible.

# 12

Rain lashed Piccadilly. Langley stood under the awnings of a gentleman's outfitters and squinted at the wet list in his hand. He could still just make out the words despite the spidering ink.

All around, the autumn shower forced people to seek shelter where they could. Those caught umbrella-free huddled together in doorways, uncomfortable at the enforced proximity. For all London's allure it discouraged easy friendships, Langley thought. More. There was something about the city that actively encouraged mistrust. Thieves and gentlemen, snakes and saints, hobos and heroes. It was impossible to tell who was who on these teeming streets. Apart from Molly. She was solid. He checked his watch. He needed to move; there was much to do. Stuffing the list in his pocket, he hunched his shoulders and ran the three hundred yards to Fortnum & Mason. He arrived at the shop's grand entrance, cursing and sodden. Even this simplest of tasks – a shopping trip – was proving troublesome.

The place was busy with rain refugees and housekeepers, its air infused with tea, cinnamon and damp wool. All around him, tables were stacked with delicacies: figs, biltongs, perfumes and pies were piled high under hanging lamps. He pushed his way to the back of the ground floor, his tweed jacket clinging to his back. Mackintosh, he thought, mackintosh.

The job was clear. As quartermaster for the Russian expedition he needed to procure supplies and arrange their delivery across the route. He was to order enough provisions for three men for a six-week tramp, with contingency food for another four weeks if circumstances required. Local porters would be used to transport the supplies; vegetables, spices and rice could be bought out there.

It was a miracle they'd got this far. Some almighty row had put the trip in jeopardy. Max wouldn't give details but he'd called things off, ashen-faced, the following day. Langley had never seen him so cowed; a high collar inadequately covered a bruise on his neck. But things changed again that morning. Whispered confirmation from Max. The expedition was going ahead again with a stop-off in Serbia along the way. He looked no less shaken. But they were Russia-bound. Quite what the atmosphere would be like, Langley didn't know. Some pact had been forged. The trip felt like a clay pot hastily repaired with glue, just about holding together but liable to collapse at any point.

Given this frailty, Langley had felt embarrassed about enquiring what kind of food to order before he'd left the studio. He'd scribbled down Max's every word: meats, pates, fruits, tinned dairy products and fancy goods. It was a new world. An exciting one. He was to order one sealed 'chop box' per man per week, Max had said. Chop boxes were each man's own portable larder; tightly sealed until opened, they allowed a person an element of freedom to choose what and when he eats on a trip. By knowing that he has a week to consume the contents of the box, a traveller can 'self-ration', as Max put it, and not be forced to eat the same as the other members of the party. Apparently Rusty called them 'food coffins' as there was always something dying at the bottom.

At the back of the shop Langley took a staircase to the basement, squinting as harsh gas mantles replaced the shopfloor's warm glow. The temperature dropped as he descended. At the back of the low-ceilinged room, swaying from two chains, was a sign that read 'Expeditions'.

He approached a clerk at a table beneath the sign. 'Good afternoon.'

'Sir,' the clerk said.

'My name's Joe Langley. I've a large order to place for a trip departing Southampton for Serbia next week.'

The assistant nodded as he ran his forefinger down the inside spine of an order book. He raised his pen as if to start writing and glanced up over his glasses. 'Your party?'

'The London Gramophone Corporation.'

The clerk looked up. 'I see.'

Langley sat opposite him and read from the soggy list in his hand. One job, he thought. Don't mess it up. 'So, per chop... chop box... we require one jar of Elvas plums, one fruit cake, one jar of chicken breasts in jelly.'

The clerk jotted in a neat column.

'Half a stilton, one pâté de foie gras, one game pie... One sugar-cured Yank... Sorry, this list is wet. Sugar-cured York ham, dressed for the table, one glass of rolled ox tongues, half a...'

The clerk raised the pen patiently.

'...cheddar loaf, half a cheddar loaf. One box of oatmeal biscuits. Crystallised oranges, soft...'

The words on the list had almost entirely merged together. He laughed nervously. He hadn't even packed and he was faltering.

'Um, bon-bon…violent fonpants.'

The clerk coughed. 'Violet fondants, sir? Bon-bon violet fondants?'

'Those. One bottle li…'

It was useless. At its driest the list looked like the Persian script he had seen in the reference books lying around Max's office.

'One bottle of brandy and one bottle of champagne, sir? That is Mr Cadenza's usual order when he travels.'

'Very good,' Langley said as he forced the mulchy list into his pocket.

'And will you take the two weeks' supply of boxes with you, as is custom, with the rest shipped ahead to our agents in Belgrade?'

'We will. Yes.'

'And where are you going after Belgrade?'

'To Russia. We'll be recording in a place called Nizhny Novgorod. On the steppe.' He spelt it out, twice, making sure that the clerk wrote it down correctly.

'Very good, Mr Langley.' The clerk stood and firmly shook his hand. 'I will ensure that everything is arranged as you'd like.'

The food ordered, Langley headed upstairs to the clothing department. Owning the correct equipment was paramount; if the food was wrong then at least he'd look the part. He knew that his entire month's wages would disappear at a stroke, but he would rather be hungry in Clapham than embarrassed in the field. He was measured for boots, a pith helmet and a two-piece khaki drill suit. He also picked up a mackintosh and a Fortmason woollen bush jumper. Both mandatory, he felt. Determined not to be caught out, he ordered a military hammock chair with a detachable pillow that weighed just eight pounds. They would be delivered to Southampton with the first of the chop boxes.

Two last things were required: a pad on which to write to Molly, and reading material. On a display table Langley spotted a novella he'd heard people mention but knew little about. It didn't look too thick. Perfect for dipping in and out of, he thought. He flashed *Heart of Darkness* to the cashier and slipped it into his pocket.

The rain had eased when he left the shop, cheered up no end by the spree. He walked back down Piccadilly as light in spirit as he was in funds. Whatever else was going on, one thing was indisputable: he was an adventurer now.

⦿⦿⦿⦿⦿⦿

Max raised the clipboard from his knees and nodded to Rusty over his desk. It was as familiar a sight as his own face in the mirror. But the glass was fractured, the reflection altered. 'Shall we?'

Rusty lifted a notepad, his face stony. He fastidiously ignored Max's high collar and the purple contusion beneath.

'Let's start with stores. We'll need some new zinc blanks. Do we know how many…' Max paused. *Survived* was the wrong word. He didn't want Rusty to think he was prodding him about the attack. '…are down there?'

'Nine.'

'Contact our man in Barrow, please. Order another thirty. Beeswax?'

'Plenty.'

'Oilcloth?'

'Nineteen square yards.'

Max winced as the top of his collar sank into the mulchy flesh of his bruise. It was a peach, the legacy of the fight. Their future seemed equally contused. He tried to ignore the pain. They were inflicting terrible falsehoods on each other by pretending everything was fine. But the alternative was worse: a complete breakdown of their relationship. The pretence of civility was at least a step towards healing. 'Is the travelling rig clean?'

'Yes.'

'Acid?'

'Three gallons.' Rusty spoke haltingly, as if guided by a languid metronome.

'Fine. Make sure the bell jars are tightly sealed please. We might have to pretend they're medical supplies. I'm told they're fussy at the Russian border.'

'Right you are,' Rusty whispered.

Max laid his checklist on the desk. The last three days had been hell. But they'd somehow arrived at the most fragile of truces. As he looked at Rusty he wanted to reach over and ruffle his hair; talk to him like he normally did; rip open the stifling cocoon into which they'd bound themselves. An honest scrap was better than forced politeness. But they'd had the scrap. And this was where they found themselves. Creeping on ice.

He supposed getting Rusty into the office was an achievement in itself. He'd waited for a day after the fight for them both to calm down. Then he'd visited and begged him to believe in him; to see that what he'd done was for both of their benefits. Using every ounce of his persuasive powers, he spent an hour laying out the attainable steps to success now that the company had money. He'd promised Rusty half the proceeds from any eventual sale of the business should it happen. Cash, immediately. At the end of the hour – grudgingly, his cheek twitching, his anger apparently spent – Rusty agreed to come to Russia.

The tramp wouldn't be easy; his cousin's presence didn't mean he'd come round to his point of view. As they'd spoken neither had apologised for what they'd done. Despite Rusty's reaction,

Max felt guilt but no regret; selling Chaveley had been sensible. Prudent. Forward-thinking. Mutually beneficial. Likewise, Rusty showed no remorse for wiping out half the studio. It was as though they were two exhausted fighters huddling in the middle of the ring, reliant on each other despite the harm they'd inflicted. Max suspected both thought they were the bigger man.

But going through their checklists still felt like a charade. Max missed the pre-tour jangle; that nervous excitement that preceded the leap into the unknown. It thickened the blood and lengthened the stride. 'Two horns or three?'

'Three.' Rusty shrugged. 'May as well.'

'Good idea.' Attempting to pep things up, Max reached for a scroll of map on the floor beside his desk. Perhaps studying the route as they had before would engender some enthusiasm.

As Max unscrolled the map, he leaned over the desk to avoid eye contact with Rusty. 'I know you haven't forgiven me,' he said softly. 'But as I said last night, thank you for giving me the chance.'

Rusty sniffed. It was acknowledgement of the comment, at least.

Max stabbed his finger to the west of Russia. 'We're stopping here, by the way.'

'Serbia?'

'Slavic rain songs are a jewel. You know that. And there's a rich tradition of them south of Belgrade. We were almost passing. It seemed obvious.' He traced the Danube with his finger and flicked his eyes up so they caught Rusty's. They were now conversing.

Rusty blinked. 'Passing? But Serbia's not on the way to Russia. We go via the Baltic, surely?'

'We would normally. But I've arranged to take the southern route. If what I've heard about this singing is true...'

'Rain songs?'

'Yes. Young girls called Dodolas sing wild hymns to invoke water during a drought. Isn't that something?'

Rusty's brow creased like damp buckskin. 'Singers cause rain?' he said coldly.

'People will love them. And our shanties. Imagine the sensation we'll cause.' Max thought for a moment about his next move. *Sod it*. Reaching over the desk, he placed a hand on his cousin's shoulder and squeezed. 'We'll come back from Russia with jewels worthy of the House of Fabergé.'

It was a move too far. Rusty twisted away angrily.

Straightening, Max clapped his hands together and looked down the map. An uneasy silence descended on the room. The stillness was frigid and biting, its quietness unbearable. Max slowly traced the Danube once again. It was longer than he remembered. Germany to the Black Sea. He peeked up at Rusty. He was in the room. That was enough.

# PART FOUR

⁌⁌⁌⁌⁌⁌

# REVOLUTION

## October 1899

# 13

Delilah Green,
121 Middleton Road,
Dalston, London

Maximilian Cadenza,
GPO Moscow,
Russia

3 October, 1899

Dear Max,

I do hope you get this before you go gallivanting down the Volga! I long to hear about your big adventure.

Are you effortlessly sliding into the Russian way of life? Vodka for breakfast and gramophone recitals to assorted babushkas in the evening? I can just picture it. I'm sure you're charming them all!

Everything in London is fine. Talking of new cultural horizons, I got a recall to the Peckham Crown yesterday, which was nice. I go in on Monday. The (reasonably) bright lights of south-east London might be calling! Better than the Paragon anyway. Last week my wig fell off during the Japanese number and Wilson tore a strip off me in the interval. Cheeky oily bastard. I think all the girls are as fed up as me. Molly's on the lookout for other roles. She won't be far behind me in leaving, I bet!

How's Rusty? And Langley? They behaving?

No news on the slayer, I'm afraid. The papers seem to be following the Haymarket prostitute line. I've stopped reading them to be honest. It's all gore and sensation.

This feels daft to write but London's not the same without you. It feels a bit like a party with the host missing. I miss walking with you, and laughing, and talking.

Look after yourself. And write, you silly fool!

Crotchets and quavers,

Delilah x

P.S. Still keen to...you know. Hope you've decided...

಄಄಄಄

Maximilian Cadenza,
Kovrov, Russia

Delilah Green,
121 Middleton Road,
Dalston, London

14 October, 1899

I'd swim the Volga
And ford the Tiber
For a night in the arms
Of my dear Delilah!

*Sweetness,*

*Greetings from the dining room at Kovrov railway station, a few days east of Moscow and a week from our destination. I'm writing from the first still surface I've found in days. How I miss a stable table! Thank you for your wonderful letter. It made my heart sing.*

*You say you miss me, and how I miss you too. London seems so distant. Despite everything, I miss its chaotic swirl. As we travel over arid plain after arid plain I envy the permanence of the Thames' mellow flow. Mainly because it's always near you. I wish I was next to you now in Rules or Simpson's or Limehouse or on a bench or up a dome (!), cosy and close.*

*I'm glad the auditions are going well. You'll rule that stage like the Queen. Peckham won't know what's hit it. Still no fresh developments over the slayer, you say? How D.I. Boot – and Fleet Street – must be losing their minds.*

*We're having quite a time out here. We're en route to a town called Nizhny Novgorod down where the mighty Volga meets the Oka. There's a commercial fair down where the rivers intersect. Half a million traders from Europe, Asia, everywhere. Boatmen up from the Caspian. They call it the wallet of Russia. There'll be wonderful music – I can hardly wait to hear the earthy rumbles of the shanties, sung in their natural environment. A jewel awaits!*

*Rusty is…being Rusty. But there have been no major flare-ups, and that is something. I think he's alright. I hope he now at least understands the freedom we have after what I did. We are a team after all, always have been. Langley, I'm learning, is the best type of man: dependable, honest and hard-working. His enthusiasm has almost made me forgive him the absurd amount of kit he's brought out with him.*

*Our stop-off in Serbia was wonderful – also yielded a jewel (I'm* ticking them off the list at some rate). We went to an eerie hamlet close to a village called Konak. It was suffering a terrible drought and there were seemingly no children. We waited for days, tired and dirty. But filth is a down payment on enlightenment, as any pilgrim will tell you.

One morning a troupe of young girls arrived just like I knew they would. They wore white dresses with black embroidered waistcoats and cradled bundles of foliage in their arms. And they were singing their hearts out, invoking the rain! The sweetest hymn I've heard; what it lacked in polish was made up in vigour. These girls spun in a circle around a girl in the middle – the dodola, or rainmaker. As they spun, women emerged from each house and emptied buckets of water on them. But their singing, Delilah! A curio, but what a sound.

When they finished I looked up. Had a cloud appeared? I'm sure I saw one. The girls repeated the song for our machine. It was perfect. Magic and passion right there.

Rusty didn't like the detour that we made to capture it one bit. He called me obsessed. But, goodness, it was worth taking the long way round. I'm convinced people back home will love it.

What else can I tell you? The air is cold and crisp, as brutally enlivening as the endless vodka you alluded to. One's nostrils feel reborn! And despite many hours of trying on the train, I still can't play the accordion. It parps and whines like a breathless mutt.

Take care, my darling. Days stretch ahead like the endless railway track but I think of you more than I dare say.

Crotchets and quavers,

MC x


P.S. Of course I haven't forgotten your request.

'It would help immeasurably if these wheels were actually round.' Tiny splinters prickled Max's grip as Grigori Pechkin's donkey wagon picked its way down Nizhny Novgorod's main avenue and towards the river. Like everything else in Russia, the wheels beneath it were almost the same as at home but not quite. The cart lolloped as it progressed, causing the occupants ranged behind its driver to gently pendulate as they clung to its riveted planks. As the bell jar of acid clinked against the recording equipment piled up behind him, Max made his elbow heavier on the demonstration gramophone on his lap. The horn was firm between his legs. Every two seconds the brittle shoulder of Langley's safari suit nudged his own. 'Wouldn't you say, Mr Langley? Round wheels?'

Langley nodded nervously. 'Yes, boss.'

He stopped in the middle of asking Rusty the same question. Arms folded, he slumped on his other side, sucking joylessly on his pipe. Max leaned forward and nudged Pechkin's arm. Their hotel's wiry proprietor was a godsend. He had, for a fee, agreed to be their driver, translator and guide. 'Almost there, Mr Pechkin?'

A nod and a gesture. Perhaps.

The façades of the few grand houses that lined the town's main street softened from crimson to peach and from mustard to yellow as the sun rose. The outline of a modest palace's onion dome punctured the blue sky, alone in its divine ambitions. This place was an outpost. A fragment of St Petersburg in miniature. The spacious street was in stark contrast to the ramshackle hillock of lanes behind them in which Pechkin's hotel was located. Grandeur and shabbiness, cheek by jowl. But it wasn't London shabbiness; it felt older, almost medieval. Max knew that what lay ahead would be different still. On a vast dusty plain over the river was the fair. His pulse quickened as a faint rumble ahead rose in volume. A mountain of furs on the cart in front blocked his view, but it sounded like a herd of buffalo rampaging just over the horizon. This was it.

The lollop of the wheels changed tone as clay gave way to wood. They were onto a bridge. The town had suddenly stopped at the riverbank, as though cut off against its will by a mightier force. Max smiled as, on either side of the rickety crossing, the Volga stretched away like an imperial carpet. Steamers, tugs and riverboats formed haphazard patterns as they jostled for position. On the other side of the bridge, Max knew, lay untold treasures. As the wagon clattered across the river he tightened his hold on the demonstration gramophone on his knee, a slight faintness coming over him.

A jam of carts slowed their progress as they approached the other end of the bridge. Max's knee jigged involuntarily as Pechkin inched the cart forwards. This was excitement's cruellest punishment: the closer one got to a desired destination, the slower one travelled. The anticipation was torture. With every second the fair's noise increased in volume. Close to bursting, Max shouted in joy as wood finally gave way to clay once more and they descended a small ramp onto the plain.

A burning vapour. He clamped his eyes shut. As he tentatively opened his lids, his pupils sizzled as though flicked with lime juice. It was as though they'd hit a foul wall; the stench of livestock, animal skin, spices, bubbling fat and human waste co-mingled and bolstered each other in an overpowering jumble. Max was pulled backwards as Langley and Rusty recoiled at the same invisible wave. He'd read about this kind of gathering. It was somewhere in the Book of Exodus in the Old Testament.

Rubbing a tear away, he breathed in shallow bursts. Sand

engulfed the cart as it progressed among tents and a gently growing crowd. All around, the rumble of commerce grew. Smoke rose from a thousand pots. He countered his giddiness by breathing more heavily. The vast temporary city pulsed as it thickened. But although makeshift, it felt rooted and ancient. As the mass of humanity intensified, the specific began to emerge from the general. To one side, Max made out traders from the desert and hawkers from Ulaanbaatar. To his other, Afghans selling daggers and Tatars trading rugs. Among the chaos, he felt strangely relieved at his own insignificance. They were a tiny tribe among thousands. He turned to Rusty. 'Did you know that Cossacks have over eight million melodies in their musical canon? Eight million.'

Rusty lowered his sleeve from his mouth. 'A cannon? That would be useful.'

Max shuffled forward and nudged Pechkin again. 'Over there.' He gestured through the fug to a line of masts and cranes up ahead to the left. Pechkin nodded. He was a good man. And while his establishment up in old Nizhny was far from perfect – small with tiny beds and no storage, meaning that the men had to keep the equipment in their bedrooms – his vehicle had certainly saved the day; there was far too much apparatus for the men to carry themselves.

The cart rattled towards the dock on the fair's eastern flank, where countless vessels were disgorging their cargo. Here, among the ships backed up bow-to-stern along the bank, they'd find sailors willing to sing. Max tapped out a rhythm on the demonstration machine. He had seen a Russian shanty in sheet music form, a song written for barge-haulers on this very river, but could only imagine the power of hearing it in its cradle. 'Left, Mr Pechkin. Left.'

Clinking and rocking as they approached the river, Max

accepted a handful of dry leaves from a man in a wicker hat. He inhaled, intoxicated. 'Fancy that! Tea from an actual Chinaman.'

All along the bank, cranes swung over belching boats, relieving them of their bounty. Winches strained, their ropes creaking like the tightening strings of a violin.

Max shuddered as Pechkin stopped the cart behind a pile of cotton bales. Time to bottle quicksilver. As he jumped down, he realised he had no idea how precisely they'd do it. He had one rule of thumb though. The trick was to make potential singers feel as though he was doing them a favour by recording them, when the opposite was in fact the case.

'Rusty. Mr Langley. Set up the rig. I'll find some rivermen.'

Walking along the dock was like walking through a dream. Max had imagined this for months. But while the sense of anticipation was as he'd hoped, the colours and shapes were different. Things were darker, bigger, colder. Running his moustache through his fingers he knew that the initial moment of interruption would be the hardest. With his odd request he'd be halting strangers in their work. And these were not clerks; these were bears of men. Starved of sleep. Weeks without women. But that was the beauty; their singing would be raw, urgent, the purest shanties ever captured. He was soliciting for magic. But he had to convince them first.

Fingers tingling, he walked for some time, past slumbering bodies and workers too busy to disturb. Then in the shadow of a tug, gathered around a pile of tusks, he saw a dozen or so men in faded oilskins. Baggy blue hats hung off the back of their heads. They stood powerful, bonded, a gang. The tallest of them was breaking up a loaf of black bread and distributing it to the others.

He nudged Pechkin. 'Sailors?'

'Caspian.' Pechkin signalled their hats.

'Come.' Pure fear rarely gripped Max. It was always diluted, tempered. But as he walked towards the group, he felt its heavy cloak. He reached into his pocket and held a pouch of tobacco in front of him, a feeble outrider. As he approached, the leader glared at him with a look so cold it almost froze his heart. Max stood still as the man stepped forward and ripped the pouch from his hand.

Max bowed and turned to Pechkin. 'Say 'Brave men, would you like to be famous the world over?" Seconds felt like minutes as Pechkin mulled the request. '*Say it.*'

The exchange sounded tentative. Confrontational.

'They ask what you want.'

Slowly, he pointed at each man individually and sung a long note, nodding affirmation as he did so. He swallowed as a dozen glares gripped him. From his breast pocket he pulled a bundle of roubles. He repeated the pointing gesture, sang once more and waved the notes. On the way, he'd wondered about holding auditions. The moment had passed. It didn't matter. If the singing didn't pass muster, he'd simply find another group. Money mattered a little less these days.

'Three songs.' He held his fingers aloft. 'Three.'

The leader beckoned Pechkin in. A chat was followed by a laugh. Then a hearty cheer. Clapping in delight, Max led the men back to the cotton bales where the machine was assembled. He grinned at Rusty and Langley as they watched him approach with a line of giants behind him, a Pied Piper in reverse.

In the shadow of a belching tug, Max tried to arrange the sailors in a crescent around the rig, close enough so they could be heard but each equidistant from the opening so no one voice dominated. Ignoring him, they craned over the machine, prodding the recording horn and turning table. In a flash, Rusty squeezed himself between the sailors and the machine, curling after his arm like child protecting a sandcastle from a wave. 'Don't touch. Please.'

Max smiled at the intervention. Fearless Rusty. Perhaps there's passion there after all. He snapped the group to attention and instructed Rusty to unwrap a zinc blank from its oilcloth satchel. 'Gentlemen, when you're ready.'

The boatmen composed themselves around the machine. A second ring of spectators gathered further back, circling the circle. Following a count from the leader, they sang. Max raised a hand to his mouth as his breath caught. He felt the song more than he heard it; it pushed him back like a gust.

'*Vnees po matooshka po Volga.*'

'A love song to Mother Volga,' Pechkin nodded.

The song rumbled like celestial thunder. The closest thing Max had heard to it was in the Welsh valleys, but its harmonies were wilder, its melodies rougher. Pure passion chanted through black teeth.

The song ended. Max stepped towards the machine and clapped. 'More. Another.' The circle of spectators had grown. He received the nod from Rusty and signalled for them to go again.

Dripping with repressed desire, a song about the first night back on shore came next. It was followed by a lament about a ship wrecked on ice; slow and heart breaking with harmonies from the depths, bass stacked on bass. Max closed his eyes and let the voices shudder through him. This is it, he thought. The essence. If anyone doubted that music has the capacity to shock, let them hear this. A rare sensation gripped him; privilege. This is what I do. And it is worth every minute, every struggle, every argument. He wished the song would last for ever.

It did not. It ended, and he felt oddly bereft as though a long-cherished gift had been ripped from his arms. Rusty removed the zinc and nodded that all was fine. Max walked to the leader and proffered his hand. 'Mr Pechkin, thank him. Tell him that, God willing, the pressed discs will appear in London, and perhaps even back in Russia, shortly.'

A hand thumped on his shoulder and he tasted salty tallow as the boatman pulled in for an embrace. Max levered himself back from the damp apron and clasped the man around the shoulders. 'Thank you.' Six jewels down. He smiled. Sometimes the roughest shone brightest.

He watched as Rusty raised his forceps and dunked the last zinc in a tray of acid. The tang of lightly burning metal filled the air as the liquid hissed its way into the wax grooves. Max catalogued the recordings and Langley stored the masters in a fresh crate. He never tired of the ritual.

As they loaded the cart, Max saw the leader point to the demonstration gramophone lying on the ground. He was agitating for something.

'What's he saying?'

Pechkin pointed to his ear.

'A demonstration? What do we think?' Max looked at Rusty. There was time. Things had gone smoothly. 'Very well. Capital idea.' He lifted the demonstration gramophone from the clay and rested it on a crate. As he selected *Music of the Sands* from a packing case, a rough shoulder shunted him aside.

'Allow me.' Rusty wound the machine's crank, unsheathed a different disc and set the turning table in motion. Max stood helpless as a tinkling piano and male Cockney voice, high and untrained, drifted over the banks of the Volga. It was a nonsense song called *Wicky Wacky Woo*. Rusty must have slipped it into the cases before they left London. Ashamed at the uneven reciprocation – folk songs of the sea for this dross, the authentic for the contrived – Max pinched his toes together and winced.

The sailors crowded around the crate.

'*Until the moon turns pink and the sun turns blue, It's you and me and my Wicky Wacky Woo.*'

It started with jabs and whoops. Within half a minute, the boatmen were twisting in delight. Some held their stomachs. One hit his thigh with such force that Max feared a snapped femur. He gently shook his head. It was quite the strangest sight he'd ever seen.

A frenzied cheer rose as the song finished. He walked to the gramophone to remove the disc. However once again, like a puppy shown love, Rusty bounded to the rig.

'I'll do it.'

Max watched as Rusty lifted the stylus. But rather than set it in its cradle and lift the disc from the turning table, he returned the needle to the start of the song. A lick of the lips as he wound the crank. A wink and a smirk. Once again, the sound of Cockney nonsense echoed off the ships' hulls.

# 14

From the hotel roof up in Nizhny Novgorod's old town, Max watched the tented city shimmer on the distant plain. Campfires glinted in the dusk. Drumbeats echoed. Even from this distance, the sprawl looked so vast he was amazed they'd successfully navigated it.

The brandy evaporated on his tongue, leaving him to inhale its fiery fumes. He could not recall a warmer satisfaction.

Plates chaffed behind him as Pechkin cleared a trestle table on the centre of the roof. Dinner had consisted of loaves of bread, roasted figs and hard-boiled eggs, acquired locally, with jellied chicken and game pie from the chop boxes. Midway along the table a half-eaten stilton rose like a mildewed centrepiece. A Tsar's buffet, Max had called it. With some ceremony, he'd struck off another jewel from his list as they'd eaten.

Next to the table, Rusty swayed gently in the breeze, the brandy bottle swinging at his side. His pipe was wedged upside down behind his ear, its bowl hanging over the top like a strange tribal adornment.

Today was life-changing. Such days were rare. Max gazed down from the balustrade. Somewhere in that haze his sailors were bedding down for the night. Had they realised the magnitude of what they'd done? Did they have any idea of what they'd gifted the world? Those songs. The rush from capturing them was like sipping wine for the first time, or finding love. Six jewels to go. Now, so attainable. So easy. On the way back to the hotel he'd made a decision. Wilma. He'd do it.

'Good music. It makes your heart beat faster. Don't you think?'

Rusty raised his fist to his breast and mimicked a beating heart. 'Yeah. Crowds, dirt and urine make mine go crazy.'

'I'm serious. That singing today mesmerised me. And those girls in Serbia – the *dodolas* – didn't they intrigue you with what they were trying to do? With their desire for rain?'

Rusty snorted. 'Rain is caused by precipitation and air turbulence. I should've had a word with them.'

Max shrugged. 'Who is to say how rain is caused? If it comes, it comes. Water is water, be it by science or by song.'

'Oh, do me a favour. What did you think, Dr Livingstone?'

Langley looked up from his round of Patience on the floor. 'Me?'

'Yeah. Speak, Streak.'

'I liked those tinsmiths with the hunting horns today, you remember? On the way out. Each played a different note but taken together they formed a rich chord. It was a sort of soothing cacophony.'

Rusty shook his head. 'Freak. I'll take… *Until the moon turns pink and the sun turns blue, It's you and me and my Wicky Wacky Woo.*' He stepped from side to side like a Mayday hobby horse.

Max placed his glass on the floor. Dancing Rusty. A rare day indeed. He stepped back from the balustrade and walked towards the trapdoor in the corner of the roof that led down into the hotel. 'Gentlemen, I'm tired. Time to retire. One way or another, today has been rather eventful.'

'*It's you and me and my…*' Rusty waltzed next to the table, performing to himself.

'Oh, and please keep the noise down when you're finished up here.' Max pointed to his feet. His room was on the top floor, meaning that the others had to descend the narrow wooden staircase outside his door to reach their rooms.

Langley lowered his cards. 'Goodnight, boss,'

'And don't forget.' Rusty gestured at Max.

'What?'

'Rain.'

'Rain?'

'Is caused by precipitation and air turbulence.'

෴෴෴෴

Max took a lantern from a hook at the top of the stairs and picked his way down to his room. Closing the door behind him, he was relieved to have some peace. He thought of home as he unbuttoned his waistcoat. The trip had been a success. Two jewels. Precisely what they'd come for. He looked across his cramped quarters. Piles of recording equipment cluttered the room; he could barely see the floor beyond his small bed for bell jars, crates of zincs and piles of oilcloth. It didn't matter. Pechkin had done them proud. One more night and they'd be gone.

He pulled back the sheet and extinguished the lamp, relishing his bed's dark safety. Now a soft hum, the tribal rhythms from the fair outside gently permeated the walls. The hum became a lullaby as he drifted to a far-off place, faintly aware of footsteps on the stairs outside. The men descending from the roof. He counted one door closing below, then another. Then no more as the world closed itself off to him.

A face. Vast and round, caked in white greasepaint and frozen in terror. Above, a hand. It holds back the head while a second hand caresses the neck. A scream as a stylus needle meets the skin. It rises in volume as the needle is inserted. Yet Balducci stands. A blue hat hangs off his head, baggy and soiled. He slaps his thigh at the spiralling disc before him, the terror gone. A dance. But now a second scream. Louder than the first as a fresh needle pierces his neck. His face is frozen in terror once more. Then laughter. A dance. A third needle. A fourth. A fifth...

Max sat upright in bed, his hands entwined in linen. He blinked himself conscious. Twisting his head in the darkness, the room's proportions came back to him. The hotel. Nizhny Novgorod. And yet the screams continued. Human pain, as guttural as it was urgent. The source could not suck air into their lungs quickly enough. A brief silence was broken by a howl that rose in pitch and volume. He felt his walls shake as doors below were yanked and slammed. Familiar voices thickened the cacophony; feet thumped on the stairs.

Fumbling for the box of matches on his bedside table, he lit the gas lamp. With light came some clarity. The noise emanated from below. Curiously, it seemed to be coming from the foot of his bed. Lifting the lamp, Max crawled to the end of his mattress. An acrid stench blasted away the remaining fug of sleep. He lowered the light over the bed's end. Beyond its iron legs, an area of the floor had disappeared. In place of the floorboards, a gaping hole hissed and smoked. The hole was surrounded by a thin pool of sizzling liquid. At the pool's fringe, rocking gently on its side, was an empty bell jar. Engraved into the glass were a skull and crossbones and two words: sulphuric acid.

A fresh scream told of pain beyond agony. 'Jesus fucking Christ. *Jesus fucking Christ.*' He knew that voice. The acid had fallen, like an evil spirit, from a place of safety to one of untold harm.

*Rusty.*

Through the floor's charred wooden slats he saw enough to make out his cousin convulsing on a bed below. Mottled skin bubbled on his right shoulder. A bulging neck vein. Max saw an arm – Langley's – holding down the writhing man.

'Rus… Rusty.' He glanced at the empty jar on the floor. He must have knocked it with his feet as he slept.

He jumped from the bed and ran downstairs, all thoughts paused. In the half-light of Rusty's room, the man's head was thrust back in terror. His right arm appeared both red-raw and wet from shoulder to hand. On his forearm, white met pink where the bed-shirt had fused to his skin. He was biting down on some sort of circular metal tube to stop the pain. The tone arm of a gramophone. The smell was familiar and foul: a freshly basted joint of meat.

'Here, move.' Max edged Langley out of the way. Rusty's torment was total. 'Rusty. It's me. Listen, you have significant burns to your arm. The acid will keep burning for some time. But we will make the pain go. I promise.'

Pechkin ran in, surveyed the carnage and immediately ran out. 'Doctor.'

Max turned to Langley, silently urging him to become the man he knew he could be. 'Go downstairs and fill a bucket with tepid water. Bring it up and then do it again. Also, rip up a fresh bed sheet. Go.'

Rusty's eyes roved across the ceiling. Keep him talking, Max thought. 'Rusty. You are going to be alright. I'm here. Tell me, what's the Devon house called?' It was the first thing he thought of. 'The *house*.'

Two growled syllables emerged from the back of Rusty's

throat. It was not a word, it was a curse. But at least he was listening. Max looked up. Poison was still dripping from the ceiling. He dragged the bed into the centre of the room.

From infant to man he'd seen Rusty screw up his face in pain, anger or frustration on an almost daily basis. But he had never seen this. Max turned as Langley entered with a bucket of water and started ripping up a bed sheet.

'The pail. Here.'

Taking the bucket, Max dipped the first piece of material in the water. He held the cloth as close to the skin of Rusty's arm as he could without touching it. He squeezed. Even though the droplets fell less than an inch, the pain of contact made him convulse on the mattress, twisting the sordid sheet beneath him with his good hand.

He soothed Rusty's forehead. 'It's the only way.'

Langley handed over strip after strip and Max applied water. Clean material every time. Max developed a system: a stroke to the forehead to signal application, a second stroke to signal it was over. 'Where's the bloody doctor?' Half an hour passed as he applied squeeze after squeeze to the raw arm.

Langley worked quietly and efficiently, bringing more water. His chin was flecked with vomit. Max was unsure when he'd puked, but it added to the competing stenches in the room.

The doctor finally arrived, a hefty man wearing a greatcoat over his nightshirt. Through Pechkin he instructed Langley to heat bricks in the kitchen and bring them up to keep Rusty's bed warm to prevent him from going into shock. Max stood over the bed with the doctor and Pechkin, glaring at Rusty's arm. It was marbled like a reptile's.

'Is he going to be alright?'

'He will be.' Pechkin nodded.

'And the arm?'

'It should heal, perhaps.'

As the doctor examined Rusty, Max lifted up a rolled bed sheet from a chair in the corner of the room to sit. As his hand slid into the sheet's fold, his fingers met with a clammy moistness. Langley's vomit. He dropped the sheet and sat on the ground, exhausted. He heard Rusty mewl. How could this have happened? He must have knocked the bell jar of acid as he slept. The beds were small. It was the only explanation. How could he have been so stupid as to keep acid in the sleeping quarters? He clenched his teeth to stifle the surge. But it came. In the room's dark corner, he wept. He wanted to tell his cousin that the pain was shared, that he felt the agony too: in his stomach, in his heart, on his own shoulder. But, then, how could it be shared? Rusty's arm was mutilated. His was not.

A tap to the shoulder and Max was beckoned to the bed. He watched as the doctor mixed a syrup of collodion and castor oil in a tin cup. The paste's tart fumes made the thick air almost too rank to breathe. He braced himself when the doctor picked up a horsehair brush in preparation for applying the solution. It was as bad as he'd feared. The screams returned, louder, as the doctor applied the syrup to Rusty's arm, favouring brevity over delicacy. Max mopped his cousin's brow as the doctor brushed. The solution dried mercifully quickly to form a translucent film over the burns.

Max held Rusty's arm as the doctor bound it in cotton wadding. 'You're protected now. The pain will subside.'

Pechkin, who had left the room before the solution was mixed, returned with a tray of tea. Without hesitation Max took him aside and promised to pay for any building work or furniture. He also promised to send an Empress gramophone and some recordings from the fair. It was the best he could think of.

The doctor departed and Max sipped his tea, watching Rusty. He was lying on his good side, shaking. But his breathing appeared regular, as if he was finally drifting off to sleep. They had done all they could; the man was warm, his wound dressed and the worst over.

Max closed his eyes.

At some point the time would come to think about the weeks that lay ahead: how best to transport Rusty home – via sea from St Petersburg was surely the quickest way, how to care for him on that journey, how to explain to Mary what happened. But not now. Every question led to a dozen more. He was too tired.

He walked to Rusty, now sleeping. There was nothing more to be done. He beckoned to Langley and they returned to their bedrooms. As he climbed he was struck by the building's quietness; it was completely at odds with the commotion of the previous hour. He got into his bed and extinguished the lamp. Once more he was enveloped by a strange peace. Even the fair's drums had fallen silent. Under his sheet, he raised his knees to his chest and wrapped his arms around them. Pulling his legs close, he mouthed a silent scream. One thing was for certain. The peace would only be temporary.

⚭⚭⚭⚭⚭

'I really don't mind. You stay here… Look after…' Langley nodded down to the carriage's lower berth.

'Are you sure?' Max's voice had not risen above a whisper in days.

'Yes. It's the least I can do.'

'Very well. Take a good few discs.' Langley left the carriage with the demonstration gramophone under one arm and a box of discs under the other. Max imagined he'd be gone for a few hours; Torzhok railway station – indistinguishable from the others, and their home until they continued towards St Petersburg that evening – was some distance from the town. 'Good luck. Wait. Posters.'

Langley returned and Max stuffed a roll under his arm. He had printed their London address next to the image of the couple listening to the machine so people could order by mail. Market square demonstrations often proved fruitless. But he was pleased Langley – blooded now, one of them – was trying. Seeds could sprout in unfamiliar soil.

Max closed the door behind him and shivered. The drab carriage had become a hospital ward; a grey box, its silence as chilling as the air, its atmosphere thick with sorrow. The carriage reeked of cheap game, the collodion adding a vinegary sharpness. No wonder Langley volunteered to go. Max looked down at Rusty on the berth. Swaddled in rugs, he had barely moved since the train left Moscow. The burns forced him to lie on his side facing the wall, all expression hidden. Two days of stillness. On top of the rugs, resting like a fragile cocoon, was his arm. A web of bandages was blotched with pus and discharge from beneath, pink in some places, ruby in others. The gentle rise and fall of his shoulder provided the only sign that he was alive. Wound aside, he'd refused to be washed. On the occasions when Max had seen his face – to feed him or dab his brow as he changed dressings – it was etched with a curdled new look; somewhere between pain and bewilderment. Max hadn't seen the look for years. It suggested a different Rusty, a man as wounded within as he was on the outside.

He sat on the berth opposite, instincts jostling. His desire to protect was held back by a sickening burden of responsibility. It almost felt wrong, hypocritical, to nurse when he'd also inflicted the damage; to be both assailant and healer, traducer and soother. Yet he'd do anything to help him, to ease his pain, to comfort him. He stood and poured himself a cup of water from a jug in the corner. Practical concerns rendered his thoughts moot; at some point soon, certainly before the train departed, he would have to re-dress the wounds again. The ritual involved peeling off the film of collodion and castor oil – taking care not to take skin with it – and lancing any blisters. After exposing the arm to air for an hour, a new solution needed to be applied, with a webbing of cotton laid over the top. It was the saddest task he'd ever performed.

He drained his glass, refilled it and approached Rusty. 'Here, old boy. Water.'

There was no reply. He lowered his hand to touch Rusty's back but withdrew it inches from his body. As he sat and sipped the water himself, the night's events went around inside his head again. He recalled going to bed exhausted and waking up to screams. The angle of his limbs, the small bed. He'd knocked the bell jar as he slept; it was the only explanation. But he wished he could remember more. Like the wretched hole itself, the middle part was missing. He started again. Went to bed exhausted. Woke up to screams.

Over the aisle, Rusty stirred; a muffled coughing from beneath the cover.

'Rusty?' Max stood, leaned over the aisle and held his ear in close. 'Rus?'

He craned closer still. Whispers from a parched mouth.

'Maimed by dripping acid. Now there's a tale for the grandchildren.'

Max thought he heard a faint laugh. He rested his hand on his cousin's hip and leaned in to speak. 'That's the spirit. It'll only add to your legend. How... How are you feeling?'

'Sprightly as a ballerina. How do you think I'm feeling?'

Max said nothing but arched over his body and held the cup to his lips. Rusty lifted his neck and twisted his head towards him, drinking sideways until the cup was dry. Max fashioned a cradle with his hand to catch the drool dripping down his cheek. Cupping it, he carefully withdrew his hands and sat over the aisle.

Rusty cleared his throat. 'Tell me something, Max.'

'Anything.'

'What did you think of me growing up?'

Max sat up, blind-sided by the question. 'What?'

'Growing up. What did you make of me?'

Poor fellow. Pain and boredom must have given him cause to reflect. Unexpected though the question was, he decided to follow the conversation's path. 'Growing up... Well. I'd say you were headstrong.'

'And?'

'And you were funny. Inventive, *always*. You were your own person.'

'*My own person*,' Rusty repeated. 'More.'

'I don't know. Gosh. You grew on me, I suppose. You started as something of an irritant if I'm being honest. Then you became a companion, then a friend. Then my best friend. My partner in crime.'

'From irritant to partner in crime.' Rusty chuckled to the wall. 'They were good, those days, weren't they? Playing at Chaveley.' He paused. 'Before things changed.'

Max exhaled. They never spoke of it. 'Your parents?'

'Being orphaned. That.'

'Yes. They were good days.'

Rusty shifted on his bed. 'You took me to the pub that night. Do you remember? In Combe Martin.'

Max shuffled uncomfortably. The night of Tobias and

Isabella's deaths. Of course he remembered. But he had no idea why Rusty was bringing it up now.

'The Pack o' Cards,' Rusty added.

No one had uttered the name of the pub in the eight years since the accident.

'Max?'

'I remember. Yes.'

'Then Mother and Father looked for us. On the cliff.'

Max nodded. 'They did.' A stillness descended once more. It was as though Rusty's pain had led him to breach his own long-held boundaries. As though, with his back to Max and thousands of miles from home, it was somehow all right to talk about these things. Max sometimes wondered if, deep down, Rusty blamed him for their deaths. It was his idea to go to the tavern. Had they stayed in the house, Tobias and Isabella would never have gone to the clifftop. He blinked back a tear. It escaped and dropped onto his knee. Both had locked the specific events away in a box and buried them deep in their mind, allowing the intervening years to moss over the catches.

'You never quite got used to me coming to live with you, did you?'

Unsure he'd heard him correctly, Max edged forward. 'What?'

'You didn't, though, did you? After my parents died. I interrupted things. Got in the way.'

'*No*. Rusty, hush. You're being silly.'

'You can be honest, Max. We've been through enough.'

'Rusty, *please*.' This was daft. 'All this... What happened was tragic, and of course I wish it hadn't happened. But you coming to live with us was...'

'Was?'

'A continuum. Of you and me. It made us stronger. It cemented everything.'

'Made us stronger.'

'Yes. You must see that.' His voice rose, effusive. 'We became even closer. You're my best friend.'

'Promise?'

'Of course.'

Rusty drew a long breath that seemed to last for minutes. His tone darkened. 'So if I'm your best friend, why did you do this to me?'

His words froze in the air.

'What?' He can't have meant them. 'Rusty, I didn't do it to you. It was an accident. The bell jar was at the end of my bed. I knocked it over with my foot as I slept.'

'You kicked it.'

'Kicked…? I was asleep. It was an *accident*. And I am so sorry.' He reached across and laid a hand on Rusty's hip again. His cousin rolled forward, causing the hand to flop onto the berth. Max stood and busied himself, his hands trembling. 'The doctor said your arm will be fine. No loss of movement.' It was a stupid thing so say; but talk was better than silence.

'No loss of movement. Pass the concertina and I'll do a jig.'

Max looked down to the berth, unsure of how to react. Rusty was moving differently. Initially he thought he was shivering due to the chill. But as he craned in, he heard a soft rattle. Sobbing.

'Stop.' He kneaded Rusty's leg through the blanket. 'There's no need for that. We've got each other.'

There were no words for some time as Rusty gently shook. Helpless, Max leaned over and cleaned the mess of tears and mucus from his face.

'We're a team. It's us against the bastards, remember?'

This delicate wounded bundle. He wanted to lie next to him on the bunk and hold him close; to warm him, hug him, reassure him. But he couldn't. He mustn't. Any contact with the injury would result in untold pain. Picking a bag from under his seat, he sat and began preparing the paste to redress the wounds. After a minute the sobbing subsided and Rusty fell quiet. For a while the metallic swirl of spoon in cup was the only sound.

Rusty cleared his throat. 'Tell me something else.'

'Of course.'

'Are you in love?'

Follow the conversation, Max thought. The man is not himself. 'In love?'

'With her. Delilah.'

Max put down the paste. 'I don't know. I'm most fond of her as you know. Love, though?'

'How do you feel when she walks into the room?'

'I suppose I feel relaxed. I feel myself.'

'Go on.'

Max edged forwards on his berth. He was still talking to Rusty's back, but was thankful that the conversation had moved on. 'Alright. It's as though everything is amplified when we're together. Everything's heightened. I suppose I used to feel like that when I played the piano. Alive.'

'Tell me more.'

*Follow it.* 'Very well. She makes life feel normal. The best kind of normal there is. And when she goes away life starts being…'

'Not normal?'

'Not normal.'

'Do you take a little extra effort with your appearance before you see her?'

Max smiled. 'Of course.'

'Collywobbles in your stomach that she might run off with someone else?'

'Yes.'

'And who's the first person you think of when you wake up?'

'Well…her.'

He watched the back of Rusty's head slowly nod. 'Always?'

'It's silly, I know.'

Rusty paused. 'You're in love, you daft bastard.'

'You know, I think that perhaps I am.' He'd never analysed it in such a way. Rusty was right. He was. His shoulders eased and he relaxed. It felt good talking about her. More, it felt good talking to him about her. He and Rusty hadn't had a conversation this frank for months. Perhaps it was a tentative signal of forgiveness for Chaveley. Max warmed. But as he looked at the bottle of collodion at his feet a terrible guilt descended. He shouldn't be feeling this content, not with Rusty in such pain. He started to mix the paste again. 'But, of course, it's not all easy with Delilah. Aspects are tricky.'

'Like?'

'She attracts unwanted attention. And her recording request has rather put me on the spot.'

As though prodded with a stick, Rusty snapped his head around so his profile was visible against the wall. 'Delilah's asked to record?'

Max shrunk back, surprised at the animation. He'd not seen Rusty's lips move in speech for days. 'She has. I'm torn. We have our jewels, you see. And business and pleasure are troublesome bedfellows.' He saw a wince dance across Rusty's face. Evidently a new twinge of pain.

'The jewels,' Rusty said. 'Yes. Perhaps stick to them. Magic and passion and all that.'

Max nodded. 'So you think I should say no? I'm minded to.'

'It's up to you.' Rusty became lost in thought for a moment. 'But why alter your strategy when we've come so far? The wind's in your sails. Stick to the mission, I would.'

Stick to the mission. 'Yes I think I agree.' As Rusty turned his head to the wall again, Max was sure he glimpsed the curl of a smile. 'What?'

'Nothing.' Rusty gently rearranged the blanket under his arm. 'Now. Are you going to re-dress these fucking wounds or do I have to do it myself?'

# 15

The wad of hay rolled around the camel's mouth, moistening but never diminishing. Max followed the clump with his eyes, hypnotised. Standing bone-weary in the late autumn sun, just inches from the animal's flaring nostrils, he counted off the three priorities he'd set himself since returning: taking Rusty home and settling him in, sleeping, and seeing Delilah. He'd achieved the first two within six hours of arriving at Victoria Station. Poor Mary. He'd never forget her horrified face when he peeled off Rusty's bandage. His arm resembled a freshly-skinned rabbit. Tacky to the touch. Relaying the instructions for dressing the wound was grim. He'd stayed for hours to ensure that Rusty was comfortable; sitting by his bed, handing him mint tea, reminiscing about the past until he eventually dropped off to sleep. He'd gone up to Highgate to achieve the second priority. Sleep. The invisible doctor. He was out for two whole days. Mama had woken him with a pot of coffee and a slab of walnut cake. She'd visited Rusty while he slept. Still and silent, she'd said. But Max's rest, he knew, was merely a necessary hurdle before his third priority. So he found himself at London Zoo, befuddled, with a dromedary in front of him and an ebullient singer at his side.

Seeing Delilah was like rediscovering Mozart; her beguiling energy was impossible to conjure from afar, hard though he'd tried. Some spirits were too mischievous for the mind to contain. There was a lightness there but a thrilling complexity too; it had almost taken his breath away when he'd met her at the gate. Rusty was right on the train after all. Perhaps he was in love. And yet he was seeing her as if through a fog, as though the brutality of events had lowered a cloud over him. No matter how hard he tried, he felt as though he was playing himself rather than being himself. He wished he possessed the stamina to give her the attention she deserved. He'd find it somewhere. He always did.

Slabs of enamel clattered like falling rocks as the camel chewed. Yet, curiously, the hay still remained. Max watched it go round and round, still undiminishing. His elbow was yanked from his body. The prettiest cadence fluttered in his ear.

'Can you fathom that, Max? Five shows a week.'

'Eh? Five?'

'At the Peckham Crown.'

'Well, well.' He turned, blinking, and watched her jade pupils sparkle. 'That really is fabulous news.'

'I know.' She inched up her hem and curtseyed. 'And I've got the Holloway Empire audition next week. There's talk of a role.'

He silently repeated her words to ensure he knew their meaning. It was as though his ear was adapting to a forgotten key.

'Mr Wilson wasn't best pleased. He said I owed the Paragon more time.'

Wilson. He'd not thought of him for a while either. 'How is he?'

She threw him a look. A polite but definite warning off.

'Behaving.'

'Come on.' As he offered her his arm he caught her scent. He thought he'd remembered it in Russia but it was fresher and sweeter than he'd recalled. They ambled down the path towards the monkey house. A mellowness lightened his fatigue. Walking was good. 'I've missed you,' he said eventually.

'You silly beggar. I've missed you too.' She looked at him. 'I worried.'

'You needn't have. We only had one minor disaster.' He looked at his feet. Making light of it was wrong. They both knew it was a catastrophe.

'Is he alright?'

'I'm afraid he's not.' A throb emanated from the crook of his elbow where Delilah's hand gently rested. It was Rusty's sorest part.

'Accidents happen, Max.'

Glancing across, her eyes were wells of genuine compassion. No bitterness, anger or suspicion. Her concern was pure and empathic. In that instant the fog lifted a touch and he felt present. Not brutally present like during the Chinese meal, but he felt with her. Together. A couple. He mouthed a thank you. He owed it to her not to brood or seek pity. None of this was her fault. As they approached the monkey house he stopped in the pathway and, glancing around, softly pulled her close. He faced her, scanning the constellation of freckles on her forehead. Looking at her now, the previous weeks vanished. Although he cursed his tiredness, seeing her felt like something approaching bliss.

His eye was caught by a weeping willow tree on the manicured lawn behind her. He took her arm and led her onto a grassy bank and up towards the tree's canopy. Sweeping the tendrils aside, he led her into the tree's private space. They were alone;

unseeing and unseen. Emerald light glinted throughout the dome as the curtain of branches fell back into place.

She smiled as he placed his hands around her waist. Saying nothing, they both edged forwards until their hips met. He barely had to move his face forward for the kiss.

His own smile meant that teeth, rather than lips, met first. But the clumsiness was fleeting; in a trice he was engaged in an embrace of such ecstasy that he was glad of the branches' protection. She tasted both soft and lively; as lush as a ripened peach. The kiss wasn't as he remembered; it was many times better. Her hand caressed his cheek, invoking him towards her. He was truly awake now. Succumbing to the need for air, he drew back, adoring her delicate sigh. Her hips remained pressed to his, their fusion alive with future promise. Together they stood. As he touched his tongue to his lip to taste her once more, she leaned in and kissed him again.

For a minute they held each other. His carnal desires had been in abeyance for so long, events outside this bubble so rotten, that – briefly, pathetically – he felt tearful. He'd forgotten that such unalloyed joy could exist. With his arms still around her waist, he locked his hands behind her.

'Is this altogether gentlemanly?' He knew full well that it was not.

She pushed herself into him and faintly raised a brow. 'Feels gentlemanly to me.'

Arms still around her, he touched his forehead on hers and once again they kissed. Overhead, somewhere above the tree, he heard a flock of birds screech in unison. An airborne choir. A lovers' canticle. His fingers met at the small of her back. Through the material of her dress he caressed the warm, low hollows of her spine.

He pulled back and smiled. Despite the desire, this was not

the place for new intimacies. Fearing that passion could spill over, he unhooked his arms from her waist. 'Let's go.'

Turning, he composed himself and stepped towards the tree's green canopy. A hand gripped his, anchoring him in place. He turned back to her. 'What?'

A coy smile played on her lips. 'It sustains and reverberates.'

'What does?' As soon as he'd spoken he recognised the words as his. It was his description of sound waves in the whispering gallery.

She raised a hand to her heart and blushed. 'It.' The word was a ghost. She barely mouthed it. But he heard it, heavier and louder than any word he'd heard before. As she uncovered her heart, she spun away, embarrassed. When she turned back, a soft grin had spread. 'Come on.' She winked, a disarming synthesis of bashful and brazen.

Max parted the hanging branches and walked, as if on air. The sky seemed a touch clearer, the wittering from the animals a fraction calmer, as he walked from the tree and led her back to the path.

They strolled in silence, as though promenading had been their sole activity all afternoon. His mouth did not yet feel his own. Deliciously, it still tasted shared. They arrived at a junction. 'Arthropods or amphibians?' he said.

'Amphibians. So apart from missing me and the incident, did you enjoy it?'

Enjoy was too strong a word, given what happened. However, one aspect of the trip had surpassed his expectations. The music. Capturing those jewels had stoked his fire, which raged with a greater intensity than ever. The songs from the sailors and the Slavic girls were exultant and vital; he found it hard to articulate, but they touched on something elemental. They'd spurred him. Thanks to them he was now half way through his list. Six to go. 'It had its moments. The music was extraordinary. But between the highs of recording were prolonged troughs of boredom. It was dull at times.'

'Poor boy. I still think it sounds terribly glamorous.'

'Crates, customs and carriages? Glamorous? No. I'd say being on stage is far more glamorous than convincing sailors to sing into a horn.'

'Not in the places I work.' She laughed.

He imagined her standing at the footlights, arms aloft, her head thrust back as she sang. 'But there's glamour, is there not, in performance? In the lights, the audience, the music? You're… up there…for everyone to see.'

"Everyone'? Every one man and his dog, more like.' She looked to the heavens. 'Maybe soon.'

'Nonsense. You're already doing it. You're a star.' He meant it. She was. He felt her arm grip his. For the first time that day, it didn't feel wrong.

What a jumble these days were. Max wondered if his soul had ever been so jostled by competing emotions. Guilt for Rusty, warmth for Delilah, weariness from the journey, euphoria from the jewels. It was impossible to unpick. But for the first time in a while he felt unfazed. He decided to let the bouillabaisse simmer undisturbed. He was sure that order would return soon. The last few hours had been glorious. That was enough.

'So…'

Delilah's inquisitive tone surprised him. It sounded youthful and tentative, in stark contrast to the firm surety of earlier. But in that single word he knew what she was about to say. Panic nipped at his stomach. With everything going on, he hadn't adequately prepared for this.

'So…' he repeated.

'Did you manage to think about me recording? You said in your letters that you hadn't quite made your mind up.'

He smiled. He wasn't sure why but it was all he could think to do.

'What? Max?'

He walked with his head straight as his mind whirred. 'Of course I've thought about it. To hear your voice on shellac would be wonderful.' He was aware of a skip at his side. 'But, with everything going on, now's just a little… It isn't the right time. Soon, but…not now.'

'Oh.' She slowly unlinked her arm from his. 'That's a shame.'

'You have a wonderful voice. Heavenly. You really do. But things are tricky.' Still looking ahead, he ascertained no fresh reaction as she walked beside him. He knew that she'd appreciate his honesty. 'You know that I have this list. And I have resolved to record everything on it. I'm nearly there.'

'Are you pulling my leg?'

'I'm not, my dear. The wind's in my sails, you see. And until I complete the list… And what with Rusty, I simply can't allow myself to be distracted. They're my jewels. I can't alter my strategy when I've come this far. It's all about music that will fire people's imagination. Songs with unusual stories behind them, sung with passion by extraordinary singers. I must stick to my mission.'

He was about to mention the joy of capturing the *dodola* girls when he became aware that she'd stopped walking. He turned. She'd paused just behind him. Her left cheek muscle was pulled taught to her mouth, making her lips resemble a sideways teardrop.

She glared at him, her brow morphing into a frown. 'I beg your pardon?'

'Stick to my mission.'

'*Extraordinary* singers?'

He wondered what she was talking about. Her face crumpled, her eyes moistening. 'Well, yes. Extra...' He stopped himself. Of course. Wrong word. Poorly selected. In using it, he hadn't dreamed of suggesting that she was the opposite, that her voice was merely ordinary. He raised a hand but her face had fallen further. 'No. Of course you're a wonderful singer. I wasn't... What I meant was, I'm after music that is out of the ordinary. Music with some kind of cultural resonance.'

Her face was a tangle of disappointment. 'But you just said I'm a star.'

Watching her, he felt every crease. Thousands of miles of Russian railroad had passed beneath him as he had thought about her sweet face. And now this. 'Delilah. Forgive me.'

'I suppose I don't sing with passion either?' She folded her arms.

He shook his head. The words had tumbled terribly. But surely she understood? It wasn't as though she was unaware of his strategy. And the intention behind his words was completely in accordance with that, even if their form was flatulent. Surely she'd forgive him the disconnect between head and mouth?

She glared at him. He watched her as a second, more devastating element crept in: coldness. He could do nothing as the previous two hours seemed to fall away. With a hurt frown, she turned and walked back towards the camel enclosure.

'Delilah.' He followed her down the path. '*Delilah.*' As his strides lengthened, so did hers. Even when he caught up with her, she turned her head away, blocking him out. 'Please. This is *silly.*'

He skipped behind her, desperate to be let back in. They passed the weeping willow tree. It was stripped of meaning now. Just a tree. She turned down a short track that led towards the exit gate crowned with a London Zoo arch. Stopping suddenly, she spun to face him.

'A simple favour.' She was now angry, as fired up as he'd ever seen her. 'I've only ever asked one thing of you, Max. One thing. You're as bad as the rest of them.' She turned and walked towards the arch.

'Delil–'

'You're obsessed.' She didn't bother to face him. Just shouted as she walked. 'Your stupid jewels. Your stupid industry. Your stupid magic and passion. Your stupid machine.'

He watched her walk through the arch and head for a row of hansoms over the road. This was too extreme. It was daft. He stopped in the path, unsure of what she'd want him to do. Even if he knew, was doing what she wanted the right thing in the circumstances? Or would doing the opposite speed her return to him? Unable to decide, he watched her clamber into the cab. Within seconds, the dust from the horse's hooves disappeared around a corner.

He blinked in shock. The entire exchange had occurred so quickly he wondered if he'd dreamed it. Perhaps time was suspended. Perhaps he was still in bed, or the camel's ponderous chewing had sent him into a trance.

In due course, he suspected that he would understand what had just happened. But right now it made no sense. Standing alone on the path, he became aware of his own shaking head. Surely she knew his strategy; why did she think he'd deviate from it? Snatches of the conversation returned. So clumsy in retrospect. Somewhere over the horizon, the day's as-yet-unknown legacy was forming like a cloud. Precipitation and air turbulence.

As he ambled towards the gate he glanced up and watched a murmuration of starlings fold in on itself and swoop blithely upwards. Their cry was the same as the one he'd heard above the tree, but this time it was shrill and pained.

୧୭ରେ⊕୧

Max raised his collar and sank into his seat. From the back row of the Lyceum's stalls, he followed the upwards curve of the theatre's peeling proscenium arch. Scorched gas mantles hung like beehives from a crudely inserted horizontal beam beneath its apex. Soft phosphorescence from their lime-drenched wicks merely illuminated the auditorium's decay. Once Franklin's flagship theatre, the Lyceum had become his shabbiest temple. From a beacon of modernity to an antiquated fleapit in two decades. Not that the man knew or cared. Max scanned the backs of the heads in front of him. Oiled partings, elaborate brooches, opera hats. The building's owner was sitting somewhere among them, waiting for Wilma.

Max squinted at the stage. It beggared belief that in a matter of minutes one of Europe's finest violin players would perform just a few feet above an underground passage that linked the theatre to a brothel behind. Burleigh Street girls were notorious. After a night on stage and still in costume, they'd crawl across to sing for clients in private, fuck them, then charge them the earth. If they could pocket a watch chain or gold cufflinks along the way, then all the better. One night; numerous ways to swell Franklin's coffers. This was no place for Wilma. Max wondered whether rapture and rot had ever co-existed so closely.

Wilma had flowered in his mind in the two days since the zoo. She was the reason he'd sneaked in. Strangely, after what happened with Delilah, it felt even more like his duty to record her. Delilah had called him obsessed. Perhaps he was, but he hadn't lied: his jewels were his priority, and Wilma topped the list. He'd decided to record Wilma in the euphoria of Russia before the accident. He wouldn't be derailed. The truth had cost him his sweetheart, temporarily at least. Why not salvage something from the wreck, however tricky it may prove? Dear Delilah. The slightest thought of that afternoon devastated him. He felt rotten about his choice of words. Given the chance to explain, she'd understand. Could he have found time to record her and release her ditties? Of course he could have. Should he have? No. His conscience was as clear as his quest. But it didn't stop him from missing her, from feeling utterly floored by apparently meaningless triggers; a passing scent or an overheard phrase. Twice in two days he'd visited her house in Dalston to apologise and to clarify. She wasn't there. Perhaps she'd moved; he knew she'd been talking about it. He'd left a note at the Paragon but in the fug of the zoo he couldn't remember whether she'd already left for the Peckham Crown. So he'd left a note there too. They'd work this out. What they had was special. It sustained and reverberated. Perhaps she'd end up apologising to him. She'd called him stupid five times. This – what was it? – this *argument* was a rip in the map. Soon they'd patch it up and continue on their journey. He was sure of it.

Stagehands bearing long poles snuffed out all but one of the gas mantles, causing the lime-light to cast a single circle on the stage floor below. As the light beneath the arch dimmed, shell-shaped brackets along the stage's lip flamed yellow, the hiss of their concealed gas tubes demanding silence from the audience. A stout woman walked briskly towards the lime-light, her eyes cast down. She halted in the pool's centre. Roughly handsome beneath tightly-bound dark hair, she wore a corduroy dress from neck to ankle. Pearls hung from her ears. Looking older than her forty years, she acknowledged the applause with an unsmiling bow and raised her violin to her chin. Wilma

Wagensperg. The Viennese virtuoso. Max clasped his hands together. Three years of silence, then this, the first of eight recitals over the Christmas period. A matinée gala. He checked to make sure he wasn't being watched. The crowd was too rapt. In front of him, rows of expectant heads craned to look at the musician. She wasn't alone on stage. Flanking her at a distance, two black-clad guards kept watch. Franklin's men, positioned to prevent any unwelcome offers from reaching her. Max sank an inch lower in his chair, aware that he might be the reason for their stationing. But this was Wilma. This was Bach. Franklin's big draw. And his next jewel.

A crunching clang filled the auditorium. Brutal and discordant, it suggested that Wilma had dropped her bow on the strings. But it was a ploy, Bach's glorious musical fraud on the listener. The eruption dissipated and was followed by the clearest playing Max had ever heard. It was urgent and confounding, like aural mathematics, but it was also as free as air and as pure as that Russian vodka. If this didn't soothe him, nothing would.

She gently wrestled with her violin but nurtured it too, as though it was a petulant child. Max marvelled that she could wrangle such phrasing and expression from so basic an instrument: cat gut stretched over maple. Her fingering was sublime, a legacy of lessons with Joseph Joachim in Berlin. The beauty of her playing contrasted with the flayed surroundings.

Max adored Bach's violin sonatas. He could never pinpoint to where they transported him, but it was always somewhere miles from wherever he was. Somewhere brighter, higher, closer to the truth. He pictured Franklin's smug face up at the front, gently nodding at his own genius in luring her to Covent Garden. Scanning the heads in front of him, Max wondered once again which belonged to the old impresario. It was a sea of bejewelled buns and oiled hair. Wilma was a virtual recluse in Vienna; she'd never responded to Max's letters. And yet that man had coaxed her. The Lyceum was packed, its ticket prices larcenous. Both Franklin and Wilma would make fortunes from this. Max imagined him grinning spiritlessly at the hoopla he'd caused as he totted up the cash.

He would do it. He'd convince her to record, by hook or by crook. Sitting there as she played, what had once seemed foolhardy and dangerous now seemed attainable. She was in London and he had nothing to lose. With six jewels down, why should he not try? He'd have to get round her security and ensure her safety. That was paramount, for everyone's sake. After the show he'd go to see Rusty and they'd devise a plan. A firm course of action would aid his recovery. Max shifted on his seat. Done properly, there was no reason why Franklin should hear about it. They'd do things differently this time. Total secrecy. And he had the Chaveley cash. His thoughts crystallised as Wilma played, ideas tumbling over and over in his mind.

A second sonata followed, then a third, each eclipsing the others in its beauty. A harpsichordist joined her. Max timed the Sonata in F minor, carefully counting the seconds. He knew it to be Wilma's favourite. Two minutes and twenty. Perfect. Applause erupted through the Lyceum when she'd finished. Wilma nodded and raised her bow to silence the audience. She moved on to a partita, the one in D minor. As she played, Max clipped open his pocket watch and tilted it to the light. Time was getting tight; he knew this to be the last piece before the interval, and he had to leave before the house lights were raised. He couldn't risk being seen. It would raise Franklin's suspicion, and he could only imagine the force with which the man would react.

Max stood, gently folding the seat behind him to prevent

it from springing shut. The height gave him a better view of the heads in front of him. They ranged towards the stage like a silent army. As he turned to leave he saw the unmistakable silhouette of Franklin's head in the front row. Hair oiled back, slowly nodding. As he'd thought. The philistine was revelling in the glory. He was flanked by two women, who seemed equally taken with the playing.

Max crept from the auditorium. It was only when he was outside on the cobbles, about to hail a hansom to Rusty's house, that a strange notion occurred. The lady to Franklin's right had her hair clasped in a large jewelled barrette. It was just like one that Mama owned.

⑥⑦⑨⑥⑦⑨

Max was surprised to find Rusty sitting at his kitchen table. He assumed he'd still be in bed. The arm of a shirt had been hacked off at the shoulder, revealing his bare flesh. The scarlet marbling had started to scab, like stew left in the cold overnight. Coffee on the stove failed to over-ride the whiff of collodion in the air. The smell was horribly familiar. But more noticeable still was Rusty's face. He looked like a changed man, a stranger.

'How's the patient?' Max placed a bundle of paper-wrapped crocuses on the Chaveley dresser and walked to the table. 'Mary not here?'

Sometimes, growing up, it had been perfectly possible to pierce Rusty's moods with silly face or word. Within seconds, the faintest smile would penetrate the hardness and any issue would be forgotten. Max knew immediately this was not one of those occasions. He followed Rusty's eyeline, trying to work out what he was focusing on. It was nothing; an empty spot in the middle of the table.

'You'll never guess where I've just been.' In the silence, Max pulled up a chair – busying himself as he placed it – and sat at the table. 'Wilma Wagensperg. At the Lyceum. Rusty, we have to do this. It'll be incredible. He was there. But we can do this. I know we can.'

Rusty didn't move.

'And guess who I saw sitting next to Franklin. Honestly... Rus?' Max frowned. His cousin remained as still as a statue.

'You cunt.'

'I'm sorry?' Max craned in to look at his cousin. As he did so, Rusty turned to meet his gaze. His eyes were like a dead man's.

'Nah.'

'What?'

Rusty shook his head. '*Nah.*'

'I don't understand.'

'I've just been to the Post Office, Max.' His voice was slow, scarred. 'Settled my future.'

'What do you mean?'

Rusty clenched his jaw. As on the train in Russia, it was as though his external pain had found a new home within. But this pain wouldn't heal. It was embedded, unmoveable. 'I've just written a letter to our friend Mr Hague. Remember him?'

Max did. The fair in Victoria Park. The wiry man with the phonographs. Peckham. He frowned.

'He's been after me for months. And now I've said yes.'

'To what?'

'Taken him up on his offer.'

'I'm sorry. I don't follow.'

'I've accepted a job at The International Phonograph Company.'

Max paused. 'Phonographs?'

'That's right. Head of development for Mr Hague.'

He felt his heart thump in his ribcage. 'Head of… You can't.'

A look approaching glee briefly danced across Rusty's face. 'I can and I have. Your loyal assistant is now your competitor. Just fancy that. Deep pockets, has Mr Hague.'

Max straightened on the chair. '*Phonographs?*'

'Yes. With a brief to do whatever you do, but better.'

'No.'

Rusty screwed up his face as though Max's reaction was incomprehensible. 'You betray me for £700. Then you maim me. Then you tell me I can't?'

Max shook his head. This was a ruse.

'You're done for, Max.' Rusty nodded, his voice gaining momentum. 'You don't know what I'm capable of. You don't know what I've done. He's a wealthy man is Hague. And you've pushed me to him.'

'Hague?' Rusty was prone to making rash decisions. He'd calm down. Max watched as a new determination crossed his cousin's face. He was utterly resolute.

'You never cared about me. Not now, not growing up, never.'

This again. 'This is nonsense. Rusty, please.'

'Nonsense?'

'Look. If this is about the money… We don't have to invest it all in the business.'

Max rocked backwards as Rusty's good fist crashed on the table. He half stood, legs bent, teeth exposed. 'This isn't about the money.'

He'd never seen his cousin's jaw grind with such bitterness. 'I'm sorry, Rusty. Sorry.' His voice weakened. 'But it's us against the world, remember?'

'*Us?*' Still half standing, Rusty wiped a glob of white sludge from the corner of his lip. 'It's never been *us*, Max. It's been you and your little orphan sidekick. Trotting behind you like a dutiful mutt.'

'*No.*'

'Everything you've ever done has been for you, Max. Not me. You. Not any more. I'll be signing up artists within days. My own *jewels.*' He threw out the last word with sarcastic relish.

'Signing?'

Rusty nodded down to his arm. 'Despite this I've been a busy boy. Been making plans. I know you better than you know yourself, and I've had a lot of time to think.' His tone blackened. 'I'm taking you on at your own game. Be under no illusion, *maestro.* I will beat you.'

Max opened his mouth to speak but the ability to think rationally had deserted him.

Rusty smirked. 'The International Phonograph Company's an ambitious outfit. My resolve is stronger than yours. Your goose is cooked.'

Through the thickening lens of his tears, Max watched Rusty's head convulse in shallow bursts. 'Rusty. Please. Don't do this.'

Standing fully, Rusty raised his good arm and pointed it at the door. As he inhaled, his whole body swelled.

'Can't we...' Max wiped his eyes on his cuff.

With the brutality of a lightning fork, Rusty exploded. '*Get out of my house.*'

# 16

The drawing room was eerily quiet. Max placed Mama's sherry on the arm of her chair, sat on the sofa and watched the fire dance in the hearth. He'd told her about Rusty. It was two days ago but this was the first time he felt able to cut through the confusion and speak to anyone.

Rusty had gone. Everything was different. He'd scarcely let himself believe it, every minute he'd expected a knock on the door or a tap on the shoulder from a laughing Rusty. A shadow box. A hug. A drink. A pledge of allegiance. A plan for dominance tomorrow. But no knock or tap came. Yesterday afternoon in the studio had proven unbearable. Stale baccy smoke infused every corner and every inch of material in the room, its sweetness gone but its presence a constant reminder of its progenitor. Max found himself breathing ever-deeper through his nose as the afternoon passed, desperate for a suggestion of life in the odour, desperate for fresh, honeyed smoke.

'That boy,' Mama whispered.

'He said I'd never cared about him. Now or growing up.'

'Don't listen to him. Don't. You loved him and looked after him. We all did.'

He drained his glass and listened to the fire pop. Life since Russia had been bleak. One week and two terrible arguments. Where was the respite? He watched Mama. She seemed equally confused. She'd understood his decision to sell Chaveley; he wasn't sure how fond she'd ever really been of the house. But Rusty. The betrayal was on her too.

He caressed the nub of his finger. Why did life deal in subtraction? Things only seemed to happen as a result of loss. He'd disposed of the house. The bell jar had disposed of its contents. Now both Delilah and Rusty had disposed of him. Where was the growth? The rebirth? How did good things flourish? Max put his empty sherry glass on the rug at his feet. He needed a proper drink.

'He's always been unpredictable.' Mama tutted softly.

'This time he means it.'

'Then let him run off. Let him try to take you on. You'll get the better of him. Always have done.'

He nodded. Just sometimes she said precisely what was required. An image flashed into his mind, lucid and colourful. The bear and the monkey. Two automatons with different mechanisms, gifted by Papa at Chaveley. It was as though he was holding them in his hands, the green of Chaveley's throbbing lawn behind them. He remembered the smell of dried glue on felt, the bone-like protrusions of the motors within as they played. The monkey jerkily drew on its cigarette as chalk dust puffed from bellows within. The bear turned its head and swigged from the bottle, its Fez hanging jauntily. Two machines. Different mechanisms. It ended in sabotage.

Mama looked mournful, as though she'd failed at some task. This wasn't her fault. Max picked up his glass and stood.

'Here's an odd thing.' He walked to the drinks table and filled his glass, his back to her. 'You weren't – I'm aware that this may sound strange – but you weren't at the Lyceum two afternoons ago were you? Silly, but I thought I glimpsed you at the Wilma Wagensperg recital.'

She said nothing.

'At the front. Wearing your barrette.'

A whispered answer. 'I was.'

He turned. She was fidgeting with her glass. 'Oh. How so? More sherry?'

'I was a guest. No thank you.'

'A guest?' He returned to the sofa and lowered himself.

'Yes. Of Barna… Of Mr Franklin.'

Max blinked as two worlds collided. 'I see.'

'And you?' She seemed taken aback that he was there.

'I just popped in. On my way to the studio. I was passing. Bach.' He stopped there.

She gave him the look. 'He's a companion, Max. Nothing more. You know that. He invited me along.' She paused. 'I thought her playing was sublime.'

'Quite.' He bit his lip and watched as, using her stick to bear her weight, she stood and walked across the drawing room towards him. She reached across and planted a kiss on his cheek.

'I'm going for a walk.'

He did not know if it was a kiss of apology, encouragement, acceptance, forgiveness or something else entirely. As she reached the door, she turned.

'Watch Rusty, Max. He has a dark soul.'

CRODCRO

Max always felt safe at the corner table in The Nell Gwynne. The tap room was tucked down a discreet alley off the Strand, meaning that its Tudor windows were shielded from prying eyes. It was equally hard to see people inside, so dark were its nooks. No one of note ever came here anyway, just drunks and harpies. It reeked of fried haddock, hawked on thigh trays by leather-aproned children. But the Nell was warm. In the gloom, a haven. He felt less safe, however, in whisky. The first dram or two were fine. More than fine, they were a treat. But once as a young man he'd done a measure from every bottle along the top shelf at Simpson's. He'd woken up in Bloomsbury Square twenty hours later, his mouth like a peat bog. He eyed the bottle of Talisker on the table in front of him. Sometimes oblivion had its attractions.

He picked up the pamphlet next to the bottle. A sheet of cheap paper folded in two. *Engineering News*. He poured himself a generous second measure and scanned its articles. While its front page and much of its second concerned themselves with a drilling scandal regarding Underground contractors – cheap machinery, broken rotor blades, dead workers – a quarter of the third page was dedicated to matters closer to home: Rusty's departure. It was official. Max winced as he reread the headline. *Blow for London Gramophone Corporation as engineer jumps ship*. The tangibility of the printed word hurt; he could no longer dismiss it as a nightmare. The writer had even sourced a photograph to accompany the piece. It showed Max and Rusty at Wilton's Music Hall the previous year. While Rusty was grinning and saluting, Max had his eyes to the ground, the loser.

Steeling himself, he read it for a third time. *The London Gramophone Corporation's plans to dominate the talking machine market were dealt a blow last week when long-standing sound engineer Ronald 'Rusty' Cadenza defected to ambitious competitor The International Phonograph Company, which is gaining a foothold in the UK market with its rival model of machine.*

'Foothold,' Max muttered.

*Details are unclear, but Mr R Cadenza is understood to have made his first signing to The International Phonograph Company. Maximilian Cadenza, founder of The London Gramophone Corporation and Ronald's cousin, now faces an uphill struggle. The move caps a challenging year for him. In the summer, Corporation tenor Alfredo Balducci was brutally slain in the so-called Opera Slayer case.*

He dropped the paper and drank. 'Uphill struggle.' How could Rusty? Brute, turncoat and now braggart to the press. He'd bet the photo was Rusty's, gleefully handed over.

The Talisker's heat mirrored his rising anger. How would his musicians and suppliers react? Surely his reasonable character would act as a modest counterpoint to any negativity surrounding Rusty's move? If he wasn't exactly popular, he was known to be reliable. With a vision. An image that had kept him awake last night re-entered his mind. Rusty was bashing the low keys of a grand piano, shouting. *'My resolve is stronger. Be under no illusion, maestro. I will beat you.'* The piano's hammers pounded on warped strings, their ghastly low echoes filling the air. He shook his head. At least they had Wilma. They'd capture her. In total secrecy, they'd record her and make her a star. The industry of human happiness would be theirs. Neither Rusty nor Franklin could deprive him of that.

'Hello.'

Max looked up. 'Old boy. You came.' He couldn't remember being happier to see Langley.

The lad squeezed around the corner table and sat next to him. 'Whisky?'

'Please.'

Max poured into a second glass.

'Are you alright, boss? You look terrible.'

'Thank you.' Max smiled and palmed the pamphlet across the table. He watched him read. 'Everything's nicely fucked.'

'He's actually done it. You thought it might have been a bluff.' Langley's lips moved as he read. He mouthed an extra word at the end.

Max nodded. 'Bastard's about right.'

'What's his plan?'

'Said he's going head to head with us. There'll be no quarter given.' It felt strange talking about Rusty as a distant third person. It somehow added to the threat.

'Determined, is he?'

Max mimicked an explosion. 'You could say that. Signing singers already.'

'So what happens now?'

'Dear boy. Sometimes when you're adrift on a sea of shit you simply have to paddle harder. We get the remaining Balducci pressed up and we sell the hell out of it. *And…*' Max reached into his breast pocket and swung his leather pouch between his fingers. 'Wilma.'

'Wagensperg?'

'I'm not sure how we'll get her, but we will. So long as I have blood in my veins.'

Langley sat back cautiously, as though confronted by a wounded predator he dared not alarm. He cocked his head and rearranged himself on his stool. 'You don't think that, perhaps, after everything, it might be time to…'

'To what?'

'Well, after Balducci and the accident, perhaps to…'

'Give up?'

'Pursue a less risky path.'

'Don't be so sensible, Mr Langley. We've got jewels to record. There's no reason…*he'll* find out. Utter secrecy. You and me. We can do this.' Max swallowed a mouthful of whisky. Pressings of the Russian shanties and *dodola* girls had been in the shops a week. Sales modest. They wouldn't be with Wilma. 'You glare at me like I'm a madman.'

'No. I'm just…'

'This is how I see it. Wilma's on this list, isn't she?'

Langley nodded.

'And have I ever given you any reason to assume that I won't – somehow – record everyone on it, one way or another?'

'No.'

'Good. We therefore have two options. We can sail for Vienna at some point in the future and try to convince her to record. If she ever opens the door. Or hasn't retired. Or moved to another city. Or we try to do it here while she's still in London.'

Langley nodded. 'But what about Franklin? He'll be waiting.'

'This'll be different. Trust me. We'll find a way.' He poured two generous helpings of Talisker. 'It's you and me against the world, Mr Langley.' It sounded wrong. Phoney. He regretted saying it. Even Langley stared down at the table.

'We just carry on?'

Max nodded. 'Why would we not? Forget Rusty. Music waits for no man.' He sipped, sinking into the wooziness. The tavern's dark embrace was increasingly comforting.

Langley shifted awkwardly on his stool. 'Molly told me about your chat with Delilah.'

Max clasped his eyes shut. He should have guessed the news would travel. 'Ah.'

'I'm sorry.'

'A small glitch. Another one. A slight difference of opinion.'

Langley nodded. 'She took it badly I gather.'

'Is that what…' Of course people talked. His heart sank as he imagined the verbal toasting she'd given him. A blast of solidified resentment and character assassination, wrapped in a vivid layer of cockney colour. He had no idea why, but in an effort to make light of it he stretched the corners of his mouth down in mock horror, as though they were tethered to the floor by invisible twine. But there was nothing light about it. It was ghastly. Torture. 'She's ignoring me.' Max rocked his glass on the table. He wished he could turn back the clock. He smiled weakly. 'I'm not sure she quite knows what she means to me. I need her back.'

Langley nodded. 'How are you going to do that?'

'I have no idea,' Max said, refilling their glasses. 'I'm hoping Mr Talisker will tell me.'

෴෴෴

Delilah walked slowly down the square's path, calming her breathing as she went. She'd never done anything like this before. With one step she wished her legs would speed her to the man on the bench. Yet with the next she wished she was walking in the opposite direction, back home, back to anonymity. She'd only seen him a few days ago. It felt strange, still. But he'd demanded a meeting and she was intrigued to know what he had to say.

She'd dressed demurely, matching her least fussy dress with her plainest bonnet. It was important not to give him the impression that she was in any way his. This relationship – was it even a relationship? – this *thing* that they had, had to progress on her terms, not his. As she approached the bench, she fixed her face with a carefree grin.

'Hello Rusty.'

'Hello Delilah. Please. Sit.' He gestured with his good arm.

She sat next to him and watched as he carefully adjusted his sling. The skin visible over the top was cracked like lava crust, revealing shiny red matter beneath. She looked around. The square of large houses behind Mile End Road was as quiet a meeting spot as he'd suggested. But she wasn't clear why he'd insisted on meeting here.

'How does it feel?'

'How does what feel?'

'To be a recording artist.'

'Oh. Yes. Good. It feels good.' It felt unreal, as though she'd been sucked up by a whirlwind. She'd signed the contract three days previously. Her surprise at seeing Rusty at the stage door of the Peckham Crown was nothing compared to the shock at reading the agreement he held in his hand. It was all there. A gift. Laid out and ready to sign. A two-year cylinder contract with The International Phonograph Company, with a six pounds-a-year salary plus a royalty of one shilling for every ten cylinders sold. Things like this didn't happen to her. It was like a dream. Putting her signature at the bottom felt incredible; it was just the circumstances that felt awkward. She still didn't know if Max knew. That first night she barely slept, wondering if she'd done the right thing and whether the deal would, as he'd promised, change her life. The next day she decided it would.

Everything was new, different and dizzying. That second morning Rusty had whisked her to his company's studio in Soho. She was almost unable to resist. She'd recorded *The Drunken Judge* ten times. As cylinders could only be recorded individually, it was all about volume, he'd said. The promises came thick and fast. Posters all over town, a showcase at the Trocadero, playbacks in the park. She had no reason not to believe him. It was thrillingly exciting. But she knew of Rusty's reputation. She cautioned herself to tread carefully in this new world.

'And you liked our studio in Poland Street? Soho's better than Covent Garden I reckon.' Rusty lit his pipe.

'It's a wonderful studio, yes.'

'I know. Like I said, forget all Max's talk about gramophones.' He shot a sideways palm out in front of him as though carving into the future. 'It's all about phonographs.'

She nodded.

'And I've got two active recording rigs in my place. Twice what he has.'

Unsure of what to make of this strange brag, she nodded. 'Were you happy with what we captured?' Even the language was new.

'Yeah, you sing very well, I must say. Nice tone.'

'Thank you.'

'I said you'd love it. You've made a wise choice.'

She had. The more she'd thought about it, the more she knew he was right. It felt as though her world had suddenly snapped open; light flooded where once it peeked. That morning, perhaps prematurely, she'd even allowed herself to look at new digs in Whitechapel. Two rooms. Hot running water. Foolish, she knew. And not cheap. But now possibly attainable.

'The girls can't believe it. I think they're a little jealous.'

He smiled. Perhaps, like performing on stage, the anticipation of Rusty was worse than the reality. Opportunities such as this didn't come along often.

'Of course they're jealous. Ignore them.' Rusty sucked from his pipe. 'How are the rehearsals going?'

'I'm still auditioning for The Holloway. The Camberwell too. It's looking hopeful.'

'The timing could work well. We can mention any shows you're in on our publicity posters. Get people to go and hear you in the flesh. May boost sales.'

Boost sales. It sounded good. She added the detail to the letter to her father she was composing in her head. 'That would be nice.'

'Nice? It's not a question of being nice, girl. This is all your own doing. You're the talent. Have a bit of confidence, eh?'

'Of course.' She looked at him, this curious man smoking on the bench. There was no question that he was awkward in form – his torso was broad and squat, giving him a vaguely cowed appearance. But the aggression and anger that Max had spoken of seemed daft. He was less animated than his cousin, that was true. But a turbulent envoy for all the world's victims? She couldn't see it.

'Now. The reason I called you here today.'

'Yes?'

'I need to check something.'

'What's that?'

He turned to face her. 'I need to know – *properly* know – that you're genuinely with me.'

'Of course I am. I signed the contract. Two years...'

'No, girl.' He waved his pipe. 'You and him. You had this thing. Don't worry. I understand. But I need to know you're committed to me and The International Phonograph Company.'

'Max?'

'Yes.' His face was blank but serious. She had no idea whether he was trying to convey a particular emotion or cover one up. The maze of these men's relationship was impenetrable.

'Rusty, I'm committed. This is a wonderful opportunity.' She thought back to the studio. She couldn't imagine never doing it again.

He removed the pipe from his mouth and spoke quickly, as though invisibly prodded. 'Because no one's forcing you to do this. You can walk away from this any time you want, Delilah.

Go back to being nobody. I'll rip the contract up and no one will be any the wiser.' He shrugged. 'It gets terribly cold at the Crown over winter.'

She raised a hand to stop him, surprised at his agitation. 'Listen. He's tried to get in touch. I've not responded.' She'd thought about it and she'd wanted to. But then Rusty had arrived on her doorstep, contract in hand. She clasped her gloved hands together and spoke slowly, looking Rusty in the eye. 'This is what I want.'

'Eh? Can't hear you.' He craned in.

'This. *This* is what I want.'

He smiled. 'Good girl.'

As she surveyed the square in front of her, a crow swooped down onto a pile of leaves near her feet and picked at a wren's carcass. The downwards force of the crow's beak forced the skeleton to bounce up and down on the ground like a marionette.

Rusty stretched out his legs and spread his good arm across the back of the bench. 'So. At the earliest opportunity, we'll get back in the studio. How does that suit you?'

'That would be good.'

'And in the meantime we can get those posters printed. How do you want to be billed?'

'I can't say I've really thought about it.' She wasn't sure why she felt the need to lie.

'Delilah Green: Stage *sensation*? Singing *star*?'

Dimples pierced her cheeks. 'Rusty!'

'*Heroine of Holloway*?'

'Enough. You make me sound like the next Lillie Langtry.'

'You could be.'

She shook her head and clasped her eyes shut. This was too much. 'You decide,' she laughed.

'That's my girl,' he nodded. 'You're in good hands.'

Delilah looked at the pile of fallen leaves near her feet. The crow now had the wren's carcass in its mouth. She watched as the black creature bounded away and took flight into the autumn sky, its catch firmly in its grip.

⁂

'News.' Max stood from his desk to open the small window behind him. He'd slept in the office more regularly than usual; the whiff of slumbering body hung heavily. The street outside and the market behind it were unnaturally quiet. Even Covent Garden rested on a Sunday. 'I've found a way of approaching Wilma,' he said as he sat.

Langley shifted on the chaise opposite. 'Go on.' The seat wasn't yet his. Too much lank and limb compared to its previous occupant. Too good a posture. But man and furniture would find a new equilibrium soon.

'Franklin's throwing a party for her on New Year's Eve. To say thank you at the end of her run and to welcome in the new century. Hundreds there.'

'And?'

'And we're going.'

Langley glared at him.

'We'll not be seen.' His resolve to capture her playing had hardened like shellac off a stamp.

'A party? How do you know?'

'He's invited Mama. I saw the invitation at home. Or, I should say, I *found* the invitation at home. In a drawer. I was tidying. Anyway, it's why I've been sleeping...' He nodded to the chaise. Distance was best. The family was fragile enough; he could neither endure further conversations with Mama about her friendship with Franklin nor risk his plans to record Wilma.

As well as the gramophone paraphernalia, his office was dotted with his personal effects. A flannel hung from the hook which once held the old sitar.

'What kind of party?'

'On a boat in Greenwich. Reels, the works. Big jamboree for the 1900s.'

Langley scrunched his nose. 'What do you mean 'we'll not be seen'?'

'Therein lies the genius of this little plan. It's fancy dress.'

Langley frowned. 'Fancy dress.'

'Yes. So we won't be there. We hide in plain sight.'

Langley said nothing.

'Everyone will be off-guard. Drunk. It's perfect. Meanwhile you and I must devise a bullet-proof way of recording her. We were sloppy last time. If we can convince her to record, then we must also convince her that it will be safe and she will face no danger. Clear?'

'Of course.' Langley sat back, taking a measure of things. 'And you're completely sure about this?'

'I haven't got much else going on at the moment, have I?'

Langley paused. 'No word?'

Max glanced at him and looked to the floor. 'Nothing.' She'd good as disappeared. He'd sought her out all over town and drawn blanks. Their time together now felt like a cruel joke, a trick of the mind. He reached over his desk and picked up a thick sheath of fibrous papers from beneath a hairbrush. Bach sheet music. The violin sonatas. He weighed them as a prospector would a precious metal, as though their mass denoted some future value.

A tinkling sound wafted through the window, breaking the fragile peace. It was a muted piano, distant, as though played from behind a closed door. Its high notes gently ruptured like smashed cocktail glasses. Max craned his ear to the noise. 'You hear that?'

The stiller they sat, the clearer the music became. A singing voice joined in. A woman's.

In a flash Max stood, strode to the window and looked out. Tavistock Street's cobbles were clear, the market beyond them a wasteland of pigeon-soiled trestle tables. As he cursed his overactive mind, the voice came back stronger. It had a wicked trill and the occasional dropped vowel. His stomach hardened. He knew the voice. It belonged to Delilah. It was the song about the drunken judge.

He scratched the base of his neck and scanned the street below. This was madness. She was hunting him, haunting him. He was about to turn when his palm slammed onto the cold pane. Down to his left, on a corner of deserted cobbles, was Rusty. A phonograph sat at his feet with its horn directed up to the window, its cylinder rotating. Rooted to the spot in a thick winter coat, Rusty held his left hand at shoulder height. It rippled in a jaunty wave.

Max pressed his second palm to the window and leaned in. The cylinder's sound ricocheted off the buildings. '*And he didn't feel a thing, until he woke up in Peking.*' He recoiled into Langley, who had moved and was craning behind him. Delilah. Rusty had recorded her.

Pursing his lips, he spun around Langley and walked behind his desk, away from the scene, the noise, the poisonous notion. He calmly sat on the chaise. There'd be a rational explanation for this. There had to be. Surely. Wouldn't there? He sat for a second. Then he squeezed his eyes shut as the truth dawned. There was no rational explanation. He covered his ears, hoping to parry the unpalatable realisations away. But they crashed onto him like heavy masonry. Rusty had recorded Delilah. He opened his eyes and looked to Langley for help. The lad was gazing out of the window.

'Mr Langley?' The words had no shape.

Langley turned, his face pale.

Max gazed at his desk. He had only seen Delilah at the zoo just over a week ago. She must have made this recording in the days since then. But how? The timescale was too short for Rusty to have organised everything. Unless he'd planned it in advance. He couldn't have. Max riffled through his memory, but recollections were strewn like shards in the debris of the last few weeks. Was it possible? Then he recalled something. The train in Russia. As he'd prepared to dress Rusty's wounds in Torzhok he'd told him of Delilah's desire to record. Rusty had told him not to. Then he smiled as he turned to the wall. Was that the moment? That must have been when this black malice took root. Rusty had planned this since then.

As if punishing him, Delilah's unmistakable voice continued to sail through the window. With it, another realisation descended on Max, more painful than the first. Delilah had willingly gone with Rusty. With evident joy, she had stood in front of his contraption and sung. After everything they'd had. After all that they'd shared.

Walking back to the window, he heaved it shut with such force that a crack appeared. With clawed fingers so brittle they hurt, he dug his nails into his head to contain the unravelling. Silently grimacing, he fell to his knees.

# PART FIVE

# MOVEMENTS

## December 1899

# 17

The night air over the Thames swirled thick with cordite, burning Max's throat and stinging his eyes. From the deck of SS *Cassius*, he watched schooners disgorge their coloured volcanoes; rockets, fountains and Roman candles. It was less a river, more a screeching inferno. Beyond, halos from makeshift catherine wheels on the shore blocked the view of the Greenwich Observatory high on the hill. This was a New Year's Eve like no other. The last of the nineteenth century. Max had read about fire ceremonies. For a moment, he imagined they were moored in the mist of the Hooghly or the Ganges as Diwali celebrations exploded all around. Only the biting cold brought him back to London. An indistinguishable rumble rose and subsided on the wind as the celebrations were repeated up and down the river. He waged that the eggy pong of sodium and charred saltpetre stretched all the way from Tilbury to Shiplake. And it was still only ten o'clock.

The *Cassius* was resting in just enough water to prevent her from listing in the low tide. A cat's cradle of streamers and flags stretched along the boat's length from the dark recesses of the stern in which Max and Langley skulked. Below the fluttering pageantry, half way up the boat, the ship's ballroom was filling up. Through open doors, Max watched dozens of guests arrive, all friends and associates of Franklin. Beyond a row of tables set with silver punch bowls, a stage was hung with a banner: *Farewell, Wilma! Welcome 1900!* Each entrant to the ballroom was greeted with a coo or a cheer as the ingenuity of their costume was assessed. Highwaymen, clowns, lionesses, tarts, cavemen carrying papier mâché clubs. Surveying the motley mob, Max wondered whether the costumes were strictly necessary. On the stage, a four-piece band rehearsed Scottish reels.

He yanked the brim of his top hat over his wig to wedge it, horsehair itching his neck. Pulling his mauve frockcoat tight, he bent to study his reflection in a mirrored bollard. Still unrecognisable. Under his moustache, his lips were painted cherry-red. His eyes were lost in kohl and his cheeks were slathered in white make-up, the handiwork all his. He smiled; he made a fine Hatter. The make-up, cool against his skin, felt protective, like an extra layer of defence. There was something else. After the most moribund Christmas he could remember, it was a novelty to be someone else. Even for a few hours. He'd spent those bleak days joylessly running things through his head over and over again. As far as he could conclude, two events had occurred separately: he'd upset Delilah at the zoo and Rusty had been given a mandate to sign artists. Both events were, to varying degrees, his fault. But somehow they'd catastrophically collided. Delilah's motive was clear: to record. He hadn't appreciated how much she'd wanted it, and he felt devastated. A fool. And Rusty's motive? Pure malice. By Boxing Day, Max had driven himself demented thinking about it. He'd sought dark solace in a den off Limehouse's Ratcliffe Highway, somewhere he'd seen in a previous life, somewhere he'd visited once before. It was miles from his usual haunts so anonymity was guaranteed. Like wearing a mauve jacket and horsehair wig, it was a blissful form of escape. Against this heap of disappointment, securing Wilma had started to feel like an obsession.

A wooden board dug into his arm. He turned and looked Langley up and down. 'Still uncomfortable?'

'Don't. I'm not sure how I'll walk.' The large red heart on the sandwich board hanging from Langley's shoulders caught the light. His orange face was topped by a red skullcap. He looked as ridiculous as he did unidentifiable.

'I suppose you'll have to shuffle the deck.' Max smirked at the pun. Attempts at humour had been thin on the ground recently. It elicited no response. He nudged Langley. 'Shuffle the deck...? Ace of Hearts?'

Ignoring him, Langley nodded to the ballroom. 'Let's hold off for a while.' He was right. The room was not yet full enough for them to become absorbed in the melee.

Queen Elizabeth, her sceptre fashioned from a pig's bladder atop a bamboo stick, strode into the ballroom. She was followed by a man in a deerstalker and a tweed Inverness overcoat. He sucked on a large S-shaped pipe.

'Holmes. Very modern.' A detective at a Franklin party. There's irony. Max wondered how many real peelers and judges were in the ballroom, drinking champagne funded by the crimes they were paid to halt. He scanned the room for either Wilma or her host; one to be wooed, the other avoided. He'd not asked her, but Mama might be in there too. Doubtful. She hadn't mentioned it over Christmas and it wasn't really her kind of party. Too rowdy and brash, not her sort of people. But it remained a possibility. If he saw her, he'd avoid her too.

Mirth levels rose as tenders dropped off more guests, the

incumbents whooping at each new guise. As Max watched the people arrive, he realised he was wrong. There was, in fact, no novelty here at all. Only cowardice. We're on the cusp of a new century, he thought, a new world full of unimaginable opportunities, and yet we're digging inwards, pretending to be other people. This party was nothing more than a final swerve of reality, a final look away before this new world presented itself and challenged people to shape it as they liked. In temporarily erasing who they were, guests were granting themselves permission not to think about it until the morning. It was a charter for detachment.

Concern nibbled at his stomach. It was almost eleven and, as far as he could tell, there was no sign of Wilma. He was sure that a wave of fuss and her stature would give her away. Perhaps her stage fright extended to parties.

Fireworks tore into the smoke above. Invisible from the boat's stern, the thickening crowds on the shore had started to sing and chant expectantly, the rowdiest choir Max had ever heard. They stood and watched, rubbing their arms against the cold. Eventually, as rocket after rocket and fountain after fountain marked time's passing, Max felt Langley's nudge. 'Boss.' He nodded at the ballroom.

A stout woman had entered followed by two minders. She was standing awkwardly by the stage, circled by a group of guests. A ripple of applause spread through the ballroom. It was unmistakably Wilma; she wore a fitted doublet and trousers, rounded above the knee like a gourd. From her ears hung the same pearl earrings she'd worn at the recital. She nodded coldly, reluctantly accepting the praise. Max licked his lips. This would be unconventional but it might just work. 'Come on.'

As he stepped from the shadows he felt Langley's hand on his shoulder. 'Tread carefully. Please.'

'Yes, yes. Follow me.'

He led Langley across the deck to the ballroom, its clock now nearing half past eleven. Entering the room felt simultaneously dangerous and a relief. Uninvited but unrecognisable, they were the room's invisible outlaws. Max handed Langley a glass of punch from the table and led him into the crowd of jesters and harlequins, princesses and thieves. Firework fumes and brandy vapour danced among the fiddles. It was perfect. Everyone was too absorbed in the bonhomie for trouble, the room too packed for individuals to stand out. He toasted Langley and swayed to the music.

An A major chord from the stage brought a cheer. A dastardly ascending fiddle followed. Max knew this reel. It was The Mason's Apron. Under instruction from the band leader on stage, the crowd created a circle in the room's centre and individuals coupled up. In this moment of chaos, Max saw a window of disruption. He whispered to Langley to keep watch and darted towards the stage, to where Wilma was standing. With a studied nonchalance, he placed himself in front of her, ignoring her minders as any tipsy guest would.

He put his arm around her back. 'You won't know the Gay Gordons, Miss Wagensperg. But may I have the pleasure of teaching you?' Before she could answer he guided her into the circle of dancers. 'It's a silly reel but you'll get used to it.'

The dance started immediately. Placing himself at her side so they faced the same direction, he reached his arm over her shoulder. 'Give me your hand.' Too bewildered to refuse, she raised her palm into his. He held her other hand in front of them. 'Just do what I do.' He guided her forward for four steps before pivoting her and taking her backwards for the same count. His mouth dried. The precious cargo was in his hands.

He leaned into her, smelling a trace of rosemary on her neck.

'Wilma. Promise me you'll ignore everything you've heard?'

She looked at him and frowned. 'Heard? Who are you?' Her voice was clipped and humourless.

He pivoted her again and walked forwards. 'My name is Maximilian Cadenza and I work at The London Gramophone Corporation.'

She peeked around her. 'Mr Cadenza. You can't.' He felt her grip loosen as she tried to leave his hold. With a pang of shame, he gently tightened his.

'Can't, Miss Wagensperg?'

'You can't be here. Mr Franklin has warned me not to talk to you.'

He pulled her into an awkward polka around the floor, her clogs clipping his boots as they turned. Gathering her closely enough into him that he felt the slats of her shorts nuzzle into his frockcoat, he spoke slowly and directly. 'Ignore him and listen to me. Your playing is sublime. Fearless. Please allow me to take you from his grubby world and deposit you in heaven. Forget a few shows in London. I could turn you into the global sensation you deserve to be. Just let me record you.' As they returned to the dance's first move – four steps forward – he looked at her. Although it had failed to spread to the rest of her face, he saw a gleam in her eyes. It suggested that he'd touched on a buried ambition. It certainly suggested that no one had spoken to her in this way before.

'Please, Mr Cadenza. I really must insist.' She spoke formally, eyes still darting, almost as though she hoped someone would overhear her rejection. 'I admire the gramophone and its possibilities. But I can not. I really must…'

He gathered her in a ballroom hold again. 'Play once for my machine and the world will hear you forever. Think about it. No more stages.' He held her close. '*No more stage fright.*'

She swallowed. 'It's dangerous. I know what happened.'

'I can guarantee your safety.'

'How?

'I have a copper-bottomed plan. I promise you. I will share it with you should you accept. Where are you staying?'

'The Langham.'

He craned in so close that her pearl earring bounced off his lips. 'I will also make you rich beyond the dreams of avarice. Every shop from New York to New Zealand will sell your discs.' As he stopped speaking he loosened his hold on her hands. To his delight her palms remained pressed into his.

She looked up at him.

'I will pay you one hundred pounds for four recordings. That's almost 2,500 Krone. Plus a ten per cent royalty for every disc sold.'

She turned under his arm and shook her head.

He'd expected a hard bargain. Franklin would have paid her handsomely to coax her to London. His offer would have to be equally generous. 'Very well. One hundred and fifty pounds and ten per cent.' That was close to 4,000 Krone. It would be almost the last of the Chaveley money.

Growing familiar with the moves, she took four paces at his side and shook her head again. 'Two hundred. Twenty percent.'

That would be all the money gone. The coffers would be empty. But as he ran the numbers in his head, a glorious Bach sonata smothered The Mason's Apron. This was Wilma. The sonata soared. They'd recoup the outlay through sales. 'Two hundred. Twenty percent. As you wish,' he whispered.

She nodded. Her face was still but he could sense the machinations beneath the surface. A seed had been planted. That was enough for tonight.

'Please consider that my final offer, Miss Wagensperg. But let me know your answer soon, won't you?' He slipped a square of paper into the folds of her shorts. The studio address. 'Heaven awaits.' He gave her hands the faintest of squeezes and released them mid-dance. She glared at him. A shallow inhale. With a small bow he stepped away from her, walking to the side of the ballroom as the music continued. He felt her eyes on his back. Without turning, he shouldered his way out of sight. He found Langley in the crowd, knocked on his sandwich board, and led him out onto the deck's expectant December air.

⚬⚭⚬⚭⚬⚭⚬

'That could have gone a lot worse.' Max leaned over the bow's balustrade and waited for a tender to take them ashore. Message relayed, he wanted to leave the Cassius as soon as possible. If they left now they'd be in a Greenwich tavern shortly after midnight.

'What did she say?'

'Not much. But she didn't say no. I expect an answer soon.' He had no idea of the outcome. But something about her reaction emboldened him.

The clamour of celebration rumbled from the banks, growing louder with every passing minute. The endless flotilla of barges up the Thames sent rolling swells across the river. Above the water, in a fragile concession to peace, firework smoke had settled into a layer of man-made fog.

Yet again, Max wondered what Delilah was up to. He couldn't help it on this landmark eve, this momentous clank of time's infinite clock, this night like no other. He thought back to a year ago. He and Rusty had celebrated the new year at the Troc with Mary and a small group of component suppliers. Money was tight but he and Rusty were tighter. Fifty hours after the celebrations started, the pair of them woke up on the office sofa, fully-clothed and entwined. How different things were now. Was it possible to hate someone and miss them at the same time? He scanned the water, seeing no sign of the tender. They should have paid a boatman in advance. But leaving had seemed a minor detail earlier. An unbearable itch spread across his head. Twisting his wig back and forth only aggravated it. So he tugged his top hat and wig off, stuffing them under his arm.

He turned as a cheer went up in the ballroom behind them. The bandleader announced that it was two minutes to midnight. A few people started to spill outside, ready to watch a new salvo of rockets light up the foggy sky.

'Looks like we'll be seeing in the new century from here.'

Langley put out his hand and whispered, 'Happy new year, boss.'

Max shook it. The man was proving to be a rock. 'And you.'

On the bank, dozens of fires roared into life. Max followed the lights all the way up the hill to where he knew the Observatory stood. Location of the prime meridian. Zero longitude. Where things started. It felt strangely apt celebrating a new epoch in the shadow of the building that dictated the world's charts, maps and time. In that instant it felt not just like the cusp of a new century but the beginnings of a complete rebirth, simultaneously thrilling and daunting. He wished they'd brought a bottle of Moët or a hipflask. Drink was a must but he didn't want to risk going back to the ballroom.

'Max? Is that you?'

He turned. Although surprised, the voice sounded jauntier than usual. Mama was shuffling across the deck towards him. He leaned back into the balustrade and instinctively replaced his wig. He barely recognised her. She wore a yellow Regency era dress with frilled bows on the sleeves; it was quite the most colourful thing he'd seen on her in months. The top of her walking stick was tied with matching ribbon. She was accompanied by a man dressed as Pierrot the Clown, his arm hovering behind the small of her back.

She approached. 'It *is* you. Hello, Mr Langley. What on earth are you two doing here?'

'Mama.' The word caught in Max's mouth. He always knew there was a danger she'd be here but he never thought she'd actually come. Equally surprising was her demeanour; she was cheerful, like the Mama of old. Her voice was leavened by champagne.

Raising her stick to the clown, she said carefully, 'You know Mr Franklin, of course.'

Max froze. He hadn't realised. Beneath a black beret, Franklin's face was blotted white apart from a dark tear curling under his left eye. Two over-sized pom-poms weighed down his smock, slightly cowing his demeanour. Max looked him up and down. It was him. But shorn of his sharp suits and entourage, he seemed different. Lessened. It didn't stop Max's mind from racing. This was bad.

Franklin opened his palms as he approached. 'Maximilian. Mr Langley. Welcome.' He smiled, his tone avuncular.

Max sensed Langley's shock next to him. If the water was any calmer, he would have grabbed his colleague, leapt overboard and swum to the bank.

'Heard your Tatars. Quite the dirge. I do hope you're enjoying the party. Got a drink?'

Max didn't move. Franklin's phony charm would have been hard enough to deal with on a normal day. But the strangeness of the situation made it unbearable. Max silently cursed the pair of them; Mama for exposing him and Franklin for putting on his act. His cheeks glowed warm; he was even more furious with himself for possibly blowing Wilma's cover.

Franklin turned to Mama and whispered in her ear. She nodded with a smile, turned around and walked back to the ballroom. Max bristled. When Mama was some distance away, Franklin stepped forwards and grimaced, his teeth dark against his alabaster face. 'You're testing me, boys.'

Max shrank back, unsure of what to say. Then he noticed Franklin's make-up. At close quarters, it looked hastily applied. Blotches of shrivelled skin were visible through the sponge work. It was a small thing but it was grotesque. Bizarre. And he found that it altered his perception. The ruthless brute faded. Franklin was momentarily an emperor dethroned; an ageing man in an ill-fitting clown costume. Even his rose cologne smelt watery. In the distance Mama's yellow dress caught Max's eye. A second thought occurred. Her presence on the boat, while surprising, acted as a brake on Franklin's true character. So long as she was here, he'd have to be the man that she knew: the benevolent entrepreneur; the patron of the arts; the builder of careers. The cold man that Max knew him to be would have to remain hidden. Franklin had boxed himself into a corner.

A banger exploded overhead. Max stepped towards Franklin until they stood toe-to-toe. Once again he looked him up and down. 'These things are terribly uncomfortable.' He raised a hand and ripped off his wig again. The sudden movement caused Franklin to flinch. It was the slightest twitch. But it was all Max needed to see. He'd made the man start, and it felt like a victory. 'That's better.' He felt Langley stand behind him, towering and silent.

Franklin leaned in. 'Listen carefully. If you're here to convince my artist to record, I strongly advise you not to.'

A countdown started in the ballroom. '*Twenty, nineteen...*'

Max shook his head. 'That would be impossible, Mr Franklin.'

'Why?'

He glanced back to Langley. 'We sail for New York next week.'

'*Sixteen, fifteen...*'

'New York?'

'Harlem. That's our focus now.'

'From what I gather you've already lost your ginger and your girl. If you're lying you'll lose a lot more.'

'You'll have to trust me on this, won't you?'

'*Ten, nine...*'

Max stared at the man standing inches away from him. His eyes had narrowed as if he was mulling a response. But Max saw a flash of yellow returning from the ballroom. With nothing to lose, he beckoned Franklin in. 'You know, old man, that in a matter of seconds the entire world as you know it will be over.'

'What did you say?'

Max licked his lips. 'Every single thing you've built will belong to a dead century.'

Franklin bristled.

'And in a year or two you'll join it in the ground. And as you rot, London will dance on your stinking corpse.' He glanced behind Franklin and smiled, opening his hands in welcome as Franklin himself had done two minutes earlier. 'Hello, Mama. Good timing.'

'Here we are.' A waiter walked at her side carrying a tray of champagne. Max took a glass and handed it to Franklin.

'*Three, two...*'

The ballroom erupted in gaiety as a wave of noise hit the boat from the shore. From the *Cassius*'s foredeck the first of twenty flares was released, one for each century. They scarred the smoky sky red as riotous singing floated back out over the river. *Auld Lang Syne.*

Max turned to look at Langley and his cherry-lips spread

into a smile. They both took glasses and slugged. The singing in the ballroom was growing louder and faster as *Auld Lang Syne* entered its second round.

'*Should auld acquaintance be forgot and never brought to mind*?'

Max walked to his mother and kissed her cheek. Turning to Franklin, who hadn't moved since Mama returned, he raised his glass and smiled. 'And a very happy new year to you.'

# 18

Deliveries thrilled Max. New shapes, new smells, new possibilities. He counted the dark boxes on the studio floor in the rig's shadow. Twelve, each with a lid adorned with a hinge at one end and a clasp at the other, each a gift from the week-old century, each another step into the future.

He opened one box. Inside, five squat cakes were slotted into a neat rack: new wax masterdiscs. He lifted one out and bumped his finger across its dark resistant surface. It was eight inches across, the extra inch allowing half a minute more music. He smiled at the simplicity of the equation. Space for time. Pressing the cool wax to his cheek, he imagined the prospects. But the new discs' arrival heralded more than added time; they transformed the process. Wax masters could be etched directly by a cutting stylus. The cakes were lighter, more responsive, easier to create a negative from. Farewell mongrel technology: no more zinc masters, swaddled in oilcloth like newborns; no more coating the discs in benzene and beeswax; and no more bell jars of sulphuric acid to burn the grooves or anything else. He looked at the stack of old equipment piled in the studio's corner. Vital yesterday, obsolete today. Progress was a cruel assassin. Five months, he thought. If the waxes had arrived five months earlier then perhaps Rusty would still be here. Perhaps.

He replaced the wax cake in the box and walked to the studio's corner to fetch his coat. He was hungry, it was time for supper. As he pulled the garment on he heard faint steps outside the studio door. They were too tentative for Langley. A timid knock followed. He walked to the door and opened it. A short figure, its head swamped by a vast hood, squeezed through like a phantom. Max shut the door, his eyes following the figure into the room. Tremoring hands peeked from beneath the cloak and, rising upwards, pulled the hood back. The faintest trace of rosemary tickled the air. It was Wilma, her face as white as snow.

'We are safe? I have seven minutes. Probably six now.' Her clipped words were so quiet they barely existed.

'Of course.' Max walked across the studio and pulled the curtains across its high windows. His heart thumped as he offered to take her cloak. This could only mean one thing.

She shook her head. 'I must be quick.' Her hair was scraped up into a bun, lending her a severe air.

'Where are your chaperones?'

'Dispersed. Temporarily. They go to smoke or drink for twenty minutes at this time every day on the assumption I am dozing in my room.' She spoke at pace. 'You see, for the last fifteen days I have slept every afternoon. But not today. I snuck out.'

How very disciplined, Max thought. Even her deceit is timetabled.

Wilma looked from the rig to the tattered tent billowing from the studio's ceiling. Her hands still quivering, she carefully circled the entire machine, her eyes darting between spindle and crank, between turning table and recording horn. She swallowed. 'Two hundred pounds for four recordings and twenty per cent, you said.'

'That's my offer.'

Stopping in front of Max, she pressed her fingers together and sliced the air, half praying, half imploring. 'First tell me your plan. I need to know I'm safe. You have to understand.'

Taking the stool from the piano platform, he placed it for Wilma to sit. As she lowered herself, she huddled in her cloak.

'It's quite simple. As far as the world knows, Mr Langley and I are sailing for New York within days.' He nodded to the old gear in the corner. It wasn't totally useless. 'I'm sending decoy equipment to Southampton. Packed, stacked and marked for Manhattan. I've already told Franklin we're going.'

'And he believes you?'

'I believe so, yes. Then we disappear from view. We return here and record quickly in the dead of night. You leave London as soon as we've finished. Then we press up the discs and sell them.' He was still considering shipping the old equipment all the way to the States just to be sure. He didn't need it back.

'Mr Franklin.' She shivered slightly as she said his name.

'What of him?'

'He made me write a letter. To promise I will not record.'

'A letter?' He wondered what good ink on paper would do. It certainly wouldn't stop him.

'He made me swear.' As soon as she said it, she turned her head to the rig, fixing her gaze on the recording horn. She shot Max a look before casting her eyes to the ground. 'What you said about the stage fright. About records allowing me to perform less,' she whispered. 'It is something I want very much.'

She was his, if he could convince her. Max bent and lifted one of the new boxes. Opening it, he picked out a brown wax cake and handed it to her. 'Two and a half minutes.'

She turned the wax in her hands, unsure what to make of it.

'Two and a half minutes of uninterrupted music, Wilma. That's unheard of. And you'll be the first.'

Her frown suggested she failed to see the connection between the object in her hands and the prospect of breaking new ground. He knelt next to her so he was looking up into her eyes.

'That violin sonata in F minor. The one with the harpsichord. The one you love.'

She nodded. 'Vivace.'

'Yes. Bach wrote it two minutes and twenty seconds long.'

'That is correct.' A faint smile played across her face as she thought of it.

'Until *this* wax was invented it was impossible to record that piece in its entirety. Two minutes was all we had. Now we can. You can.'

She held his gaze.

'Four recordings, Wilma. We could be done in half an hour but they'll last forever. An indelible mark. Think of the legacy. Think of the freedom.' His own voice disappeared to almost nothing. 'Think of the *magic*.'

Her eyes flickered between Max, the rig and the disc in her hand. She bounced her finger across the wax's soft surface. 'Who?'

'Who what?'

'Who will know about this?'

'Myself, Mr Langley and our accompanist Mr Wilson.' He'd been reluctant to use the man again. But he knew the system and played well. And despite his oily character he could keep a secret.

'No one else?'

'Not a soul. Until we release the discs.' His eyes widened. 'Then the whole world will know.'

She handed him the wax, stood and walked around the rig once more, like a monk examining an altar. A full circle in silence, the hooves on the cobbles outside the only noise. She returned to him and nodded, her pearl-drop earrings swaying. 'All right.'

He clenched his eyes shut. This was momentous. After everything, a new beginning. He rested his hands on her shoulders. 'Oh Wilma. That is wonderful.' Tonight he'd celebrate. Somewhere special. Somewhere he could think. He knew precisely where he'd go. 'You won't regret this. Now, before you go, let's talk about timings.'

CONGLOMERATE

Never had he relished a guilty thrill more. The dark promise that greeted him as he pulled aside the heavy brocade curtain was enthralling; its allure magnified tenfold by the knowledge that he shouldn't be there in the first place.

The stench greeted him next. Sweat, rum and a syrupy smoke, like spiced marzipan. As Max walked down the dim hut's central corridor towards the soft sound, the chaos of the Limehouse docks outside receded. But evidence of voyage was everywhere. Chinese lanterns hung haphazardly overhead. The matting beneath his feet softly crunched as its dried West Indian palms slipped their weave. The lair was laid out like an army dormitory; on either side of the hut dozens of low bunks were set end to end, each with a squat candle on its stead. On every mattress, a coiled figure. Sailors, stevedores and longshoremen; skins of every hue. The occupants moved slowly, their actions not their own; all were simultaneously present and absent. Some fiddled with the ephemera of escape resting on platforms next to the beds where opium lamps flickered. Others lay on their sides, rags propping up their heads as they inhaled the poison from their long pipes. Others still had long been spirited away; lying on their backs in a lush aftermath, one knee up, one leg dangling, crook of elbow over face. Gone. As Max stepped down the corridor he saw half-naked men, thrill-seekers and lowlifes. He was now one of them.

His first visit to the opium den on the night he learned of Delilah's recording had been accompanied by nerves and little else. It had been rash. But he craved proximity to her, and being next to the Chinese restaurant – the scene of his fondest hour – allowed him to almost touch the memories. On his second visit on Boxing Day, his most recent, an element of excitement had crept in. And if it didn't quite feel familiar on this third visit, there was at least an absence of justification. This was now something he did. This was his treat. He deserved it. And particularly after a night like tonight. He'd secured Wilma. There was so much to absorb, so much to think about. The hour was late but the lure was irresistible.

He reached the end of the dormitory and raised his arm to find the edge of a second curtain. Pulling it aside, he stepped into the very definition of peace. The square space at the hut's end was lit by a pair of candelabras and dotted with battered wingback chairs. Occupying the centre of the space, a single table was crammed with bottles – cane liquor, hooch and whisky – and bowls of walnuts and dried jackfruit. In the shadows behind the table, his back to the wall, an Indian boy heaved the bellows of a harmonium back and forth, his forehead blackened with charcoal. The female singer sitting next to him wore a dark sari embellished with gold, a flamboyant ring hanging from her nose. Occasionally she sucked from a delicate pipe. Max had asked the proprietor about them last time; travelling musicians and stowaways often played in the hut on the promise of a free ball and an attentive audience.

It seemed to him that the true essence of London lay in this makeshift saloon's tangle of debauchery and stillness, music and life. It gave him the thrilling rush of a swimmer just out of his depth.

The wingbacks were occupied so he took a seat at the table next to the owner, who was hunched over circling palms. In front of him sat a tin cup of dark marbles ready to be heated and dropped, smelting, into the bowls of customers' pipes. The tin rattled as each new ball fell from the owner's hands. He smiled toothlessly at Max and gestured at the bowl, palms black with resin. Max shook his head, pointed to the bottles and threw a coin across the table. Just grog tonight. He'd tried opium on his first visit; a small ball. It had given him a glorious bump that both warmed and freed him. He'd liked it too much. But he'd vowed not to do any more until things were calmer. Control was important. It didn't stop him loving the place and wanting to wallow in its smooth nook, floating in the wake of its wrecked patrons and enjoying their sublime dislocation by proxy. In his mind it was no different to those European tourists who flocked to the temples of Benares. Could a Christian appreciate the splendour of a Hindu temple, even though he followed a different creed? Of course. Could a Moslem marvel at the dome of St Paul's? Naturally. He poured himself a glass of cane liquor and listened as the singer's spiralling voice wrapped around the harmonium's drone like ivy. He drank once but it burned twice: when he swallowed and when he exhaled afterwards. It was bitter but strong. He topped up his glass. He deserved this.

The days ahead would be busy. Wilma had agreed to record in two days' time, in the dead hours of Saturday morning. It gave him and Langley enough time to clean the gear and test the waxes. They also had to lay the New York decoy. Before he'd headed east he'd run through the plan with Langley. He'd grasped the finer details, his earlier reservations gone. They could do this. They could take Bach to the world and make their names in the process. But smooth running was crucial. Cold logistics held the key to this jewel.

After emptying his second glass Max was trapped in the sweet spot between tiredness and elation. Letting go like this produced a splendid brand of contentment; in a hut deep in the bowels of his city he was, for a few hours at least, untouchable.

Unprompted, the owner placed a cup of tea in front of him. Max looked up and thanked him; the shack was that kind of place. Lighting a cigarette, he watched its smoke mingle with the cup's steam. He sipped. The tea was strong, thick and sweet, a delicious counterpoint to the liquor's sourness. He thrust his head back and let the hut's murky allure thicken. He waited for the tea to cool and drained the cup. Closing his eyes, he allowed his mild inebriation to propel him into the shack's hypnotic orbit. Slowly, he drifted off.

A jolt shook the table. He woke with a start and wiped the ash worm of his long-dead cigarette from his lap. As he blinked the fug away, he became aware of a man sitting opposite him.

'This place is right up your street.'

'Rusty.' Max pulled himself upright. '*Rusty?*' The cloud of baccy smoke engulfing the table told him he was not dreaming.

Rusty looked around, nodding. 'Dank. Smelly. Weird.'

'How did you know I was here?'

'How do you think? I followed you.' Rusty poured liquor into Max's glass and raised it. 'Good health.'

Having not seem him for weeks, Rusty characteristics seemed brutally emphasised. His enmity was palpable; his swagger obvious; his hair shocking; the scar beneath his cuff gruesome. Max wondered if these facets had grown in recent weeks or whether years of daily contact had blinded him to them. As though blasted by cold air, the room's charm faded. Its darkness suddenly felt oppressive. 'You can't be here. Go.'

Rusty chuckled. 'Behave.' He beckoned to the owner for his own glass and pointed to the musicians. 'Your kind of music too. *Interesting.*'

Max tried to stand but his legs were heavy. He reached for another cigarette and glared at his cousin over the table. His presence was unconscionable. He felt his anger rise. 'When?' he spat.

'Your Delilah? You gifted her to me. On that train. Keen as mustard, she was.'

He was right. Rusty had been fishing as he'd lain there. 'You bastard.'

'Me? After Chaveley?' He raised his hand. A warped red diamond protruded from his cuff. 'After this?'

'How dare you. It was an accident.'

Rusty shook his head. 'You took something from me, Max. So I took something from you. She's great in the studio, you know. Right little gem. Or should that be jewel?'

Neither man said anything.

Rusty leaned in. 'So how many?'

'How many what?'

'How many copies of the Russians have you sold?'

'They're still being pressed.' It was a lie. They'd sold just sixty.

'And those flower girls?'

Max cast his eyes to the ground. The palm matting appeared softer then before, almost like carpet. He looked up to see Rusty's open palm hovering inches from his face over the table, his digits splayed.

'Five.'

Frowning, Max mouthed the word back to Rusty, irritated

he'd been drawn into the conversation.

'Five hundred. I've sold five hundred cylinders in as many weeks.'

'This isn't a game, Rusty.'

'Oh, that's precisely what it is. And of those sales, a fifth of them were your Delilah.' A languid smirk. 'Sorry. *My* Delilah.'

The words jabbed. Max's back slackened, lowering him into his chair. He grimaced. 'She'll see through you.'

'I doubt it. We're flying.'

Max flicked ash on the table. 'You must leave. There's nothing meaningful in the world that you could possibly say to me, nor I to you.'

Rusty shrugged.

Once again Max considered standing but stubbornness got the better of him. Despite the unwelcome surprise, this was his place. His discovery. His sanctuary. He wouldn't be bamboozled out. He filled his glass, stared over the table and decided to change tack. 'Tell me, have you heard of the Ainu people of Japan?'

'What?'

'An island people. Proud. Happy.'

Rusty lit his pipe, saying nothing.

'Every year Ainu villagers catch a baby bear. They see it as a deity in animal form. They take this bear into their village and nurture it. The children play with it. The women suckle it.'

'So?'

'Cubs grow, Rusty. They become big and strong. They scratch people. Their embrace starts to crush. Eventually cub becomes bigger than villager. Can you guess what they do?'

'Ask it to sing?'

'They lock the bear in a wooden cage and they kill it. A gruesome sacrifice. They shoot arrows into it and squeeze its neck until it snaps.' He squeezed his hands together. 'It's boiled meat is eaten by every villager.'

'What the fuck are you talking about?'.

'You see Delilah as a cub, don't you? Something you can control. No threat. And perhaps right now she isn't one. But you haven't counted on her growing. You haven't realised that one day she'll be big. Too big for you to handle. You'll lose her because she'll crush you. As will every artist you sign.'

Rusty raised his hand. '*Fuck you*, Max. Don't tell me about my artists and don't tell me how to run my business. Those days are gone.'

Max shook his head. The man had devilry in his eyes. He didn't like it. 'Why are you here?'

'I'm here to find out what my competition's up to. See if I'm missing anything.'

He smiled at the naivety. He'd reveal nothing. 'Ah, yes. Our little tête-à-tête in your kitchen. Allow me a second to recall it.' He paused, pretending to have forgotten the conversation that had obsessed him for weeks. 'You said you're going to take me on at my own game. Beat me with your resolve.'

He smiled. 'And here I am.' Rusty yanked the pipe from his mouth. 'Don't doubt me, Max. I'm going to show the world that you're not as special as you think you are.'

Child, Max thought. He peeked around. Despite his anger, a degree of foggy grace had descended on the room. Shadows danced on the walls behind the candelabras. The only measure of time's passage came from the harmonium and the singer. Max didn't stop Rusty when he refilled their glasses; it suddenly felt like too much effort. Inch by inch the bottle drained. They drank in silence, adversaries across a table.

'You feeling confident?' Rusty was sitting back in his chair, watching Max.

'Of what?'

'Carrying on. With me on your back?'

He said nothing and, with some difficulty, stood. 'Piss.' The wood yielded to his touch as he steadied himself on the table, as though it was coated with unset concrete. He pulled back his hand. The sensation wasn't unpleasant, just surprising. As if walking on sand, he made his way to the small side door that led to a yard.

Rusty hadn't moved when he returned to the table. The bottle was now empty, at least he thought it was. But the sureties of size, distance and form had been replaced by cottony approximations. A film of wintry sweat glazed his forehead despite the room's warmth. It was time to leave. He turned to the curtain that would lead him to the main exit but a lingering ache deep in his belly suddenly intensified, causing him to sit. It made him feel bilious and hungry and in need of emptying his bowels all at the same time.

'You alright?' Rusty's tongue darted to his lips.

'Of course.' The ache subsided but came back stronger moments later. Not now, Max thought, not here. Soon the hum had found intense new form. He rocked forwards in the near darkness, cradling his stomach. Nausea came in waves as though his belly was being gnawed from the inside. He looked at Rusty. He'd only felt like this way once before, but in far milder form. It was the night that he heard Delilah's cylinder. His first night in the hut.

Every time Max reached a new level of discomfort, he felt a fresh coating of shivery moisture on his head. Discomfort plateaued and disappeared before coming back, heavier and hungrier. He took deep, slow breaths. He peered at Rusty again. He knew what had happened to him but couldn't speak. The bastard had dosed him.

'You need air.' Rusty's hand sank into his sweat-soaked shoulder.

He shrugged Rusty off, but found himself being lifted from his chair and guided towards the dividing curtain. To prevent himself from falling he hooked his arm over Rusty's shoulder. They walked down the corridor of mattresses to the hut's main entrance. Each step was exploratory; Max saw knees in the air, pipes on the tables. Sounds became noises, objects became shapes. He saw pipes in the air, knees on the tables.

Max closed his eyes and let his pupils settle backwards.

⚬⊱⊰⚬⊱⊰⚬

The cool air encased Max's face like a wet rag. He opened his eyes, gave his wrist to Rusty and picked his way along the dock's cobbles, listening to the soft lapping of the Thames. Above, stars took it in turns to shine the brightest.

'This way.'

He let Rusty lead him up a lane away from the river. The black edifices of the warehouses juddered with every step. He ripped his wrist away and, needing to sit, lowered himself onto a stack of wooden crates. Stillness helped. Coming outside was a good idea.

For some minutes Max sat and listened to his breathing. As he wiped a warmer, more bearable sheen of perspiration from his head he noticed that the aching in his stomach had subsided. An anesthetised sensation that was not altogether disagreeable replaced it; it was as though a blanket had been placed over his shoulders, warming his entire body. He tried to focus on Rusty but, like everything, his face was swirling and twisting like water down a plughole.

'You…'

'What's that?' Rusty leaned in.

'You've…'

'You're fine.'

Max felt a warm palm under his armpit. He was lifted from the crates, and Rusty gestured up the lane. 'Come on. Let's bimble.'

The lane become a narrow tunnel as they walked, lights from beneath doors turning every cobble into a distinguishable monument.

'London,' Max said.

'London, indeed. Do you need anything?'

'Nothing.' His spine tingled as he felt Rusty's hand on his back.

Around a corner, a group of dockers had gathered around a sputtering kerosene lamp. A man plucked a banjo in the light's honeyed glow. As Max rested against cool bricks to watch, colours started to misbehave. He tried to blink them into compliance but couldn't. A mosaic formed in front of his eyes: the red of the dockers' shirts, the yellow of the flame, the white of the banjo, the bruised blue of the wall behind. They hung momentarily in a pattern as if in a kaleidoscope, then, with each beat of his heart, shattered into new forms. As they rearranged themselves, the shards briefly became porous circles, spinning prettily.

Max felt a hand clasp his forearm. He reached across and rubbed the soft knuckle, kneading each nub in turn. The voice suggested they kept walking. Everything pulsed: the cobbles underfoot, the buildings around them, the clear winter sky. Sounds came from nowhere and everywhere; instruments, voices, traffic, gulls. Each noise was precise and in perfect harmony with the others. They walked on.

'Things make sense, don't they?' Max hadn't wanted a reply.

But he was sure that one came.

'They will soon.'

They reached a bench outside a warehouse and sat. Max liked the way that the letters over the warehouse's door were rendered in splendid gold and green calligraphy. Clasping his hands behind his head, he gazed at the sky. Within seconds the stars were as bright as diamonds. The longer his eyes stayed fixed on one area of the sky, the more interesting things became; four stars would become six, then nine. Soon they were bouncing off each other like charged metal filings. He understood precisely why they behaved that way: they were trying to escape. It was obvious. He lit a cigarette and explained to Rusty how stars worked. His words were emphatic, his explanation detailed.

'You're so right,' Rusty said when he'd finished. 'It's a shame. They're trying to escape their natural place.'

Max said nothing, absorbed in his view.

'So how are you feeling?' Rusty stuffed his pipe. 'Enjoy your tea? I told them to make it nice and strong.'

The bench's arm yielded like velvet as Max caressed it. He turned to his cousin. 'I always preferred the bear, you know.'

'What?'

'You didn't know that, did you? I liked its fez. You thought I liked the smoking monkey. But I didn't like the monkey. It was always the bear.'

'The bear.'

'I've never told you that.'

'You haven't.' Rusty stretched his feet out. 'Now. Tell me something else.'

Max thrust his head back and his eyes followed the stars as they fizzed and exploded. 'Anything.'

'Upcoming recording activity.'

Round and round they danced. 'What of it?' He grinned as

he felt Rusty's hand softly massage his shoulder.

'Who've you got coming in?'

⚜

Brown morphed into red. Red to green, gloriously rich. He could feel his body straining to escape but he couldn't move. Wooden slats beneath him dug into his back as the weight on top of him bore down. Someone's knees on his shoulders. His head was angled awkwardly between the bench's arm and its seat, cocked unnaturally. But those colours. They were all he could see. Green morphed into brown then back to red. Occasionally everything flashed white. That was when the pain came. Over his eye. Burning pain, unlike anything he'd ever felt. Wet too. Liquid fire.

But those colours.

# 19

**D**elilah watched Rusty slide the cylinder onto the phonograph's mandrel and set the machine. There was something hypnotic about his economy of movement; every action was meaningful – the laying back of the stylus block, the angling of the horn, the tightening of butterfly screws. It was a conversation between man and machine, its mystery making it all the more mesmerising.

The metallic tang of motor grease filled the room. Nothing she saw in front of her spoke of music. Engineering, yes. Mechanics, absolutely. Watching Rusty, she may as well have been standing in a backstreet workshop, not a newly fitted out recording studio in Soho. Its high windows and fitted carpet seemed incongruous in the face of such oily graft, as though they'd been specified for a different building. She glanced at the blank cylinders stacked up next to the spare phonograph against the wall behind Rusty. They were equally bereft of music. Six inch lengths of barren pipe awaiting transformation.

Rusty oiled the spindle along which the cutting stylus travelled. As she watched his fingers stroke and pinch, she realised. The thing that would transform these cold objects into living, vibrant entities was her. Three minutes of her singing would give lifeless machinery purpose. The responsibility momentarily stole her breath. She hummed softly, warming her larynx. Reaching behind her, she felt for the piano's keyboard. Cold ivory on her fingers. Eighty-eight notes, and her voice. They'd turn science into art.

Suddenly the gulf between the end and the means seemed too wide. It wasn't enough to simply expect her voice to be captured; she wanted to understand how that transference occurred. She looked at Rusty with envy; she wanted to speak the same silent language with the machine that he spoke. It seemed brutally unfair that she couldn't.

'Rusty.'

He looked up from the machine and grunted.

'Teach me how it works.'

ɛᴄᴏᴅɛᴄᴏᴅ

With every prod to his body Max sensed the weakening of sleep's snug protection. He fought against each nudge, wrapping himself in slumber's diminishing warmth, desperate to keep the light at bay. It was too late. One by one his faculties flickered alive. Mouth dry as cotton. Head pounding. Neck aching. While his left eye claggily opened, his right would not. He raised a disorientated hand to it and pain shot through him. A fleshy patty rose from his eye socket, sticky to the touch. A voice hovered somewhere close. Rough fabric from the jacket draped over him itched his chin. Through his left eye he saw Langley's chin hovering inches above his face.

'Blimey. I thought you'd never wake up.'

Groaning, Max heaved himself into an upright position on the office chaise. Everything in the room around him felt distant:

his ears were muffled, as though waxed up; his head throbbed in time with his heart; dried drool welded his moustache to his lips. 'Water, please.'

He took a glass from Langley and drained it, recoiling at his own smell. Apples on the turn.

Langley leaned over him. 'We'll need to have that looked at. It's nasty.'

As he sat still and winced, scattered memories came back to him. The bench. Slats pressing into his back. 'What day is it?'

'Friday.'

'Eh?'

'It's Friday. Lunchtime.'

'What happened?'

'You tell me. Someone dropped you off outside this morning.'

'Who?'

'No idea. They didn't hang around.' Langley walked slowly around the office, his voice subdued and tired.

Max lifted the jacket from his body. He was wearing the same shirt and trousers he'd worn when Wilma visited. Fragments returned. The shack. Rusty.

Shirt-cuffs rolled up, Langley dampened a cloth from a jug in the corner. 'Look I really think we should alert the police. You've been assaulted.'

'No.' He grimaced as he twisted his neck towards Langley. Shacks like that had been outlawed for twenty years. 'Hold on. Friday lunchtime?'

'Yes.'

'Hell.' He stood from the chaise with a panicked heave. Blood rushed from his head and he fell forward, resting his elbows on his desk. 'Wilma.' She was due to arrive in just over twelve hours. Their plan relied on utter precision. He cursed his weakness. 'The decoy. New York.'

'Don't worry.' Langley said flatly, sitting Max back down on the chaise. 'It's taken care of.'

'Out there?'

'Yes.'

Max edged him out of the way and stood. Wincing with each step, he walked around the desk to the window. Down on the cobbles, piled in an obtrusive stack, was the obsolete recording equipment. To the crates of zinc masters, packing cases and rolls of oilcloth from the studio, Langley had added a suitcase and a travel trunk. An old recording horn protruded from the heap. Two grubby boys sat guard, bouncing a rubber ball between them. The mound was attracting the attention of curious passers by; he hoped some of them were Franklin's scouts. 'Is the gear marked up?'

'It couldn't be clearer. Southampton to New York.'

'And everything's ready in the studio?'

'Almost.'

'Good man, Langley. Thank you.' Poor lad. Having to nurse him as well as sort everything out. He flushed with embarrassment; he'd become the liability. He'd make it up to him.

As Max stepped back, he caught his reflection in the cracked window. Smears of dirt criss-crossed his face. A scuzzy cherry pinched his right eye shut, his lashes a gummy line bisecting it. That shack. The stench. The energy. The woman in the sari with the ring hanging from her nose. Rusty had dosed his tea. They'd made it nice and strong.

Elements returned. He'd pissed. They'd walked. He recalled shapes and sensations and a strange energy but nothing concrete. A banjo's twang. Gulls' caws. Stars. They'd talked. He couldn't remember about what. Flashes of white above his right eye.

Pulling open a desk drawer, he fumbled for a circular tin. He unscrewed its lid and scooped a finger of white powder into his mouth. Distributing the salty grit across his teeth he signalled for more water. Langley passed it. Max swirled the tooth powder into a froth, sucking it back and forth through his teeth. Trying to feel clean. Trying to erase recent memories, at least temporarily. A hint of eucalyptus perked him up. He bent to pick the waste paper bin from under the desk and spat the foam in. 'Right. Here's what will happen. I need to go home, clean myself up and pack.' The packing was real; Mama also had to believe that he was going to America. He didn't know who she spoke to these days. It would mean living in his office for a month.

'Of course.'

'I'll be back here in a few hours. Then we'll load a carriage with the apparatus, drawing as much attention to ourselves as possible. You and I will travel with it as far as Brixton, before we jump out and return here. We owe it to Wilma to make the deceit as realistic as possible.'

'I agree.'

'Have you confirmed everything with Mr Wilson?'

'Yes. He'll be here at two o'clock tomorrow morning. At the back door. He's fetching Wilma at the Langham on the way. Kitchen entrance.'

'Excellent. And while we wait for them we can test those new waxes.' He walked to the chaise and picked up his jacket.

'You're looking better already.' Langley smiled.

Max let the misconception lie. He'd rarely felt worse. His sickening weakness together with the headache and the eye-throb were too much; almost numbing. But another agony was asserting itself: the burden of responsibility of what they were about to do. It increased the discomfort tenfold. As he picked up his house keys from the desk, he paused. An aching hollowness twisted through him; nerves like he'd rarely known. The future of the company, the purity of his vision, rested on tonight. The twist intensified. If he'd eaten anything in the last two days he was sure he'd be looking at it now on the desk's surface.

He turned to Langley, who was ordering the Bach sheet music on the chaise. 'Thank you again for…everything. I'm sorry.' Puffing his cheeks, he summoned all the energy he could muster. 'Let's do this.'

❦❦❦❦❦

What's more important, Max thought as he paced around the primed rig: the chord or the note that precedes it? For twenty minutes he'd mulled the question. Matters of musical theory were an effective way of passing the time, of diverting the mind from other things. He reached into his waistcoat and clipped open his pocket watch, holding it up to his good eye. Twenty-five minutes past two in the morning. They should be here by now.

Returning the watch, he walked around the recording horn, cleaned and poised but as deprived of sound as the Covent Garden night outside. Of course the chord was the thing. But without the note before it, there was no context. No springboard. No sense of advancement. They were yoked, devoid of meaning without each other. He spun as the studio door rustled open, for an instant believing the wait to be over. But it was Langley, frowning.

'Any sign?' He clasped his eyes shut; his head still pounded.

Langley shook his head. 'Back door's unlocked, as we thought. No sign.'

'Where are they?' Max strode to the fireplace and threw on a fresh log. A consistent heat was crucial. On a low table a few feet back from the fire lay six blank masterdiscs, their wax surfaces warmed to the perfect softness for capturing the cutting stylus's etchings.

'No idea.' Langley sat heavily on the piano stool.

A dull but growing fear was edging out the nervous excitement of an hour before. The men exchanged glances, neither needing to express their deepest concern. Max fumbled in his pocket for a cigarette. It wouldn't help his coruscating headache but it might fend off the tiredness. His head was fast becoming scrambled; waking up in that fuggy daze, the eye, packing, the Brixton decoy and setting up the studio had heaped exhaustion on exhaustion. They couldn't have prepared more thoroughly. On the evening's carriage ride deep into south London with the gear, Max had even instructed the driver to take them past four of Franklin's theatres. Short of actually getting on the steamer to New York themselves, he could not imagine laying a stronger scent of departure. He lit his cigarette, walked to the window and reached up for the curtain. He inched it back, his eyes level with the pavement. The street outside was deserted, distant hooves and far-off laughter the only sounds. It was night's quietest hour, that time when even the darkness slumbered undisturbed.

Drawing heavily on his cigarette, he shook his head. Mr Wilson had agreed to meet Wilma at the kitchen entrance at a quarter to two to escort her to the studio. Something was definitely wrong.

Max walked to the turning table and gently spun it. Yellow parchment sheets rested expectantly on a music stand next to the rig. Bach's Sonata Number Six in G Major sat on top; its plaintive opening notes almost leaping from the page. Three more treasures lay beneath. He pictured Wilma's fingers, loose and free. He reached for his pocket watch. Half past two. He swallowed and resumed his pacing.

'Tell me, Mr Langley. What's more important? The chord or the note that precedes it?'

# 20

A burst of ratta-tats woke Max. He sat upright, one eye still closed, and immediately shivered at the studio's chill. It was light outside. The fire was a smouldering ash mountain. On the table in front of it, melted brown waxes lay as flat as Napoli pizzas, their formless edges touching. The banging grew in volume, followed by muffled cries of his name from behind the door. He stood and scanned the studio. Sheet music was strewn across the floor having toppled from its stand. His face slackened as he remembered. They'd never come; Langley had departed at four and he'd stayed in case they arrived. He clicked his watch open. Eleven in the morning.

As he stepped towards the door it burst open with almighty force. Four men entered as though pushed from behind. Blue suits buttoned to the neck, midriff buckles gleaming, truncheons and whistles. Max winced as he paced backwards towards the rig, his back not yet recovered from six hours of fitful sleep on the hard floor. Walking slowly behind the peelers, like a soloist entering after his chorus, was a man he hadn't seen for a while. His throat dried. Detective Inspector Boot wore a dark greatcoat and tall bowler. His sideburns framed cold and ruddy cheeks, his eyes were dark, his mouth severe.

'Mr Cadenza, would you be so kind as to come with us?'

The policemen silently surrounded him. 'What's happened?' He immediately coughed, hoping to disguise the quiver in his voice. He bent down to pick up his jacket from the piano stool.

'Just come with us.'

He was ready to oblige. However heavy hands clamped him by the arms and walked him to the door.

Outside, ravens circled under low clouds. Max raised his collar, hoping no one saw him. The Saturday flower market was in full swing; the sweet vanilla scent of lilies seemed cruelly carefree as he was bundled onto the bench of a police cart the size of a small horse tram. A peeler sat either side of him.

'Where are we going? Boot?'

All eyes faced forward.

He picked at his calloused finger, further questions halting at his lips. He had neither been accused of anything nor cuffed. Yet his chest was tight and an icy sheen cooled his forehead. Sitting in front of him, Boot maintained a stony silence, occasionally mumbling to himself.

Hooves on cobbles announced their departure like a gun salute. Max hunched his shoulders, thankful to be obscured by uniformed men as they headed down towards the Embankment. Turning east, they broke into a trot – the street's clay at least muffling the noise – and headed up towards St Paul's. Its dome loomed magnificently. But the context was mangled; Max turned his head, memories of it too luscious for today. They continued east, past the City's trading houses and the flinty keeps of the Tower of London. In the distance, becoming clearer, he saw the chimneys and warehouse roofs of Limehouse. He must have done this journey yesterday but in reverse, as his unknown chaperone deposited him back to the studio. His eye stung at the thought and his stomach tightened further. Outside, London was degrading with every clip of the horses' hooves. Grand frontages were disappearing. Soon they were among the dosshouses, taverns and dens of the Ratcliffe Highway. The buildings were a tangle of improvised brickwork and shoddy buttressing. Doors slammed and backs turned as people saw the cart approach. They took a sharp right and headed down towards the docks. Max didn't know the streets but he recognised the buildings' shapes, their proportions, their dark energy. It was like delving back into a hazy nightmare. The faecal pong of cold morning air over the Thames was horribly familiar. His knuckles tightened around his forearm as the cart pulled up at a stretch of roughly shingled beach, one bend of the river west of Limehouse.

'Out.' Boot shuffled his great frame along the front bench. The vehicle trembled as he jumped the short distance onto the dark sludge.

Max stepped down and stood by the cart, his eyes adjusting to the iceberg-white sky. He surveyed the stretch of water and followed its rugged shoreline back towards the City. A glacial cold suddenly gripped his feet. Looking down he saw that moats had formed around his heels where he'd sunk into the mud. Water seeped in through his boots' stitching.

'This way.'

Pacing west behind Boot, hugging his jacket to him, Max saw that a small crowd had gathered in the distance. He glanced around. The four policemen were walking two paces behind him. If Boot was a trawler, they were its net. Max wondered what that made him.

Pebbles and bottletops crunched into the muddy sand as they approached the crowd; dockers, scavengers, a man with a muzzled Doberman on a chain. They were held back by a line of uniformed officers, their arms linked to form a cordon. Beyond the police, some way further down the beach, a smaller group huddled around something. Gulls massed over it, possessive and protective.

Against a biting wind, they were allowed through the first police cordon. Once past it, Max saw that the second group were ranged around a dark angular pile. It rose from the shingles like a beached sea monster, partially covered with wet material. It was when one of the huddle stepped aside that he had a clear view for the first time.

The triangle of a naked leg, bent at the knee, was blotched and softly bloated. Two paces later, Max saw a second leg. A body. He frowned and broke into a fractured run; feet slipping within his boots, the boots themselves clagging in the mud. His heart raced. The face, he thought. Where's the face? Passing Boot, he reached the group and shouldered his way in, falling to his knees as he did so. The body lay on its side facing him. It was a man, naked from the waist down. One knee pointed skywards as though he was lounging. His penis lolled pathetically, a white acorn. His arms were bound behind him, his face obscured by a curtain of matted hair.

Max gasped and gripped his mouth.

Lying behind the man, back-to-back as if in mirror image, was a second, smaller body. A woman's arms were stretched behind her back, her wrists were bound to the man's like a gruesomely conjoined twin. Max pulled back the man's hair. Crooked yellow teeth roared from a rictus mouth. His eyes bulged in their sockets. It was Mr Wilson. Scrambling around the body, not daring to breathe, he cleared hair from the woman's body's face and silently screamed. It was as he feared. Her swollen features were frigid in pain. Wilma Wagensperg. A ripped corduroy dress only partially covered her breasts. Both her earlobes were ripped and bloodied, violently redeemed of what had dangled from them.

Max clawed her cheeks, absurdly willing her back to life. He said her name, repeating it until it became a continuous word, then an urgent rune. He brushed her hair from her face, stroking it upright, back to how it always was. Again and again he stroked it, the repetition of contact his only answer. Her belly beneath the corduroy was gently distended.

It had been his job to protect her. For a second time, he had failed. In a flash he was ripped away, strong hands lifting him upright.

'A mudlark found them this morning.' Boot was standing behind him. He signalled to a young girl sitting on the ground nearby, her knees up to her face as she tried to block out the world. 'They've been in the water since last night or the night before. It seems clear that you know these people, Mr Cadenza.'

A lone gull swooped, its wing grazing Wilson's knee.

'Mr Cadenza?'

'Of course I know them.'

'Care to name them?'

'What?' He turned, bewildered, to look at Boot.

'*Names.*'

Max pointed to the man. 'Edwin Wilson. Wilma Wagensperg. Can't you cover them up?'

'Do you know anything about this?'

'Of course not.'

'Care to take a closer look?'

'What do you mean?'

Boot took a deep breath. 'The wrists.'

Max bent down and grimaced. Above purple hands, the bodies' wrists were strung together like a pork loin. Wan flesh protruded between coils of tightly bound steel wire. One end of the wire, just above its ghastly knot, was thicker than the rest. It looped through a small ball. A violin string.

'Did you know where she was staying, Mr Cadenza?'

'The Langham.' He blinked. 'I think.'

'This has all the hallmarks of a ritual murder.' He paused. 'Rather like our friend Alfredo Balducci. This all seems terribly familiar. Wouldn't you say?'

Max stood as the full weight of Boot's comment became clear. It was ridiculous; so outlandish that in defiance of everything – his thumping heart, his disgust, the biting cold – his lips curled into a smile. 'Detective inspector, as I told you last year, I have absolutely no…'

'Ms Wagensperg's a renowned violin player, isn't she?'

He nodded.

'And you recently asked her to record a disc.' Boot's delivery was accusatory.

'Well, yes, I did…'

'And she said no,' Boot interjected.

'Wrong. She said yes.'

Boot shook his head and raised his voice, making sure the assembled group could clearly hear. 'You also accused Mr Wilson last year of behaving inappropriately towards your friend, Miss Delilah Green. Isn't that correct, Mr Cadenza?'

'Absolutely not.'

'You were seen down here two nights ago.' The certainty underscoring Boot's tone hardened. He almost sounded pleased with himself. 'Developed a taste for opium, I gather.'

Frantically rubbing his numb hands against an icy gust, Max felt his head swarm. As he watched Boot nod, he knew what was coming. He tried to close his ears to the world but the whipping wind screamed like a klaxon. A large hand gripped his left wrist and moved it behind his back. 'No. Come on.' He turned to see a peeler at his shoulder. They'd see reason. A second hand gripped his right wrist and held it to his left. He felt the cold touch of iron as cuffs were clasped shut.

'Don't worry.' Boot walked towards him. 'There's plenty more.' The tails of his greatcoat flapped wildly and he pointed back to the police cart. 'I think we'd better go up to the station. Don't you?'

᷒᷒᷒᷒᷒

The reek of piss and posies from the corridor outside tickled Max's nostrils, their unforgettable alliance causing the last five months to melt away. The bare walls and sticky floor of Boot's office hadn't changed either. He sat on a stool, blinking rapidly and trying to control his quivering hands. They were still bound behind his back. He'd never worn ruffles before; they stung with every jitter. Across a square table, he watched Boot pull out a chair. Despite the similarities, this felt completely different from last time. More serious. Sinister.

'I somehow thought we'd meet again like this.' Boot laid a notebook and some papers on the table with the confidence of a cardsharp on his game. His greatcoat off, he used a palm to cantilever his chin while he unbuttoned the top of his navy tunic. 'Where shall we start, I wonder?'

As Max looked around the office he noticed that the gramophone was still in the corner. The first time he saw it he'd been vaguely flattered that Boot had bought one. This time it seemed to mock him, sitting on its table like a curious piece of evidence, somehow linking him with this mess. He twisted his body so Boot could see his cuffed hands. 'Would you please remove these?' His voice sounded anaemic bouncing off the walls. 'They're terribly uncomfortable.' The ruffles were also pointless; he'd not try to escape. He had nothing to hide. Besides, he was hobbled by tiredness and shock; he wouldn't get very far.

'What happened to your eye?' Boot frowned, ignoring him.

'I was assaulted.'

'Where?'

Partway through a pause to consider the correct answer, he realised that the pause itself suggested impropriety. 'Limehouse.'

Boot arched a brow. 'How about we start at New Year's Eve?' He ordered his papers. 'Will you confirm to me that you attended a party thrown by Barnabas Franklin for Miss Wagensperg on the Thames near Greenwich? On the SS *Cassius*.'

Complete frankness was key. Besides, he was seen. 'I did.'

'And you attended as an uninvited guest. Is that correct?'

Max nodded.

'Why? Surely a man like you – popular, *charismatic* – was inundated with invitations that evening of all evenings?'

*Complete frankness.* 'Mr Langley and I wanted to convince Miss Wagensperg to record for our company. And I wasn't, as it happens.'

'Wasn't what?'

'Inundated.'

'So did you ask Miss Wagensperg to record for you?'

'Yes.'

Boot nodded. 'I know you did. We found this in her hotel room.' He held up a scrap of paper. It was the studio address that Max had slipped into the folds of her shorts as he'd left. 'And you gave this to her on New Year's Eve?'

'Yes. The reason I gave it to her, detective inspector, was because she agreed to record. She wanted to do it. Ask Mr Langley.'

'She agreed, you say?'

Max frowned. 'Hold on. How do you know I was there

on New Year's Eve? At the party? I could have given her that address any time.'

'We received a complaint, Mr Cadenza. The following day.'

'A complaint? From whom?'

'From Mr Franklin. Says you threatened him that night.'

'Oh, please, detective inspector.' Spit arced over the table.

Reading from his notebook, Boot shook his head. 'You told him that soon he'll be dead in the ground and you'd be dancing on his stinking corpse.' He glanced up. 'Did you say that?'

'I was talking figuratively.'

Boot glared at him.

'I was talking about his business. His outlook. About change. The new century.' He nodded towards the gramophone. 'I was being competitive.'

'*Dance on your stinking corpse.*' Boot let the phrase hang in the air. 'I spoke to Mr Franklin again early this morning. He gave me this.'

Max craned forward to read a second piece of paper that Boot slid across the table. It was the letter from Wilma to Franklin, dated January 2nd. The one she'd mentioned, promising not to record for anyone.

'Miss Wagensperg states here, in a letter written after the party, that she had no intention of recording a disc with you or anyone else. No intention at all. How do you explain that?'

The room's temperature dropped. Max sat back. Whatever their relationship, this contact between Boot and Franklin felt ominous. 'It was a bluff. She agreed to record for us and wrote the letter to put Franklin off the scent.' He told himself to slow down. His quickened delivery helped no one.

'A bluff?'

'Yes. She knew of the consequences if he found out she planned to work with us. She'd seen what had happened to

Balducci.' But he had found out. The beach. Purple hands. Wrists coiled with violin string. His eyes moistened.

Boot shook his head. 'Wilma Wagensperg is a serious musician, known for her sincerity. Over here on a professional tour. Why would she lie to the man who's hosting her in his theatres?'

'He's a thug.' He spat out the last word.

Boot read from his notebook. '*Dance on your stinking corpse.*' He looked up. 'Who's the thug, I wonder? Now, do you have any proof that she agreed to record with you, Mr Cadenza? A contract, perhaps?'

He swallowed. 'Verbal.'

'I'm sorry?'

'It was verbal.'

Boot smiled. 'Was it now? That's almost as convenient as that non-existent business card.'

Closing his eyes, Max saw himself as if from outside his body. He was standing next to a pit with Boot standing behind him. With a shove, Boot pushed him into the hole. Everything darkened. From the dank pit he looked up. Boot was glaring down, the only light behind him.

The detective cleared his throat and moved his pencil down his pad, as though working through a list. 'Mr Wilson.'

'What of him?'

'Tell me how you knew him.'

Max sighed. 'Edwin Wilson is – was – an accompanist I sometimes use. He was to play with Wilma at the recording.'

'He was also the musical director at the Paragon Theatre of Varieties, where Miss Delilah Green used to sing. Is that correct?'

'I believe so.'

'At the end of July last year you argued with Mr Wilson

in Simpson's, didn't you? You called him a snake for making advances towards Miss Green. You were seen.'

Max was back in the pit. He looked up; the light faded slightly as Boot heaved a cover over its opening. 'It was nothing. We work together. We drank afterwards. We're friends.'

Tapping a sideburn, Boot mulled his comments. 'If someone behaved in such a way towards Mrs Boot I'm not sure I'd drink with him. But then perhaps you and I inhabit different moral universes, eh? Now. Turkish? Chinese? Indian?'

*Moral universes.* Max gritted his teeth at the man's pious pontificating. As nausea rose through him, he realised Boot was waiting for an answer. 'What?'

'Turkish, Chinese or Indian?'

'I don't understand what you're saying.'

'Which kind of opium do you prefer?'

'Really, I've only ever...'

Boot grinned over the table. 'Three times you've been seen at a den in Limehouse. The last time was two nights ago. Which is around the time that these murders occurred.'

Time froze. He shook his head. The light above the pit faded to almost nothing as the cover edged across. 'Now hold on just a moment.'

'I'm told you were in quite a state. Needed help walking.'

Max's mouth dried. To connect a night in that shack with murder was preposterous. Outrageous. Then, like a bolt, a lifeline. He sat up straight, his chin jutting. 'I was with Rusty. Ask him.' Despite all that had passed between them, the man would back him up in the face of the law. They shared blood.

'Your cousin Ronald Cadenza?

'Yes. Ask him.'

'I've already spoken to him. Before we came to find you this morning.'

Max sighed. 'Good. I was with him all night.'

Boot looked at his notebook. 'I'm afraid not. Your cousin says he went down to Limehouse to find you and take you home. For your own safety. He was worried about your state of mind. Your spiralling opium use, as he put it. You left the shack together at around one twenty in the morning and he tried to walk you from the area. But he says you refused to leave. Insisted on staying on a bench somewhere.'

'Lies.'

'Which part?'

He squeezed his eyes shut to filter out all but the parts pertinent to Boot. 'First of all, Rusty gave me the opium.' He instantly regretted saying it as an incredulous guffaw echoed off the walls and Boot's palm landed on the table. The fact was largely irrelevant. He scrambled to regain ground. 'It's not true that he simply tried to walk me home. He didn't. We stayed down there, together. We talked all night.' The half-lie flew from his mouth. Rusty had left him at some point. He just couldn't remember when. Was a small fib excusable? 'Go and ask him again. Please.'

Boot lifted his notebook. 'It's all here. Mary Cadenza says her husband returned at around three in the morning. So you didn't talk all night, did you?' He threw the book down. 'There's no point in looking at me like that, Mr Cadenza. I'm only doing my job.'

Max said nothing.

'The bench.' Boot's voice grew irritable. 'You remained on the bench?'

He nodded.

'And you'd taken opium?'

He reluctantly nodded again. As Boot leaned back in his chair, Max lurched forwards, wrenching his wrists apart. Iron met bone as he tried to twist his hands free from the cuffs. He growled, clawing his fingers in vain. Down in the pit, all was pitch black.

'Here's what I think happened.' Boot stood and rested on his knuckles. 'You've had a difficult few months and this obsession you've had with recording Mr Franklin's musicians has grown in you. It goes all the way back to your father. Some childhood fixation you've had.'

Max shook his head.

'The reasons are neither here nor there. But it's clear that it consumes you.'

'No. Franklin's part of a wider... My jewels. You know that.'

Boot wafted the air. 'But Franklin's not yielded to you. You're not denting him. So when Miss Wagensperg refused to be recorded on New Year's Eve, something snapped. Two days later, high on opium, you went on a spree. Went to the Langham, coaxed her out and killed her. Then you killed your old foe Mr Wilson. One or both put up a fight. You bound them up with violin string and threw them in the Thames at Limehouse as some kind of bizarre message to Franklin.'

'No!' Max shouted. 'It was *to me*. A message *to me*. Franklin was warning me off. You have to believe me. He found out that Wilma and Wilson were coming to the studio and he killed them to stop them.'

Boot paced around his table and disappeared from view behind Max. He felt his breath in his ear. 'We've had a similar discussion before, haven't we Mr Cadenza? About Signor Balducci. I'm the victim, you said. Franklin's a killer and he's sending me a message.'

Max pulled against the cuffs again, rocking on the stool. A cold dab as a brass button from Boot's jacket brushed the back of his head. He recoiled as, from nowhere, his left eye's bloody orange vision became black. Boot's cold fingers sank into the bruised mound of his socket. Pain ripped through him as a second hand clamped his chin in place. One finger bent into a fish hook, gauging his mulchy skin. Boot massaged the weak flesh in all directions. Max yelled at the agony, trying in vain to writhe free.

'Everything I've said is true,' Boot whispered.

Black became orange again. The hand under his chin disappeared and Max slumped to the floor.

'Why did you pretend to go to New York yesterday?' Boot walked back round to his desk.

'What?' Tears made the pain worse.

'New York.'

'A decoy,' he said, almost too weak to talk. 'To fool Franklin.'

'Or perhaps to fool everyone else? To make people think you weren't around. You're a competitive man, Mr Cadenza. You're also a jealous opiate user. You can't stand the fact that someone like Mr Franklin is more successful than you.'

He shook his head and clambered to his knees.

'You can't stand that he's preventing you from making a success of your machines. So you kill what you can't have.'

'You've got this wrong,' Max wailed. '*You have to believe me.*'

He watched Boot rest his knuckles on the table and lean into them once more. Risen on his knees, Max knew what was coming. He strained once more against the cuffs.

'Maximilian Cadenza. I'm charging you with the murders of Edwin Wilson, Wilma Wagensperg and Alfredo Balducci.'

# PART SIX

# CRESCENDOS

## February 1900

# 21

**D**elilah stretched one foot behind her and tugged the stool into the folds of her petticoat. She shuffled towards her dressing table, the weight of her curls held from her forehead by a makeshift chiffon turban. As she wiped the stage paint from her face, white revealed white. The skin under her cheekbones hung sallow. Perhaps it was the harsh light from the gas mantles in these dressing room. She scrubbed. What did it matter? Tiredness was a consequence of success. If she was physically lessened due to her routine, what of it? The daily dash between the rehearsal room and The Camberwell Palace of Varieties would exhaust anyone. None of it mattered. Her name was painted in foot-high letters outside. Letters couldn't tire. On top of this, those new digs were almost within reach. The deposit was all but raised. Reclining in her own bath four months hence, the shiny brass of the hot water tap an inch from her toe, would she look back and remember how tired she was from her first flush of success? Not likely. She'd pick up the champagne glass resting by the tub and raise it through the steam to the heavens.

A burst of laughter from the girls next door caused her to hold her sponge still. There was little wrong with The Camberwell but the walls backstage were too thin. The other soloists frequently complained. She blinked and returned to her face. Shivering at the cloth's touch, she wondered what it would be like back next door with the chorus. Cluttered and noisy, no doubt. Flailing elbows and a carpet of discarded clothes.

She stood and reached for her corset, bought from the smartest corsetière on Westbourne Grove with her first cylinder money. With her deposit savings and the occasional luxury necessity, almost all that money was gone now, as were the cylinders themselves. Five hundred snapped up in a month; the speed of the sales had been dizzying. Fresh blanks were due any day soon. It would mean a return to Rusty's studio. More singing, more earning. She loved both. Smiling, she wrapped the corset around her, its leather lining cool to the touch. As her fingers worked down its eyes and hooks, she felt air between its whalebone slats and her skin. There was no question: her schedule had taken its toll. The Palace's second season was the talk of south London, or at least this part of it. She'd been pinched from The Peckham Crown as soon as her cylinders started selling. Hattie in *The Belle of Bohemia*. Nine shows a week, including matinées. If it weren't for the flat, she might have stopped there. But she'd also accepted the understudy role up in north London at weekends. It could only help.

Pulling her dress on, she glanced at herself in the dressing table mirror. She immediately looked down, cursing herself for asking the question. It was always at this time of day. Always now. *What would he say?* He'd grin. He'd be proud. He'd say what a fool he'd been. He'd hold her. She thumped her heel on the ground as if stamping out the thoughts. They were pointless. Everything had changed. Yet the idea of Max awaiting trial in Newgate devastated her. Occasionally the vision of him in his cell would ambush her from nowhere, stop her from doing anything. He'd been there weeks. Poor Max; falling while she climbed. Somewhere their fortunes had crossed. She sighed angrily and – once again – forbade herself from thinking of it again. Only one thing mattered: the singing and the cylinders. They were her future. They had to be. She was only in the foothills. There were bigger roles out there. Better ones. There were two-foot-high painted letters.

Gathering her coat and holdall, she walked out into the corridor, ignoring the laughter seeping from the chorus's changing room. At the stage door she brushed the concierge's arm and stepped into the night. As usual, a small crowd had gathered outside. Once, near the start of the run, she'd been halted and asked for an autograph. Tonight, as she had every night since, she moved away from the door with a purposeful yet open stroll, perfectly calibrated to encourage any person who wanted to come forward. None did.

She walked down Denmark Hill to wait for the omnibus back to Ridley Road. Every night, these steps required the greatest mental adjustment. The street's silence and her sudden anonymity contrasted harshly with the generous adulation of the audience half an hour earlier. How cruelly London denuded an actor of her status. How readily.

'Delilah.' A voice from nowhere.

She turned. 'Rusty.' He wore a new suit – dark blue serge, cut to fit. She hadn't seen him for weeks.

He strode towards her, baring teeth as he smiled. 'How are you, girl?'

'I'm well. Thank you.' As she reached out to touch his arm she caught the familiar odour of mildewed honey. But there was something different about him. His presence seemed better defined. In the place of his baggy sack coat he had properly shaped shoulders. Lines followed his body's contours rather than obscured it. With that came the suggestion of something. Power.

'Glad I caught you. Come over here. I've got news.'

They walked to a pavement cabin near the theatre that sold hot drinks and pies. She sat at a table and pointed at the theatre's illuminated façade. Her name was there on the marquee; not the most prominent, but there, nonetheless. 'What do you think?'

He winked at her. 'So proud.' Walking to the cabin, he bought two cups of tea.

She took a shawl from her bag and watched him flick a coin up to the vendor. It still thrilled her that this is what she did. She took a cup from him. 'And how are you, Rusty?'

'Tickety boo. Couldn't be better.'

There was something else different about him. A fresh confidence had crept into his voice, tempering the menace of old. He sat with poise. It clung to his surface, like rosewater on brine.

'Good news. We're ready for the next push,' he said. 'The new blanks arrive from America next week. It means we can get back in the studio.'

She placed down her tea. Finally. 'That's fabulous. Oh, I'm so pleased.'

'We've got the world at our feet. I've got exciting plans, now that you're a star.' He nodded at the theatre.

'Hush.' She smiled.

'And I've booked us a place at a playback in Victoria Park next month. We can showcase you.'

*Showcase.* She loved that word.

'There's only a dozen of the recorded cylinders left. We need to work. Hard. How are they going anyway?'

'The shows?'

He nodded.

'Exhausting.' She shrugged then looked at him. '*And sold out.*' She waited for his smirk. It forced a grin of her own. Her father had even come to an early performance. They'd talked afterwards.

'Now listen to my plan. We start in the studio as soon as possible. Gather a crop. Make the most of all this. You free to record next week as soon as the blanks arrive?'

'Tuesday and Thursday afternoons.'

'Grand.'

Although life was busier than any time she could remember, those early days in the studio with Rusty had been special. She'd felt unencumbered, free. Following her request, he'd taught her how a phonograph worked. Getting back in there would be good.

'Think of the numbers you'd like to record,' he said.

*I already have.* She started re-jigging the list again. It had become her favourite game.

As she watched Rusty sip his tea, a nervousness descended. She pulled her shawl tighter and, raising her cup, fired a wall of steam over the table as she thought about it. She knew she had to ask. Placing down the cup, she tucked her hair behind her ear.

'Is there any news?' she said quietly.

'Eh?'

She curled her toes. 'Max.'

In a flash his face changed. It darkened as through control had been wrestled away from him. He almost looked disappointed. 'Don't you worry about him.'

'But is he alright? You must have heard.'

'Listen, Delilah. This is about me and you now.'

'I know. But it doesn't mean…'

He sat forward. 'Forget Max,' he snapped. 'The stage is mine. Ours.'

'Don't you care what happens to him?'

Rusty stared at her, unmoving, before his tone softened. 'Of course I care. He's my own flesh and blood, isn't he? We have to let justice run its course. There's talk of bail.'

'Bail?'

He swiped the air. 'Don't think about him, Delilah. It's not worth the candle.' A hint of menace returned. 'He sure as hell isn't thinking about you.'

Sitting straight, she picked up her tea and exhaled through her nose, sending another steam cloud into the air between them. The words hurt. She liked Rusty. He'd hoiked her up when no one else would. She wouldn't be where she was without his help. But at times she felt he saw life as a game. He seemed like a child in a nursery, his only objective to come out on top. Except this wasn't a game. It was brutally, horribly real.

The clipping of a horse's hooves ricocheted off the theatre wall. Delilah looked around. A lone horse carriage was approaching down the street, probably the evening's last.

'That's my bus. I must get it.'

Rusty put down his tea. 'So everything's in order then. We push on. Happy?'

'Of course.' She stood and walked around the table. Unsure of how to say farewell, she put her arm out and shook his hand. 'Thank you, Rusty.'

'I'll come and find you next week.' He bowed his head in a way she had never seen before. It was borderline noble. 'Until then.'

She walked from the table and raised her hand to the carriage's driver. The vehicle pulled to a halt and she broke into a trot.

The bus was empty apart from a gaggle of young ladies

towards the back. Delilah sat on a bench just behind the driver's cabin. As the carriage pulled away, she stared through the window back at Rusty. He was still at the table, pouring the remnants of her tea into his cup. The theatre – her name – receded from view.

*Showcase.* Victoria Park would be fabulous. She thought about what she'd sing in the studio and what they'd play to the crowd in the park. How things had changed. Only six months ago, she was a member of that crowd. She sank into her shawl and let the prospect warm her. It was only when the bus crossed the Thames to Dalston that her thoughts shifted again. She felt the strange gnawing that she'd experienced too many times recently. It was like a niggling hunger that was not confined to her stomach. She closed her eyes, hoping it might disappear. But it didn't. The carriage hit a bump and she once again cursed herself for being so weak. Why would she think of him now, just minutes after she'd mapped out her future? Rusty was right: he sure as hell wasn't thinking of her. She gazed out of the window at the river's maudlin passage. But try as she might, she couldn't dislodge Max from her head.

⋘⋙

His fingers were foul tools, caked in grime for weeks, useless. Bending a hand forward, he used the nub of his wrist to knock a fly from his forehead. Extending his forearm, he rubbed his jailcrop; the hair had been too tempting for lice. He'd watched the curls fall to the floor, his identity diminishing with each chop. The cut had cost him his collar studs and cufflinks. The moustache remained, shortened, although he hadn't seen his reflection for weeks.

Max's suit reeked like everything else at Newgate. It was an all-pervasive smell, so dense it itched the skin; a co-mingling of rotten fish and sweat, of putrid wounds and the shit of men with unselective cravings. Twice he'd paid a man in the yard to wash his clothes. But soap and water were as useless as hope in this godforsaken place.

He stared at the barred window, his swollen eye finally subsided. No bigger than a gramophone box, the opening provided the cell's only light. He shuffled on the stool to get comfortable; his arse had been numb since he'd flinched the seat earlier. Standing would mean losing it again and it could be days before he got it back. It was impossible to sit up straight on the bunks around the cell's walls. Yells rebounded from every surface; the corridor linking the cells was a giant echo chamber, as if every loudmouth from Billingsgate to Bermondsey had been banged up.

Thirty-two days. Thirty-two days since his life had been brutally ripped away from him. He hadn't believed it at first. A joke, surely. A game. But for thirty-two days he'd been in this cell with three others. Close to eight hundred hours, he'd calculated. Over eighteen thousand plays of a new wax disc. All that time, waiting for his trial date to be set and bail to be decided upon. And today was the day. Today he'd hear if he'd done it; if he'd be bailed before he had the chance to clear his name in front of a judge. He doubted he would. Boot had it in for him. When he'd pieced together his theory in the Bow Street interview room, it had sounded horribly convincing. Brick by brick the detective inspector had built a plausible edifice that had made the truth seem almost irrelevant. His theories were baseless. All sizzle, no sausage. And Rusty. Why had he not helped and stood up for him? That was the greatest travesty of all. Out-manoeuvred and out-sold by his own relative, then hung out to dry. Yet all this contemplation meant nothing at Newgate, where once a week the whipcrack of the gallows provided the dawn chorus. Then there was the money. For countless nights he'd lain awake, wondering at what price his freedom – if offered – would be set. He'd smuggled a note out to Langley instructing him to have the sole surviving Balducci pressed onto shellac. Its rarity would ensure cash. And there was just over two hundred pounds left from Chaveley. There was a grim irony here: he only had that money because he'd never had to pay Wilma the agreed sum. Her drowning was both the reason he was here and the reason he'd get out.

Re-evaluating and reminiscing had become a compulsion since he'd arrived. In life he'd always tried to look ahead not backwards; dredging was for canals. But every day here he'd pass the time by imagining his list, locked away with his other possessions in some prison vault. He'd picture lifting the dog-eared piece of paper from his wallet's inner pouch and – with the precision of a watchmaker – carefully opening it on his palm. He'd cast his eye down its patchwork of squares, barely held together by their fibrous hinges. The words, there in black and white, eternal. His twelve jewels. He'd captured six. Half. Half wasn't bad. Half meant equilibrium. He'd re-live the recordings' chronology, raking over memories and relishing the scraps. Spain had been first. Seville. Miguel Sandoval's vigorous flamenco on *Music of the Sands*, captured in an orange grove under flaming skies. Next came the baroque choir at Amiens, uplifting and elemental beneath a mighty nave, followed by the heavenly drone of the Nethy Bridge bagpipers. Or was Nethy Bridge before Amiens?

Then, as he was revelling in the sounds, his body would lurch as he remembered. Two of the artistes were dead. Balducci and Wilma. Snuffed out by Franklin's poisonous tentacles. Wilson too, collateral damage of the man's control and jealousy. While

Balducci's music lived on via one recording, Wilma's legacy was as silent as the ground in which she lay. Nightly he'd wonder what he could have done differently. And then the chronology would once again occupy him. It was surely Amiens. Amiens was before Nethy Bridge.

He saw Delilah all the time. She was a constant presence. He talked to her, picking over morsels of their conversations for hours, chewing on them a multitude of ways, only shutting up when spat on or shouted at by his cell mates. He remembered particular phrases or folds of her dress. But smells were impossible to recall, no matter how hard he tried to summon them. Cherries and cut grass. He could never get it, and it broke him.

A clanging bell forced him to sit up on the stool. The new man, a forger, was pissing in a tin bucket next to him. Max stood, moved the stool to the other side of the room and sat. Resting his head against the wall, he closed his eyes. The further he leaned his head back, the less putrid he found the air. He tried to picture life outside. Most of all he missed music. The sweetest freedom in the world surely lay in the ability to choose what to listen to. The freedom to roam, to speak, to pray, to write were nothing next to this. Music was the great transporter. But the music in his head had fallen silent. Monitoring his breathing, he thought of Harlem. When he'd cleared his name, he and Langley would go. They'd capture hot rags in underground clubs then drink until dawn. He imagined leaving London; he imagined the vast spaces of the sea; he imagined freedom. Slowly, he drifted off.

A dull clunk at the door startled him awake. His cell mates cawed and rattled their beds as a jailor entered. Max shielded his eyes from the burst of lantern light from the corridor outside.

'Cadenza.'

He steadied himself on the wall as he stood, aware of the jailor walking towards him.

'Come with me,' he gestured. 'You've been bailed.'

❧❧❧

'One hundred and eighty pounds. Mr Langley brought it in as soon as they set it. It's less than I thought but it's still almost everything he and I have.' Max gently prodded at his face in the fireplace mirror. He was washed, freshly shaven and in a clean Pontings suit. Yet it still wasn't him there in the Highbury drawing room. It was a poorly impostor. Half a man. Without his hair, he looked stripped, a ghoul. The room also felt wrong. Its elements were too ordered and clean. Its green walls too uniform. He didn't deserve to be there. Although physically away from Newgate, part of him was still in it, and it in him.

There was a stranger, too, in the armchair. He quietly watched her reflection in the mirror, his questions burning stronger than he'd imagined they would. Mama had cried when he arrived and clasped her hands to his cheeks, but said little since. Her eyes were dark wells. Dressed in thick grey, she looked a world away from the figure he'd seen at the New Year party; a regression. She had the same haunted look that she had in the weeks after Papa died; lost in a mire of grief. But her appearance failed to answer his questions. They churned within him until they entangled themselves in their own fiery coils.

Turning from the hearth, he walked to her and knelt. He rested a hand on hers. 'Mama. There's something I must ask.' He barely recognised the patina of civilised speech. The luxury of inflection and the extravagance of contemplation had been absent for weeks. He coughed to clear his throat; his lungs quietly rumbled as if underwater. 'I know we've rarely spoken of your friendship with Mr Franklin. But if you know something – *anything* – about what happened you must tell me.'

Her dark eyes met his but her face remained blank. He still couldn't tell: did her sadness spring from sorrow for him or shame about him? Had she sided with that brute and already started mourning the son she once had?

He leaned in, squeezing her hand, imploring. 'Mama?'

Like a mighty branch snapping, her composure cracked.

'Oh, Max.' Fresh tears filled her eyes. She shook her head. 'I haven't seen him since the boat that night.'

'New Year's Eve?'

She nodded. 'I saw the way he looked at you and it terrified me.' She moved her hand from beneath his and cupped his face. 'You have to understand, he was just an acquaintance. An old friend. I'm lonely. I never…'

He settled back, overcome.

'I genuinely don't know anything, Max. If I did, I'd tell you.' She moved her palms to her lap and fidgeted, mouthing various words before speaking with a soft steeliness. 'Listen to me. I don't know the ins and outs of what happened. I promise, I don't. But I believe one thing. I believe that you had no part in these killings.'

His own eyes welled up. It was the first time in weeks that anyone had spoken to him like this, their words founded on the presumption of innocence. Mama smiled at him in a way he hadn't seen for years. Looking at her, he suddenly felt overwhelmed at the kindness in her face. And kindness, he knew, was the worst possible thing for a man at the end of his tether; it had the potential for transforming concrete into jelly, precipitating a collapse. He felt his cheeks tickle with emotion.

'I could hang,' he whispered.

Mama shook her head. 'When's the trial?'

'A month.'

She nodded and looked to the floor.

Standing, he tried to clear the fog. Something surged within; it was a sudden compulsion to see things practically; a growing impulse, having taken succour from her words, to tackle the days ahead and not fear them. He walked back to the hearth and spoke slowly. 'This is what I'm going to do. In a few days' time, when my energy has returned, I'm going to temporarily stand aside at the company. Hand over my duties to Mr Langley.'

She glanced at him.

'I have to. For the time being. I don't have the fight in me to run it. And who'd buy a machine from a man accused of murder? Mr Langley is more than capable of taking charge. I'm then going to dedicate all my time, all my reserves, to clearing my name.' It all sounded so simple when he ran through it in his head. But the words broke his heart. And, God willing, his leave of absence would only be temporary. He gnawed on his finger's nub. None of this would be easy. Others' scrutiny, their curiosity, would be endless.

He watched Mama's knuckles glow white as she gripped her chair's arms.

'Have you seen Rusty?' he asked.

'No. Neither hide nor hair.' A faraway look descended. She shook her head. 'Those gramophones. They're just machines.'

'Mama, please.' He knew she meant it kindly.

'You always thought they were going to change the world. But they haven't. They've done the opposite. They've brought you nothing but misery.'

Max looked at the gramophone in the corner. It had sat silent for months, a thin layer of dust coating its turning table. Perhaps she was right. Perhaps, sitting there, the contraption was just an awkward aggregate of its constituent parts: a mahogany box supporting an over-sized flowering horn, taking up space. What had it really brought to his life? War with Rusty. The Limehouse beach. The bound wrists of double murder victims. Balducci slain on his bed. She was right. That box was a cost not an asset. A risk not a reward. A weapon in its own right.

'We're drowning in useless progress,' she continued. 'Do you know, Harrods now has a mechanical staircase. Can you imagine?' A humourless smile spread. 'You have to understand, Max, that what your generation does confounds me. And you'd be a fool to assume that one day you won't be confounded too. In years to come, some machine will come along that you'll deem completely unnecessary. And you'll try to understand its value and you will fail. When that time comes I will be long gone. But when it happens you will know exactly what I am talking about.'

He stood at the hearth, saying nothing.

Mama pecked the air as if to speak. Eventually, blinking, the words came. Each one was formed slowly, as though she was reciting them in her mind first. 'This situation you're in…'

'What of it?'

'You must win this, Max. Do you hear? You are not a fool. You are resourceful and charming. And you must use every ounce of your initiative to prove the police wrong. You are exceptional.' She paused to allow a catch in her throat to pass. 'You are my son.'

He watched her, unsure of how to respond.

'Use this month wisely. Be the Max I used to know.'

He wanted to reply but could not.

She nodded and repeated. 'Be the Max I used to know.'

# 22

I t's good of you to come.'

'It's nice to be here.' Max smiled and looked away in an attempt to save Langley's blushes. He'd caught the lad looking at his cropped hair as he'd approached, just as he'd done at Newgate when he arrived with the bail money. Without question Max would have done the same. He nodded skywards. 'My. Look at this place.'

The Holloway Empire announced itself like the loudest scream in London. Not yet open three months, its foyer was a riot of electric lighting, mirrored surfaces and curved silver lines. In its stupefying modernity, it didn't even need to mock the dull gold, heavy drapery and gas mantles of Franklin's Covent Garden. It was too far ahead, a new breed of independent theatre; its every aspect, its thousands of bulbs, bragged of a thrilling future. But it needed to calm down. The tang of metal was still too lively, its sheen almost too bright. They made Max's head ache. Everything was too dizzying. Three days ago he was in Newgate in a filthy suit. And here he was in a dinner jacket, its starched collar loose after weeks of oatmeal gruel, watching reflections of reflections disappear into the distance.

Langley had insisted that he join him. In the hansom from the prison to Highgate, fresh from dropping off the bail money, he'd almost begged him to come. His treat. The weekend was one of Molly's last performances before she moved to The Edgware, he'd said. In the face of tiredness and the blizzard of forgotten experiences – the rush of air, the glimpse of sky, the sound of laughter on the street – Max was too overwhelmed to refuse. Besides, he owed it to Langley. As well as gathering the money and fetching him from the clink, the man would be a vital support to him in the months ahead; as the custodian of the company, as a confidante, as a character witness at the trial. In the circumstances, accepting his invitation was the least he could do. He'd try to enjoy it.

Turning to the wall behind him, Max cast his eyes down the poster for the night's entertainment. *Palmarama*. The Holloway had received rave notices for its musical about lust and inheritance in a perfume factory on a Polynesian island. Molly's name was at the foot of the poster, adorning a decorated perfume bottle. 'How is she? Nervous?'

'Extremely.' Langley seemed a touch apprehensive, as though he himself was about to take the stage.

Max nudged his arm. 'Don't worry, old boy. I gather the show's a musk-see.' It was a daft, shaming pun, made worse because he'd forced himself to make it. His heart sank even more at Langley's appalled expression.

'Shall we?' Langley nodded up to the grand circle and boxes.

Shoe leather on mosaic steps produced a comforting shush, like the sound of a brush crossing a snare drum. Max didn't know why, but its gentle magic made him smile. As they climbed, he caught his wan visage in the mirrors. He still looked a fraud; a waif pretending to be Max Cadenza.

'Here.' Langley held open the box's door. From their seats the auditorium opened out like a carmine canyon. Max looked up at the ceiling's dome, a relief in a faux Indian style. Elephants bore bejewelled maharanis around its base in a Londoner's interpretation of the East. The dome's size and artful affectations scared Max; they were in such contrast to the low dripping ceiling under which he'd slept for the past month. He could scarcely believe the two co-existed in the same city. Reality and escapism, three miles and forty hours apart.

As the lights dimmed he peeked at Langley next to him. He shifted apprehensively in his seat, looking straight ahead.

*Palmarama* was everything Max expected: a florid libretto, characters cartoon-like in their enthusiasm, and a set consisting of palm trees, sandbanks and a rolling blue ocean. It was loud, colourful and completely daft. Prior to prison he would have dismissed it as nonsense. But there was something refreshing about its unapologetic glee. He sat forward when Molly came on as Edith, sister of the wronged heiress of the island of Palmarama. Poor girl. Up against greedy industrialists and a mysterious aristocrat called Lady Wallop, who had arrived uninvited in search of a husband and a secret perfume recipe. But as upbeat song followed upbeat song, the colours and the joy started to fade. As the minutes passed, pockets of darkness became apparent. Soon, despite the levity, Max started to seek out the bleakness. It was there in the black spaces between the stage flats. It was there in the rumble of the timpani. It was there in the faces of the island's carved statues, standing open-mouthed and ominous, fending off all-comers. It was as though he was mining for misery, compulsively willing it, scared of embracing the colour. He knew why. There was affinity in misery. In that darkness his future lay.

With a thumping inevitability, Boot and the trial entered his thoughts. Once again, he started laying out the facts in his defence. His freedom would depend on his ability to recount in detail every incident over the last six months; every confrontation and every argument, no matter how small or inconsequential. A shrill note startled him. Blinking, he looked to the stage below. Molly was sitting between two flats singing a lament called *Your Love is Like a Fragrant Balm*. Behind her, a chorus line of girls in grass skirts fluttered fans and swayed. As the song ended Max became aware of a new character lurking on the stage behind the chorus, a broad wicker hat obscuring her face. She carried a bunch of bougainvilleas and walked with evil intent. Lady Wallop, here to ruin the island's sweet equilibrium. He sat forward, relieved at last to see some actual strife on stage. Lady Wallop strode centre-stage, stood behind Molly and removed her hat. Shaking out coils of chestnut hair, she burst into song.

It was Delilah.

Max's hand jerked to his chest. He snapped his head around to Langley, looking for an expression of shock to match his own. But Langley was glaring at the stage as if he hadn't noticed her, his face as frozen as one of the South Seas statues. Max's chin slowly fell as the truth dawned. This was no coincidence. It was deliberate.

Heads turned as he abruptly stood, his seat snapping shut. 'How dare you?' he hissed as he turned to the box's door and heaved it open. It explained Langley's nerves and his insistence that he came.

Outside he walked towards a small bar, his palms smothering his crop in confusion. The box's door had barely shut behind him when he heard it open again.

Max spun. 'What the hell are you doing?'

Langley's hands were raised in a bid for forbearance as he walked towards him. 'Molly and I… *I* thought that it may perhaps do you good to see her. After…you know…everything.'

'Do me good? What's she doing here? She's not even in this play,' he spat.

'She understudies. Lady Wallop. At weekends.'

'And you knew?'

'Of course.' Langley shuffled awkwardly, as though the carpet's orange swirls were hot embers.

'And precisely how does seeing her do me good? Are you trying to torment me?' Max pulled out a handkerchief and coughed into it.

'I know how much she means to you. And Molly said she's been a little out of sorts recently. I thought if there was even a chance you two could talk…'

'Talk? *Talk*? About what?'

'We thought we could all go for grog afterwards. Just to see if there's…you know.'

Max fixed him with a gaze and shrugged. He didn't know.

'To see if there's a way back for you two. You parted on such bad terms.'

Max frowned as he stuffed his handkerchief back into his pocket. 'Is Rusty here too?'

'Of course not.' Langley looked surprised, as though he wouldn't be so daft.

'Does Delilah know?'

'Know what?'

'That I'm here.'

Langley shook his head.

Max clasped his eyes shut and walked two paces closer to the bar. He paused and turned back to his colleague. 'Mr Langley. Think about this. I have recently been bailed from jail on a murder charge. Sorry, *charges*. Delilah is now enjoying success as a stage and cylinder artiste. For mercy's sake, what possible purpose would be served by us seeing one another?'

Before Langley could answer, Max walked to the bar and picked up a glass of champagne. He slugged it open-mouthed, its bubbles unfamiliar and coarse. A loud burst of applause came from the auditorium, followed by a low rumble. The interval. He was aware of Langley beside him. 'Do you really think that I need half-cocked attempts by others to marshal my emotions? Now of all times?'

'No,' Langley whispered. 'I'm sorry.'

'Did you think that I'd run backstage and melt into her arms like a lovelorn *Palmaraman*? This is entrapment.'

Langley picked up a glass and drank himself, eyes down like a cowed child.

As the bar filled with audience members, Max wondered what to do. Throw a punch at Langley? Tempting, but not entirely sensible. Shout down at the stage once the second half started? Too public. A surprising thought entered his mind. Staring at Langley through thin eyes, he assessed its outlandishness. It was certainly the thing that Langley would least expect him to do. He reached to the bar for another glass. 'You know, perhaps you're right.'

'What?'

'Talk.' Max nodded.

'Boss?'

'Talk. To Delilah. Right now. It's a wonderful idea.' Turning to the bar's mirror, he pulled his waistcoat straight. 'Seeing that surprises are the order of the day. Excuse me.' He nudged passed Langley and walked towards the stairs down to the foyer, weaving through theatregoers.

'Where are you going?' Langley followed him.

'I'm going to her dressing room.'

'*Now*?'

Head up, Max walked with pace. 'No time like the present, as they say. This is what you wanted, isn't it? I should thank you really. There's plenty I have to say to her.'

Langley's feet shushed on the mosaic stairs behind Max. 'Don't you perhaps think you should wait until the play's over?'

'Why? She'll be in her dressing room at this very moment. Twiddling her thumbs.' He took the stairs two at a time.

By the time he reached the foyer Max realised Langley had stopped following him. He was alone, driven on by an unstoppable impetus. No drama, he thought as he made his way across the floor towards the theatre's revolving doors; just a few home truths. Once outside, he'd nip down the side alley to the stage door.

This was the right thing to do.

He'd surprise Delilah.

⳩⳩⳩⳩⳩

If he'd had time to order his thoughts, he might have stopped halfway down the corridor. As it was, Max pushed into the dressing room unprepared. He thought it didn't matter; detail was anathema to spontaneity. He knew how he *felt*.

He walked in to find Delilah sitting on Molly's dressing table, facing into the centre of the room. Her back was flush against a large make-up mirror, her body framed by a crescent of incandescent bulbs that emphasised her profile. A bunch of paper bougainvilleas rested on her lap. The tail end of a carefree laugh filled the room. At Delilah's feet, Molly perched on a low chair, changing her wig.

Max hovered by the door. Molly turned first. With a curious gurgle she stood and walked towards him, brushing past – eyes averted – and closing the door behind her as she left the room.

He didn't see Delilah's expression; the lights behind her made it impossible. But the absolute stillness of her body told him all that he needed to know. The next sound he heard was the rustle of bougainvilleas hitting the floor.

He remained fixed to the spot. On seeing the familiar stranger across the room, he realised that – contrary to everything he hoped – he didn't know how he felt at all. This was strange. And rash. He doubted he could have walked the short distance to the chair even if he'd wanted to. He tried to smile but his jaw twitched as though his mouth was full of moths. 'Delilah.' His tone was flat, neither chastening nor beseeching.

During the weeks in the cell he'd planned what he'd say if he ever bumped into her: he'd damn her for signing with Rusty and he'd curse her treachery. He'd acknowledge her commendable ambition then rubbish the route down which she'd travelled. But here in her presence, the words evaporated. Their logic disappeared. He stepped tentatively towards her. She remained silent, her head bowed. As he approached she closed her eyes and turned from him. Her breathing was deep and wary. He sat gingerly on the low chair vacated by Molly.

'My dear girl,' he said softly.

In the quiet of the dressing room, it occurred to him that far from admonishing her as he'd planned, he wished that he could gather her up and, somehow, take her back to that day at London Zoo. If a way existed of wiping out all that happened since he'd do it. He'd give anything for the power to reset things. From his seat he could see her lowered face through fallen corkscrews of hair.

'Delilah?'

He shifted forward on the chair and craned to gauge her expression. A vault burst open as her scent flickered in his nostrils, its sweetness only slightly altered by her stage make-up. The tightness of the dressing room's space meant that his head was just a foot from hers. As he traced her soft features, her eyes opened. On seeing him she leaned back against the mirror, the bulbs' harsh light illuminating her face from the sides and above.

He felt her eyes on his face, and watched them widen then pinch as she took in his gaunt features. After a minute a warm hand touched his head, another his cheek. 'Max. I'm sorry.' She looked as if she was about say something more. Instead she withdrew her palms and held them at shoulder-height, her face crumbling. Tears dropped onto her lap where the flowers had sat. 'I'm sorry,' she repeated.

'May I ask why?'

She frowned. '*Why?*'

He hadn't meant to say it. Being there was enough. But in an unexpected rush – as though his mind was compelling him to take the chance that had consumed him for months – his pre-planned words flooded back into his head. 'Yes. *Why?* Did a little flattery corrupt your mind?' Again, he heard the words flow unfiltered from his mouth before he had a chance to weigh them.

Her frown deepened as she repeated the words. 'Corrupt my mind?'

He nodded. A corruption was what had occurred, both technically and morally. He'd spent days in Newgate thinking about it. 'What kind of person are you?' It was another practised line. But the words did not tally with what he felt. They sounded alien, like a record playing backwards.

Her face hardened, as though blindsided by the conversation's direction. A scowl replaced the frown. 'He took a chance on me, Max. Can't you see that? After you said no. Chasing your blessed jewels. He gave me what I'd always wanted: a chance to sing, to record, to make something of myself. *That's* the kind of person I am.'

It was a daft question. He tried to interrupt but could not. He knew what she meant, and it hurt.

'Back at The Paragon I was one of a dozen people fighting for a line in a song. I was just another girl in another chorus. And then he came along. *He picked me.* And it's working, Max. Look.' She gestured around the room, keeping her hands raised and defiant.

He hung his head. He couldn't even get this conversation right. Sitting there, he saw things with absolute clarity. Had he not dismissed her initial request to record with The London Gramophone Corporation, she would not have found herself in hock to Rusty. If he'd committed her to shellac, perhaps they'd still be together. As the architect of his own downfall he'd acted superlatively. What a fool. He imagined watching himself on that pathway at the zoo, pontificating and theorising, scything Delilah's ambitions with his words. An imbecile couldn't have done worse. How could he have got it so wrong? Self-loathing and regret tore at him, their twin blades sharpened by his own hand. Looking up at her, he knew there was nothing he could say. Even if, sitting here in front of her, he offered to ask Langley to record her at the company in his temporary absence, it was too late. Why would she even consider such an offer? She was set fair with Rusty. Settled. Happy. He felt a grim air of intractability descend. A shamed smile danced on his lips. He closed his eyes and mouthed an apology.

She cleared her throat. 'Why are you here, anyway?'

'Here?'

'Yeah, tonight.'

'Came with Mr Langley. Although he forgot to...' He gestured between them.

She smirked and softly shook her head as a bell rang outside. It was time to leave; the second half of *Palmarama* was about to start. He glanced up and saw that her expression had changed; her earlier defiance had given way to something else. It was a look he hadn't seen for some time, like a rope stretching back to the past. He recognised it. Compassion. It was the same look with which she'd handed him chopsticks when he'd fumbled, the same stare that preceded the kiss in the tree, the same glance that accompanied her pauses when they'd spoken, carefree, for hours.

'Are you going to be all right, Max?'

He forced a smile. 'Of course I am.'

Standing from the dressing table, she cast her eyes down and fiddled with her frock's lace. He stood too, so they were inches apart. She moistened her lips, on the cusp of saying something. Watching, waiting, his stomach churned. But no words came.

In silence they faced each other. As he was about to turn to the door he felt her palm on his cheek once more. She held his gaze as her thumb gently caressed his skin. Briefly, he lowered his forehead onto hers, surprised that she didn't resist. He inhaled; cherries and summer lawns. As he mulled what could have been, standing there became too much. He stepped away and walked the few paces to the door. He reached for the handle.

'Max…'

He turned. He couldn't be sure but her expression seemed tempered with a modicum of regret.

'Look after yourself.' A smile, weak but not forced, played on her lips.

He interpreted her words to mean goodbye. Pulling the door open, he stepped into the corridor and closed it behind him.

Langley was sitting on the studio floor surrounded by parcels when Max entered. The rig towered behind him, mothballed under a vast dust sheet. With the canopy overhead and the wares piled on the floor, the place resembled a souk. But there was no life here. Max shivered. He hadn't been in the room since the morning of his arrest. His cradle, his laboratory. Eeriness hung heavily. The room was too cold, for starters. There was something else. Silence. Despite the mid-morning hour, it was as quiet as midnight.

Langley stood abruptly. 'Boss. Can I just say how sorry I am…'

Max raised his hand from the crate of trinkets wedged under his arm. 'Nonsense. You thought you were helping. Don't mention it.' In a strange way the conversation with Delilah had cleared his head. It had hurt, but at least lingering hopes could now be put to bed. He supposed that Langley had done him a favour. 'And I'm sorry I snapped at you. It was all a bit of a surprise.'

'Did you…'

'Have meaningful dialogue?' He chuckled and shook his head. That chapter had closed. 'You carry on.'

'What's that?' Langley eyed the box under his arm.

'A few things from the office upstairs. I've been meaning to tell you.'

'Tell me what?'

'That I'm taking some time away from this. Just until the trial's done. To clear my name.' He knew what was coming and he felt mildly ridiculous and bestowing saying it, like a father addressing a son. 'I thought that perhaps you could run things on a caretaker basis. You know, keep things ticking over.'

'Me?'

'You're more than capable, old boy. It would be a tremendous help. Besides, I'll be back soon.' He swallowed.

'Well…'

Max swore he saw the lad grow an unneeded inch there on the studio floor.

'Yes. I'd be… Of course. But are you sure about this?'

'Stepping aside?' Dear naive boy. 'Mr Langley, do you really think in your wildest dreams that anyone will want to be associated with the company with me attached?' Max shook his head. Carrying on at present was impossible. 'All my energy must go towards proving my innocence. It must.' In talking about it, Max felt reasonably sanguine. He wasn't sure why. Unimaginable battles lay ahead.

Wanting to be businesslike, Langley bent to pick one of the open parcels from the floor. It contained a pile of fresh shellac discs, their centres stamped with the company's logo. He passed one to Max. 'You might want to look at this.'

Max took it with his free hand. 'Well, I never.' It was the sole surviving Balducci. *Pari Siamo* from *Rigoletto*. Pressed up.

'And look here.' Langley held up a letter. 'An order for dozens.'

The letter was headed Whiteleys of Bayswater. William Whiteley, the department store's managing director, had written personally.

'Stone me.' Max smiled faintly. Only as Balducci's murder trial was about to get underway could London finally listen to the poor soul. He felt bad for thinking of the much-needed working capital the sales would bring in. 'Looks as though you'll be busy after all.' He slipped a copy of the disc into his crate.

Langley raised another letter. 'Oh, and we've had confirmation for that playback in Victoria Park.'

'Again.' Max pointed a finger at Langley as if to confer responsibility. It would be his show. As he watched his charge sort the parcels, he felt a bump of pride. He'd be a fine steward of the company, such as it was. He suspected that under his humility Langley knew it too. Max wished that, just for the afternoon, he could drop his guard and help. Spend a final day talking about opera and recording horns, reminiscing about the past and planning for a rebuilt future. There was so much still to do. But he could not do it. Not with the Bailey to prepare for.

'Listen, I was thinking when I was…*un-busy*…' Max said. 'The Strangers' Home for Asiatics in St Giles. There may be rich musical pickings there. Jewelettes and curios, if nothing more. It's worth scouting. And it's safe to say you definitely won't be treading on Rusty's toes.'

'Thanks, boss.' Langley paused from counting out the Balduccis on the work bench and smiled apologetically at his choice of word.

'Talking of that…' Reaching into his breast pocket, Max fingered the soft leather of his battered pouch. Years of dreaming. Months of graft. Twelve jewels. He pulled out the wallet and lobbed it towards Langley. 'For what it's worth.'

Langley turned and watched the pouch skid across the floor towards him. He looked at Max. 'Is this…?'

Max nodded. 'All yours for now. Boss.'

Footsteps echoed down the steps beyond the studio door.

'Are you expecting anyone?'

'No,' Langley said.

A familiar whistle accompanied the steps. Max frowned as a key clinked in the lock before being withdrawn, redundant. A tentative push. Slowly the door swung open.

Rusty stood in the frame, a surprised sneer spreading across his face.

'Well I never. The clowns are in the big top.' He strutted in, unbuttoning his tailored blue jacket. Pipe clasped between his lips, he looked Max up and down. 'Jesus. Prison food not to your taste?'

It had been weeks since Max had heard his gravelly drawl. But more alarming was his poise. He looked charged. Purposeful. Max pointed at the door. 'Out.'

Rusty raised his hands. 'Don't want any drama. I've simply come to pick up my soldering iron. Alright, Streak?' He approached Max and peered into the crate under his arm. 'Packing up?'

Max swallowed and told himself to remain staunch, dignified. He would have done so, but for the smell. The familiar sweet-stale odour of baccy smoke brought the past into the room. The inescapable musk filled the studio, representing all that had happened between them and all that could not be forgotten. The smell blasted through Max's defences, tearing at his soul. You can't be here, he thought. Not here in my sanctuary on my last day. With a discordant clang his box hit the floor as he thrust his hand at Rusty's hair. But the lunge was slow and his cousin pirouetted out of the way, leaving Max grabbing at thin air.

'Temper, temper.' Rusty straightened his jacket.

'You evil shit.'

'Perhaps. But I'm an evil shit with a job. And a future. What've you got?' He walked to the workbench and picked up his soldering iron.

Max didn't try to stop him. Instead he looked to the ground. The crate's contents lay strewn at his feet: letters, books, a broken xylophone, the Balducci disc. 'Why didn't you defend me?'

'What?'

'To Boot. Why did you let him believe I killed?'

Rusty turned with his iron and tutted. 'Come come, Max. Don't lower the tone.'

Stepping towards his cousin, Max lifted a trembling hand.

'Please. Tell him I didn't do it. Tell him I don't have it in me.'

Unmoving, Rusty sucked on his pipe, letting a thickening cloud of smoke envelop his head. He said nothing, as though contemplating a heavy thought. Slowly, he drew the pipe from his lips and pointed it at Max. 'You know what tickles me most?' he said. 'In a few weeks' time, you'll be in court and I'll be in the studio recording my Delilah.' He re-inserted his pipe and raised his eyebrows.

'Why are you doing this to me?'

Clasping his soldering iron in his armpit, Rusty inched the right sleeve of his jacket up his arm. He unbuttoned his shirt cuff and heaved it towards his elbow. No longer an injury, he lifted his reptilian arm, its permanent scales craggy and uneven in the light. 'This. For starters.'

'But Rus...'

Rusty stepped towards him. 'I'm doing this for all the times you patronised me. Took me places, talked to me, assuming your way was the only way. *Magic and passion.* That night.'

'Which night?'

'Combe Martin. That was your idea.'

The night his parents died. Max's eyes glazed and he shook his head. 'No. I loved you, Rusty.'

'I don't think you ever really cared.' Sadness gave way to a grimace. 'You could dangle, Max. Funny how life turns out.'

A bursting heat rose and Max threw himself across the floor towards Rusty. Before he made contact a palm landed on his chest, slowing his progress. It was followed by a willowy frame as Langley inserted himself between the men.

'You need to leave.' Langley glared at Rusty, his face twitching.

A sneer returned. 'Gladly.' Rusty stood for a second, nodding at Max. Saying nothing, he turned to the door and walked out.

The blast of air as Langley slammed it shut behind him sent a ripple through the canopy above. 'Halfwit.'

Head bowed, Max bent down, exhausted. He picked up the personal effects scattered across the floor. He wished he'd thumped him. The man was baiting him like a bear. He shook as he picked up the xylophone's shattered frame, mumbling an apology to Langley. It was unedifying, he murmured. Distasteful. He glanced across to the machine, *his* machine. Walking to it, he yanked off the dustsheet with a single tug. Its horn was cold to the touch. And crooked. And imperfect. Yet so utterly full of promise. The rig embodied everything he held dear and everything he'd lost. He rested his hand on the turning table and closed his eyes. Music flooded his ears as he pictured it spinning, rendering, capturing.

In that brief moment of contact, he felt complete.

# 23

You could dangle. *Dangle.* Rusty's word echoed round his head. Tormented him. Did two more ominous syllables co-exist? He tried to block it out as the final mellifluous plucks from an Ottomanian zither sailed across the drawing room from the gramophone in the corner. Baghdad, 1897. A brief moment of release. The disc reached its shuddering climax as rattles and cymbals drowned out the zither. He savoured every dying second until the horn hissed and the stylus reached the record's empty centre. As the needle hit the label it tripped, jumping back to repeat the final barren groove again and again, filling the room with a hypnotic d-gl, d-gl, d-gl. Max closed his eyes. The repetitive noise became all-consuming. It grew louder, boring into him. Dangle, dangle, dangle.

Leaping from the sofa, he strode to the machine and drew back the tone arm. He'd never known life to feel so bleak; so lacking in harmony; so shorn of fidelity. And his private woes were about to become public. The trial would have everyone's chins wagging, the gossip stoked by Rusty. His absence from normal life as he prepared himself for the ordeal would start to be noticed; at venues, around the Garden, at the empty corner table of Simpson's. Lifting the disc from the turning table, his mind automatically flipped back to events leading up to his arrest. Reminiscing by rote. He hated it. But it was simply what happened now. Re-evaluating. Looking for ways to prove the police wrong. They'd dismissed Langley's word. Too close to Max, they'd said. The more he churned conversations and incidents around his head, the less he could see a way out of the maze. Was there a point when misery became intractable? When fear became irreversible?

As he slipped the Baghdad record back in its sleeve, he remembered. The Balducci. He'd brought the copy home with his other trinkets from the office. It was there in the box by the door. He retrieved it and unsheathed the shellac. Walking back to the gramophone, he studied its central label. Gold lettering on black. Curled around its entire circumference was the company name, the 'n' of 'Corporation' almost touching the 'T' of 'The'. A crude image of a diamond sat above the central hole. Max's jewel, the print taken from his own drawing. And beneath the hole, stacked in three lines of text, read the words: *Alfredo Balducci sings Pari Siamo by Guiseppe Verdi*. Max's forearms tingled. He was carrying more than a record. The disc contained one of the man's last ever songs. More. It contained some of his last ever breaths. Light danced off the grooves. This was his legacy. His requiem.

Setting down the disc, he wound the gramophone's side spindle. As he released the motor he lowered the stylus onto its outer edge and walked back to the sofa. That day was incredible. It was the start of the team: he and Rusty and Langley, together capturing music for the first time. They'd almost been carried on air through Leicester Square as they headed to Café Royal afterwards, such was the joy. Then, Franklin. The confrontation. Max recalled his and Rusty's excited glares at each other, cousins bonded in their quest. Franklin's sneering face, his entitled air. Intoxication followed. He and Rusty had argued, and Rusty had stormed out. But they'd made up in Rules a few hours later. The evening was a typical jumble of excess and tussle, celebration and braggadocio.

Balducci's voice burst from the horn, as low and powerful as Max remembered. He translated the Italian in his head as he listened. Rigoletto's lament. The dark hymn about his similarity to a murderer.

*We are two of a kind.* Balducci's voice groaned with passion, rising from the depths. *My weapon is my tongue, his is a dagger.*

The piano came in, trembling beneath the voice. Max blinked. Wilson. The record contained not one dead musician but two. As Balducci's voice intensified, Max started to mouth the translation.

*I am a man of laughter. He strikes the fatal blow.*

He froze.

For two minutes he sat, unwilling to unpick the thought that had landed in his mind. But it stained instantly, its brief flash instantly blackening his brain. Barely daring to think, he stood and strode to the gramophone. Balducci fell silent as he lifted the stylus and placed it at the start of the song again. He clasped his eyes shut and listened once more. The voice from the depths. Low and powerful.

*We are two of a kind. My weapon is my tongue, his is a dagger.*

❦❦❦❦❦

He'd changed his mind. She was his only salvation from all this. He had to see her.

After he'd listened to the Balducci, he'd drunk two large brandies. All he could think of was Delilah. She'd swirled and screamed around his head, caressed him and cried at him. He'd hailed a hansom from Highgate to The Camberwell Palace of Varieties. It was half past four when he'd arrived at the theatre, and there were no matinées on a Monday. So he'd sat with his back to the wall at the entrance of the stage door alleyway. Twice, passers-by had dropped coins at his feet. The rolling sixpences had barely caused him to look up.

It was now six o'clock and he hadn't moved. His knees were at his chin, his feet were turned inwards. He nervously patted the ground with his palms, beating out a rhythm. He'd expected her around five, after her session in Soho and in preparation for the evening's shows. But she hadn't come. He didn't mind. At least there was a purpose to this wait. He hoped.

He smoked a cigarette and, like a costermonger laying out his cart, placed each nugget of information out in front of him, starting with the biggest. But the small ones were no less important. Supposition filled the gaps. He stared at the neatly laid cart for many minutes. Then he picked up the nuggets and laid them out again in a different pattern, testing alternative permutations. He smoked some more, before once more taking the nuggets and starting again.

At a quarter to six, she arrived.

He watched her walk towards the theatre, a fur collar swaddling her neck. As in the dressing room at the Holloway, it felt strangely familiar to see her. She was in a rush, her delicate but determined poise as it had always been. Errant coils of hair danced down her face and in her wake. She wore her usual look of serene determination. It was the Delilah he knew before the world changed. He studied her face as she approached, remembering nuances, expressions and inflections. Not one of these revealed themselves when she saw him; they were smothered by a scowl as she stopped abruptly at the mouth of the alleyway.

'Max?' She glanced behind her to see if anyone was watching.

He steadied himself on the wall and stood. 'I need to talk to you. I've been an utter fool. I thought that this didn't matter. But it does. Hugely.'

She shook her head and walked down the alley. 'We said all we needed to a few nights ago.'

'Please. We must speak,' he said to her back as he scrambled behind her. 'I need you.'

He almost bumped into her as she stopped walking. She spun around angrily.

'Stop it. Just stop.'

Words tumbled through his mind. He ordered them as quickly as he could but she raised a gloved hand before he spoke.

'You can't just arrive like this, Max.' The steeliness in her voice was absolute.

'I appreciate...'

'I don't have a minute to myself. I'm recording every hour that God sends. Shows galore. Playback preparation. I can't do this.'

'I'm sorry to impose. But you have to listen to me.'

A stamp echoed down the alley. 'No. I don't. I don't have to listen to you.'

'Please.'

She stepped towards the stage door but paused and turned back to him, her head shaking. 'You need to stop dreaming, Max.'

He frowned. 'Dreaming?'

'You want the world to be a perfect whole, don't you? You want all the parts to fit neatly together, like one of your machines. But life isn't like that'. Her voice softened. 'It simply isn't.'

Wondering if she remembered, he raised his hand to his heart. He was prepared for it to appear desperate; the dewy-eyed rambling of a broken man. But it was the single most beautiful thing anyone had ever said to him. 'Love's like sound, Delilah. It sustains and reverberates.' The emerald dapples of the weeping willow came back to him.

She nodded, her voice falling to a whisper. 'You're right. It is.' She held his gaze for a second. 'And just like sound, love eventually fades.'

Blinking as an unbearable darkness descended, he stepped to her and, reaching out, formed a mitten over her clasped hands with his own. She flinched at the contact. 'You have to listen to me.' He gently squeezed her hands and told himself not to mess this up. These were likely to be the last words he ever spoke to her. He knew that. But he somehow had to convey part of himself to her.

He looked at her, imploring her to give him this moment. It was time to empty his heart. It was time to tell her everything he felt, however preposterous, however dangerous.

# 24

**Y**ou shouldn't be encouraging me. Mary'll have my guts for garters.'

Delilah ignored Rusty and poured another drink.

'We're supposed to be working,' he said.

'Hush. Just one more then we'll go back.' She flashed him a playful smile. 'We deserve it.'

She topped up her own tankard and laid down the jug of porter on the table, carefully shielding the lace trim of her sleeve as she did so. The tavern was empty apart from two other people at the bar; this corner of Soho rarely came alive until later in the afternoon. Delilah watched as fat particles of sawdust from the floor cavorted in the shafts of afternoon sun. Today was a good day. Today would cement everything.

'You happy with this morning?' He teased down a baton of hair.

'Of course.' Twenty-five cylinders down by lunchtime, all recorded and packaged up in tubes. Canned music, right there. It was the most she'd ever done in a morning. The music had flowed in a way she could never have imagined. 'I particularly enjoyed doing *Glorious Tim Bobbin*.'

'Good, that.'

'And *The Barnes Bluebell*.'

'Delilah, they were all fabulous. We're fair set for Sunday.' Rusty drew heavily on his ale and sat back to stuff his pipe.

Her first playback. 'I'm excited. A little nervous too.'

'Nah. Forget nerves. It's easy. We stand there and play the cylinders. You look pretty. They swoon. I sell stock.' He rubbed his palms together.

'Well if it's *that* easy...' She emptied the remains of the jug into their cups. He didn't stop her.

'I've done posters everywhere. Should be a hell of a crowd.'

Did she ever imagine herself doing her own playback in Victoria Park? Not in a month of Sundays. She thought ahead to standing behind the machines as an audience listened. She smiled again across the table. 'I'm glad you agreed to this. I think we deserve a little celebration. To your good health.'

He drank, thumped the tankard on the table and wiped his chin.

'So what's your favourite part?' she said.

'Eh?'

'Of recording.'

He shrugged.

'Oh come on, Rusty. Don't be a grump.'

She watched him light his pipe. Plumes engulfed him. She held her breath as she waited for the cloud of malty tar to pass.

'Logic, I suppose,' he said, shrugging again. 'I like the logic.'

Resting her elbows on the table, she leaned forwards. 'Explain.'

'The logic of the rig. It's like a, sort of, big jigsaw puzzle. The length of the horn, the width of the diaphragm, the layout of the studio. One thing affects the other. The speed of the revolutions. It's the science of it that I like.'

'Funny. I thought it was about *magic and passion*.' She laughed.

'Tripe.'

She immediately felt guilty. Poor Max. The conversation outside the theatre the previous evening had been painful and sad. She glanced down.

'Magic and passion,' Rusty repeated. 'Does he think Harry bleedin' Houdini lives in the recording machine? The man's off his onion.'

Delilah picked gently at her cuff. 'Rusty, I really shouldn't tell you this. But I saw him yesterday. He seemed a little…manic.'

'Yesterday?'

'It was odd. He'd been there for some time outside The Camberwell, waiting. He begged me to stop recording with you.'

'Idiot.'

'He looked awful. Told me he still had…feelings for me.' The conversation had kept her awake for most of the night. His words were hard to dislodge. Her lack of sleep made the day's crop of recordings an even greater feat.

Rusty cut the air with his pipe. 'Forget him. He's got bigger things to worry about. We're sitting pretty.'

'I know.' She nodded and thought ahead to Sunday's playback. 'I know.'

As she watched Rusty smoke, she realised that she'd come round to his way of seeing things. Life wasn't just about taking chances as they arose. It was also about clearing the path of potential distractions.

'But although he's preoccupied,' Rusty adopted a formal tone, 'I hope he'll be unable to ignore the stench of success from The International Phonograph Company.'

She stifled a laugh. 'Oh, he won't. Tell me something.'

'Go on.'

'You and Max. What was it that started all this? This…
business between you two.'

Rusty snorted, as if the question contained the whole world.
He chewed on his pipe. 'Things he's said and done. Family. His
manner. Chaveley. This.' With a finger he traced the arrowhead
of scarified skin on his wrist. She noticed a flash of melancholy
in his eyes. 'Being almost equal but somehow not.'

'Have you always fought?'

'Always. On and off. From our first breeches onwards.' He
looked at her and raised his eyebrows and sneered, all sorrow
gone. 'I tend to win though.'

'I'm beginning to see that.'

'Like I said, he's an idiot. He's got what he deserved.'

She rested her chin on her fist. 'So when his studio was
smashed up… Was that really you?'

He grinned wickedly.

'*Rusty!*'

He nodded to his mottled wrist and weighed his words.
'Before Russia. I may or may not have paid a little visit to his
studio. Rearranged things a little.'

'That *was* you?' Delilah sat back, suddenly feeling a touch
uneasy. She didn't want Rusty to think she was prying. 'Come
on. Back to the studio.' She drained her ale. 'Any more grog and
I shan't be able to speak, let alone sing.'

'Right you are. Let's get a few more out of you.'

'Twenty more today? Thirty?'

'Steady on, girl.'

She winked across the table and lifted her coat from the
back of her seat. Now was the perfect time to leave. There was a
pleasant abandon to things; the recordings would flow.

She followed Rusty to the tavern's door, thanking him as he
pulled it open and stood aside to let her through. Although

bright, the afternoon's chill took her by surprise. As they crossed Poland Street and turned down the cobbled alleyway that led to the studio, she slipped her arm into his. He didn't resist. In time with her steps, she sang Lady Wallop's refrain from *Palmarama*. She repeated it, looking at him to see if its florid tune was annoying him yet.

'Behave,' he said with a smirk as they reached the studio door. 'In.'

She entered and crossed the small hall into the recording room, elated and ready to go. Her body tingled; drinking in the afternoon was a rare treat. The studio was ordered and tidy, just as they'd left it. She thought back to their conversation in the pub. Logic. Glancing around, she could see it now.

Along one of the studio's walls, dozens of blank cylinders lay in neat racks, waiting to be etched. Along the opposite wall was a rack of completed recordings. Rusty had labelled them all, ready for sale at the playback. There was one phonograph machine in the centre of the room, its recording horn sideways on to an upright piano, so as to capture both Delilah's voice and her playing. A second, reserve machine was in the studio's corner under the window. Logic, she nodded.

Delilah hung her coat behind the door as Rusty removed his jacket and rolled up his shirt sleeves. He busied himself behind the central machine, checking for errant wax shavings prior to sliding on a blank cylinder. Stretching, she walked to the piano and dragged the stool from beneath the keyboard ledge. With a satisfied slump, she sat and lolled her head to one side.

'Thoughts?' he said as he loaded the machine.

'I thought *Bird in a Gilded Cage*.'

'*Gilded Cage*. Very well.'

He lined up the stylus with the end of the tube, set the phonograph's spindle in motion and sat on a stool by the machine, watching Delilah. 'Ready?'

Nodding, she took a deep breath and allowed her fingers to feel their way along the keyboard. The drink had loosened her up nicely. She'd enjoy this performance. She pinched her eyes shut and, when she heard the thud of the stylus land on the cylinder, played. The tune was pretty, mournful. Three bars in, she drew a deep breath.

'*The ballroom was filled with fashion's throng, it shone with a thousand lights, and there was a woman who passed along, the fairest of all the sights.*'

As she sang she opened her eyes and shared a smile with Rusty.

'*She's only a bird in a gilded cage, a beautiful sight to see. You may think she's happy and free from care; she's not, though she seems to be.*'

She watched Rusty lean over the phonograph to check the stylus was travelling along the feedscrew unencumbered. All was well. As she launched into the second verse, she felt a rush of air in her face, as cold as it was unexpected. It was most curious. Craning her neck, she looked over the top of the piano to see that the studio door was open. She was sure she saw Rusty close it. Keen not to lose her rhythm, she returned to the keyboard and the singing. But a piercing screech over-rode the music as Rusty stood from his stool. The piano fell silent as she pulled her left then her right hands from the keyboard. The recording ruined, she rose. There, leaning against the doorframe, was a figure as unheralded as he was familiar.

'Darlings!' Max was wearing the same attire as the evening before, but he was significantly more dishevelled.

'What the fuck are you doing here?' Rusty's face ruddied.

'You dropped by my studio. I'm doing the same.' Max mimicked the gentle buzz of a soldering iron.

'You're drunk.'

Delilah covered her mouth. He was a sorry sight; he clearly hadn't slept, his eyes were bloodshot.

Max took a pace into the studio. Immediately he stepped back and hooked his arm around the doorframe. He pointed at Rusty. 'I'm here to tell you that I hate you.' He moved his finger across to Delilah. 'And I'm here to tell you that I hate you.' The familiar bounce in his voice had been replaced by a slurred monotone.

Tentatively unhooking his arm, he made his crooked trajectory into the studio. 'I'm drunk? What of it?'

Rusty walked to the phonograph and lifted the stylus from its mandrel. With a yank, he removed the cylinder and threw it on the floor. It clunked and rolled to a halt under the piano. He strode back to where his cousin was standing.

'Leave.'

'Shan't.'

'Out!' They stood toe to toe.

'No.'

Delilah slammed her hand on the piano top. These men. Boys. 'Please, Max. You're embarrassing yourself.'

He ignored her and slowly lifted his right palm until it was perpendicular to his side. He held it in position like a policeman directing traffic before swinging it up into Rusty's cheek. The crack of skin on skin filled the studio.

Delilah's fingers twisted into her hair. She could see Rusty's forearm muscles clench and unclench as he readied his fists at his side.

'You need to leave now,' he whispered.

Max shook his head. 'Did you know that your little starlet's a treacherous whore?' He nodded towards Delilah before firing a shower of spit in Rusty's face.

Delilah saw both men flinch, and closed her eyes. The sight was too much to bear. A snarl became a thud before all hell broke loose. She squeezed her eyes tighter and shrieked. Two bulldogs in a pen would have made less of a primal din. The straining and the banging, the sources of which she could initially envisage, quickly became indeterminate as the noise whipped itself into a brutal cacophony.

'Stop.' She couldn't hear herself over the noise. 'Just *stop*.'

A howl preceded silence; not peaceful silence but the silence of aftermath, an ominous pause. Delilah opened her eyes. Panting like a febrile savage, his shirt removed, Rusty was hovering over Max on his knees. His right arm glistened scarlet from shoulder to wrist, melted wax over muscle. The arch of his left hand pinned Max's throat to the ground. Max lay still on his back, his nose bloodied.

Delilah recoiled. Slowly, Max twisted his head against Rusty's grip and looked at her. He strained to speak. 'For God's sake, go and stand out of harm's way.'

Rusty nodded. 'Move, girl.'

Eyes moist, Delilah ran from the piano. She took refuge in the corner of the studio under the window, her hands trembling.

༺ ༻

A snake traversing hot sand. Max watched the vein in Rusty's forehead flicker and whip above him, its actions seemingly its own. He could taste the iron tang of the blood blocking his nose. Gasping for air through his mouth, he twisted his neck, seeking that fragment of space that would let him breathe more easily. But Rusty's entire weight seemed to be bearing down on his claw. As Max writhed, the back of his head scraped raw against the wooden floor.

Desperate, he forced a finger into the shifting cavity between neck and hand. Then two fingers, then three. The second he felt the pressure abate, he wrenched Rusty's hand away from his neck. As he drank in the air and struggled to free himself, the hand landed back down, but this time over his open mouth. He bit, hard. The leathery knuckle between his teeth became warm and wet as Rusty's blood mingled with his own. A gruff scream filled the room, and he tasted air once more. He gulped it in as his cousin leapt back, holding his hand to his chest.

Max scuttled to his feet and took a pace towards the piano. He raised a hand to assess the damage to his face. The respite was brief. Before he knew it Rusty lurched towards him, spun him by the shirt and landed a rough uppercut to the ribs. A flash of reptilian arm. Max bent double, his breath stolen. As his body jack-knifed, his cheekbone crunched into the ball of Rusty's knee. He saw black and fell to the floor. When he came to he was lying on his side. Panting. All he heard was someone else's panting. He was aware of feet pacing the length of his body.

'Oh, you're taking some liberty.' A new ugliness had seized Rusty's voice. 'What do I do with you, eh?' Do I ignore you and sling you out? That would be the sensible thing to do.'

Max looked up. Rusty's naked torso shone with sweat. Half man, half beast.

'Nah. I won't do that. Do I give you what you want? Give you the girl back? Nah, not that either. Or do I...do I *damage* you?'

A yell from the corner.

'Shut it, Delilah.'

Max tried to swallow but the trickle of blood in his throat had become a torrent. He turned his head to the side and let it run onto the floor. He noticed that Rusty had stopped pacing; the soles of his boots were static, just inches from his face. A boot slowly lifted. He braced himself for imminent pain. But none came. Max raised his head to see what was happening. Before he knew it a heavy heel crashed down on his hip. A numbing spasm shook him. He grabbed his hip and screamed. This torture was worse than he expected. Delilah. She mustn't see the extent of his pain. He rolled over and shouted towards the piano.

'Delilah. Leave. Get out. Go.'

'Don't tell her what to *do*.' Rusty landed his boot in the bony underside of Max's leg, where thigh met buttock. He leaned down. 'She ain't yours to tell.'

Max saw that Delilah hadn't moved from the corner. He coughed and rolled onto his back, his agony total. Struggling to breathe, he reverted to his side and saw Rusty's boots pacing once more.

'Misplaced pride, Max. That's what you've got,' Rusty growled between gasps. 'Even now, even when you're finished, you think you can do as you please and walk in here. Well, you can't. You're nothing.'

Using every ounce of his strength, Max raised himself onto his elbows. Coughing away blood, he watched Rusty pace in a circle, mumbling and nodding as though congratulating himself. The noble victim. Yet also the child, demanding attention with his fury. The years fell away. The nursery in Chaveley. Rusty crying on his mother's lap. Max shook his head. 'I'm more than you'll ever be.'

Rusty stopped pacing. The snake returned to his forehead. 'You think so?' he shouted, his eyes dark holes. 'Look at you. Not so much of a maestro now, are you? Let me tell you something, Max. All the bad things that have happened to you have happened because of me.'

'Poppycock.' Bloodied slaver peppered Max's chin.

'You know nothing.' Rusty leaned in. 'I'm the orphaned cousin who ruined your life.'

Max laughed. 'Please.'

Rusty bent lower. 'The break-in when all your precious masters got mangled? I folded them like paper. That was for Chaveley.' He grinned towards Delilah. 'You see, you sold what was rightfully mine. You always thought you were better than me. Why would I let you get away with that?'

Willing away the pain, Max lifted himself further. 'You're incapable of hurting me.'

'Incapable? You have no idea what I'm capable of.'

'*Nothing*. You're capable of *nothing*.' His voice strained as he shouted. 'You've ridden on my coattails all your sorry life. You're pathetic.'

A fresh wildness burned in Rusty's eyes, hinting of hellfire untold. He raised his mottled arm and raged. 'Oh yeah? What about Balducci, eh?'

Max glared at him.

'Who do you think led Franklin's men to him at the Savoy? The old bastard didn't have a clue where he was.'

Max didn't move.

'The night you insulted my parents. *Swimming*, you said. Eight years dead and you make a fucking joke of it? You think I'd let something like that go?' Rusty bent low, his eyes glowing. 'Not capable of anything? *I was there as they killed Balducci*, Max. I knew how losing that fat fool would hurt you. *Me.*'

'What?'

Rusty lifted his finger to his larynx and slowly pressed his flesh, his voice thick with relish. 'Inserted a needle myself.'

Max glared at him, stupefied. A wail from Delilah filled the studio.

'Shut up, girl! Thing is, there's no proof. You and I provided each other's alibis, remember?'

'I don't believe you.' He slumped backwards. *'I don't believe you.'*

'Yeah. And that's not all.' Rusty nodded manically. 'Your friends Wilma and Wilson?'

A boot's heavy sole landed on Max's stomach.

'*Me*, Max. How d'you think Franklin knew of their plans? Eh? *I* took his gang to intercept those miserable bastards. We drowned them before they could record for you.'

Max lurched violently under Rusty's foot. He wiped the puke from his mouth. 'No.' Barely a whisper.

'You told me all your plans down in Limehouse. To the last detail. Opium loosens the tongue something rotten.'

The boot grew heavier on his torso. Max mewled, trying to shut his words out.

'Like I said.' Rusty licked his lips and paused between words, relishing each one. 'All. The. Bad. Things. That have happened. To. You. Have happened. Because of. *Me*.'

The boot was released and Max felt two hands heave him up by the lapels. He held up his own in bitter resignation. 'Rus...'

'Get out of my studio. *Scram*.'

Unable to look back at Delilah, he was dragged to the door. Rusty heaved it open with the force of a whirlwind and pushed him through. Collapsing to the hallway floor, he rolled away as the door slammed behind him.

With dwindling energy, Max counted his ever-weakening breaths, clinging to them, relying on them to keep him in the present. He lay in a sordid heap in the hallway. Time stood still. It was only the sound of voices in the room that prevented him from drifting away. He tried to crawl back to the door, fearing that in his anger Rusty would turn on Delilah. But the pain was too great. Heaving himself along by the elbows, he dragged himself half way there, craning his neck to listen. Through the door he heard Rusty's voice. It had softened.

'It wasn't that bad,' he heard him say.

Delilah was weeping. He caught whispered snatches. 'A shadow of himself…desperate.'

Movement followed. He heard the shuffling of a stool on the floor. Then – unexpectedly – piano music. A mournful tune drifted under the door. After three bars he heard a voice, intense and on the edge of cracking.

'*She's only a bird in a gilded cage, a beautiful sight to see. You may think she's happy and free from care; she's not, though she seems to be.*'

There was too much to make sense of through the immediate cloud of pain. Only in the coming days would the impact of the afternoon become clear. Max sat against the wall and pulled his knees up to his chest. Rusty.

The song finished.

'One more?' he heard Rusty quietly ask.

'No.' Delilah lowered the piano lid. 'No more.'

'You sure?'

'Yes.' Her voice cracked. 'That'll do for today.'

# 25

The Den was rowdier than Max imagined; a semi-lit riot of raised skirts and dirty hollers, Irish fiddles and clammy air. Every step hurt as he carefully picked his way through its crush, aware that the merest contact with a curtseying harlot or drunk reveller would result in agony. The stiffness in his thigh and the tautness of his neck had worsened overnight. Breathing through an open mouth, he kept his eyes on the single door ahead. All the tables were occupied, their salvers of greasy meat being ignored in favour of more human fare. The doors of the chambers around him clattered open and shut. Punters' eyes widened as he passed them. Even the most solicitous slum whore gyred away as he shambled through.

The dry blood still blocking his nose gave way and a warm trickle moistened his moustache. He stopped to block it with a handkerchief, thinking of dams breached. Of emperors dethroned. He reached the door. Two men stood guard on either side. Max sped up and reached for the handle.

'I need to see him.'

Walking straight in, he pushed the door closed behind him, blocking out the fiddle and the filth. A stoked fire illuminated gold palm-leaf wallpaper. To Franklin an office, to Max a gaudy tomb. Four men turned to face him and a mumbled conversation trailed off. The backs of a dozen picture frames crowded the desk in front of him, all ranged for the sole pleasure of its occupant. And there he was, sitting heavily, imperious in a black smoking jacket.

Franklin glared up, the gem of his cravat pin glinting in the firelight. Incredulity morphed into shock at the moment of recognition. Shock became confusion as Max nodded.

'Mr Franklin.' He stepped towards the desk.

'Get out.' Franklin frowned, eyeing his battered features.

Max glanced around as guards stood either side of him. 'One question. Please. Just one.'

'Questions are dangerous, Maximilian.'

'Is there anything you'd like to tell me about the murders of Alfredo Balducci and Wilma Wagensperg?'

Franklin winced and slowly rose from his chair. Before the guards could clasp him, Max lifted his hands to his shoulders in surrender and stepped closer to Franklin's desk. Leaning over it, he offered an outstretched palm.

'No? In which case, I've come to say goodbye.'

෴෴෴෴෴

Max's fingernails matched the bark; gnarled and brown. Spreading his fingers across the tree, he wished he'd had time for a scrub. Today was important. He estimated the crowd was already two hundred strong, a mixture of experts and waverers, the curious and the converted. He skulked back behind the tree; it was best for everyone that he stayed away from the action. Any movement hurt. Two days had only ripened the bruise on his hip. Black as tar at the point of impact, it crept outwards a dull purple, like an ink drop on vellum. His nose was fudgy, still too warm to touch. Somehow he'd managed to shave; it had made him feel marginally more respectable. He told himself to breathe deeply. It might stop the shaking. After this no more. This was it.

He watched Delilah busy herself around The International Phonograph Company's booth one hundred yards away. She checked the horn's trajectory one moment, fiddled with the machine's mandrel the next. That crook, that self-confessed criminal, stood with her, pacing. Max ground his teeth as he followed Rusty's movements. He shouldn't be there. He *couldn't*. From the depths of his soul he damned his bones. *After this, no more.* Every so often Rusty drummed his fingers down his hair with a rapid-fire patting. A word to Delilah. She nodded and smiled. Max had only seen that frock once before. It was the light blue one with a white lace trim. It matched the spring sky overhead and spoke to him of new beginnings, of hope. She'd worn it when they'd eaten Chinese food and visited the dome. How important she looked right now next to her machine. How enhanced. Since his last time in the park, she'd found her voice and he'd lost his.

His eyes flicked between the playback's four tents. In front of each was a table laden with talking machines: gramophones and phonographs, ornate and modest. He imagined all the music they'd captured between them; all those hours, all that work. Perhaps it was his tiredness, but looking now as an outsider from afar, they seemed strangely limited. The boxes looked so small, their horns so tight, the piles of discs and cylinders captured to date so meagre. Maybe his enforced distance brought a new perspective. But the technology on display – the sounds stacked on those tables – had to be just the beginning. They *had* to be. They'd come such a short way. Those flimsy machines were vessels, not cargo; the means not the end. Despite his desire to stay back, he was suddenly struck by a sense of urgency. He thought of the infinite melodies stretching centuries into the future. He thought of the endless invention, of wondrous music as-yet unimagined. His shoulders tightened. There was so much to do. On days like today, the park should be his.

The poster tacked to the tree trunk announced a Grand Playback. For once, it was a bill that did not exaggerate.

> 'Listen to talking machines from the biggest manufacturers in one place. Sounds from the London stage! Music from Paris! Treats of the Orient! Victoria Park, February 21st 1900.'

It was the same bill that he'd seen all over town for the past few weeks. The poster had done its job; the park was packed. Mary hovered meekly next to Rusty's tent. One marquee along, ignoring his neighbours, Langley paced around the Corporation's table. He'd play Balducci on the Regal. That would be fitting. Perhaps the Russian shanty. *Music of the Sands* to finish things off.

At the crowd's thinning fringe, leaning against a marble drinking fountain, Max saw the silhouette of Detective Inspector Boot, his softly pom-pomming cheeks belying the sadism he knew him capable of. Gathering evidence. Sniffing around. A dull ache pulled at Max's eye as he recalled that day in Boot's room. If Boot did the job he was paid to do then Max's nightmare would be over. Two uniformed colleagues stood with him. They scanned the crowd as though primed for action. Max slunk back around the tree.

Blasts from an accordion interrupted the throng's chatter. The sound came from a machine outside Pathé Frères' tent. It was starting. At last. The crowd's eyes turned to the Pathé tent as the playback got underway. Max supposed the tune had a jolly Gallic bounce; its Parisian charm was no doubt designed to whet people's appetites for the upcoming Exposition Universelle. But he'd always suspected that Pathé didn't stand a chance over here. Their machines were too complicated by half, all fancy cranks and buff gilding. He was unsurprised when, after a minute, talk subsumed the music. How cruel this fickle public is. But how crucial, too. As the disc played, he watched Rusty in front of his booth, deep in conversation with Delilah. Up next. She was pointing at herself, as if imploring him. The conversation continued as the accordion fell silent. An agreement evidently reached, Rusty stepped forward to The International Phonograph Company's table and clapped. Max gnawed the nub of his finger. Rusty's big moment. The crowd hushed. He craned around the tree; he'd never heard Rusty speak in public before.

'And now, people of London, here is the playback you've been waiting for.'

*Good* people of London, surely, Max thought. He watched Rusty oafishly raise his arms, a chimpanzee playing a ringmaster. He wondered if others were seeing through it too.

'I would like to introduce my greatest discovery. Magic and passion right here, ladies and gentlemen. Magic and passion.'

How dare he? Max cringed in pain as he involuntarily lurched forward. This was rank appropriation. Only agony and better judgement forced him to grab the trunk and hold himself back. Those were *his* words; words that had been regularly and routinely derided by Rusty over the years. The brute was now claiming them as his own, wrapping them in borrowed gestures and purported enthusiasm. Max breathed deeply and told himself to calm down. Not now. Not yet.

Rusty continued. 'It gives me great pleasure to introduce

Delilah Green, currently performing at The Camberwell Palace of Varieties. She's the real thing, folks. And guess what? She's a local girl. Stepney.' He waited for the clapping to die down before an element of surprise crept in. 'Now, she's just asked to introduce her own recording. So, without further ado…I give you Delilah Green.'

Delilah. As Max had hoped, a modest cheer rose and she stepped up to the phonograph table. To everyone else there she would have appeared the picture of confidence, but Max saw the tell-tale signs of jitters. A final, unnecessary fiddle with a coil of hair. A coy straightening of her dress's seam. She'd done them both when they first met and the charm had floored him. He watched as Rusty walked to join Mary close to where Langley was standing, leaving the table to Delilah. She carefully selected a cylinder and looked over to her boss.

'Thank you, Rusty.' Delilah tipped the cylinder from its tube and smiled nervously. 'Ladies and gentlemen, I'm very happy to be here.' Her voice caught. She paused to gently clear her throat. 'As soon as I recorded this I couldn't wait for you to hear it.'

She slid the tube on to the phonograph's mandrel and rested the stylus at one end, taking her time to place it correctly. She was about to release the machine's motor when she leaned down to check the needle's position once again.

'Get on with it!' Rusty glanced around him, baring his teeth as he grinned. Smirking, Mary nudged him in the ribs.

Another coil. 'I hope you enjoy it.'

A hiss as the cylinder began to rotate. Max craned around the trunk. He heard the needle lock into the groove, and the sound of the studio's hollow echo – like wind passing through a cave – sailed from the phonograph. Now, he told himself. Wincing in discomfort, he stepped away from the tree and limped towards the crowd.

The horn crackled into life as the recording played. But it was not the sound of piano. It was the rumble of indistinguishable movement. Then, as if tearing the very air apart, a wild voice screeched from the machine.

'*Don't tell her what to do.*'

Max nodded to himself; the clarity was excellent. He walked on as a thud filled the air – the sound of leather making contact with something far softer, something fleshier. It was followed by a muffled cry of pain. He pushed into the crowd as quickly as his leg would allow. People were looking at each other. This was not the sweet singing voice of the girl from Stepney.

The recording continued. '*She ain't yours to tell.*'

With his head down, Max limped towards the tents. He halted and looked up. Perfect. He could clearly see Rusty, standing a few yards away from the table at the fringe of the crowd. His features were pinched in confusion.

'*Misplaced pride, Max. That's what you've got. Even now, even when you're finished, you think you can do as you please and walk in here.*' The breathing was heavy, raw. '*You're nothing.*'

That instant, Rusty's expression changed. It snapped from bafflement to recognition. A look of horror descended. He recognised his own gruff voice only too well.

Rusty glanced around and, with a panicked skitter, leapt towards the phonograph. Before he could reach it, Langley stepped behind him and looped an arm into his. Heaving him back by the elbow, he hooked his other arm around his chest. A peeler threw his helmet to the ground and rushed to join him. Together they held Rusty back, the snake in his forehead fattening as he strained.

The cylinder continued to turn. Max heard his own voice as he made his way to the front of the crowd. '*Poppycock.*'

He stopped just to the side of the table and a few metres from

Rusty. Delilah stood over the phonograph, lost in thought. Max's heart thumped as he watched her. The heroine of the piece. She'd executed the plan like clockwork that afternoon in the studio: rushing to the corner; affecting panic; turning on the second recording machine. Max looked back to Rusty across the small expanse of grass that separated them. It was three metres maximum, but Rusty remained tethered to the spot by his captors' grip, scanning the crowd. Any second now. A low growl filled the air when he saw Max, his face ruddying as though choked at the neck.

With mock indignation, Max raised his finger to his lips. 'Hush, old boy. People won't be able to hear us.' He clasped his eyes shut. There was no joy in this. But cornered, he'd had to do it.

*I'm the orphaned cousin who ruined your life. The break-in when all your precious masters got mangled? I folded them like paper.*

Another growl as Rusty tried to drown out the sound.

*'That was for Chaveley. You sold what was rightfully mine. You always thought you were better than me. Why would I let you get away with that?'*

In a flurry of whispers and nods, the crowd around Max had cottoned on. The playback was no longer about the music. A mumble spread outwards from the machine. A wave of hushes followed, silencing the park. Max looked to Boot. He glanced back, frowning. Max had promised him a playback he'd never forget. He hadn't told him why. Max heard his own voice again. It sounded strained, desperate.

*'Nothing. You're capable of nothing. You've ridden on my coattails all your sorry life. You're pathetic.'*

*'Oh yeah? What about Balducci, eh?'*

A fresh murmur rippled out at the name. Max stood still as a sustained shushing followed it, filtering out in a wave of its own, sounds chasing sounds. Necks craned around him.

*'Who do you think led Franklin's men to him at the Savoy? The old bastard didn't have a clue where he was.'*

As a collective gasp erupted, Rusty shouted to block what he knew was coming. It was no good. The recording was loud; his studio had excellent acoustics.

*'The night you insulted my parents. Swimming, you said. Eight years dead and you make a fucking joke of it? You think I'd let something like that go? I was there as they killed Balducci, Max. I knew how losing that fat fool would hurt you. Me.'*

As Max had in the studio, the crowd around him seemed to inhale as one. He stumbled forward as people jostled behind him to get nearer the horn. He shouted a plea for quiet, needing Boot to hear.

*'Inserted a needle myself.'*

A hand in the air to quell the noise. Just one more minute. One final crescendo. The crowd obeyed.

*'Yeah. And that's not all. Your friends Wilma and Wilson?'*

Rusty's recorded voice – triumphant and vicious – hung in the air. Max braced himself.

*'Me, Max. How d'you think Franklin knew of their plans? Eh? I took his gang to intercept those miserable bastards. We drowned them before they could record for you. Opium loosens the tongue something rotten.'*

This time there were no gasps. Just stunned silence.

*'All the bad things that have happened to you…happened because of me.'*

Max waited for the pop as Delilah lifted the stylus from the mandrel. Time itself seemed to stop; no one moved.

Then pandemonium erupted.

In the chaos of jeers and shoving, Langley and the policeman must have loosened their grip on Rusty. Escaping from a tangle of flailing arms, he threw himself at the machine. Delilah scurried backwards but it was not her he was after. With a primitive howl Rusty rained blow after blow on the phonograph's mandrel, his fist white and taut. The cylinder and the spindle beneath snapped, sending pieces of wax high into the air. Subsequent blows reduced what remained to dozens of shards. Fragments of his confession littered the table and the ground around it.

Langley and the peeler caught up with Rusty. Each took an arm. Hauling him back, they gripped him tightly.

'Smash away.' Max walked to the table. 'It will have no consequence. Not only do we have hundreds of witnesses here, but I've been shopping. Bought a few of your machines.'

Rusty glared at him. 'What?'

'Delilah loaned me her cylinder last night. I was up until dawn in the studio with Mr Langley here making copies from machine to machine. Fiddlesome things. But we have dozens.' He raised his dark fingernails, blackened by hours of handling wax cylinders. He looked at Rusty and swallowed. He'd had to do it to save his skin. He didn't want to say the words, but his way out relied on everyone there knowing the truth. 'That's some feat, Rusty. You've given us the world's first recording of an accomplice to murder confessing his crimes. I can think of many people who'll want to hear that. Clever thing, technology. Wouldn't you say?'

Unable to maintain eye contact, Max looked down. Were the past to creep into his thoughts, he wasn't sure he'd keep his composure. He'd framed his cousin. But the alternative was a noose around his neck. His shoulder fell as a chubby palm landed on it. Boot had pushed his way through the crowd. Max turned. 'I told you it would be worth your while.'

'Ever the showman.' Boot looked shellshocked, as if aware of the upheaval he'd now be obliged to cause. As well as implicating himself, Rusty had told the world of Franklin's involvement. An indelible confession. And it would fall to Boot to bring his empire down. He now had no option. As it fell, Covent Garden – *London* – would be redrawn. The night before in The Den, Max had given Franklin the chance to confess with perhaps a quieter resolution. He'd refused to do so, so Max had said goodbye.

'I have to say, your plan seemed a touch far-fetched.' Boot said. 'Not the way I'd do things, of course. But thank you.'

Max's eye twitched. I know the way you do things, he thought. He still didn't trust him. 'Oh, and just to be clear detective inspector, I'll be putting cylinders in the post to your superiors. And the newspapers. Just to ensure everyone's fully in the picture.'

Rusty's body convulsed, tiny shakes rippling through him, as a policeman replaced Langley at his shoulder. Mary stood close by, motionless, her lips pursed in sorrow as Rusty mouthed a silent word to her.

Max walked to him. 'Your Delilah's a clever girl. A dab hand in the studio.'

Spit arced from Rusty's mouth, landing short. The gob drooped from the grass. With every fibre of his being Max wished this final play hadn't been necessary. A glaze of tears ruddied his vision. But when the revelation came, he had to act on it.

The chime of loose cuffs filled the clearing. Rusty glanced around him as Boot secured his hands behind his back.

Max stared at his feet. The sickening thought that Rusty was instrumental in the murders had hit him like a freight train during the second listen of *Pari Siamo* in the drawing room a few days ago. *We are two of a kind: my weapon is my tongue, his is a dagger*. What if the blood they shared had blinded him to his cousin's underlying darkness? Made him always find excuses for it? Max the tongue, Rusty the dagger. The truth lay in the music all along. What if Rusty's blind anger had taken him straight to Franklin to tell him of Balducci's recording? And what if Rusty knew that a word with Franklin would see Wilma and Wilson meeting the same fate as the Italian? Max would be chief suspect. He'd sat, terrified, in the drawing room as these thoughts had occurred. It was the gramophone in the corner that shook him from his stupor. That machine. The snarer of sound. Looking at it, he knew what he had to do. It was simply a case of laying the trap. A talking machine would capture the truth. A talking machine would secure his future.

'On you go.' Boot nudged Rusty forward as peelers in front cleared a tunnel through the crowd. Mary walked behind Boot, shocked and timid, her eyes darting. A police carriage waited beyond the park's gate.

As Rusty started walking, he threw a look at Max. Confusion peeked through the anger; his brow furrowed over a twitching nose. Years tumbled. Max turned, unable to watch. The ground beneath him suddenly became the lawn at Chaveley. London's thick air was replaced by a sea breeze. Rusty was sitting on the grass next to him, surrounded by cranks and springs. Like now, his nose twitched under a furrowed brow. A boy, absorbed in the joy of deconstruction. Two toys. The bear and the monkey.

Rusty turned one last time. 'Max?'

He closed his eyes. This wasn't how things were meant to be. It was he and Rusty against the bastards. But time was a ruthless conductor. He'd learned that. Time could alter the tone of things and change life's rhythm on a whim. With one flick of the baton, it could transform the shape of everything. And he suspected it would continue to do so for ever.

He watched Rusty disappear through the gate, the man's future and past now permanently etched together in a thousand scratched grooves. Max looked at the music machines ranged on the tables. In capture, release. In sound, freedom. But it was a release so startling, a freedom so weighed down by sadness and the unravelling of lives fully lived, that he felt no triumph. Instead, he felt the weight of responsibility. A vibration on wax. A delicate line indistinguishable to the human eye. These were what he traded in. But in them lay a power even more awesome than he ever imagined.

His eyes scanned the crowd, seeking out Delilah. She was standing alone by the broken phonograph machine. He silently begged her to look at him. In all the plotting he hadn't considered the aftermath.

He kept his eyes on her until she found him. A mutual gaze, long and inconclusive. He raised his eyebrows in a tentative enquiry. The faintest smile played on her lips. It seemed intended as the grin of a co-conspirator. But to Max it looked strained. He wondered what true feelings it was masking, and how deep they ran. Guilt, shock, relief, anger. Any would be understandable. That conversation outside The Camberwell had been the hardest of his life.

*'And just like sound, love eventually fades.'*

*Clasping her hand between his, he stepped towards her. 'You have to listen to me.'*

*'Please, Max. Don't do this.'*

*He looked to the alley's end to check that the stage door was firmly closed. Eyes fixed on Delilah's, he lowered his voice. 'It was Rusty.'*

*'What was?'*

*'The murders.'*

*Her face pinched in confusion. She shook her head. 'No…
You're being daft. No.'*

*'On my life, Delilah, listen. I'll tell you everything. Then I need
you to do something for me…'*

But she hadn't done it for him. Not really. As they planned the
trap, he realised she was doing it as much out of obedience to
her sense of right as anything else. Momentum established, she
couldn't be stopped. Taking Rusty to the pub to loosen him up.
That was her idea. Max acting drunk and slapping Rusty. Hers,
too. While she took no relish in any of it, she saw it through with
inexhaustible commitment. It was typically, brilliantly, Delilah.

Rising chatter stirred Max from his thoughts. A strange
atmosphere had descended on the park. Although the crowd
had thinned, many remained, as though there was more to
come. The sideshow had become the show. But now that was
over, they wanted something else. Delilah caught his eye again
and nodded across at The London Gramophone Corporation's
table. She shrugged.

Heads turned to Max. Prods on his back. A ripple of applause.
Over on the company's table, the horn of the Empress yawned
silently, invitingly. Beyond it lay a stack of shellacs. A glance to
Delilah. A nod of encouragement. Ignoring his throbbing leg
he limped towards the company's table. Rubbing his eyes, he
turned to face the audience. Tentatively, he raised his hands to
his side.

'Ladies and…' His throat was too dry. He drew saliva across
his mouth. 'Ladies and gentlemen. We present to you a new
technology for a new century.' He was surprised at how easily
the words came. He pointed down at the table and raised his
voice. 'In your own homes, in place of the rustle of a newspaper
or the scratch of a nib you can listen to choirs, orchestras and

marching bands. Gramophones make walls melt.'

An elderly lady in front of him turned to her friend and cooed, their bonnets gently clashing.

'You, madam. Have you ever had opera for breakfast?'

She pursed her lips in an embarrassed smile and shook her head. A bump of confidence.

'We'll bring you music from Stepney to Harlem, from Covent Garden to Kyoto.' He spread his arms. 'Welcome to the industry of human happiness.'

The opening chords of the Russian shanty sailed from the horn. He turned. Langley was standing proudly behind the machine, laying the disc's empty sheath on the table.

As the song played, Max watched Delilah's face. Clear-eyed and still, a calm serenity had descended. It was the same look he noticed after their climb in St Paul's; open yet resolute. He walked towards her, desperate to be allowed in, desperate to start the process of unpicking the last six months and starting again. But every step was accompanied by a dull fear. Fear that she couldn't forgive him. Fear that their closeness would never be rekindled. Fear that she wouldn't see what he knew: that he'd been a fool.

As he reached her, he offered his palm for her hand. She ignored it and looked up at him, eyes gently glinting. 'You said Stepney.'

'What?'

'You said 'music from Stepney to Harlem'.'

'I did.' A thin tangle of hair drifted across her face. In that moment, he'd have swapped his soul to reach across and tuck it behind her ear. Just for that second of intimacy, that tender touch of contact. But his arms remained static.

'What did you mean by that?'

He tried to speak but there was too much to say. It was a

pledge. He was hers. In life. In love. In music. If she'd let him in. He raised his hand and touched his heart, his mouth spreading into a smile.

She smiled back. Stepping forward, he tentatively cradled her cheek. She didn't move. He planted a kiss on her forehead. The park fell silent as the shanty ended. Max felt a ripple of anxiety. Silences were for filling. But rather than act on his instinct to talk or replace the disc, he listened. And as he did so, a weight lifted. This was not an ominous silence, begging for noise to snuff it out. Rather, it contained a soft rhythm all of its own. It was the sound of breathing. The calm pulse of a world regathering itself. The beautiful moment of solitude between the end of one thing and the beginning of another. And at its centre stood Delilah.

'Come on.' Max whispered, nodding west towards Covent Garden. 'I'd like to show you a little studio I know.'

# EPILOGUE

Mr Ronald Cadenza
4 Church Crescent
London E

Mr Maximilian Cadenza
18 Calabria Road
London N

4 September, 1930

Dear Rusty,

I am sure that it will surprise you to receive this letter. I have surprised myself somewhat in sitting down to write it. However, I have given much thought to putting pen to paper in recent weeks. So much time has passed since our difficulties. There have certainly been events in the intervening years that have put all that into perspective. Humanity is a cruel thing.

I prayed that you wouldn't hang, and I was happy when you didn't. I mean that sincerely. Your lawyer was a clever man. I trust that you have enjoyed life since your release as much as you have been able to.

I am writing to you to honour something that I promised many years ago. You might have read about this in the press, but last year I sold The London Gramophone Corporation to our rival The Gramophone Company, or His Master's Voice as people insist on calling it. I am nearly 60 now and it was time to take a back seat. The funds from the sale recently came through. I always said that the company was half-owned by you, and despite everything that happened, I am a man of my word. So I enclose a cheque. After taxes and costs, it amounts to £8,000. Please enjoy it.

Memory is a funny thing, Rusty. Last month I found a box of personal effects as I cleared out the attic in Highbury. (Mama has been gone for a decade but I am only now finally selling the house). This box took me back. Among the items in it were a Regal tone arm, receipts from Fortnums and Russian train tickets! You will recall our differences as deeply as I do. But I look back fondly on much that happened in those years. The more that time progresses, the more I think that we were at the start of something big. The world has become a lot smaller in recent years and a lot sadder too. I can't imagine that the excitement we felt as we ventured to new places would be felt to such a degree by visitors today. I genuinely believe that we were, in our own small way, pioneers.

We are experiencing a time of rapid technological change. As I'm sure you know, cylinders ceased being produced commercially last year (I was right!). And acoustic recording as you and I knew it is now over. I shall never forget when I first heard a recording made using an electrical microphone five or so years ago. That very instant I knew that the way I saw things, the way we saw things, was from a bygone age. Sounds we could not have dreamed of capturing through the horn of a gramophone can now be picked up and reproduced perfectly through a microphone.

This change has consequences, mind. People like us who captured sound using instinct and experience are being edged out by a new breed, folk who record using a hardback manual and help from our friends at the Central Electricity Board. Children born in the year we started are now in their early 30s, probably over their prime already! Someone once warned me that new technology would one day come along and confound me. It's funny; I didn't believe her at the time. How life clatters on.

Despite selling the company, I am not retired. The terms of the sale ensured that I remain with the enlarged group. I now command a relatively senior position at The Gramophone Company. My superior is Fred Gaisberg, whom I have always *admired. To an even greater degree than us, he has been around since the beginning (our logo is still that white terrier sniffing that recording horn. Marking out its territory, as you put it!). There is more change afoot. The plan, still in its early stages, is for The Gramophone Company to form a large new company with Columbia Records to knock out the competition. We will be called Electric and Musical Industries. The industry of human happiness just keeps getting bigger! It saddens me somewhat that the intimate culture we once held dear will be replaced by something grander and more corporate. But I suspect that 'EMI' will be for the best.*

*Delilah sends her regards. The children are both well.*

*I must get on now as there is an important meeting this afternoon. The Gramophone Company is searching for a new recording studio, as we have outgrown our current facility. One option under consideration by Mr Gaisberg and colleagues is a large building that some of us walk past on our way to work. There's a heated debate internally over whether to buy it. I think it would make a superb studio. It has ample space for big orchestras and would be well suited for electrical recording; a crucible for future magic and passion! The building is tucked away in a quiet residential street in St John's Wood. It's called Abbey Road. I think we might be onto something.*

*Yours,*
*Max*

# Jewels:
## Capture these and you have the world

**1** Japanese *shamisen* orchestra
**2** The flamenco guitar of Miguel Sandoval (Seville 7/ 1898)
**3** Harlem ragtime
**4** The bagpipers of Nethy Bridge (Highlands 12/ 1898)
**5** Bach sonatas – Wilma Wagensperg
**6** Baroque choir (Amiens 1/ 1899)
**7** Sitar raga
**8** Opera arias – Alfredo Balducci (London 7/ 1899)
**9** Serbian Dodola girls (Belgrade 10/ 1899)
**10** Cornish crowdy-crawn
**11** Russia Volga shanty (Nizhny Novgorod 11/ 1899)
**12** Beethoven symphony

# The London Gramophone Corporation: log of recordings 1898-1903

| Country | Recordings | Present | Sales (as of Dec 1903) |
|---|---|---|---|
| England | 95 | MC, RC, JL | 120,772 |
| Scotland | 29 | MC/RC, MC/JL | 64,006 |
| India | 17 | MC, JL | 56,746 |
| Russia | 8 | MC, RC, JL | 2,012 |
| Spain | 5 | MC, RC | 3,982 |
| Serbia | 1 | MC, RC, JL | 989 |
| New York | 25 | MC, JL, DG | 33,896 |
| France | 7 | MC, RC | 13,138 |

*Personnel: MC – Maximilian Cadenza, RB – Ronald Cadenza,*
*JL – Joe Langley, DG – Delilah Green*

# AUTHOR'S NOTES

I'd like to say a big thank you to Jo Hughes at the EMI Group Archive Trust for her time and enthusiasm in showing me the vast treasure trove of old gramophones and recordings at the Trust's facility in Hayes. From the splendid Monarch gramophone that Captain Scott took on his Terra Nova expedition to the South Pole in 1910 to the early edible discs made from chocolate, it's a music lover's paradise. It was an honour and a thrill to see these items at first hand having written and thought about them for so long. Thank you too to Dr Andrea Tanner, the archivist at Fortnum & Mason, for giving me a glimpse into the world of expeditions in the 1890s and teaching me about chop boxes.

To the purists, an apology. While I have tried to be accurate with the chronology of technological advances in the novel, I have had to be flexible in places for the sake of the story. For example, wax master discs replaced zincs in the UK at some point around 1902 (not 1900). And phonographs were perhaps more common at the end of the 1890s than I suggest. However, I've attempted to capture the spirit of the age, and in particular the intense competition between talking machine companies. Format wars have always fascinated me. The gramophone versus phonograph battle was the VHS vs Betamax or iPhone vs Galaxy stand-off of its day.

The seed of this book was sown in October 2011 when I went to a concert in London organised by the Honest Jon's record label and Damon Albarn, who has links with the label. The evening, called Another Honest Jon's Chop Up, was a chaotic but largely joyous jam session that took in genres from afrobeat to disco and funk to folk and featured musicians from around the world – from Nigerian drummer Tony Allen to Malian singer Fatoumata Diawara to Flea from the Red Hot Chili

Peppers. Max would have loved it, thinking about it. Anyway, among the music that the label releases are compilation albums of very early gramophone recordings, many of which are from the EMI Archive. It was from a trestle table in the foyer outside this concert that I bought a CD of such recordings. In the sleeve notes I read about these fearless and slightly bonkers adventurers who travelled the world to capture sound for new-fangled 'talking machines'. It sparked something in me. I imagined all the stories involved. All the belief. All the rivalry. All the magic and passion.

The people who created the recorded music industry were true disrupters and pioneers, risking life, limb and a dollop of public opprobrium in pursuit of their vision. I wonder if people like Charles Cros, Thomas Edison, Emile Berliner, George Gouraud, Arthur Clarke, Frank Capps, the Pathé brothers, Fred Gaisberg, Sinkler Darby and William Barry Owen had any idea that their ideas and endeavours would change the world to the extent that they did. These people launched the 'industry of human happiness' and laid the foundations of the music industry as we know it today. In an age when a song can be streamed through the air at the touch of a button, I wonder if we perhaps take the convenience of music for granted these days. Maybe because we can listen to any song whenever we want, we don't always value it quite as much as we should.

In researching this novel I read dozens of books, websites, and historical and academic papers. Particularly useful were The Sound of the Hound website, Hugo Ströbaum's meticulous Recording Pioneers website and Michael S Kinnear's accounts of early Indian recordings (great sources of information about this era). Also, George Kennan's 1883 paper about the trade fair at Nizhny Novgorod, printed in the Journal of the American Geographical Society of New York, provided some fascinating information about this extraordinary gathering. Lastly, the diaries of The Gramophone Company founder Fred Gaisberg – Music on Record – and Jerrold Northrop Moore's biography of Gaisberg – Sound Revolutions – were useful research tools. Indeed, some of Gaisberg's real-life recording adventures over 100 years ago influenced some of my characters' escapades; on a trip to Russia in 1900, for example, a bucket of acid sprang a leak and burned through a hotel floor. Given that Gaisberg was among the fathers of the recorded music industry, I felt it only fitting that Max Cadenza should end up working for him at the end of the book.

While neither The London Gramophone Corporation nor The International Phonograph Company existed, it is true that The Gramophone Company and Columbia merged to form EMI in 1931. The establishment of Abbey Road studios that I mention in the Epilogue also happened as I described. I hope music historians will forgive the merging of my fictional 'tributary' with a factual 'river' at the end.

For Victorian London, I learned much from Gavin Weightman and Steve Humphries' The Making of Modern London and from Kellow Chesney's The Victorian Underworld.

This novel would not have happened without Chris Wakling and Anna Davis at Curtis Brown Creative, and the writing group that grew out of that 2012 course. Fiona, Lisa, Chris, Maria, Paul, Sara-Mae and Dan – those cold Monday nights were worth it. A big shout out to my other early readers: Craig Keeley, George Potts, Zanna Hall, Euan Thorneycroft and Jack Tennant. Alice Saunders, my wonderful agent at Lucas Alexander Whitley, has been a total rock and an unstinting supporter of this, and I can't thank her enough. Ifan Bates, thanks for the brilliant cover design. Lastly, to Scott Pack, Dan Hiscocks and all at Lightning Books: thank you for your passion. I'm so happy to be working with you.

On a personal note, to family and friends who've been enthused by the idea of this – too many to mention, but hello Mum, Dad and Lucy – I love you and ta-da! It happened. To all my wonderful cousins, rest assured that the Max/Rusty relationship is based on nothing but my imagination (although, James A, the 'dead crows' incident is something I can picture them having done!). Laura Morgan and Hannah Vowles: you are, and always will be, the best of the best. And finally, Zanna. My everything. Without you I'd be a tone arm with no stylus. A disc with no groove. A talking machine with no horn. Thank you.